SPEARHEAD LAKE, BOOK 3

E.L. STEVENS

TRIGGER WARNINGS

LOSS OF A SPOUSE

LOSS OF A CHILD

BETRAYAL

CHEATING

RECOUNT OF CHILD ABUSE

NOTE FROM THE AUTHOR

While this book *can* be read as a standalone novel, I would strongly advise reading book one and two first. (georgia and constantine)

A side note:

There are people who will just never get over *it*.

And then there are people that *say* they could never get over it, but then find a way to forgive.

Both of those viewpoints are valid.

For Debra June,
for fostering my life long love of books.

Thank you.

CONTENTS

THEN

ONE

ALEX

September 22, 2010

ETA: Approximately 22 minutes. Palms get damp. My heart rate increases. Then, right on cue, there's a burn in my chest.

This isn't something that happens to everybody, but it happens to me.

Some guys practically sprint home. But not me. I drag. I methodically and slowly move through the compound, taking time to tie up any and all loose ends. *Anyone need a debrief? Need a buddy to go see the medic? The psych? Need a ride?* Everyone knows that I'm the one to come to.

They probably think I do it in the name of brotherhood. And maybe I do, a bit. But mostly, I do it to avoid what's waiting for me. At home.

I avoid home. Not that I'd call the condo home. That's just a place I sometimes sleep. *Sometimes.* If I can avoid it, I will.

"So, you ever gonna answer me?" Blanks is staring at me like I'm an idiot. He's been waxing poetic about cryptocurrency the entire drive. Mentally, I'd tuned him out at mile marker 52.

"Sure." I stare back at the road. As each landmark we pass grows in familiarity, so does my blood pressure.

"Sure is your answer? Or sure, you're gonna answer me?" If I give in, maybe he'll stop talking about this. It'll buy me 16 minutes of silence, I hope.

"Sure is my answer. There's 500 euros in my rucksack. It's yours...if you can shut the fuck up the rest of the drive." Blanks breaks out in a huge grin and doesn't say a word. Frankly, I would've given him a 1000 for ten minutes of silence, but he doesn't need to know that.

Six more exits, eight and a half minutes approximately. The silence inside the cab of my truck is deafening now. No music while we drive. That's a rule, everyone knows it. Blanks still asks on occasion, but my answer never changes. I need to be able to hear. *Stay alert. Stay alive.*

It's a simple mantra, but one I swear by. *It's one that's gotten me this far...*

Blanks lives two condos over in the small North Carolina town we're currently stationed at, so there's almost never a time he drives himself to and from the compound. I don't mind it because he's a lingerer, too.

His reasons are different from mine, though. He's got no one at home to go to. No one to call. No one to see. If he's not at the unit, he's alone. Doesn't date either, doesn't try, doesn't want to. He's a bit like a younger me, except happier. He's me, with a smile.

Turning off our exit, we pass the Waffle House and just

like clockwork, just like every time we pass the dilapidated restaurant, my body knows and my stomach turns. A small sweat breaks out on the back of my neck. My jaw tightens. My thumb starts thumping against the steering wheel nervously.

I've got less than three minutes now. Approximately two and a quarter minutes if I averaged it. And I have.

Blanks sees the shift. He always does, but today he doesn't say shit. He wants that 500 euros.

I pull into my assigned parking space, kill the engine, then stare straight ahead at the brown and beige condos where they're probably waiting for me. With smiles and cheer. Because they always are. And I always ruin it. Every damn time.

The sound of Blanks slamming the door shut pulls me out of the void I slip into whenever I come home. *Again*, it's not *home*. Never home. Whenever I *come back* — that's more appropriate.

Swallowing the guilt and anxiety I step out of the truck, grabbing the euros still hidden in a discreet pocket, then pass them off to Blanks.

"What should we call it?" he asks, a smile on his face. He's not oblivious to what I'm going through, but this is how he copes. He makes plans for the future. When things get hard, when shit hits the fan, like it did in this last mission, Blanks doesn't get down. Instead he focuses on tomorrow. Making plans, manifesting that he'll be around to do...it. Whatever *it* is.

"Whatever you want it to be." Couldn't care less. I'm probably flushing $650 down the drain. Bitcoin, or whatever the fuck he talks about incessantly is probably just a fad that'll be dead in a year and a half, but it bought me 16 minutes of silence. Silence I desperately needed.

Blanks slams a hand down on my shoulder, giving me a good look in the eyes. There's a lot that passes between us without a single word being said. Aside from Damian, he's probably the only person that gets me.

His brows furrow: *One, I'm sorry about Corey. Two, I'm sorry you're about to go in there and be miserable. Three, stop being miserable, you fucking twat. You have a wife and a little girl in there that love the fuck out of you.*

His eyes say all that, and I give a brief nod.

Pulling my ball cap down a little further, I block out his knowing eyes, and he releases me to grab my rucksack and kit.

Hoisting his own bag over his shoulder, he turns and leaves. No other words needed, and no goodbyes. I don't do goodbyes. At least not well.

He walks two doors down, unlocks his front door, then disappears into his solitary world.

Seven paces. Five or six seconds. That's the distance from my parking spot to my front door. That's all that separates me from my family. But that's just what *literally* separates us. There's a lot more to it than that. There's worlds and lifetimes between us. Fuck, a whole other universe because I live...on a different plane than most people.

Most people live in the "normal" world. That's where Amy does her living, on the normal plane. I liked that about her at first. Gave her a certain innocence.

Me, though? I live on my own plane of existence. No one else there but me. Sometimes I can slip into her world with her, or maybe it's just that our existences intersect briefly.

Two planes intersecting at a point for the briefest of moments in time before veering off in opposite directions.

Those times are fleeting and rare, but that's what Amy stays for – the rare times I slip into her world of existence and act like I'm free.

I can count the number of times it's happened on one hand.

It's four.

And fuck, if it wasn't bliss each time. But just like a demon escaping hell, you gotta go back eventually, and I always do. I slip away from her and slide back into my singular existence.

We might have been a mistake. *Hell, my whole life feels like a mistake sometimes.*

Staring at the brown painted front door, I try to get myself right, for them, but fuck if I don't hate coming back.

Nothing is as bad as the first day. I mean, it never really gets "better," but *this*, the first day, is always the worst. The first "hey." The first hug. From there it just spirals. Or maybe I spiral because after the first apprehensive hello, I'll remember that neither of us ever really knew each other in the first place. And I'll realize it wasn't just the distance of the latest rotation, it's just who we both are. And now we know each other even less, because I'm out *there*, doing, living, working, fighting. And Amy is just — at home. Being a mom. And doesn't that just make me the asshole? Is that all I think she *is*? That's all she does?

I'm sure she's busy living life — her own life — but I don't care most days to know what she does. So now that makes me the asshole *and* a shitty fucking husband. *Not that that comes as any surprise considering where I came from.*

And that's not even including Tally. What about her?

I'm surprised by the front door swinging open revealing Amy, staring at me, holding our daughter in her arms. When I look at her, it feels like maybe I'm seeing her for the first time. *No, that's not it.* It's that I'm looking into the eyes of a stranger. *Fuck,* that makes me feel some sort of way. But definitely not sad. I definitely don't feel the same way she's looking back at me now.

"Hey," I say, tentatively.

She looks away, avoiding eye contact. That's supposed to be my M.O., not hers. It's pretty fucking telling, though. And it's not because I know her so intimately either. It's because reading people is essential to my work. '*Stay alert, stay alive*' doesn't just refer to your surroundings.

So when she tucks her bottom lip in and fights a tremble, trying to hide it by adjusting Tally in her arms, I start to get a little nervous. *Not as nervous as I probably should be, though...*

When she doesn't say anything a second later, I step towards her. "Amy?" I bring myself closer to her physically, but there's still a barrier there. On my side. But for the first time, I feel it on her end as well.

"We're leaving, Alex." She's quiet, but there's a strength to her voice. It surprises me, and I'm almost...*proud?*

"Where are you headed?" I ask like she might be going to the grocery store, but I know that's not the case. First thing I noticed when the front door opened was Amy's sad eyes, second thing I noticed was Tally's shoes were on, third thing I noticed was the suitcases and Pack 'n Play lined up against the wall.

"To my mom's." She raises her eyes back to me. Same sad

look, yet she's resolved about this. It's the most life I've seen in her in a year and a half. Not since I left Amy with a 6-week-old infant in a new town for three months, where I came back to find her slightly lifeless. A bit subdued. *I know. It was fucked up. I know it.*

"For how long?" Again, I'm asking when I already know.

"Indefinitely." *Good for her.* I just nod.

"What about Tally?" I see the fear flash across her eyes, and then it's there in her voice.

"Tallulah is coming with me." No surprise there. I'm rarely here, but that's when the faintest hint of pain starts cropping up. Tally is still my girl.

She's being sweet right now, no clue her little world is crumbling on the threshold of this brown condo. She's tucked against Amy's side, tugging gently at her mother's hair, making smiley faces at me. But she doesn't reach out for me. I notice that. I know it's my fault. Never around enough.

"Why'd you wait?" She knew I'd be home today. It's a Sunday. Would've made more sense to leave on a Friday, avoid traffic and a confrontation entirely. Honestly, a letter would have sufficed.

This time it's anger that flashes across her face. It's pointed at me, and I have to admit it's well deserved. That was a dick thing to say.

"I wasn't going to just leave you without saying anything...a-and I thought you'd want to say goodbye to Tally. At least..." Her tone is...unkind. Or maybe it's wrecked. *Fuck,* maybe it's both.

I don't want to say goodbye to Tally. Not because I don't do goodbyes, but now that the likelihood of them leaving is hitting, I don't want Tally to go. *I know, I didn't say Amy, but they're a package deal.*

Amy holds out our daughter for me, so I drop my bags just inside the front door, right next to hers, and take Tally in my arms. I hold her tight, pressing my forehead against hers. She's a lot like me. Quiet for a baby. Technically a toddler, but she'll always be my baby. Her hair is a golden blonde, short with a few curls at the ends. She actually looks like my little sister Britain did at this age.

"Tally, you're gonna go with mom today, okay?" I ask her, she nods. Doesn't talk much, again, like me. "I love you, Tallulah June," I whisper against her soft hair, swaying with her slightly. Her little hands grip my biceps. And we do what we always do, her and I. We speak without words.

I pull her against my body a bit tighter. *I love you so much, Tally.* And she reaches up a hand to run her small fingers against my stubbled jaw. *I love you too, Daddy.* I let time fall away because what else is there to do?

Amy leaving with Tally is probably the right thing. She deserves better than me not existing with her — just around her. That's shitty. For everyone. Especially for Tally.

Amy gently clears her throat from where she's been watching us. Probably with some regret and guilt, if I know her. But she shouldn't feel guilty, I should. I could have tried harder, been better. But instead of saying that to her, letting there be some closure or helpful words, she reaches out for Tallulah and I pass our daughter to her.

"Can you help me load up?" she asks quietly, politely, the same way you'd ask a stranger. *A stranger.* I nod. Not exactly happy to help, but something akin to that.

A light drizzle starts so I grab multiple suitcases at once to speed up the process while Amy buckles Tally into her carseat.

I check the weather app as the drops of water hitting the brim of my hat grow in size. There's a storm pushing through this afternoon.

"Amy, I don't think you should go." I stop her with a hand on her forearm as she walks to the driver's door. She looks up at me, surprised, hopeful even. "There's a storm coming through. You should wait till tomorrow." And just like a storm showing up and moving through quickly, the storm dormant inside Amy breaks loose. She scoffs at me, pulling her arm free of my grip.

"No, Alex, I'm leaving *now*. I'm done waiting, and hoping, and praying for different. I-I thought you'd at least fight for me to stay for Tallulah's sake, but you couldn't even do that," she looks away from me before finishing, "could you?" And then the tears begin to stream down her face. It's the most emotion Amy's shown me aside from the day Tally was born. I think about reaching out for her, but if I was Amy, would I want a stranger to hug me right now? No. I would want the easiest goodbye possible, no stringing her along. I've got to let her get on the road. She has a solid 5-hour drive ahead of her.

I get a pang of worry in my gut about it, a sour feeling, but what do you expect me to do? I can't solve three years of hurting her while we stand next to her loaded-down car in the rain.

She's staring at me now, willing me for something... anything...but...*fuck!* I don't know what she wants me to do. I just came home and she's springing this on me. She knows the first day is the worst. I'm not acclimated. My mind is somewhere else, fighting some other battle. But I just can't muster the strength to give her the one she wants. *I'm the fucking worst.*

She sees the resignation on me, and nods. Accepting our fates. Accepting that I'm me. I'm broken, and she's going to save herself from this broken life once and for all.

"Goodbye, Alex," she says, somehow managing to fill the words with love and hope. She's a good person at the end of the day. Far better than me, that's for sure.

I try to swallow and push away whatever this feeling is welling up inside of me. It's shitty. I can't put a name to it, but it's shit, I know that.

I watch my wife buckle up, close her door, and reverse out of her parking spot. Her small red SUV pulls out onto the main road, all while I just stand there, frozen.

I'm thinking about some of the other guys in the unit, how they'd handle what just happened. I think at least one or two would act the same as me. More in shock than anything else, but most would have lost it.

Migo would have begged, fallen to his knees, cried – done whatever was needed to keep his wife and kids. He would have bartered his soul to the devil.

Sacks would lose his shit, albeit a bit differently. He'd think there was someone else. Still, he'd try and get Meg to stay.

And then Blanks...I don't know what Blanks would do.

"WHAT THE FUCK ARE YOU DOING, MAN?" Speak of the devil. He walks up to me, in what is now a heavy downpour and shoves me. "Get in your fucking car, man!" His words are venomous.

"WAKE UP, ALEX!" he yells at me again when I don't

move. *Wake up, Alex.* I hear it in a different voice. It's no longer Blanks' deep tone, it's my mother's. It's Georgia's voice. *Wake up, Alex.*

Like getting hit by a bus, every emotion and thought and feeling I should have had catch up to me. "FUCK!" I yell, heading for my truck. Blanks does, too. He's a good brother, won't let me do this alone.

I don't know how long I zoned out after they left. Five minutes, maybe fifteen?

"Red SUV, Virginia plates, QRB-4591. How long was I zoned out for?" I ask while Blanks keeps his head on a swivel as we hit the interstate.

"Longer than you should have been," he says back to me, harshly.

"God damnit, Blanks. HOW LONG?" I raise my voice, and it startles him. I don't raise my voice at people like this. That's not who I am. *That is* not *who I am.*

"17 minutes give or take." Blanks doesn't bring up my outburst, just keeps his eyes on the road. That means she's got maybe fifteen miles on us, at best. With this rain, more likely ten or eleven.

I call her cell, hoping I can convince her to turn around, but she declines. *Fuck.* I finally did it. I pushed her to the breaking point. Amy has always been soft, genuinely sweet, but all it took to break her was my fucked-up, half-life and three years of neglect.

Most drivers are being safe, driving five under the speed limit with the rain coming down this hard, but I'm doing ten over, trying to make up time. She should only be two miles ahead at this rate.

"Fuck!" I slam a palm down on the steering wheel as

brake lights start reflecting against my windshield. It goes on for as far as my eye can see, bringing us to a complete stand-still on the highway.

I bounce my palm impatiently against the wheel, then turn on the radio for probably the first time in this car, flipping to the AM station for highway information. Before I can even hear the reporter, first response sirens sound in the distance, and it's like all the air gets sucked right out of me. I look at Blanks, and he looks at me. The silent conversation is happening again.

Calm down. They're probably just sitting in this traffic, too. Try calling her again.

I hit her contact on my phone and it rings. And it rings. And it rings. *"Hi, you've reached Amy Palomino.* (Baby giggles in the background.) *We're a bit busy at the moment,* (she laughs when the baby laughs louder) *but I'll call you back as soon as I can, promise!"* I look at Blanks, and he sees it on my face.

"She's probably on the phone with her mom," he says, but I shake my head at him. *No, she's not.* Chills run up and down my arms as I throw my truck in park then throw open my door. I don't even bother to shut it, just bolting the second my feet make impact with the asphalt.

Blanks is already yelling at me. "Don't do this! Come back! They're fine!" His voice fades as my feet move me faster down the highway. He honks the horn twice, and is still yelling at me, but that's because he doesn't know what I know. When I heard the first siren, I think I knew. The way Tally and I speak without words, and *know*, it's the same way I knew.

Pumping my arms and pushing my legs, I'm running a

5-minute mile easily, even in this rain. I clock myself gauging the distance, head on a swivel looking for a little red SUV.

But each minute that passes, and her red SUV doesn't come into view, is like someone throwing a shovel of dirt on your coffin. You're already in the ground, sure, but each shovel is just more proof you're never coming out of this.

It's at four minutes and 39 seconds that I see carnage. There's an 18-wheeler and at least eight other cars...at least one of them red. Hard to tell what shape or type of car it is now.

Don't need to see it, though, because I know. Just like I've known.

I weave between parked vehicles the last quarter mile, running like my life depends on it. Probably running faster. I've run like my life depended on it before, and I'm beating any personal records now, bar none.

There's smoke in the air, paramedics, overturned vehicles, and then I pass the first casualty. It's a small white Honda, crushed beyond what the mind can comprehend. I selfishly don't even look to see if there's someone still in there. When I think back on this, I'll feel fucked about it because I might be more qualified to handle a disaster than every person standing on this highway. Of which there are many, at least 12. Some are "good samaritans" trying to help, but I don't want their help. Don't need it. And some are first responders.

Just need to get to that red SUV. And now that I'm closer, I can tell. It's a red SUV. It *was* a red SUV. I'm breathing hard, soaked to the core, but I'm moving towards the red vehicle like nothing, *no one*, has ever existed outside of this moment. The rest of the world goes quiet while my vision tunnels.

At the moment, there's paramedics and firefighters working on the little red SUV. No other car *except* hers is getting worked on. That's either the best sign...or the worst.

"Sir! You can't come over here!" Someone is yelling at me. *Don't give a fuck.* I come to an abrupt stop when I'm face to face with...aftermath. Metal and glass crunch underneath my boots, a siren blares in the distance. Then I freeze and stop breathing altogether when I realize: There's no one in the driver's seat. *There's no more windshield either.* I look around frantically for my wife that's no longer in the car.

Because her body...is on the ground. Covered by a tarp.

I run over and rip the tarp back, and people really start yelling at me now.

"Sir! STOP! YOU CANNOT DO THAT!" *Still don't care.*

Amy. I start crying. It's involuntary. Haven't cried since *that* day.

My body slips into shock. I know it, but I'm powerless against it. So when someone grabs me by the arm to pull me up and away, I fold easily and go with them. Didn't even realize I was on all fours on the ground till then.

"That's my wife," I say. To him? To the universe? I don't know what's really happening right now.

"What?" he asks in return. It's loud, there's machinery prying metal apart, rain pounding against every surface, people yelling – *screaming* – for help.

"THAT'S MY WIFE!" I point to the mangled body on the ground. *That was my wife.*

The firefighter stops trying to drag me away. He looks around trying to gauge something I'm not yet aware of.

"Alright," he resigns. "Come to the truck." He tries to shoulder me towards a vehicle, an ambulance, but I know what he's doing. He's trying to shield me.

"Where's my daughter?"

"Sir, I want you to take a seat and we'll get you a blanket." The guy is really doing a great job at being compassionate, good bedside manor, really.

It doesn't take much to break free of his grip and run over to what's left of Amy's car. I'm there just in time to see the jaws of life prying apart red pieces of metal. Really just remnants of a passenger door.

As soon as there's an opening large enough, three firefighters and a paramedic clamber forward, towards the toddler still strapped into her carseat.

The paramedic turns around first, putting the back of a gloved hand to her mouth, a look on her face I'll never forget. Instantly, I know I'll remember her always. This paramedic, a woman in her late thirties I'd guess, now wears a face that's a mix of devastation...and revulsion. It's haunting how even in the rain I can see her tears.

A guttural sob, a cry, a battle roar escapes me and I fall to the asphalt. *I knew.* I fucking knew the moment it happened. I felt Tally go.

I let them go.

I watched them go.

I packed their car.

I did nothing to stop this and in doing so, *I* sealed their fate.

TWO

JESS

June 6, 2012

I let the last box fall on top of my twin bed and then plop down next to it, falling back. Laid out, staring up at the ceiling, I'm met by the warm eyes of Lance Bass staring back down at me. *Fuck me.* I laugh out loud. This is ridiculous.

No one ever tells you how shitty it feels to move out, go to college, spread your wings — just to move back home four years later. I know the point is to not move home, I understand that, but this is New York City. Free rent is better than any other kind of rent. Plus you're in the city. *Duh.*

"May!" I call out through my open door.

"Yes, baby?" She comes to stand in the entryway of my bedroom with a fresh cup of tea in hand.

"Can you bring me the broom? I can't sleep in here with this poster staring at me." She laughs.

"You have no idea how many times your mother stopped

me from ripping that thing down over the years." She sighs, gets a bit sad for a moment, then wanders back down the hall for the broom.

Mom let me indulge in all my boy band crazes. Well, I guess just boy craziness. Period. (One didn't need to be in a band for me to be crazy about them.)

Once May is back with the broom, I stand on the bed and try to scrape it off. *How the fuck did a five-foot-four thing like me even get this on my 12-foot ceiling?* Actually, I do know how. Sheer determination, I imagine.

May leans against the doorframe of our NOHO loft, watching me. It's not the apartment I grew up in, but we moved here after Mom made tenure at NYU. It was right before high school, which meant 13-year-old Jess got to decorate the shit out of her bedroom. And did she ever.

There's hideous, psychedelic-inspired flowers painted on one wall. Jonas Brothers, Backstreet Boys, and Eminem posters are plastered on another. My twin bed is decked out in PB teen, and yeah, I think I may have been living the life straight out of some Mary-Kate and Ashley movie.

Except in this movie, I have two moms and a dad I don't live with, a pet rat, and an insane obsession with Anna Wintour. (And I do mean 13-year-old-Jess, not current Jess.) So maybe not exactly like an Olsen twin movie.

"Current Jess" still has two moms, but only lives with one of them. And a dad who passed away after my freshman year of college. No more pet rats, no more obsession with Anna Wintour. *Still obsessed with Vogue?* Yes. *But with Anna?* No. But I guess I'm still living in 13-year-old-Jess' bedroom...so there's that.

The broom finally catches a corner of the poster, and I rip it off triumphantly. May still hasn't moved.

"I'm going to visit Jules this afternoon. Probably pick up Thai on the way home. That work for you?" she asks. I give her a warm smile.

"Yeah, that sounds good."

"You could come with me, if you want..." *I don't want.* I don't really have to say it because May already knows and she doesn't wait for my response. "No, right. That's okay. You go on your own time. I'll be back around seven." May moves like she might come in and hug me goodbye, but hesitates and walks out instead.

When May visits with mom, I'm sort of an afterthought. I think they forget I'm there sometimes. I know it's not on purpose, of course, but if my mom is having a good day, she wants to bathe in May's attention. It's just better for everyone if I sit out. My feelings don't get hurt, it doesn't put May and I at odds with each other, and well, my mom likely won't remember the encounter at all.

She lives in a care facility now, Jules does. One that assists with memory care. It's for the best. May couldn't be her full-time caregiver anymore, and they didn't want the burden to fall on me. Not that my mom is a burden, they just wanted me to have a normal life. Always. They always tried to give me a "normal" life. And it was. Normal to me.

I grew up with three loving parents. Two I lived with full time, and one I saw during the summer and on holidays. But I never felt I lacked for love or anything at all, really. My dad might not have lived in the same house as me, but he called me all the time. Wrote me emails when he worked from the road. Bought me a souvenir from every college campus he ever visited, and told me he loved me every chance he got. As far as parental relationships go, I feel like I got pretty lucky.

And then I lived with Jules and May full time. Julia is my mother, as in she gave birth to me, and May is my mom. I always describe it to people like this: Picture Meredith Grey and Cristina Yang, but they're professors instead of doctors, and they're also lesbians. That's my moms in a nutshell.

I crumple up the poster and toss it in the trash. No offense, Lance, just light eyes and frosted tips don't really do it for me anymore. I take a quick look around the space and take note of the few things I could change to make the space feel more grown up. *Paint, new desk chair, new bedding, new lamps, new art – basically a whole new room.* That's alright, it'll give me a project to focus on.

I didn't come back to this apartment much once I started college. Summers were spent at my dad's house, even after he passed. Then a lot of holidays, Julia and May would come to me. Don't get me wrong, I missed the city (the city will always be home), but it wasn't like I missed this place. Sometimes this place is just a reminder of when things started going south for Mom.

Things like finding her keys in the freezer. Or waking up in the middle of the night to see the front door left wide open. It was little oopsies like that that started adding up until eventually, one day, Julia forgot...me.

I walked into the apartment like I did every day senior year. Just praying to get to the end of the semester. *Once I graduate, it's peace out NYC, hello college campus.*

My mom was in the kitchen, so I went to say hi and grab a glass of water.

The look on her face when she saw me should have told

me right away something was wrong. She looked crazed. She had eyes that went too wide, mid bite into a sandwich just hanging halfway to her face.

"What are you doing in here?" She asked me in a voice that sounded so unlike her normal, calming lilt.

"Uh, getting a glass of water?" I posed it back at her. I couldn't piece together what was happening at the time. It's just not something you ever really think about, you know? You don't expect to come home one day, and find that your parent just...forgot who you are.

"This is my house, you need to leave!" Mom said back to me in a raised voice. It hurt. I was confused. She was confused. It sucked.

I immediately called May thinking maybe I'd missed something. *Are they kicking me out? Did they find out about the rave I went to and I'm in trouble?* Let's be honest, no, they wouldn't kick me out over that. May and Jules are hippies at their core, and partying was kind of their thing in the 70s. *Maybe they know I had sex with David (pronounced Da-veed)?* First off, of course they know. They know everything about me, and they certainly wouldn't fault me seeing as May started slipping fresh condoms in my dresser every few years starting at the age of 13.

I stepped outside the front door, tears rolling down my face silently. Thankfully, May picked up after the first ring. Sort of like she anticipated this call.

"May?" I kind of cried out.

"Oh, JJ, what happened?" May asked.

"Is it something I did? I came home, and Mom told me to leave, that this was her house." I was still crying, but May was silent.

"Can you come to my office? I have a meeting I can't miss, but then I'll meet you there and we can talk? And JJ, I promise you haven't done anything wrong. Jules is...well, I'll explain when I see you."

"Yup." It came out sniffly.

I walked the four blocks to the NYU campus. I waited an hour for May, and when she came back, she told me that Mom had early onset Alzheimer's. And then we cried and held each other for a long time.

After that, things changed for us. May took her sabbatical, and so did Jules. May shielded me from my Mom's worst days and brought me in with them on the good, but still it was a struggle. I think when I left for school it was a relief all around.

I went to college where my dad was the long-standing men's lacrosse coach. He'd worked there my whole life. A small university in Kentucky, near Louisville, and I loved it. It wasn't New York, but for the first time in my life, that was a perk, not a deterrent.

I was undoubtedly a city girl through and through, but something about the city darkened my last few years there. Just like if a tree falls in the woods and no one is around. Well, if Jules couldn't remember my childhood, the latest Broadway show we saw, our memories, did they really happen?

The first year at college was great. Spending time with Dad, making new friends, hooking up with new guys, parties — it was college. Then for spring break, Jules and May came to visit. They stayed with Dad and me, and it was like seeing a new side of each parent.

The second day in, Jules had a bad day. She couldn't

remember May, but she remembered my dad and it was heartbreaking. For each of them. I never realized until that day how much my dad still loved my mom, how my mom might have once loved my dad, and how it *killed* May to see this alternate reality play out before her. I felt for each one of them, but probably no one more than my dad.

He might have dated after my mom. I wouldn't know, it's not something I thought to ask, but he never introduced me to anyone, talked about anyone, nothing. I don't remember anything from my childhood that would suggest there were other women, or men (no discrimination), or love, period.

What I will remember is the way my dad stroked Jules' cheek when she embraced him that day. The way you'd embrace a lover. He looked into her hazel eyes, and I could see it written all over him. There hadn't been another for him *because* of her.

He brushed his thumb across her cheek, held her chin in his hand and Jules looked at him adoringly. All while May and I stood by and watched. That's not something I'd wish for anybody to see, least of all May.

May might not have birthed me, but she was my mom. My protector, my nurturer, my ally, and I watched that day crush her soul.

I don't know exactly what happened between Jules, May, and my dad back then. I just know my mom moved to Kentucky in the late 80's, but was back in NYC for my birth in 1990. That's it. Just one big gray area of time I'm not privy to in my parents' lives. And seeing the three of them that day, it made sense. The whole situation reeked of pain.

All these years later, I still haven't gotten the nerve to ask May what happened. She's really the only one left I *could* ask, and she'd only be able to tell her part of the story, which might be the reason why.

I take a seat at my small desk with a pinboard hung above it. It's littered with photos of Jules, May, and me. There's a photo of Dad and I decked out in scarlet for one of his playoff games. A few photos of old friends from prom, and a few from past vacations.

It's the photo of my dad and his sister with me and my cousin that gives me pause, though. I was never super close with that side of my family. It was a bit weird if I'm honest, but I was close with Amy. I always loved her. She was like the big sister I never had. God, I haven't talked to her in ages. I think last I heard she had a baby and a husband, but that was like three years ago, and okay, I'm an asshole. Sure, my dad passed away, but I could've called.

She could've called, too, but like having a baby is distracting. I get that.

I don't know whether it's the nostalgia of today, the longing for something to feel familiar, or the need to hear a friendly voice, but I pick up my phone and hit Amy's contact.

On the third ring, a gruff voice answers. "Hello?"

"Hi, uh...is Amy there?" I ask, a bit confused.

"Who is this?" The deep voice, that is decidedly male, asks back.

"This is Jess Butera. I-uh thought I called Amy Ketterman, well used to be Amy Ketterman, not sure what her married name is." I sort of laugh at that, a bit nervous. *Why?* Because the gruff deep voice is making me feel that way.

"Amy's dead." No pomp, no circumstance, no compassion, just a blatant fact. My stomach plummets. I suck in a little gasp, but stay silent. He's silent, too. Then I think for a minute, how do I know this is someone Amy knows? What if she changed her number and this is just some asshole tired of getting wrong number calls for an "Amy?"

"And *how* do you know this?" I ask, my tone accusing.

"Because I'm her husband. I *was* her husband." *Oh.* His tone is cold if not flat-out rude. Makes sense. though. I'm the asshole now.

"Oh," I say, quietly.

"Yeah, so is there something you need?" He pushes to get me off the phone, but all I can think is: *dick.* This guy's being a dick. I feel bad that Amy married an ass.

"I was just trying to talk to my cousin. I guess, is there an obituary or is there somewhere I could send flowers? I'd look it up, but I don't know her married name."

"There's nowhere to send flowers to. Don't need your flowers, don't need your sympathies." *Click.*

He fucking hung up on me. My blood boils a bit. *Fucking dickhead.* I sit back in my desk chair, still holding the phone and think about what just happened. And all I'm left with is questions.

How did she die? When? What happened to her baby? What was the baby's name? Started with a T or a G maybe? Does she live with her dad? Was that him I just talked to? Is that poor babe stuck with that asshole? How didn't I hear about this? Obviously, with Dad gone, I wouldn't have heard, but my aunt Sally could've let me know. But she didn't, and why? I think I know why. It's because she's a "bigot." (*May's word for her, not mine*). I can't really prove Sally didn't like us for that reason. It could have been because my mom broke my dad's heart and it's as simple as that. But who knows?

Ugh. I can't let this go. I tap Amy's name in my contacts again. On the fourth ring, he answers. "Yes?"

"Hi. First, that was rude. And second, Amy was my family. And I may not have been around much, but I adored her, and I need to know that her daughter is alright." There's silence on his end for a little.

"Her daughter died, too." *What the fuck?* There's a slight softening of his tone when he says this. Then he clears his throat. "Tallulah died, too." I can hear the pain, practically feel it. And a lone tear streaks down my cheek. Alright, maybe he's allowed to act like an asshole. I'd be an asshole, too.

"How?" I ask, my voice quiet. He's quiet on his end for more than a moment.

"You're not going to let this go until you know, are you?" Nope.

"You're right, I'll just keep calling." I'm not trying to sound annoying, it's just the truth.

"Car accident. They think she unbuckled her seatbelt to pick up a pacifier in the backseat during a torrential downpour, and they collided with an 18-wheeler. Both of them gone, instantly." *No.* I touch my fingers to my lips absentmindedly because there are no words that could come out of my mouth to make anything he just said better.

I try, though. "I-I'm very sad for your loss. I'm sad for Amy and I'm sad for Tallulah, and I'm sad for you." There's a choked, gruff mumble that comes through the phone. It's a bit of an affirming sound.

"Okay. I-I'll let you go then," I say, not entirely sure he's still on the line after some time has passed.

"Okay," is all he says, then hangs up. I set my phone

down on my desk and spend the rest of the afternoon thinking about life and how precarious it is. How transient and *heartbreaking* the world can be. How I'm homesick even though I'm sitting in my childhood home. I'm thinking how...I should be with Jules and May right now.

I grab my purse and head towards Mom's care facility with purpose in my stride.

THREE

JESS

December 25, 2012

It would be a bald-faced lie to say I haven't thought about my phone call with Amy's husband at least once a week. It's stuck with me for some reason, and I can't shake the nagging feeling tugging at me. Pulling me.

So with nothing to lose, I text Alexander via Amy's phone.

JESS

I just wanted to say Merry Christmas. How are you doing?

AMY

Merry Christmas. Fine.

I'm doing fine, too. Thanks for asking. What are your plans for the holiday?

I'm sleeping in a crappy hostel in Istanbul.
The plan is to wake up tomorrow.

Right. Sounds dreamy. Why Istanbul?

Work.

Ahh, super spy or something, right?

Or something. If I was a super spy, I
wouldn't have told you I was in Istanbul
though.

Well, maybe it's a ruse? Throw prying eyes
off your scent?

That's not how that works...

Okay, well, glad to hear you're surviving if
not thriving on your European holiday.

Also, not a holiday, but thanks.

😊

April 15, 2013

JESS

Hello. Just checking in to see how you are?

AMY

Fine.

...

?

I'm fine, too, thanks for asking.

Great.

It's her birthday today.

I know.

So I'm just checking in to see how you are.

I said I was fine.

Right you are.

September 18, 2013

JESS
Hi. How are you?

AMY
Fine.

...

And how are you?

Better now, thank you. (Also, I'm fine.)

I'm reaching out because I wanted to know where Amy and Tallulah are buried?

Fairfax Memorial Park. Ketterman plot.

Thank you.

———

September 22, 2013

. . .

It's sunny today. And hot. And humid as fuck. Whenever I imagine coming to a cemetery, I always think it should be overcast, cold, maybe rainy, but it never is. Even when I've visited my Dad, the weather's always been excellent. Well, maybe not excellent, but like, not shitty. I've never needed an umbrella, and isn't that always how it is in the movies? Someone dressed in black, hovering over a gravestone as rain drops plop down on their umbrella?

Well, I'm not wearing black today either. I love black, but today I felt like putting on something sunshine-y for Amy. For her little girl. I chose a wispy, floral dress from this new brand, Reformation. It looks like something Amy would have picked out for me. The buttery yellow color pops against my olive skin and hair. My dark brown (heat absorbing) hair is pulled back in a half-up do, leaving humidity dampened waves falling to the middle of my back.

I feel like Amy would have approved the whole look.

I didn't go to her funeral, obviously, and I couldn't make it last year. I was too busy settling into my new job (read: trying not to get fired) to break away. But I wanted to do this, and decided I would visit her today. To pay my respects for a life cut far too short, and say thanks for the time she spent with me. May even let me borrow the Volvo so I could take my time. Said this way, I could be without an agenda today. It was nice of her.

The drive down is about five hours, NYC to DC. Well, northern Virginia. I could've taken a train, but then getting between the train and the cemetery, timing it all, driving just won out in the end. And the drive wasn't terrible either. I listened to a 90s throwback playlist, stopped for coffee, and got flowers — two bouquets. One primarily whites and yellows, soft and buttery like Amy. And for Tallulah, I got pinks and oranges. I imagine she was just as sweet as Amy, but more vibrant.

I'd called ahead for a map and the placement of their headstones, avoiding hours wandering aimlessly. So when I arrive, it's a quick park and a short walk to where the Kettermans' plots are located.

The cemetery is hilly, and a bit...idyllic? Weird thing to think about a cemetery, but it's true. There's large oak trees scattered throughout the grounds offering shade and the hills roll gently, luring you in to meander through the neat rows of graves. *That's weird to think, right?* Right.

When I get to their row, I divert my gaze to the ground and start looking for their names. *Horace Ketterman, Eunice Ketterman, and on and on until...*Amy Palomino and Tallulah Palomino. They share a headstone, and a grave. I don't know why that makes me feel grateful, but I am, thankful, that she's not alone. She was an only child just like me. We bonded over that at a family reunion once.

My eyes well with water, but I don't really want to let loose any tears, so I don't. I sniffle a bit and hold them in.

Dropping to my knees, I let my purse fall on the soft grass and start arranging the flowers around their gravestone. While I do, I talk to her. To them.

Hi, Ames. I'm sorry I didn't make it here sooner. I didn't know. See, my dad died. And I don't know if you knew that, but I guess if you see him, tell him I said hi.

I'm so sorry that you're here, Amy. I'm sorry that you had to experience that day...with your baby, but I'm glad you're together. Your own little girl gang, right?

Remember when we formed that girl gang at Pops' 80th

birthday party? Why were all the boys in our family such pricks? Doesn't matter, we kicked their ass in flag football, and I think Pops had never been so proud to have granddaughters than he did that day.

I'm really sorry we lost touch somewhere along the way. I would've loved to have known Tallulah June. June, that wasn't for me? Was it? I don't think it was, but I can pretend, and that makes me love your little girl even more than I possibly could have already.

I sit back from my floral arranging and run my fingers over the engraved headstone. It's something I do when I visit my dad as well. I trace his name, Robert Butera, over and over. But here, today, I trace Tallulah June Palomino's name just once. I think, more than anything, I feel the most sorry for never meeting her daughter. I can't place the feeling for why that is...

"Ahem." A deep clearing of the throat startles me and my shoulders shoot up. I turn around to find a man standing a few feet back, watching me. I didn't even hear him approach. He doesn't come bearing flowers, or anything, and my hackles rise for a second since there's no one else around. *It's broad daylight, and this is not New York,* I remind myself.

I stand, dusting off my dress, and turn towards the man who has moved closer.

"Can I help you?" I ask.

"Just waiting my turn to pay my respects," he says to me in a voice I think I recognize.

"Alexander?" I ask. Even though we've texted, he's never told me his name. But I looked up the obituary after that phone call and learned that Amy's married name was Amy Palomino, *survived by Alexander Palomino.* The same

Alexander Palomino who's been awarded practically every medal for valor except the medal of honor. I've never seen pictures of him. He's not on social media. (I looked.) He's got a quiet presence in this world if he even has one at all. And everything I have found of him is written in Amy and Tallulah's obituary.

He looks down slightly, maybe bashfully or ashamed? Before he looks up at me and nods, replying simply with, "Alex."

I extend my hand to him.

"I'm Jess, Amy's cousin." I nod over my shoulder to the gravestone. Like an idiot. He nods, too, taking my hand in his and it's like my hand gets swallowed by a bear's paw. It's massive, making me feel even smaller than I already do. I'm just some lowly cousin, taking up space and time at his wife's and daughter's grave on the anniversary of their deaths.

"Nice to meet you." I give him a smile, then grab my purse. "I'll leave you three alone."

He doesn't say anything in response, just a gentle nod and I make my way down the hill towards the Volvo. Sliding into the car, I sit there and watch him. I watch the way he takes off his baseball hat and folds the bill over and over. I watch how he runs his big hands through his sandy colored hair. I watch him crouch down, his massive thighs straining against his blue jeans.

I see the way his eyes never leave that gravestone. I see how much love he pours out from his soul. I see a man mourning, deeply, the loss of his two greatest loves and I see how that must be one of the most unbearable types of grief.

Feeling like an intruder when I do this, I pull out my phone and take a picture of this man crouched and hovering over their graves. There's something about the moment I don't ever want to forget. Just another reminder of our fleeting presence here. (Just a reminder that a love like that exists.)

I pull out of my parking space and drive away, checking the rear view multiple times and never once see him shift, move, or drop his gaze away from their headstones.

September 23, 2013

JESS

Why don't you disconnect this phone line?

AMY

So that I can call and hear the voicemail recording no matter when or where I am.

Oh.

Do you always carry the phone around with you, too? You always reply pretty quickly.

Yes.

It was nice to finally meet you, put a face to the name.

Same.

December 25, 2013

JESS

Merry Christmas. How are you?

AMY

Merry Christmas. Fine.

Fine and...

How are you?

I'm okay.

Just okay?

Weird day. It's a bad day for one of my moms, which means it's a bad day for my other mom. And it's Christmas. So it's hard.

Sorry.

It could be worse. It could always be worse.

Yes, it can.

September 22, 2014

JESS

Hi.

AMY

Hey.

Will you be visiting them today?

Yes.

Do you go every year?

If I'm in the country, yes.

Okay, I hope the day is kind for you.

Thnks.

December 25, 2014

JESS

Merry Christmas

AMY

Merry Christmas.

How are you?

And so the student finally becomes the master.

Haha. I'm good. Today's a good day for my mom. So that means it's a good day for both of my moms and, well, it's Christmas.

Good.

What does that mean? Good day?
Bad day?

A good day is when my mom can remember me, can remember her wife, and can forget that some days she can't remember us at all. A bad day is when she doesn't remember. Sometimes it's me, sometimes it's my other mom, May. Sometimes it's everyone.

Sorry to hear that.

It could be worse and today's a good day. Right?

Right.

How are you? Stuck in some five-star resort in Indonesia?

Ha! Nope. In rural Georgia, doing training.

Did, did you just...laugh?

Not out loud.

Okay...

September 23, 2015

JESS

Hi. How are you?

AMY

Fine.

How was yesterday?

I'm out of the country.

I'm sorry. You should have told me. I would have gone in your place.

You would have?

Yes.

December 25, 2015

AMY

Merry Christmas. Good day or bad day?

JESS

You have rendered me speechless.

You just messaged me...of your own accord.

I did. Good day or bad day?

An okay day. We don't get many good days anymore. Just okay.

I'm sorry.

It could be worse.

Always.

How are you?

Fine.

Really?

Tally would have been almost 7.

Tally, that's beautiful. What was she like?

Quiet. Sweet. Full of life.

Sounds like her mom.

Yes.

Is today a good day or a bad day?

It's actually a good day. I don't talk about them. With anyone. Except sometimes my shrink. He'll be thrilled to hear about this conversation actually.

Then good. I'm glad.

September 20, 2016

AMY

I'm stuck. I might not be able to make it this year. Can you?

JESS

I think so.

I can make it work.

Thnks.

———

September 22, 2016

Today it's cold and overcast. Not perfect "cemetery weather" exactly, but close to it.

Aside from the weather, it's the same drill as last time. May lets me take the Volvo. I listen to Prince for the majority of the drive. I make a stop for coffee, then two bouquets of flowers.

Since the weather is drab, I opt for brighter blooms than last time. This time, I do bright yellows and oranges for Amy. And for Tally, bright pink and purples.

I wear my saddle-colored Rag and Bone booties with a dark purple DVF wrap dress. My hair is down and loose, adding warmth to my neck on this 50-degree, gloomy day and when I get out of the car to walk the short distance to their graves, I slip into my long Ralph Lauren, wool coat.

It's a quintessential fall day this time. There's a breeze rustling, turning leaves off the trees surrounding the neat rows of headstones. And when the wind whisks up and around my coat, I start walking more briskly to avoid getting too cold.

Kneeling down on the cool grass, I start by arranging the flowers. Yellows and oranges surround the side with Amy's name and pinks and purples surround the side with Tally's name. While I do, I talk to both of them this time.

Hi, girls! It's cold out here today. Feels like my nipples could practically cut glass! I know, Amy. Language. But I think Tally is old enough for some girl talk now, right? Remember that summer you were a senior in high school and I was only a freshman, and you took me with you to that kegger?

See, Tally, I'm not the only one who can be a bad influence. I giggle a bit out loud. *Shall I catch you up on my life then? Let's see here...Antony broke up with me last month. Said I didn't have enough time for him anymore. He's right. I don't have time for bullshit.*

Language! I know!

I'm working for a stylist right now. She does a lot of actors and actresses. A lot of work on broadway. And you want to know something? I hate it. I hate all of it. If I never steam another piece of clothing in my life, I think I could be really happy.

But I live in New York, rent free (still), and I have a couple close friends who I go out with occasionally. I have entirely too much casual sex. (Tally, ear muffs.) Actually, there's no such thing, Amy. The sex is good, almost glad Antony broke it off because it was getting a bit stale, to be honest.

Okay, Tally, un-earmuff yourself. I hope wherever you two are today, it's warm and sunshiney, just like the both of you.

I trace both their names silently, then dust my hands off and move to stand.

The warmth I feel at my back startles me, and he grips the back of my arms to steady me.

"Sorry, didn't mean to scare you," he says in that gruff

tone of his. I whip around and come face to face (in actuality, it's face to chest) with Alexander Palomino.

I look up at him and he looks different now. He's got a full beard that's neatly trimmed, a deep tan, and he looks like he's packed on an extra 50 pounds of muscle. He was broad and large before, but now he's larger than life. A real Thor amongst men.

"You made it," I say, staring up at him.

"Came straight from the airport," he says. I nod.

"Good." I give him a quick smile. "I'll let the three of you be alone now."

"You could stay...if you want," he says to me. But I don't want. There's a pull here, *oddly*, but I think back to the last time I came. When I watched him silently pour his heart out to the ground beneath him, and I don't want to intrude on that. This is his special place. *Their special place.*

I gently shake my head, and I can't tell with his beard, but I think his face falls slightly. "I'll see you around, Alex," I say and walk down the small hill.

When I get to the car, and slide into the driver's seat, I take a moment to admire him. *What? No.* Not admire. Just look. I was just *looking* at him. And then he turns and looks at me. And my cheeks feel hot. *The fuck?*

I don't think he can really see my facial expressions from this distance, but I give a sort of smile and a wave and I pull out of my parking spot. Glancing back in the rear view, I watch him watch me drive away.

————

December 26, 2016

AMY

I'm guessing yesterday was a bad day?
Merry (late) Christmas.

JESS

It was one of the worst bad days.

Sorry to hear.

Good day or bad day for you?

It was an okay day. I was surprised I didn't
hear from you.

Sorry.

No need.

Okay.

Let me know if you need anything.

A vacation.

Ok...

I'm not literally asking you for a vacation.
Calm down.

Ha, okay.

Was that "ha" out loud?

You know what, I actually think it was.

Oh my gawd. That means today is a good
day because I made Alexander Palomino
laugh. No matter what.

Happy to be of service.

Thank you. Truly.

I should be the one thanking you. For showing up.

No need.

February 24, 2017

JESS

Today has been the worst day.

AMY

What's wrong?

My mom, Julia, passed away today.

I'm sorry.

Can I do anything?

No, nothing. I just...needed to tell someone who would understand.

Okay. If you want to talk, you could always call me.

On your late wife's phone?

571.300.6820

Anytime, Jess.

June 6, 2017

JESS

I'm thinking about moving

Also, this is Jess.

ALEX

Where to?

And I knew who it was, Jess.

DC?

Why DC?

It's still a city, but it's not New York. Boston is too cold for me, and I don't really love the idea of living in Pennsylvania.

Do you live in NYC now?

Yes.

Why would you want to leave the greatest city on Earth?

One: right?! It is the greatest city. But two, if I'm honest, it's a couple reasons. I don't want to walk through my city and only think about the absence of someone from it. At the same time, I don't want to walk around the corner and not have a single person know my name or face. I used to live for the anonymity, but now...I want something different. I want to start over. Be someone else.

Whoa whoa, I think you just broke my phone with all those words you're throwing out there.

Too much?

No, I got excited. It's the most you've shared with me before.

You don't share much with me.

> I share the most with you.

That can't be right. And those are not butterflies I just felt right now. *No.* It's just that I've never had a guy friend before. That's *just* a friend. But I think that's what Alexander has become to me. A friend. I push the butterflies down, those misdirected pests.

> I'm honored to be that friend for you then.

> Are you local to DC?

Sometimes. I have family that live there.
Lots of people in my professional network.
A lot of friends, too.

> Well, if you hear of any job openings in your professional network, let me know?

Will do.

———

Alex
June 17, 2017

A

> Hey.

J
Hi.

I know of a job opening coming up at the start of September. It's an assistant to the head of UX design for a tech company. She's a good boss. Benefits are great. She doesn't really need you to have experience with web/app design, just have to have an eye for design.

Seriously?

Yes.

Um, I'd love an intro!

Okay, I'll forward you the opening once it comes up.

Thank you, seriously.

How are you?

I'm doing okay. Packing up my dad's house to sell it. Bigger project than I thought it would be.

Your dad?

He passed away about a year before Amy. I'm just now getting around to closing out his affairs.

I just didn't realize your dad was in the picture, that's all.

He was.

How are you?

Same as always.

You're just always fine?

> If I say yes, would you believe me?

No

> Okay then, no. But I work in a high stress environment and I don't really have the option to not be okay because there are other people depending on me being fine. They need me to be better than fine. So I just sort of am fine. All the time.

Sounds tough. Do you ever take breaks?

Only when they're mandated.

> Sure.

That's a no then, ha!

> Since when do you think you know me?

I don't know. It just sort of happened.

Huh. It just sort of happens that you're getting by, and then one day you realize she didn't text you on Christmas and you panic. You think maybe she got in a car accident and you're stressed and freaking out, and you think *why the hell am I freaking out about this* and then it hits you. Because somewhere along the way, it just sort of happened that this woman wormed her way into *my* cold, dead heart. *Fuck.*

NOW

FOUR

JESS

"Mmkay. You, my dear, are going to be chill for 15 minutes, right? So mommy can shower?" I look down at my daughter, looking sweet as pie, but knowing she's a little demon in cherub's clothing.

I've got the Pack 'n Play set up in the bathroom, filled with toys, teething rings, and an iPad playing Bluey on repeat. *Like, come on girl, cut me some slack.*

She's been teething on and off for months. And that means no one is sleeping. Which also means I've been walking around our row house like a zombie most days. But that ends now.

I'm putting my foot down. I'm pulling out all the stops, including screen time. (Judge me, I dare you.) But this mom's gotta do what this mom's gotta do. And that starts with a shower and a blow out.

I slowly back away from the Pack 'n Play like you would a

ticking time bomb, then quickly slip into the shower when she turns to look at the iPad.

I'm under the hot spray less than two minutes before she starts screaming bloody murder. *Two minutes.* My heart rate spikes at the sound. I step out of the shower, soaking wet and stare at Eden who is standing at the edge of the Pack 'n Play with crocodile tears rolling down her pink cheeks.

"Edie, we talked about this," I say in mock scolding as I throw a towel down on the tile to walk over to her. "Mommy needs 15 minutes, okay?" I try to soothe her without picking her up. If I pick her up, I'll have to hold her while I shower.

I notice that Bluey has stopped playing on the iPad. I get it. I'd be pissed, too.

"Is this what we're upset about?" I ask her. She doesn't say anything back (obviously, she's only eight months old), but she plops down on her butt while I reach over to restart the episode.

A text message comes through, and I swipe up quickly to get back to Bluey. But another text message comes through before I can even start the video again. It's Jamie. *Ugh.* I swipe the message away again and press play, but another message comes through. Again. I roll my eyes and drop my shoulders in annoyance. That's what I get for trying to use Tommy's iPad.

Grabbing my phone off the counter, I pull up the show, then put my phone straight into the hands of the babe. (Mother-of-the-year stuff right here.) Tommy would be pissed, but like...I *need* a shower. It's been a solid week since I've had an "everything shower." Things are getting desperate (and hairy) over here. And Tommy got a babysitter for tonight, which he hasn't done since...ever.

And we're going out, which we haven't done in...what feels like forever.

The wheels may have fallen off, but we're getting our shit together to-day. And that's final. I walk Tommy's iPad to his bathroom counter to set it down, just as another text message from Jamie comes through.

JAMIE

Have you told her yet?

Excuse me, what? My heart stutters in my chest.

Do you ever just *know* something is bad before you really even know? That's *this*. Instant dread.

I don't typically read Tommy's messages. I've never felt I had a reason to snoop on my husband. We have a great relationship. We're partners, we talk constantly, our sex life is pretty good, all things considered. I mean, we do have an eight month old...but I open his messages app where I have a birds-eye view of their unfolding conversation.

TOMMY

No. But I'm planning to.

T. You said you were going to tell her last week.

I know. Just Eden's not sleeping great, and it was a rough week. I didn't want to pile on.

All the alarms are going off in my mind now. Bells are ringing. Flags are waving. Tell me *what*? And "T"? I know they're friends, but something about the nickname irks me. Tommy is his nickname. He doesn't need *another* nickname.

> I'm ready for you. I held up my part of the bargain, T. Now it's your turn. We can finally do this. If you're having second thoughts, you just need to let me know.

I'm breathing rapidly now, short bursts of air, in and out. My legs are trembling. My hands are shaking. There's way too much hot saliva in my mouth.

> I'm ready for us, too. Tonight. I promise. I love you.

Oh my god. *I love you.* Three little words, each one like a dagger, stealing my breath, halting my heart, and souring everything that Tommy and I are. *Everything we were.*

I'm calling it, July 12, 2023 at 10:49 A.M. That's the moment I knew — my marriage was ending. Standing soaking wet, naked, in my bathroom while the sounds of Bluey and Bingo devolving into fits of laughter echoed around the small space, that's when I knew.

Placing both hands against the bathroom sink, I hunch forward and let the counter hold me up. I give myself a couple minutes, but that's all. Just a few minutes to feel the absolute misery and shittiness of it all. Because Jess Butera won't let this be the thing that breaks her. Not a fucking chance.

———

I'm not trying to toot my own horn or anything, but, *damnnnnn.* I don't think I've ever looked better.

As soon as I threw Tommy's iPad out our second story window, I took my everything shower. And it's like Eden knew I needed it because she calmed down and watched her Bluey religiously for the next hour. I was able to shave (every-thing), lather up my body with the fancy body oil I got from France, and give myself a killer "fuck me" blowout. I did my makeup like I was on my way to an awards gala, then piled Eden and myself in the car for a little shopping trip...on Tommy's credit card.

We hit up all my faves: Saks, Gucci, and Prada, then were back home in time for me to change for my "date" with my "husband."

I tighten the strap on my new YSL Opyum sandals, then stand and admire myself in the mirror. If I had red hair I'd look like Jessica-fucking-Rabbit in my red, strapless Bronx and Banco lace dress that pops against my extra tan-for-the-summer, olive skin.

I *am* a fucking beautiful, amazing woman. Fuck Tommy DiAngelo. Fuck Jamie. I hope they both choke on a dick.

"Wow," Tommy says from our bedroom doorway.

He smiles at me and I smile back, but I don't mean it. All I'm thinking is: *fuck you, fuck you, fuck you.* Maybe the mature thing to do would have been to call him. Let him know that I *knew.* Call off the date. Let our marriage fade away peacefully.

But then I thought about it and decided: Nope. Won't be doing that, will we?

I've given up a lot for this man. So much. And now he's going to dump me? *For Jamie???* No, I think I'll go out with a bang, looking like a million dollars, and ending the night by throwing a drink in Tommy's face. That's more my speed.

"Ready?" I ask sweetly, and he nods. It's disturbing how there's nothing off about his behavior. No hint that he's about to end our marriage and tell me he's in love with his best friend. It makes me wonder how long it's been going on because he's acting completely normal. Absolutely normal. *Fucking sociopath.*

I walk out of our bedroom and as I pass him, he places a hand at the small of my back and gives me a kiss on the cheek. *Judas.*

Our neighbor Glenn is babysitting tonight and she's already settled into the sofa in our living room with Eden in the crook of her arm while they read *The Velveteen Rabbit*. The scene makes me sad. Glenn looks a bit like Julia did.

Eden. Her little family is collapsing and she has no idea. *I had no idea either, babe.*

I give her a quick kiss on her forehead and thank Glenn before walking outside to wait in Tommy's car for him.

He's right at my back, though, slipping a hand around my waist and as we get to the car, he pulls my back against him. My stomach rolls and I have to fight off the urge to turn around and punch him. I do fight the urge because I'm curious: How's he planning to go about this? Wait until after dinner? Or just the first drink? What's the end game here? Serve me divorce papers with dessert?

"I'm so glad we're doing this," he whispers against my ear, and all I can think is: *Yeah, I bet. Big day for you, bud.* He can't see my face, so I just nod against his shoulder while feeling like I could crack any minute. But I won't. He doesn't deserve to break me.

He opens my car door, rests his hand on my leg while we drive, then drops me off while he goes to find parking. While he does, I slip into the bar that's at the alley entrance to our restaurant and take a quick shot of Don Julio for some liquid courage.

I walk back out just in time to see him walking up 9th Street towards me. A genuine looking smile on his face. *Ick.*

I used to think he was so handsome. (Okay fine, I still think he's handsome as fuck). He's svelte. (Picture Harry Styles if Harry ran marathons and shrunk an inch or two). And he dresses to the nines in Armani most days. But on top of looking fuckable, he's also intelligent and funny and...I hate that I'm losing him. I should say, I hate that I lost him. Because he's already gone to me.

I put on a mask of confidence and vow I'll make it through tonight without shedding one tear. (At least not in front of him.) *Not one goddamn tear, Jessica.*

He slips next to me, and leads me down the alley to our hidden restaurant with a hand at the small of my back the whole time. The touch burns my skin and I can feel the heat creeping up my neck to my cheeks. It's not desire, though, it's something more like rage.

But before we step into the restaurant, Tommy takes my hand, effectively pulling me to a stop. He stands practically eye to eye with me in my almost 5-inch heels.

"I don't want to ruin that lipstick, but can I kiss you?" *Considerate prick.* He glances down at my lips and I can see the longing isn't missing from his eyes. It's just like it always is.

Well, I can play this game, too.

"I thought you'd never ask," I say seductively, then lean forward to kiss him.

He's warm and tastes slightly minty. He pushes his tongue in, and I let him. The kiss is like it always is. Like we can't wait to get home and rip each other's clothes off. My stomach sinks at the image and I end the kiss with a sharp nip at his bottom lip. (Might have drawn blood.)

He pulls away a few inches and puts his fingers to his lip, staring at me slightly in shock. I play it off innocently with a devilish wink and he smiles, but it's slow. It's the first sign of the night to come. The canaries in the mine start to pass out, starved of oxygen. Somewhere, a bell tolls. A flag waves. A siren wails. Maybe he's wondering if I already know. Or maybe he's wondering if that nip was on purpose...

I starve him the opportunity to ask me as I turn and give him my back to enter the restaurant.

"I just love this restaurant," I chat with the host while they seat us. My voice is unusually sunny for this run-of-the-mill dinner. "Nope, no anniversary tonight. No special occasion. Just a night I'm sure I'll *never* forget," is my response when they ask if we're here celebrating anything.

Crickets from Tommy. He's not an idiot. He's perceptive. Between the kiss (where he probably tasted tequila on me) and that comment, he's probably understanding that I'm not as clueless as he anticipated.

Once we're seated, I notice we've been sat at a table for four. When the host only clears away one additional place setting, I glance at Tommy and raise an eyebrow. It's a question, and as much as I wanted to let this play out organically, my roiling stomach can't sit through seven courses waiting.

"Tommy? Would you like to explain?" I ask, fake sweetness coating my voice. He reaches across the table for my hand, but I don't give it. Instead, I lean back in my chair, adding additional space between us.

"Jess. I love you so much. You know that, right?" *No. I*

don't reply. I just sit there waiting, absorbing this moment. There's people all around us, enjoying their pre-dinner cocktails. There's servers bustling in between tables. The kitchen is open-air to the dining room, and the clatter of pans and people yelling out "fire!" bounces against walls and rattles around inside my brain.

But everything gets fuzzy in the lead up to *this*. Whatever comes out of his mouth next is likely to change my world, effective immediately. I should have just let this play out. I'm not ready. I don't want it. I'd take it back. But I can't.

The train has left the station.

"I want us to explore opening up our marriage."

The clatter ceases. The clinking glasses halt. The shuffle of feet stops. The kitchen turns down to a simmer. And all I see, all I hear, is my husband asking me for an open marriage.

I just keep staring at him. *Remember, Jess, no tears. Not a fucking one.*

He's looking at me expectantly. His hair is slightly moppy today, a loose piece of wavy brown hair falling forward and he pushes it back while still waiting on me.

"Why?" I think, I *hope*, I'll catch him in a lie because I'm a sick bitch that wants — no *needs* — this to hurt.

I can tell he's grappling with something internally before he finally lets *it* out. "I'm in love with Jamie." If I thought him asking for an open marriage was bad, this is the sucker punch. The kick in the stomach. *Jamie*, who's been in his life since before I was. *Jamie*, who is our child's godparent. *Jamie*, who he stays with when he works in Taiwan.

"How long?" I ask, needing to know how long I've been played a fool. Needing the pain.

He doesn't look down, or ashamed, or any of the things he should, and a part of me thinks: *Alright, good for fucking you.*

"Since always," he says apologetically, yet also sincerely.

Okay. (Read: Not okay. Nothing is okay.) I'm laying on the ground, breathless. Sucker punched. Bruised ribs from where his boot is repeatedly hitting me, and now he drives the dagger through my chest. *Direct hit.*

"Then what the fuck do you need me for?" I ask coldly. My voice is ice. My gaze is murderous. Back stiff, and ramrod straight.

He looks sad, like he's wondering, *'How could she even ask that?'* My gaze doesn't waver, though. My spine is locked, I'm poised, and not one fucking tear will be shed. He does not get to break me. Period. The end.

"I still love *you,* Jess. I love our family. I want all of us...to be a family." At that, I laugh disingenuously and shake my head.

"I cannot believe you would even ask that of me." I stand up. I'm done here. He doesn't even know me.

My only regret is I didn't wait long enough to order a drink to throw in his face.

A hand at my back sends a chill down my spine. I turn to face the gentle touch and am met with gorgeous green eyes, golden hair, tawny skin, and a million-dollar smile. (Think Theo James. I know, is it any wonder my husband is in love with him?)

"Jamie." I nod at him curtly, still standing out of my seat.

"Jess." He looks at me, then at Tommy, then back to me. "So he told you." I will not let them have this over me.

"He may have just told me, but I already knew." I reach

out to hold Jamie's arm slightly. I don't know why. I think a part of me hopes it will make Tommy jealous.

Tommy tilts his head like a lost puppy. All innocence. *Ick*. Ick. Ick.

"I'm not interested in being anyone's spare," I say, giving Tommy a sad smile. I look at Jamie to see concern reflected back at me.

"I don't want it to be an 'either or,' Jess," Tommy says to me and I roll my eyes mentally.

"I'm sure you wouldn't, Tommy." I push my chair back with my legs, pat Jamie on the chest as I go up on tiptoes and whisper in his ear, "He's all yours, buddy. Thanks for ruining my daughter's family." And then I walk away. I ignore Tommy's plea for me to stop, and when I look back, Jamie is preventing Tommy from getting up with a hand on his shoulder.

Fuck them.

I walk out of the alley and down 9th Street. I walk with abandon. I even slip out of my heels and stroll barefoot down the streets of DC. (Gross, right?) Well, I don't care. Can't care.

I walk to City Center and stop for gelato, then walk up and down the brightly lit shops. I pretend to window shop, but I don't absorb an ounce of anything I see.

Eventually, I find a planter and sit on the edge to stare off into the distance, occasionally glancing down to see if my gelato has turned to creamy soup in its cup.

My life is shuddering to a halt while the world around me...just keeps marching. Pedestrians head to the metro. Tourists stop in front of Moncler. Interns pop into Dolcezza for their pre-going-out quad espresso. It's amazing, all this forward motion. But not me.

I've never wished for a time machine before. Not when my dad died, not when Julia died. But now...I think I would go back. I'd go back to a night I wish I could forget, and see how that might have changed...everything.

But that doesn't exist. It's not real. So I pull out my phone and hover over Britain's contact. I could use my best friend right now...but damn, she doesn't need anymore stress in her life. She's just a few months pregnant. Heartbroken. She's trying to forge a new life for herself, and her kids. She doesn't need to carry my weight either. *She's unknowingly carried my mistakes for years.*

Instead, I flip to messages and do something I haven't done in a long time. Years, actually.

JESS

> Today was a bad day. My husband is in love with his best friend. He asked if I'd be their third wheel, but I won't. I refuse to do it. Not sure what I'll do now. Maybe it's time to move back to the city. Maybe May will let E and I have my old room. But I think you're right. Me coming to DC was a mistake.

Maybe I text Amy because I know in all likelihood I've just sent the message out into the ether and not to Alex, or anyone real for that matter. Which is oddly satisfying in its own right.

I'm sure Alex disconnected the line years ago. But on the off chance he didn't, there's a sort of hopeless thrill I get from texting him all my craziest thoughts and dreams (read: fears). It's freeing to tell someone who doesn't give a crap about me.

Someone who can't judge me. And even if they did, I wouldn't give a shit.

I wait a few minutes, a little bit hopeful, and when nothing comes through, I slip my phone back into my new Bottega Venetta clutch (thanks, Tommy) and start walking towards the metro. I don't bother checking for a response from "Amy" after that.

When I get to the escalator at Gallery Place, I put my shoes back on. I put on my don't-fuck-with-me-face, and head home.

Home. Fucking laughable.

FIVE

JESS

It's almost midnight when Tommy slips into our bed. *The fucking gall.* I immediately sit up and stare at him. My eyes wide. Livid. That's what I am, livid. He has the nerve to get into our bed after...*that?*

"What are you doing?" I ask harshly.

"Come here." He reaches out for me, but I lurch back and away from him. "Jess, baby, please come here." *No. No. No.* I shake my head. Finding words is all of a sudden way too hard.

He sits up and slips an arm around my midsection, pulling me towards him. I could fight back, push him away, but the shitty thing is, I need somewhere to rest my head. I need someone to hold me and tell me everything is going to be alright. I need comforting, too, and it's a miserable realization to understand that Tommy is that person for me — *was* that person for me.

Fuck him for smelling so good, too. The cologne I bought him for his birthday fills our shared space. Our shared existence. And especially fuck him for *feeling* so good, for absorbing the weight I've placed on his shoulder.

"Jess, I told you without telling you a long time ago." I stiffen in his arms, at his words. I know Tommy is bisexual. I knew that. It's never been an issue. Not once. It's the betrayal that bothers me. It's the fact that he's not *mine* and mine alone that bothers me.

Yes, I knew there was someone he was with a long time ago that he still had feelings for, but he assured me it was in the past. It would have never worked. It could *never* happen. (Never say never, huh?)

"I didn't know it was Jamie, Tommy. You left that part out." I can feel him nod against my back, then rest his chin on my shoulder.

"Jamie didn't want anyone to know. His family isn't like our family, Jess. They don't understand."

"So now that Jamie's ready, he says jump, and you do?" I ask, the hurt burning my airways.

"No," he hesitates. "I've been trying to figure this out for a long time because I love you, Jess. But I also love Jamie. He's my best friend, an-and I've wanted to be with him since I was 13." My eyes well with tears. *Not one fucking tear, Jess*, and by sheer force of will, I swallow hard and hold them in.

"How can I compete with that?" I ask. I'm progressive. I'm all for polyamory, gender fluidity, sex-positivity, blended families. But when it comes to what *I* want, I don't want to come in second place. I don't want to be watered down to just some surrogate for their dream family.

Ugh! I want to scream. *Is this how my dad felt? Just some sperm donor, some extra to the leading roles of Jules and May? I'm just the "mistake" to Tommy and Jamie, aren't I?*

"It doesn't have to be a competition, sweetheart," Tommy says, soothing me. I laugh inwardly, and roll my eyes.

I hate that I still love him, though. So when he pulls me onto his lap, I don't stop him. When he peppers me with soft kisses along my shoulders, I let him. When he slips a hand under my nightgown, he finds me wet because my body still wants him.

I know I'm a sick bitch for still wanting him, I know that. But there's this desperate part of me that has something to prove. That he still desires me. I'm still worthy. It wasn't all a lie. And I am desperate — to prove all of that.

He lays me out beneath him, sliding my nightgown up my torso as he gazes at me intently. And it's just like it's always been. There's still that same fire there. I can see where he's bulging against his briefs. Nothing is different, nothing has changed...except me knowing.

His hand grips my breast as he trails hot kisses down my abdomen, and then, like a flip of a switch, the need within us both turns primal. There's that desperation lacing each touch. There's a torment in each tug of our garments. When he rips my nightgown, the sound makes me even more wet.

There's a sort of tortured roughness when he pushes into me, and my head falls back, muscles already clenching and pulsing. *I love my husband, I love my husband's cock, I love when my husband fucks me;* the words play over in my mind.

But it's all a lie, though. *My* husband? No. He was never mine, was he?

The needy desperation of fucking turns sour and my eyes clench tight as I focus on my pleasure and mine alone. *Fuck you, Tommy DiAngelo.* I put my hand on my clit and rub, bringing myself to orgasm within seconds. He comes with me, but I've already started the disassociation and I don't care. I barely wait for him to finish emptying himself when I push him off me.

Every bad feeling seems to find me at once. It's anguish, it's disgust, it's despair. I picture Tommy and Jamie. *Does Tommy fuck Jamie like that? Is it better? Do they make love? It's not fast and hard, is it? It's not like it just was with me, I bet. Where Tommy is just dying for it to be over as quickly as possible? Probably not.*

Stumbling to the bathroom, I shut the water closet door, pee, clean up, then come back out to grab my phone off the charger.

"Where are you going?" Tommy asks, a little befuddled.

"I love you, Tommy, but I can't do this. It'll eat me alive." Even in our darkened room, I can see his face fall. "I'll be sleeping in the guest room until we figure out next steps...and you're on morning duty." I look down at my phone, *July 13th, 2023 at 1:27 A.M.* It's official *now*. My marriage is over.

————

I'm lying in bed, staring at the ceiling when I hear the first cry. It's shortly followed by the sound of Tommy shuffling down the hall to get our daughter.

Normally, I'd get her and bring her back to bed for morning cuddles. That was our routine. Get the baby, family cuddles in bed. Then Tommy would get up first to bring me a coffee that I'd drink while he got ready for the day. It sounds picturesque, right?

But that's the thing about a picture. You're getting a one dimensional view of someone's life. Just a glimpse of someone's layered and nuanced existence. A picture tells the story of a fragment of a second. That's all. Just an infinitesimal fraction of your life, representing such a small moment in time, it essentially amounts to nil in the scheme of things.

A quick snapshot glosses over the emotions, the hurt, the pain, and all the hidden secrets. (You won't find those happily displayed on your Instagram feed.)

If someone took a photo of me right now, maybe they'd see some of the truth.

Hanging in some sparse gallery, a single photo is mounted to cheap cardstock. The work of art titled: "Sad Woman Stares at Ceiling."

But if you'd have taken a photo of me at this exact time yesterday, the photo could have easily been titled *"Marital Bliss in Capitol Hill."* And even I wouldn't have known it was all a lie. (Wild, right?)

I can hear the front door opening, then there's an extra pair of footsteps that join my husband's downstairs. Joining *Tommy's* downstairs. (Have to stop referring to him as my husband, don't I?)

I feel a bit nauseated when I sit up, hands already clammy. The nervousness is coursing freely through my veins.

But I'm not as furious as I thought I'd be. (One should feel that way, right?) When the person you've married (and thought was your person) is in love with someone else, you're supposed to be burn-the-world-down pissed. And I thought I was yesterday, but today I'm finding it hard to give enough fucks to be irate.

What I am is nervous, because today is the day that starts a new life for me and for Eden. And I'm afraid that I have no idea what that looks like. Where do we live? Do I find a new job? Do I put Eden in daycare? Do we split custody? Do I babysit for their date nights? *Hate that, though.*

I softly pad out of the guest bedroom and down the stairs and...it's as bad as I imagined it would be. (Okay, maybe I am a little fucking pissed still.)

Tommy is sitting on our living room sofa against Jamie with our daughter wedged between the two of them. I've never seen a more beautiful family.

It's miserable, this feeling. Being the outsider looking in.

They're talking softly to one another and it reminds me of times I've seen them similar to this before. Times when I thought they just shared a tight bond, but now every time I'll look back on the memories, I'll wonder. I'll question. I'll grow sick with envy and jealousy. *No, thank you. Unsubscribe.*

I walk into the kitchen avoiding making eye contact with either of them and work on brewing coffee and putting together Eden's morning bottle.

It's only a minute before Jamie joins me in the kitchen. *Fucker.*

"I'm sorry, Jess." I nod, putting my back to him as I measure out formula. I want to ask: *Sorry for what???* I want to scream, but I'm holding my cards (and feelings) a little bit tighter to my chest now and won't be giving them the satisfaction of an outburst.

When I turn around to put the bottle in the warmer, I find Jamie staring at my nightgown, where it's been ripped at the hem. It's weird to see him jealous, but even weirder to know I've seen him like this before. Hundreds of times. I thought Jamie just wasn't very fond of me. And well, I suppose he wasn't. He was jealous.

"He told me the two of you had sex last night. You didn't need to come down here in a ripped nightgown to prove a point. Or make me jealous."

I rear back at the tone and the accusation, like he's slapped me. *Those are fighting words.* "Are you fucking kidding me right now, Jamie?" I clap back and he shakes his head. Not because he's saying no, but because he's shaking out of whatever just came over him.

"Jess, I'm sorry. That was way out of line..." he trails off, probably thinking of all the things he wants to say to me, but doesn't know how to. *Same.* I'm thinking of questions, I'm thinking of accusations, I'm thinking of hurtful words. But does any of it matter? *Not. At. All.*

I know it's over, regardless of what Tommy wants. Because, honestly, I'm not sure Tommy is being completely honest with himself when he says he still wants me. It wouldn't take much for him to choose, and I'm almost positive he'd choose Jamie.

I imagine a car barreling down the street towards the three of us, Jamie and I unaware, and Tommy's the only one with the power to save us. With one on either side of him, he can't save both. Who does he push to safety? *It's not me.*

I give Jamie a sad look and he knows, like I know. One random night of sex, one ripped nightgown is nothing to whatever they have.

He opens his arms, offering me a hug with a question on his face, but I shake my head. *Not yet. I'm not ready yet.* I think he understands because he drops his arms and works on making me a cup of coffee instead. Kudos to him (read: fuck all the way off, Jamie) because it's even the right shade of brown. He passes it to me, a peace offering, and *this* I'll accept.

Tommy and Eden come find us. She's a graspy little thing right now, squirming, hungry for her breakfast.

I watch, like an outsider, as Jamie takes his goddaughter (daughter?) from Tommy and sits at the kitchen island to feed her. He does it with ease. He's done it before, he'll do it again, but I think this is the first time I'm seeing him do it...as her dad. *Don't love it.* This feeling, it's a big nope. He gets to have Tommy...and my daughter? That's bullshit. I look at Tommy and he sees the fight or flight rising in me.

He pulls me to his office on the first floor, closing the door softly and I wait. No clue what he's planning to do or say.

"Jamie didn't come here this morning to see me." I scoff and give a roll of the eyes. Like hell he didn't. "He was dropping off files I need to review," he pauses, "because they want me on the Chen case...in Taiwan." Normally I get bummed when he has to go to Asia for work. But not this time. Weird, but I guess that's the new normal.

"I want you and Eden to come with us." *US.* Come with Tommy and Jamie. Third wheel for real. I can see it: We're walking in the airport, the two of them cuddled together, laughing with a giggling Eden. And then there's me, trailing behind with a diaper bag and stroller. Title of that snapshot would read: *"Gorgeous Family...and Their Nanny."* (Cute, right?)

My face is completely void when I shake my head back and forth. My eyes are glazed over because I can see how this is going to go down in the future. I can see another name for a different snapshot: *"Two Successful Lawyers with a Beautiful*

House in Capitol Hill Want Full Custody." Who wouldn't give it to them?

I'm just me. Part-time assistant to my best friend. No real assets, thanks to Tommy's lock-tight prenup and a lot of paychecks I've foolishly spent on shoes and vacations. Maybe I should have planned for this, but silly me for thinking when I got married, what does a prenup matter when I plan on staying married forever? When Tommy told me not to worry about retirement plans and credit card bills because he was taking care of me, I trusted him.

Now here we are...well, here *I* am. (There's no "we" here.)

I can see the resignation in Tommy. I can see the line in the sand. My refusal to go, him unable to force me (for now). The writing is on the wall, plain as day.

"I have to go, Jess."

"I know. But Eden and I aren't coming with you." He's never asked us to go before. Well, he's never asked me before. It used to just be me. This will be his first international trip since Eden was born.

He nods, but it's not a nod that says, *"I'm backing down."* This is a nod that says, *"I know I won't win this battle, but don't worry, I'll win the war."*

"When do you leave?" I ask.

"This weekend."

"Okay."

"Okay? That's it?" He questions my nonchalance.

I shrug. "We can talk about it, or bide our time in this false sense of peace. It's entirely up to you." And it is. I'm fine either way.

"When I come back, we'll start figuring this out, okay?"

71

He asks and I nod. This gives him time to come up with a strategy. What he's not banking on is that I'll be coming up with one, too. Not that I have any idea what that is yet...

After we left the office, I went upstairs to change. Tommy went to the kitchen and I waited until I knew Eden was done with her bottle before resurfacing. Jamie didn't linger much longer after that.

When they said their goodbyes, I purposely diverted my attention, however it would have been impossible to not hear the sound of them embracing, then kissing farewell. Still makes me feel nauseous to even think about him kissing someone else.

And then, much like a normal day would go, Tommy got ready for work. I drank my coffee and fed Eden some yogurt and raspberries with a handful of cheerios for breakfast.

When Tommy comes down, looking dapper as fuck in his Brunello Cucinelli one-and-a-half breasted suit, I have to avert my gaze because it's starting to hurt. And hurt leads to sadness, and sadness leads to tears. And I really don't want to give him that satisfaction. He doesn't deserve it.

The three of us stand at the threshold of our house, *his* house, and we say our goodbyes. Tommy blows a raspberry on Eden's belly then leans over to give me a kiss, but I turn, giving him my cheek instead. It's unfortunate how fast things can fade and change.

He inhales deeply, and I maintain my stoic stance. "I'll see you tonight?" He asks me what's normally a statement, but instead comes out as a question. It's normally, *"I'll see you tonight, babe."* And now it's a question because he's a smart man. I'd be lying if I said I wasn't already thinking of a thousand other places I could be between now and when he leaves this weekend. I'd be lying if I said that question didn't suck balls.

"Nowhere else to be," I reply with a shrug. He nods, turns to leave, but stops.

Looking back at us, he says, "I love you both." *I won't say it back.*

Instead, I lift Eden's hand to wave to her dad and say, "Eden loves you, too." Tommy reads between the lines. He looks crestfallen, but it doesn't deter him from leaving for the office. Didn't think it would.

Eden and I trudge back inside and start our own morning routine, but instead of it taking two hours to pick up the toys, make me breakfast, get Eden bathed and dressed, it takes us 45 minutes. It's amazing how motivating relationship woes can be. I can't sit still. Sitting still leads to thinking which leads to hurting which leads to sadness which leads to tears.

I will *not* sit still.

I take Eden to her Pack 'n Play that's still in our primary bathroom, and plop her down with *my* iPad while I shower. I spend my time in the shower making a list of all the museums I've been wanting to go to, but haven't gotten around to. *Yes, we'll go to the National Portrait Gallery. Get pizza at Pie. Then we'll make our way to the sculpture garden. I'll give Brit a call while Eden naps in the stroller...*

As soon as I'm wrapped in a towel, my phone starts vibrating on the edge of my vanity and I immediately swipe to answer. (It's Britain). *And yes! Another distraction.*

"Hey, babe. I was just thinking about you!" I say, overly

cheery. Should probably tone that down. Don't want to seem suspicious.

"Hi." My best friend's voice comes out weak and trembling, and I know.

"What's wrong? Is everything okay?" I know Brit, and that meager little voice tells me everything I need to know, except who I need to murder to make everything better.

"Everything is wrong, and nothing is okay," she cries out. She's crying so hard. Big gasping breaths that make my heart feel like it's being squeezed too tight.

"Oh, Britain. I'm sorry. What's going on?" I'm worried about her. She's trying so hard to be okay, and it's at her own expense. I hate this for her.

"I," she cries out again, "I can't pretend like I'm fine anymore." She keeps crying.

"Then don't. Don't pretend to be fine. You shouldn't be fine." (The coded message there is that I shouldn't be fine either. Noted.)

"I...I dropped the girls off at Sandy's this morning and she told me Liam called her. And he asked about me. Why?!" She cries, "Why would he do that?!" It comes out half shrill yell half sob. *This fucking guy.* If Britain would let me, I'd roll up to his front door and unload on him, but she won't. For whatever reason, she's still protective of him. Still protecting the guy who dumped her in the middle of a bar, at their engagement party, when she was just 5 weeks pregnant. None of that says this guy is worth protecting, however I do respect her wishes. It's just getting harder to do so.

What I want to say is, maybe stop hanging around his mom, Sandy. Maybe cut off all ties with him entirely. But Sandy has become something of a surrogate mother to her, and I think it would actually hurt her more than running the risk of hearing about him or even potentially running into him. (Him, aka Liam, the guy that destroyed her heart, body, and soul).

No, instead I say, "I have no idea, sweetheart. Is that why you're so worked up?"

"It's one of the reasons." She sniffles. "Jess, I...I'm struggling...to get out of bed in the mornings, and to keep going. It just hurts so bad." This is worse than the sucker punch, roundhouse-kick to the head, dagger-through-the-heart combo Tommy delivered last night. (That should tell me something right there.) This is so much worse. Guilt, pain, and fear run rampant through me. It only takes me a quick moment before I know what to do.

"I'll be there tonight. At the latest, tomorrow morning. Okay?" It's a no-brainer.

"Okay." That meek fucking voice. I hate it on her. I'll try my best to bolster her up, though. It's what friends are for. And the deeper I get into this life, the more I realize maybe Jules and May were on to something: Fuck this "men" bullshit. It's the women in my life who are important. It's Jules and May, it's Brit and her girls, it was Amy.

"Everything's going to be okay. Not right this moment, not even tomorrow," I try to pepper the truth in, "but soon. Everything will be okay, got it?" I want her to believe me. I need her to. *I need myself to.*

"Yep," she sniffles out.

"I'm gonna go book a flight and pack. Are you okay to go to your appointment this afternoon?" Poor babe has her 12-week scan today. She was planning to go alone. I should have been there for her, though. I *will* be there for her. I owe her.

"There's nothing wrong with rescheduling it. In fact, I recommend rescheduling it. Go to the store, get some ice cream." (Our girl loves her Ben & Jerry's.) "Then go home and put on Bridgerton." (Our girl also loves a period drama. Bridgerton is the only one I'll watch with her.) "Before you can even get to Queen Charlotte, I'll be there." I hope she takes my advice. I hope she takes a day to let herself be sad.

But it's hard when you're a mom and you're mourning. How do you balance the pain with the need to show the younger women in your life that you are strong and capable and that they should be, too? It's a catch 22. I wish Britain would see that. She can show her girls strength by crying about the fact that her heart was traumatized. You can cry and still be a strong, independent woman who is also vulnerable, and beautiful, and intelligent. (I should probably take my own advice, too.) *Oh my gawd, though, I've turned into May.* I smile a little bit. She'd be proud of me right now.

"Y-you're right. I'm going to reschedule," she says, her crying simmering down.

"Good, I'm going to let you go, but text me if you need anything. I'll see you soon, okay?"

"Okay, and Jess?" she asks.

"Yeah?"

"Thank you." *Hate that.* She shouldn't be thanking me.

"Of course. Love you." (I mean that). "We're going to be okay, okay?" We are, both of us.

She quickly says back, "Uh-huh. Love you, too. Bye." Then hangs up the phone. *Christ.* I'm glad she called, but I hate that we're all that each other really has right now. I look down at Eden aimlessly rolling back and forth with a teething ring, and I let a few tears fall.

Picking up my baby, I cuddle my face into her soft neck, inhaling her sweet scent. And I start whispering my affirmations to her. "You and I are amazing women. We come from a long line of amazing women who do amazing things with their lives. We will do the same. When we're ready, you and me. We'll do amazing things and we will be wonderful, and fulfilled, and happy, and strong, and vulnerable. All at the same time." It's in one ear and out the other with this one, but that's okay.

I set her back down and text the man who started this all, Brit's ex-husband Damian.

JESS

> You owe me. One flight to California. I'm going to see your wife who is probably going through the darkest moments of her life, and we should be there. I'm counting on you to do the right thing.

When do you want to leave?

> Ideally today. Ideally in the next three hours.

Done. I'll send a car for you.

Damian. I hate to love him, but a part of me does. I'd never tell him. Never. Not after what he did to Brit (which was leaving her for his assistant). But if it meant making Britain happy, I think he'd jump off a ragged cliff just to see her smile. He's like that.

In the end, a part of me doesn't blame him for cheating, though. He was desperately in love with his wife, and she just...couldn't love him back the same way. Ultimately, the cheating ended their marriage, but it was really just a symptom. Their marriage had ended years before, and I think Damian hoped if he could screw up big enough, it'd awaken some part of Brit that would fight for him.

It never did.

I text Tommy to let him know I'm leaving, and then with the speed and efficiency of the executive assistant that I am, I pack our bags and wait for Damian to tell me the car is on the way.

SIX

JESS

While we wait for the car to the airport, I feed and change Eden. *Again.* I line up all our suitcases by the door. I even reach out to my one and only contact in California for a reference.

JESS

> Hi Carly! Hope you're doing well. I know we haven't chatted in a while, but was hoping you could help me out. Is there a sort of Task Rabbit service near Britain's new house? I need some same-day groceries and orders delivered.

I'm surprised when she texts me back almost instantaneously. Carly is Britain and Liam's private chef. *Was their chef?* Maybe is just Liam's chef now? (And yes, they have a private chef. No, I don't have that same kind of money. Yes, I just went on a designer shopping spree, but that was on Tommy's credit card, and I deserved it. *Judge me*.)

> **CARLY**
>
> Hi Jess! It's been a while! How is Eden?! I'll send you the contact info for someone who can help you today. I'd trust them with my life, you're in good hands. I'd say it's task rabbit service adjacent 😊

I send off a slew of texts to one "James Judge" along with a few threats, but also a promise of a big tip for a job well done, then I settle in to wait. Some more. I feel like I could've run a marathon with all this nervous energy fueling me.

I'm surprised I haven't heard from Tommy, if I'm being honest. *Ugh*, I don't like this. Every time my brain slows for even the shortest moment, I drift to him. I think about him, his day. He's probably at lunch right now, maybe he and Jamie are out celebrating...

I'm stopped from deep diving that living nightmare when the front door flies open, rattling the picture frames along the wall. And...I've never seen Tommy look scared before. But he does now.

"Jess. Come on, babe. Don't do this." He advances towards me looking like my knight in shining armor, something straight out of a wet dream. (And by shining armor, I mean a silk and virgin mohair suit).

"Do what?" I ask him, quizzically.

"Leave. Go to California?" He stops to shake his head. "You can go to California, but you can't come to Taiwan with me? Your husband?" *Hmm*. Not a fan of that.

"My husband?" I raise both eyebrows. "My husband?! Who just kissed his best friend goodbye in our house this morning?" My voice is raised. (And it's not my house, it's Tommy's. That was made very, *very* clear in our prenuptial agreement.) Tommy's head rolls back and he closes his eyes, placing his hands on his hips. It's his power stance. Next his head will snap forward and he'll have a sword drawn.

"Jessica DiAngelo," head has snapped forward, metaphorical sword drawn, "I love you and our daughter. I want us to stay a family. I want us to be together, all of us. I know this isn't what you signed up for, but I feel like you should at least try. Don't we owe that to each other? To our daughter?" *Nope.*

"No." I shrug my shoulders. "I don't owe you a damn thing. I've given you everything you've ever asked for, and what'd I get? The shaft. So, no. You get to keep the house, your big bank accounts, you get the love of your life, and what do I get after giving up progressing my career to birth our child? I get booted. Out of your house, out of my bed. And I swear to God, Tommy," I start shaking my head, "if you try to take Eden from me..." I don't know what I'd do.

"Knock knock." Damian calls out from the entryway where the front door was left wide open.

"Damian?" Tommy turns to his friend while I start gathering the diaper bag and my purse. Tommy looks between the two of us, confused. "You two are going...together?" (An unlikely duo, I know.)

Damian sort of gets this bashful look and rubs at the back of his neck. He's got a bad rep. I think that's where Tommy is going with this, but I'll stop him right there if he does. He has zero legs to stand on in that regard.

When neither Damian or myself say anything back to

him, Tommy says, "Just never thought I'd see the day is all." Well, hell has frozen over. Pigs may as well fly, too.

Honestly, I'm grateful for Damian's timing. I didn't want to find out the direction our conversation was going.

"These the suitcases that are going?" Damian gestures to the three lined up by the door.

"Are we flying private or commercial?" I volley back.

"Private."

I nod in response, then roll another suitcase that was tucked away in the office. And Damian laughs at me. Tommy just watches us, his brain not willing to compute what he's seeing. Yeah, I talk a lot of shit on Damian, but when it comes to Britain and his girls, we're on the same team. Always. (Almost always).

"Jess," Tommy pleads, slipping a hand around my arm as I walk past. "I don't want it to be like this." *No shit, Sherlock.*

"We'll talk when you're back." I say it as a reminder. Because he's the one who was leaving in the first place. I pick Eden up out of the highchair, then toss my keys to Damian once he's done with the suitcases.

"Can you get her carseat out of my car, please?"

"Can do," Damian says as he walks past us, through the kitchen, to where my car is parked in the back alley.

Tommy's just standing in the middle of our hallway, still struck by the oddness of the dynamic he's witnessing between Damian and myself. There's a shocking ease and familiarity between us.

And then Tommy looks at me with a question. Head cocked, eyes slightly narrowed — I know what he's asking.

Instantly, I divert eye contact, jostling Eden in my arms

as a distraction. I won't give him the satisfaction of an answer one way or another.

With that, Tommy takes a step away from me, nodding, coming to a conclusion. And my heart breaks, just a little. I know what I'm doing. I'm allowing it to happen, but it still hurts.

"We'll talk when I'm back," he says, his tone no longer pliant and warm. Now it's cold and firm, and I imagine I'm now the enemy. His newest opponent.

It's not a place I'd like to be.

Just like Michael kisses Fredo, Tommy leans forward, pulling my face closer with a hand behind my head and he kisses me, firmly, painfully. (It's the kiss of death if you're Italian or, you know, into *The Godfather* or mafia things.) There's a hurt that crosses his face that should be on mine, but isn't. And I say nothing.

He kisses Eden with extreme gentleness and care, a stark comparison, and says "safe travels," before gliding out the front door with a light jog down our front steps.

I feel the dampness around the corners of my eyes, but that's all that materializes. There are no sobs, no desperate cries, just a sadness I'll be feeling for a long time to come.

"I feel like I got the timing of that wrong. I wasn't sure if I was supposed to interrupt before he power posed? Or after?" Damian jokes, and I laugh. I actually laugh at Damian.

"Your timing is classically shit, Damian." He nods in agreement, then slips a hand on my shoulder, squeezing gently. Any other day or time I would swat him away, but today I allow it.

"You ready?" he asks.

"As I'll ever be," I reply.

———

"Umm, is it just me or is this place kind of...shitty?" I was trying to think of a kinder word, but I don't think there is one. The only other word that comes to mind is...brown.

Damian's laugh bounces around the cab of his rented Escalade.

"I like to call this place an 'acquired taste,'" he says with a smile. (He's being much more gracious than me.)

Driving through Britain's hometown has me confused. I'm trying to match her description of the place to what I'm actually seeing. (And what I'm seeing has me depressed.)

Britain moved back here following the implosion of her life in DC. (First Damian left her for his assistant. Then she came here to get closure with her mother's death, eventually ended up falling in love with a hot zaddy who then dumped her rather rudely and very publicly. And now she's living here because she's a masochist, just like me.)

The town itself is decent sized and smack dab in the center of California, but it's farm country, which is strange to me. We're in California, not Montana, but I guess the term "California cowboy" had to come from somewhere. And if I had to guess, I'd say it was here.

I raise my eyebrows and blink rapidly as we pass a brown building with weathered siding and yellow neon that reads: *The Boot Barn.*

I haven't been here before, but I think Damian's been here twice. Maybe more?

"About how long till we get to her place?" Brit's new house isn't in town, it's on the outskirts, on a lake, Robles Lake. I know her house is beautiful (I helped pick it), so as long as I don't get suckered into riding a mechanical bull somewhere, or stuck in this sepia colored valley, all will be right with the world.

"Mmm," Damian hums, "thirty minutes or so."

"K," I nod my head and look out the window.

We pass through a small, worn downtown area before hitting the highway towards Robles Lake. The highway then eventually fades from four lanes to two, and the straights turn to hills and gentle curves. Rolling mounds, covered in dried-out, beige grasses surround us on each side and I start to get a bit claustrophobic. Wide open spaces and I'm claustrophobic. (I know. It's weird.) But *city girl* here doesn't like it. Something about no cell service and being stranded, it gives me the ick.

"Hey, thanks for taking Eden for a bit during the flight." If I'm already uncomfortable, I might as well swim in it and say thanks to Damian. He held her for a bit so I could sleep. When I woke up, they were both zonked out, snoring together. It was cute.

He turns to look at me and smiles. He's handsome. He has sort of unruly reddish hair that just works on him. He's lean and cut, a fitness fanatic, and he has these piercing blue eyes and a strong jawline. Top that off with the title of CEO and, like, I get the appeal, I really do.

"Anytime," he says. "I miss the girls being that small." His daughters haven't been that small in a decade and a half. "I missed a lot of it," he says quietly. I may not have been around during that time, but Britain told me. About the sacrifices he made, the time he poured into his company and not his family. It paid off, I guess. Sold his company for a couple hundred million last year, but if the price was not seeing your kids grow up, was it worth it?

"I miss...." He mutters as quiet as a whisper before trailing off, never finishing the sentiment. But I can infer the meaning. (Read: I miss *her*.) And there it is, Damian's character flaw. Britain is his greatest love and no one can compare, not even his fiancé Summer. (Yup, he's engaged, but still pining for his ex.) I reach over and rub his shoulder in a very platonic manner, but one that I hope says, "*I know. I won't tell.*"

This might be a weird opinion for me to have, but I think he could do better than Summer. Damian looks over and smiles at me, giving me one dimple. And yeah, he could definitely do better. Sure, Summer is textbook gorgeous, but there's something between them that just doesn't fit. I always sort of thought Summer was just the closest life raft he jumped to when he was drowning in despair from a loveless marriage. She was his easy out.

He clears his throat, simultaneously clearing the air. "So what had Tommy pulling on his big boy britches with you today?" I pull my hand back and roll my eyes. I don't really want to talk about it. I mean, I haven't even told Brit, but I know Damian can keep a secret...

"Tommy and I...well, we're over." Damian looks at me sharply. Like he's maybe confused or even shocked. He's got one eyebrow cocked. "He's in love with someone else," I say it like this explains and excuses away the entire situation. I clear my throat to drop the banger, "He's in love with Jamie." Damian's disposition shifts from shock to understanding. Like maybe he had suspected something between them before. Maybe he flat-out knew. I mean, he has known Tommy longer than me.

Damian eventually just nods, then rests a gentle hand on my thigh (as platonically as possible).

"Don't tell Brit, please?" I ask him. "She's got a lot on her plate, and I just wanna focus on helping her."

"It's safe with me," he says, giving my leg a gentle squeeze then removing his hand. "You could have called me, you know?" It had crossed my mind, but I didn't know if it would be weird because he was Tommy's friend first. I just shrug, though.

As we get closer to Britain's house (well, I assume closer because we've been in the car nearly 25 minutes), I have to get this off my chest. "Don't get too annoyed with me when I pretend to dislike you, but I gotta keep up appearances."

Damian laughs a little. "We could just tell her we're friends now. It'd be the truth...and it's been long enough..."

I get a little pang of anxiety at the thought, but play it off. "I don't know, I kind of like our banter. Where's the fun in being friends?" I shoot him a slightly mischievous look and Damian leans an arm across the car to ruffle my hair, with a certain boyish charm that says, *"You're annoying, but a great friend."* And I smile back at him, then smooth down my hair.

Looks can be deceiving. A snapshot right now might get titled: *"Couple Flirting on Scenic Drive"*, but that would be a lie six ways to Sunday, just like most snapshots are.

———

Brit gave us a quick tour of the house upon arrival, and several things: First, my best friend looks like shit. She's gorgeous, always, but she looks too thin, the bags under her eyes are dark purple, and she looks ready to cry at the drop of a hat. My stomach sank the moment I set eyes on her.

The second, this house is a fucking mansion. She keeps calling it a villa like that makes it sound quaint, but it is not. It's not even a McMansion, this is just a flat-out mansion. I would literally kill to live here. I might even get over my fear of wide open spaces because it's just that amazing.

The house is perched on a hill overlooking a sleepy lake. It's not mountainous, just hilly, and it makes me feel, or I can sort of pretend, like I'm in the Italian countryside and not podunk California — two words I would have previously never even put together.

Brit's house at Robles Lake doesn't read tired, sepia like the valley does. It feels more like a sun tan in the summer. Like the scent of the place is just perpetually sunblock and citrus. Like everyday it's sunny, and Aperol spritzes simply appear in one's hand the moment you step out onto her deck. It's refreshing.

The inside feels the same. Light, airy. White boucle against, white oak flooring. Its tall ceilings and perfectly worn furniture give off that effortless (yet expensive) California, cool vibe.

After some awkwardness about sleeping arrangements, I excused myself to spend some time putting the bedding on the Pack 'n Play while Eden explores the guest room by scooting from one place to the next. (As long as the doors are closed, she's good.)

I put away some of our clothes, then hide the suitcases in the closet. I double check that the monitor Task Rabbit-James set up is in working order. (It is.) I'm laying out diapers, the changing pad, and wipes so I'm not caught with my pants down in the middle of the night when there's a gentle knock at the door.

"Come in," I call out. I'm surprised when it's Damian who slips into my room quickly. Don't like the look on his face, though.

"She doesn't look good." His face is white as a ghost's. It makes me ache...for him. He cares for her so fucking much. It's going to kill him watching her hurt over someone else.

I agree, "She doesn't." Damian gets on all fours with Eden and plays with her while I ponder the best way forward.

"What's the game plan, Coach?" Damian asks me.

"I don't know. I think we just have to be there for her. Support her. It's the only way, right?"

From where Damian is now sprawled out on the floor, with Eden crawling over him, back and forth, over and over, he asks, "Was she ever like this...after...me?" This is going to crush him. I shake my head back and forth. I can see him swallow. It's a hard pill to get down, but it's the truth.

"Yeah, didn't think so. Kind of hoped, in some sick way..." I don't know what it is about Damian and me. I think we're a bit kindred somehow. There's some tie that binds us, and whatever it is (fine, I know what it is), we can share things with each other. Things he can't tell Tommy *or his other best friend*, he tells me, and vice versa. Sometimes there's things I don't want to burden Brit with, so I dump it on Damian.

It sounds clandestine, but it's far less nefarious. It's just two people still searching for their person.

I think.

I used to have that person (thought I had that person), but not anymore. Not for a long time.

I offer Damian a hand, hauling him to his full height. "It's not sick or twisted. I wish my husband didn't want me to be his and his boyfriend's spare. I'd rather he just let me go and burn our relationship to the ground. It's worse this way."

"Sounds like a fucking dumpster fire as it is, Jess."

I nod. "Yup. I think you're right."

Without saying anything, Damian places a warm hand at the base of my neck, and massages me gently. I'm surprised when the comfort comes. It's next level.

"Alright, let's roll out. Pizza'll be here any minute," I say, putting a reluctant end to Damian's hands that have eased some of the tension in my shoulders.

"You know pizza parties aren't actually beneficial to morale, right?" He teases me.

"Hey! Nothing else delivers here, and pizza is fucking amazing. You cook next time then!" I shove him away playfully and he laughs at me.

"Maybe I will!" he says, swiping a hand through my hair to muss it up as we walk out of the guest room.

"You get the baby!" I turn, jokingly bossing him around and he throws up his hands in mock defeat.

"*Jess?*" *Alex?* I turn around in the hall to see Alex staring right back at me.

The moment shatters when Damian walks right into me, with Eden in his arms, and starts laughing when I stumble.

I might stumble, but my eyes never waver from Alex who turns and leaves just as stealthily as he arrived. I might have thought it was an apparition purely in my mind if not for Damian saying, "Was that Alex?"

I nod. "Yeah, I think so."

SEVEN

ALEX

The fuck is she doing here? With him? Fuck's sake.

I throw open the door to my Jeep then peel out of Britain's drive. I'd just wanted to check on my sister, make sure she was eating, see if the girls needed anything. I'd known something was off the minute I walked in, though. The house was too quiet. At first I thought no one was home, so I texted my nieces to see where they were.

J

> Hey, I'm at your house, where are you guys?

C

> We're at Sandy's in Spearhead, spending the night.

E

> I think mom's in a bad way, check on her?

C

Dad and Jess are coming, they'll be there
soon.

All they needed to say was Jess and I was ready to go, but
the giggles coming from the guest suite gave me pause. There
was that old feeling, back again, stopping me in my tracks.
There's a part of me that couldn't move, frozen, standing
there, waiting. *Fine, hoping.*

And lo and behold, who stumbles out, but Jess...followed
by Damian. It was fucking suspect. I didn't mean to say
anything, but her name just sort of...came out. Haven't seen
her in a long time. Purposefully.

I avoid her like the plague. Haven't talked to her in, I
don't know, maybe 6 years? *Fine, I know exactly how long it's
been, but that's besides the fact.*

I head straight back to my mom's house because I should
probably eat. But suddenly I don't feel even remotely hungry.

What the fuck is Jess doing here?

She's like a parasite. Pesky, tough to get rid of. She uses
people. And most of the time, people don't even know they're
being used. Don't like it. Not for my sister, not for my best
friend. But just like she does, she embeds herself in your life.
Wasn't any different for Britain. It's not any different with
Damian.

Maybe it's my fault for introducing her. Getting her the
job as Britain's assistant. I'll accept the fault there, but everything else? That's on her.

It comes on quick and it's almost impossible to ignore.
But it's there, that urge to flee is making the slow rise up
my spine. Eventually it'll take root in my mind, and it'll be

all I can do to not load up a rucksack and walk away from it all.

But I promised Britain I'd be here. She's got no one looking out for her, and yeah, she might be 35 and not completely helpless, but I've seen her like this before.

This time is worse.

This heartbreak is different. This is the kind that'll put you in the fucking ground if you aren't careful.

We're runners, Brit and I. We both have the same problem. When shit hits the fan, we bolt. I retreat, she just goes. But things are changing. We're both trying. I'm trying for her and she's trying for her girls. We used to be tight until I ran away. *The last time.*

In my absence, I might as well have thrown her to the wolves because when we finally caught up again, she was just a shell of her former self, passed out on the floor of a bar in Spearhead Lake.

If that's not a wakeup call for the both of us, well, I'd wonder if we still had a heart beating in our chests.

Brit was fine in the end. Passed out because she forgets to eat...also she's pregnant and anemic, but all that tells me is, again, she needs someone looking after her. And "fine" is relative. Health-wise, she might be fine, but everything else-wise, she's fucked.

We're fucked up, I know. Both of us. Nothing about either of our childhoods was particularly good. Mine might have been bad, but then sometimes I think Brit had it worse. I knew love, but I'm not sure if she ever did.

Up until I was six, life was pretty good. My mom loved me, she didn't let my asshole father near me on the bad days, and we had friends. I was normal, running through sprinklers and playing soccer in the street with the neighborhood kids. *Shit was normal.*

Until *that* day, when life turned upside down, and everything went to shit. It was the day my mom almost died at the hands of my dad. I didn't see it, but I heard it. Still hear it in my nightmares if I'm honest.

On nights when I don't hear my mother screaming, it's the sound of the jaws of life scraping against metal.

That day changed the entire course of my life, though. And my sister's, too. She wasn't even born yet, but that day was the day Britain went from not existing to being. I hate saying it, even thinking the word because its fucking terrible, but just to give you an idea: My father Ray, he's an abuser, a rapist, and an addict.

Can't blame the abuse or the rape on his addictions, because those didn't come till later. He was just that shit of a human being.

After that day, I chose to live with him.

I was six. It was stupid, but in a way I'm grateful I chose that life. It made me who I am. I never had to worry about him hurting my mom or Britain. And all the shit he put me through ended up being the start of my training for my life in special operations.

I was already battle-worn and tough when I showed up to basic. They still broke me, but no one would ever break me to the same level that living with Ray Palomino did.

Britain escaped Ray completely, but got left to be raised as the unwanted byproduct of a night everyone wishes they could forget.

It poses the age-old question: Better to have loved and lost than to have never loved at all? I haven't figured out the answer to that yet myself. I think maybe I've been loved, but I'm not sold that I've loved. Except Tally. And Georgia, and Britain and her girls. But that's a different kind of love. That's protective love. Lay-my-life-down type of love. Not passionate love. Not sure that's happened for me. It might have, or maybe it could have, but not yet. *Hopefully at least.*

That's another reason I'm here. I'm trying to stick. Trying to see if there's a chance for the two and a half kids, picket fence, and a dog. Though I'd settle for a warm body right now...*Fuck*, I didn't mean it like that. I'd settle for a partner. *Is that better?* Maybe I don't need the "normal" shit, but I'd take someone who understands me, a friend, someone to love and be loved in return. *That's not too much to ask, is it?*

For people like me, though, it probably is. Not entirely sure I'm deserving of any of it. I've done horrible things in my life. I had a chance and I failed. I was a horrible husband, horrible father, and if it wasn't for me, the two of them might still be here.

My palms get damp and my knee starts bouncing. The itch to go is almost unbearable now. It'd be easy, too. Everything I need is at Georgia's house. I could just walk into the Sierra Nevada mountains and just...not look back. It's tempting. So goddamn tempting.

But Brit needs you. Her girls need you. I can't leave her. Again.

I pull up to my late mother's house that I inherited when she passed, which is weird because I never even lived here, but Brit did. Yet all Georgia left Brit was a box.

It's weird and it's things like that that I resent Georgia for. Like leaving my sister a box filled with notebooks? *Really, Mom? But not her childhood home?*

Not much makes sense whenever I try to examine my mom's life choices. And I've tried. All I can come up with is she was trying her best given some shit circumstances. Don't know that I'll ever agree or be on board with them, though.

I turn on the drip system to water the vegetable garden in the back, then head for the fridge. Should probably eat.

It's a fucking miracle any of the appliances in here still work. The house is sort of crumbling, but I'm planning to sell it. I'm also just sort of dragging my feet about it because this place works as well as most at the moment.

It's just a basic ranch house that was thrown together in the 70s. Was probably pretty nice in its heyday, but now it just needs work. The kitchen is a gut job, needs new siding, new roof, new flooring. Walls need to be redone and painted. I could work on it myself, but that's not really my bread and butter. Doesn't interest me, and I've got real work to do. Which reminds me, I can't keep holding Blanks off.

I pull up his last message that's a week old and an empty threat to track my ass down if I don't respond.

A

> Wouldn't be much of a tracking job…you know where I am.

B

> Now you'll text me back!? Pick up your phone asshole!

> Nah, don't feel like it.

> We owe Axe Corp an answer yesterday. If you don't want to do it, just say so.

> I don't want to do it.

You fucking prick.

Sorry.

I'm not. I knew you'd want to stop doing this shit eventually, take a break. Just tell me sooner next time, ass clown.

Also, when do I get to come visit? Your hot sister single yet?

Not single for you. Also she's sort of dating someone. I think.

The fuck, man? She moved on fast.

Nah, more like she never moved on from him at all. I give it a 27% chance at success.

God you're a debbie downer.

Yup.

So...when do I get to come visit? Meet your adoptive Daddy?

You're such a fucking ass. Constantine isn't my adoptive daddy, alright? He's just...

An adoptive daddy?

Fuck you. Don't come see me.

You can only hold me off so long!

Maybe, but I think your latest booty call/model of the week will do an alright job of it for me.

It's been two and a half weeks.

> You want a gold star?

My text is followed by ten middle finger emojis. I shrug, tossing my phone on the eat-in table then head back to the fridge. *Chicken and broccoli.* It's practically the only thing in here, so I pull it out and start prepping the food for the grill. It's the same shit I've been doing and eating for the last couple of weeks.

It's starting to get old. Maybe it's because I'm tired of the food, maybe it's because I'm tired of eating alone. But I shouldn't be. Because "alone" is good. Alone is where I thrive. I think it's the stagnation that I hate. The staying in one spot. *Maybe it's because you need to get laid and get it out of your system.* That's Blanks' voice talking, not mine.

After running into *her* today, maybe he's not wrong.

———

I step into Jimbo's for the first time since I was probably 21. Jimbo's is exactly what you'd think it'd be. Saw dust on the floor. Everything is raw wood on the interior. Same neon hanging on the walls since the gold rush of 49'. *Not literally.*

I head for the bar and some habits just die hard. *At least four exits, probably 5, 16 total windows, best vantage point is far, left-hand corner of the bar turned out at a 45 degree angle.* Bars aren't really my scene, too much can go wrong. Too many people, and it's typically too loud. But desperate times, right?

I case the joint, quickly spotting a familiar face. Not here for that, though, so I draw my ball cap down a bit more and make my way to the bartop.

I order a beer, read some news on my phone, and rudely let the bartender know I'm not interested in small talk about the Dodgers or the Giants. Neither are my teams. Baseball isn't my sport.

The hardest part about being at Jimbo's is going to be finding someone who's not already shit faced and doesn't have long dark hair. *Too painful.*

There's a lot of pretty women in here, and a tall blonde catches my eye. I noticed her when I walked in, too. Instant eye contact, and it looks like she's still interested. All good signs.

Haven't done this in a while, but here goes nothing. Literally nothing, all I have to do is pocket my phone, make brief eye contact, and wait.

And bingo. She approaches, walking like a supermodel in cowboy boots. Heel toe, heel toe. She takes the seat next to me and leans forward like she might be getting the bartender's attention, but really it's mine she's seeking. Her drink is still 3/4ths full.

She looks at me with a smile, then back towards the bartender who is dutifully ignoring her, almost like they both know the drill here. I don't care. That's fine.

"Has anyone ever told you you look like a Hemsworth brother?" *Only the last girl who picked me up.*

"Nope," I reply.

"That's surprising. You look just like that guy in Avengers." Hating this already.

"Huh, haven't seen it."

"WHAT? Get out!" She exclaims then lightly shoves at my shoulder.

"Seriously."

"Well, if you ever want a buddy to watch it with, I'd be happy to volunteer." She's being quick about this, great.

"Alright, let's do it." She's surprised when I'm quick about it, too. I make a little nod towards the back where the bathrooms are and her cheeks turn pink. I throw a twenty down on the bar, drain my beer, and walk towards the back hall that leads to the restrooms.

She's right behind me, losing her drink somewhere along the way. And right on cue, I enter one of the single bathrooms, leaving the door unlocked, and she follows right behind. She closes and locks the door on her way in.

This part's always a bit tricky. Don't love kissing on the lips, but most people are offended when you just bend them over without any foreplay. I turn my ball cap backwards, then with a gentle push, I pin her up against the door with a hand on her shoulder and one at her waist. Nudging her neck to the side, I drag my mouth down her tan skin. *Fake tan*, tastes slightly chemical, smells like too much perfume.

So I shut my eyes...and see someone else.

That always helps. I push a hand into her hair, and tug gently. I slip one hand into the front of her pants, but check her with a question before I dive further. Our eyes meet, I ask.

And she says, "Yeah, please do."

I quickly unbutton the jeans that practically hit her ribcage and push them down. With a hand holding her neck, I keep sucking and nipping and kissing, and with a hand down her pants I slide between her folds and find she's already slick.

She lets out an exaggerated moan and I close my eyes again. Turning, I move her away from the door and towards the sink. I push her jeans down to her boots, and quickly undo my belt buckle. I pull a condom out of my back pocket, roll it on, close my eyes, and with her back to my chest, I push into...*fuck*. I realize I don't even know her fucking name. Not that it matters because I'm seeing someone else right now.

It's a balance because right now sex is just clinical. I can think about someone else, but if I let it go too far, I'll start *acting* like it's someone else I'm thrusting into, and we don't want that. That behavior causes attachment. I need this to be just good enough to get us both off. Just quick enough, no one's the wiser, and just quiet enough I don't hear the moaning in my nightmares at night.

Just like I anticipated, she lets out another overly loud moan and I shush her. It's not so other people don't hear, it's so that *I* don't hear.

Need to wrap this up, so I start pressing into her, harder, riding her deeper. I push one of her hands to her clit and she starts rubbing. I feel her start to clench, so slamming my eyes tighter, I slide a hand into her long hair and tug gently, and it brings me home. Over the finish line.

I see *her*. I feel *her*. I still want *her*. I almost say *her* name, and when I open my eyes, I sober quickly.

Tall blonde is looking back at me with expectation and heart eyes, but I don't want it. Don't want to be rude, but I gotta go.

"So, do you want to come to my place to watch a movie?" she asks sweetly.

"No, I've actually gotta go. You good?" I ask. Her smile fades, but I get the feeling she knows how this goes.

"Yep, I'm good. Thanks, bubba." I get the chills because I fucking hate that nickname. All too quickly, this feels fucking dirty and disgusting, and all I want is a shower. It takes me a minute to clean up, wash hands, and then with a kiss on the cheek, I say goodbye to the tall blonde. She watches me go then locks the door behind me once I'm out in the hall.

As I leave, I take a couple glances around and *damnit*.

"Fuck." I mutter under my breath.

I can't help that I notice shit. Sometimes I wish I didn't. There's a certain bliss in ignorance, but *this*. Can't be fucking ignored.

I give him a quick tap on the shoulder and he turns around surprised to find me glaring at him.

Matt Scala is at a fucking bar, with some chick who is not my sister. *Chances of him successfully getting with Britain have just fallen to 1%.*

I nod, giving him a chance before I say anything. I think I know what's happening here, but I could be wrong. Hope I'm wrong. But odds are I'm not. Because I have eyes, ones that are trained to pick up slight nuances and deduce body language. And this, what I see now, is all fucking wrong.

"Alex!" he says, eyes a bit glossy, then drops the girl's hand that he'd been playing with underneath the table.

"What are you doing?" I ask, cold as the blue mountains on his beer can.

"Just grabbing a drink with an old friend."

I nod towards the girl. Cute. But I'm not buying the old part. She looks like she just turned 22, just past jailbait.

I scoff at him and shake my head. "Alright, we're doing this then. I'm going to ask again. What the fuck are you doing?"

Matt's demeanor shifts and his back straightens. "We were just talking." I nod, not buying it for one second.

"Mmkay. I will just say this," I lean forward, getting in his face. He's tall, but I have at least a half inch on him. "You make Britain cry, and you'll never stop crying. I'll ruin you, your business, and any chance of you ever having a happy life."

I lean back, slapping a hand down on his shoulder and say, "Make good choices, Matt." Then I walk out of that dusty shit hole.

A

> Your brother is about to do something stupid. He's at Jimbo's. If I stop him, there'll be cops and broken bones. You want to come get him? Or should I take care of it?

M

> On my way. Wait for me.

Only reason I don't leave is to make sure Matt doesn't walk out that door with jailbait on his arm. I stand up against my Jeep until Max rolls into Jimbo's gravel parking lot in an Aston Martin. Looks like being a CFO and owning a ranch pays.

Max jogs over to me, giving me a handshake.

"Max, if he fucks with Britain..." I say in warning, but he's already shaking his head.

"Nah, I won't let him either. I've got something in the works right now. Promise, I won't let him do anything stupid before then. Can't make any promises for later, though." I nod in understanding. I may have threatened Max to get Liam back here. If for no other reason than I can kick his fucking ass.

"Need me to stick around for backup?" I ask Max.

"I think I'll manage."

"K, I'll see you around, man," I say to Max as Matt comes waltzing out of Jimbo's, with his "old friend" draped around him.

"Christ's sake," I mutter under my breath at the same time Max says, "This fucking idiot."

"You warned him, didn't you?" Max asks, and I nod. He gives me a stern look. "I got it, hang back."

He walks straight up to Matt, takes the hand of the cute girl, pulling her off to the side, then shoves Matt hard, causing him to trip and fall into the gravel parking lot. Max proceeds to rip him a new asshole, and I laugh, then get in my Jeep and drive away.

Won't be doing any of this again. At least not anytime soon. And for sure not in this fucking town.

EIGHT

JESS

"You're still up?" I find Damian sprawled out on the sectional, flipping through channels in the darkened great room when I come down the stairs from Britain's bedroom. I planned to wait till Brit was asleep to sneak out, but after a deep chat and cry session about Liam, she told me to go. Probably because I was the one falling asleep.

He gives me a somber smile and says, "Yeah. Wanna watch something?" Then pats the seat beside him expectantly. *Yes.*

"Little bit. I'm tired," I say, then yawn as I walk around to sit beside him, setting the baby monitor on the coffee table first.

With Britain in bed for the night and the girls sleeping over at Sandy's, I don't give him the two seat buffer I normally would. This time, I take the seat right next to him. And when he looks at me, he smiles with a lot less sadness.

"You're taking this really well..." I note, tilting my head to examine him. He almost seems unbothered(?). I don't know if I'd take it that far, but maybe he's *finally* getting over Britain.

"Yeah. I guess it just feels like things are changing, but not necessarily for the worse. Can't really explain it right now." I just nod at his response. I can't say I agree with that sentiment. Things are definitely changing, but in my case, all things are trending *worse*.

I'm happy for him, though, for his engagement. For turning over a new leaf with Brit. *Congrats on turning the corner, Damian.* I don't say anything, though. I just turn to face the tv screen.

Without even consciously thinking about it, my head drops to his shoulder while he keeps scrolling. When he spots Casino playing, he doesn't even have to ask, he chooses it and we both settle in. My head rests heavily on his shoulder, while his hand is splayed across my leg. It's neither intimate or romantic, just comfortable. In every way. (Or maybe that's just the exhaustion talking.)

He squeezes my leg to get my attention and says, "Come, sit here," patting the floor in front of him.

"It's been a long day, I know," he says when I just look at him confused. But I don't really question, I just stand, zombie-like, then take a seat cross-legged on the floor in front of him.

With his legs on either side of me, he scoots forward and moves his hands to my neck. *Oh, fuck me.* His thumbs dig deep into my tense muscles as he pushes, then drags them down my spine, willing me to close my eyes and let go.

When he runs his hands into my hair, pushing his thumbs against my skull behind my ears, I think I moan involuntarily. *Fuck*, I should be embarrassed, but with Damian, I don't care.

He stops abruptly, and I whine, "*Whhhyyy* are you stopp*ing*?"

"You should go to sleep, it's late," he says a bit brusquely. But he's right.

Lazily, I crawl to a standing position and stretch my hands over my head, bringing my t-shirt up to my rib cage. As I do, Damian makes a choking sound.

"Are you okay?" I turn back to look at him where he has a water bottle halfway to his lips.

"Went down wrong." I just nod, but I don't move to go to my room just yet.

There's something weird happening. I know I *should* go to bed, but my legs feel like they're stuck in concrete. And I don't want to go. And lay in bed alone. And maybe have to think about my life. I'd rather stay here...with him. Where it's safe.

And the fact that neither one of us is moving now is only heightening the awkwardness.

Finally Damian breaks. "What's wrong?"

A single tear slips out before I can respond and Damian's on his feet in a heartbeat, warm arms surrounding me. He's a great hugger.

There's tears, but I'm not exactly crying. I'm also not exactly sad about Tommy as much as I'm just sad about my life. About my daughter's life. About Eden's family. I always dreamt of having that big family. With lots of kids running around and aunts and uncles. I always dreamt of getting the family I never had. And now, I know I'll never have it. At least not how I planned. Not with Tommy. And not anytime soon. And *that's* what's making me sad.

After a couple minutes of Damian just being present (he doesn't push me to talk, doesn't even move), he says, "Bed time. It's hard right this second, but not for long, okay?"

I nod against his chest and then he turns to lead me to my room, snagging the baby monitor off the coffee table as he does.

"You're a good friend, Damian." Maybe even the best. He's the only person I can be totally honest with right now.

Huh. I don't think I've ever lied to Damian before...

"I know," he says sort of smugly, making me laugh. *Cocky son of a bitch,* and I elbow him right in his abdominals.

"Oof!" He fakes a laugh and injury.

When we get to the door to my room, I turn towards him to say goodnight. But again, the words don't come. I push down the reason I'm speechless. I push that shit as far away from my mind as possible lest the words slip out against my will. I physically swallow them down, because *this,* what's happening right now, well it's not supposed to.

He's my best friend's ex-husband. He's my husband's best friend. He's engaged for fuck's sake. But all of that...and still there's a magnetism to him.

Probably because he's somehow become my closest friend with Brit in California. Probably because I know I can tell him the truth without judgment. And probably because I'm just a lonely fuck. That's it. That's the real reason.

So instead of saying something I'll regret, I tell him the partial truth. "I just don't want to be alone...at least not right now, not yet." When our eyes meet, he knows. He sees it all.

He leans forward, and with a hand cradling the back of my head, he gives me a gentle forehead kiss. Somehow it amplifies this broken-hearted feeling instead of comforting it, but I don't say anything.

"I can't, Jess," he says quietly. *Oh god.* No, of course he can't.

"I-I didn't mean it like that, Damian. I was just..." It's pointless to explain when even I don't know what the fuck I'm thinking. "Nevermind. I'll see you tomorrow." And without waiting for his reply, I slip into the room, being careful to shut the door slowly and quietly to let Eden keep sleeping.

Damian's large hand reaches out before the door can click shut, though, slipping into the room with me and causing my breath to catch.

"I'll stay for a little bit," he whispers and relief floods me.

Without another word, we both settle onto the bed, already in sweats and pjs. We lay back in tandem and then his hand reaches out for mine. I slip my hand against his, and he holds it, simultaneously holding me together without even knowing it.

I take one long blink. Then another.

His hand squeezes mine and the simple gesture reassures me, soothes me. It's my permission slip to step away from the living world.

On the next long blink, I fall hard into a dream that's equal parts fantasy and nightmare.

———

It's still dark out when I wake up to the sounds of gentle, rhythmic breathing. It takes me a second for my mind to wade through the sleepy haze and realize it's not the sound of Tommy's erratic snoring, but Damian's deep inhales and relaxed exhales.

The panic doesn't come for me. The wrongness doesn't yell at me to get up and run. It's just comfort. He stayed. Because he knew I needed it. I needed him. Brit would have done the same if roles were reversed. But it's not Brit, because I can't tell her just yet. She has enough to deal with as it is.

When I open my eyes, I realize just how close we are. We aren't cuddling, but our hands are still clasped and we're lying, facing each other. Like a sixth sense, Damian's breathing falters and his eyes flutter open.

"I'm sorry," I say after it's been a couple seconds of us staring at each other. Both of us are trying to make sense of *this*. "I know you didn't want to stay..."

"Shh..." He pulls me in closer, into a hug that melts away any residual discomfort. "Let's go make coffee before Eden and Brit wake up, yeah?" I nod against him and we both roll away from each other to head towards the kitchen.

In the light of (almost) day, this feels different than I expected. It doesn't feel like I just spent the night in bed with someone I shouldn't have. It feels exceedingly normal.

Damian moves around the kitchen, pulling out coffee mugs and turning on the Nespresso machine while I pull out a stool at the kitchen island to wait. We occasionally make eye contact and every time results in a little half smile from me or a one-dimpled grin from him.

He makes my coffee first, then his, then takes a seat at the stool beside me.

"So..." he starts, but I don't want (read: *can't* want) to see where this leads.

Clearing my throat abruptly, I say, "I won't tell anyone about last night if you don't. I know you were just helping me out. As a friend." He stares at me blankly, then nods.

He takes a sip of his coffee. Then another. And we both sit there silently watching as the sun starts to rise over the lake.

This place is definitely an acquired taste, but watching the sun crest over the golden hills, bathing the kitchen in orange and violet light, I can see myself quickly acclimating and acquiring said taste. I didn't even know a landscape like this existed. It's foreign, yes, but I think there's something beautiful about it. In the same way items, places, even people are overlooked for their normality, too.

If you dig, examine, look harder at what's actually happening, you'll see the beauty. The possibilities. The dependability in the normal. I sigh, and it pulls Damian's attention away from the picture windows.

This, my friendship with him, is one of those things, too. *Beautiful.*

Beautiful. That word doesn't get tossed around nearly enough- I put an abrupt stop to the memory playing in my mind. Nope, I'm not reliving that night. Not here, not now.

When Eden starts babbling on the baby monitor, I excuse myself to get her. I do a quick diaper change and when we get back to the kitchen, Damian's outside on the phone, pacing, like his CEO switch got flipped on.

That's okay. Because nothing more needs to be said or done about this. Period. It was just me needing comfort, and he was there to give it. The end. *Fin.* (I don't know if I'm convincing you or myself right now.)

When Brit finally comes down, I switch into best friend support mode.

I try to steer the conversation away from Liam seeing as last night ended in tears. Today, I'm taking a different approach: 1. Amp Brit up. 2. Hype up the new guy. 3. Don't talk about Liam. In that order.

The door bell ringing surprises all of us, but none so more than me when Brit let's in a fucking centerfold, panty dropper of a man. Tall-dark-and-cut traipses into her entryway with a bouquet of flowers and a bakery box.

"Stare much, Jess?" I close my hanging open mouth at Damian calling me out. I was so awestruck, I didn't even hear him come in.

"It's just not what I was expecting..." I pick up Eden out of her high chair to walk towards the living room where I have a better view of the scene unfolding before me. Damian follows.

I watch as the woman who couldn't be any more broken, goes up on her tip toes and gets a thorough tongue fucking from the man, whom I'm assuming is Matthias. (Her new beau.)

It's the burn of jealousy at the back of my throat that surprises me, too. *Fuck.* If this is making me feel some sort of way, this must be decimating Damian. When I look at him briefly, he's looking at me uncomfortably.

I clear my throat to get Brit's attention and to protect my friend who probably never needed to see this.

Brit turns back to her sheepish self when she realizes

we're in the living room with a clear view of the unfolding lust fest.

She does a quick, yet awkward introduction before pulling Matthias back out the front door.

I immediately turn to Damian, "I'm sorry you had to see that. You must be feeling—"

He puts a hand up and rears back slightly, "You have no clue what I'm feeling, Jess. No fucking clue." *So that's a yes.* He must be feeling all kinds of jealousy and hurt over what just unfolded.

And then it gets worse.

When we hear Britain moan through the front door, my stomach turns queasy for him. This is killing him. I know it.

Thankfully it ends a few minutes later when Brit floats back into the house on a high I would honestly kill for. She even has this stupid, euphoric-looking smile plastered all over her face. I mirror the smile as best I can because she deserves this, regardless of whatever is happening on this side of the living room. My jealousy, Damian's unrequited love. None of that matters right now.

"What?" she asks when no one says anything.

I laugh to break the moment and say, "Girrlll, if you don't want him, I do." Damian immediately shoots me a look I can't entirely discern, but it says something along the lines of *traitor*. I feel that pang of guilt in my stomach, but keep up the act of being the excited and supportive friend. For Brit.

Brit immediately gives a lackluster, non-apologetic apology to Damian, "Sorry you had to see that, Damian." He quickly looks at me where I'm smiling, fakely.

Then turning to Brit he says, "Yeah, I'm sorry, too. Probably could've gone the rest of my life without seeing that." He gives me a disappointed look, avoiding eye contact with Brit, then stalks away, straight to the back porch.

The pang in my gut turns to a full piercing. Even when I brush Damian off and tell Brit not to worry about him, I'm still feeling like shit. And I'm not quite sure why. I can't tell if it's because he's so hurt and pissed at Brit...or at me.

NINE

JESS

After another drama-filled morning between Liam and Brit, I'm desperate for a minute of solitude. He showed up at The Grounds this morning (where we picked up Caroline and Elodie from their sleepover) and a confrontation ensued.

Being here for her is the right thing. She fucking needs it, but at the same time, it's hard. Because I just want to scream, *"I'm not okay either! I need someone, too!"*

When I finally get Eden settled down for a nap, for the first time since I've found out about Tommy (and Jamie), I'm truly alone. I'm grateful for a moment, until I curl into a ball on my bed and check my messages.

There's one from May and one from our house cleaner. Then there's one from Jamie. (Eyeroll.)

JAMIE

> I don't know what just happened, but Tommy is beside himself. I've never seen him like this. I know you're not trying to hurt him on purpose, are you?

Gag. He's worried about me? Hurting Tommy? That's fucking laughable. I may have let Tommy think there's something more between Damian and I because fuck him. But there isn't. (You and I both know that.)

I ignore Jamie's text.

TOMMY

> I'm leaving. Hopefully I'll be back in a couple weeks. If you change your mind, I've emailed you all the information you need. Addresses, offices, my assistant there. Reach out any time.

> And I don't know what you're doing with Damian, but I'm going to hope it's not what I think, Jess. I'm still hopeful. Okay? I still love you. Do you want me to not stay at Jamie's? Just tell me.

My stomach drops out. My chest hurts. Right, of course he'd stay with Jamie. That's where he lives most of the time. He works at the Taiwan office, and I wonder: Would this have happened sooner if there weren't thousands of miles between them?

> Stay with Jamie. Stay as long as you'd like. I likely won't change my mind, but thank you for the information. If anything happens while you're gone, I'll do my best to let you know.

Dig, dig, *little dig*. I try, but if anything, I think the text reads a bit like one you'd send to your boss when you've just declined to take that business trip. Polite and to the point. And that's exactly what this is, isn't it? It's transactional, and in this equation, I'm the superfluous one.

Hurt in my chest turns to a full-blown crack, it's breaking. Officially. I've stopped moving long enough for the pain to erupt, multiply, morph into a beast all its own. And I've never felt like this before.

I grab the monitor and my phone and walk into the garage at Britain's house. It's the only place to hide now that her girls are home from their sleepover.

I press May's name and wait, she doesn't make me wait long though, bless her.

"Hi, JJ."

"May." My voice doesn't sound like my own.

"Jessie? What is it?" May asks, all quiet concern.

"Tommy is in love with Jamie." I hear a gentle "Oh" from her end of the line. "They want to be together." I can practically see May nodding along. She'll have pushed her glasses to the top of her head and crossed her arms over her chest by now. She undoubtedly has me on speaker in her office, too.

"Tommy still wants me to be with them, though...but...*I can't*." A slight cry breaks out. But once a small cry breaks out, it leads to bigger crying, because with May, I can be anything. She lets me. And that includes being a small child, and crying like the boys were being mean to me at the park.

"Of course you can't!" She says indignantly in my defense. "Does he *even* know you?!" She's bewildered at the idiocy of men, always. It makes me chuckle because I can just picture her standing in her office now, pacing the small carpet, waving her hands in the air.

"Exactly!" I exclaim.

"J, if that's not what you want, that is one hundred percent, A-OK. Fuck Tommy DiAngelo!"

"Yes! Fuck him!" I say back, feeling slightly more resolved in all of this.

"Good. That's good, Jessica!"

"Yes, I-I don't need him." I say, not entirely convincingly.

"Of course you don't. You are the daughter of Jules and Robert and May, and no woman I've raised would ever need a man. Do you hear me?" I can hear the absolute confidence in her voice. It's almost enough to instill some confidence in me.

"I hear you."

"Good. Now listen close, baby, because I know that was the pep talk, but now it's time for the real talk." My entire body falls slightly.

"Okay," I say quietly.

"Let him go," she says softly. I cry silently, placing my hand over my mouth in hopes May doesn't hear me. "Don't hang on for his sake, but especially not for yours." She delivers this so exceptionally well and so compassionately, my heart splits right down the middle.

I think perhaps I've been in a smidge of denial. I've been using avoidance, keeping busy, but the second I stopped moving, the second I was alone, there was no escaping it. And now? Now, we move into the anger phase of grief. This anger feels less reactionary and more deep-seated.

"Let him go?" I practically sob, then scoff, "So what? He can live happily ever after? And me and Eden, we're just what? Collateral damage?!"

"Never. And how dare you see yourself that way!" May scolds me. It just makes me angrier.

"I have to go, I'll call you later." I hang up without waiting for her response. I'm not mad at May. I'm just...mad. So completely consumed by a rage I've been keeping at bay because if I let myself feel it, it feels like there'll never be an end.

The air gets sucked from my lungs, and I bow over, because remaining upright no longer seems feasible. I drop the monitor and my phone on the concrete floor and remain bowed over with my hands resting on my thighs, fighting for breath.

Finding out how little control I have over my own life is earth shattering. (Fine, maybe just life shattering.) I've always seen myself as a strong, confident, independent woman. But I'm not. I've become dependent on Tommy. As my partner, my friend, my co-parent, my confidant.

I put my career (my life) on hold so we could have a child and now, I'm left with...what the fuck am I left with? (Thanks to Tommy's prenup) it's simple: not much.

I was just a pawn. I was just a placeholder. My stomach rolls.

> You know what, fuck you, Tommy. For making me an interloper in my own life. Fuck you for even asking something of me that you know I'd never be okay with. I watched my father DIE of a broken heart loving someone who could never be his. And you're asking me to stick around and do the same? FUCK YOU.

Tommy gets to look like the good guy, doesn't he? Because he wanted us to stay together, right? That's fine. Let me be the villain. I've been here before, this time I'll be the villain in *their* rendition of life.

Fuck, maybe I'll always be the bad guy. Maybe that's just my cross to bear.

———

After a couple dips in a bowl full of ice water, the swelling around my eyes starts to come down. No one will ever know I've been crying.

Yet, I still brace myself at the gentle knock on my bedroom door. It's all a lot right now. Britain's life is Messy. (Yeah, with a capital M.) And right now, I'm her safe harbor, her dumping ground, and I'm happy to do it. It's just a lot on top of what I already have. Doesn't help that she's also so helplessly in love, and it's so fucking obvious, but she just can't accept and move past and forgive. (But I also don't blame her one bit.)

I open the door and she peeks her head in. "Hi, is the babe awake?" she whispers.

"Yeah, come in." I pull her into the room while I finish toweling off my face.

"What are you using on your skin? It looks amazing." I want to tell her it's a concoction of the tears of my enemies and the plus side of having a heart of ice.

Instead, all I say is, "La Mer." She nods.

"There's, um, something I want to show you. Think you can come take a look?" she asks so innocently and sweetly.

"Of course."

Britain picks up a groggy Eden from her nap, changes her diaper and totes her upstairs to her primary suite. Setting herself and Eden up on the bed with a set of play car keys, she tosses me a phone off her bedside table.

"Read the messages from Liam," her only instructions. So I do. I read each one, and with each one, I feel more and more angry and...jealous. She has this guy by the fucking balls.

Just like Damian would jump off a cliff, Liam would buy her an island. *Then* he'd build a grandstand on the edge of said cliff, on said island, so she could sit and watch him push every one of her enemies over the edge before falling on his own sword if it might make her happy.

"So, what do you want to do about it?" I ask her once I'm finished.

"I don't know, Jess," she says, sounding completely uncertain.

"I think after today," (Liam, showing up in Spearhead. And him begging for forgiveness), "and all *this*, it's pretty clear that he loves you. And it's pretty clear to me that you still love him, too."

"I don't disagree," she says, sort of trailing off.

"So?" It's so fucking obvious.

"So...I'm seeing someone else. And it takes more than love to make a relationship work. It takes trust and communication, two things Liam has proven to me to be lacking."

My blood is boiling. "You do remember yesterday, when I could barely get you to admit you liked Matthias, right?" She literally could have lived without the guy yesterday.

"I like Matthias, there's something there." Her voice is quiet. I know she thinks she's being honest, but she's not.

"Are you trying to convince me or yourself?" It comes out a bit saltier than I mean it to. I can see it the moment it leaves my lips because her little mouth turns down in a frown.

"Are you mad at me right now?" She treads gently. I've never actually been mad at her. I'm not mad at her now. I'm just...mad.

"I'm not mad at you, but I am frustrated. You love Liam. Liam loves you." (Only someone blind and deaf could miss it.) "From what I can tell, it's the end-all-be-all type of love. The mythical kind of love you read about, but don't experience. And you're just going to mess with some other guy's emotions because you have something to prove to Liam? Yourself? It's wrong. Sit and think on it, and if afterwards you can honestly tell me you are over Liam or don't love him anymore, then you should go out with Matthias. But if you can't do that, let him go. Don't make him a pawn in your game because if the roles were reversed, you wouldn't want that either." (Clearly I'm projecting and not in a good way.) My friend looks like I've just struck her.

"This morning you were pumped about me going out with Matthias, though," she defends herself. I want to roll my eyes at her, but I can't do it. I'm misdirecting all my negative thoughts and feelings towards her. It's incredibly unfair of me.

"I think these text messages and Liam coming back make a difference. I know you're smart enough to see that whether you want it to or not, Liam being here changes things. If you feel strongly about Matthias, then wait. Wait till you're sure you can get over Liam. Otherwise you run the risk of doing things you'll regret and hurting people who don't deserve it along the way."

I sigh before continuing, "I am grumpy, so I'm sorry this is all coming out in a bitchy tone. I will always be Team Britain, so if you want to date Matthias, I will root you on. I just don't want you to make the same mistake as...someone I know. That's all." (Almost said Tommy, fuck.) I hope she hears me though, because I will always be Team B. Period. Till the end of time.

"Someone you know?" She questions me, one light brown eyebrow popping up. (Don't want to deal with this right now, can't actually.)

"Want to go swimming?" I ask, popping up from my spot on the bed like I've just had the greatest desire to throw myself under water for a little while. (Maybe even a long while.)

"What?" She shakes her head, not missing my act of deflection. "No, I want my best friend to talk to me about what's going on."

"I'm not ready. Not yet." That's all I can give without becoming an emotional wrecking ball.

"I can respect that. Honestly, I can. But not forever, okay?" She tries and succeeds at making eye contact with me.

"Okay." This is where things get difficult. Sometimes I

want to be an open book and tell her everything. About me. About her brother. But then...I clam up. I never want to lose her friendship.

"You know, I'm Team Jess, too, right?" She reminds me. I sort of half smile, and like word vomit, I push down all the things I'd love to talk to her about, but can't yet. Instead I nod. She reaches over, pushing a piece of my dark brown hair out of my eyes to make sure I can see how sincere she's being and I nod again.

"So then I guess I should make a decision about Matthias, right? Do you think I should cancel our date?" This poor babe, she's so conflicted, and all I've done is made things more convoluted for her. My role here is support, get her to the other side. It's not my job to tell her what side that is.

"I don't know, Brit," I sigh, feeling like maybe I'm about to say the wrong thing, but perhaps it's the right thing for Brit. "Maybe go on the date and get your answer that way. Maybe you go, and if it doesn't feel good, you'll know it's not what you want. Or maybe you go, and it's better than you expected, and the feelings deepen, and you realize it's worth it to move forward with Matthias." Felt wrong saying it.

"Right...yeah, I think I'm going to go. But after that I have to make a decision one way or the other. Hold me to it, please?" A part of me wants to yell at her, that she has two amazing men that aren't Matthias willing to go to bat for her, and that she should abandon this ship. But it's not my place, so I hold my tongue.

"I will," I say, then imagine how my life could have been if someone had had this talk with Tommy.

"Wanna start Queen Charlotte before dinner gets here?

I'll make you a margaritaaaa..." She asks in the most ridiculous voice, and it makes me smile.

"Duh, yes." We all roll off the bed and Eden and Brit trail behind me down the stairs.

I head for the great room to turn on the tv while Brit turns towards the kitchen where I hope she'll bring me back a margarita. She's derailed by the doorbell though.

"Are you expecting something?" she calls out to me.

"Nope!" I shout back, turning on the Apple TV.

"Hey, what are you doing here?" Brit asks the guest. I lean against the back cushions of her sectional so I can view the door, and just like I always do when I see Alex, I freeze.

He breezes in like he owns the place, but stops dead when he glimpses me. Turning around quickly, he faces his sister so that I can't hear them. And no matter how hard I strain, I can't. They exchange words, and then he trudges to the kitchen.

Brit gives me a helpless look that says, *"I'm sorry my brother is a dick,"* then places Eden in my lap to follow her brother to the other side of the house.

What I want to do is get up, walk over to where they are in the kitchen and force the issue. It's been long enough. You'd think he could stop hating me now. But I don't get the chance, because he's back, walking fast towards the front door.

Britain barely just stops him, "Wait! Wait! Wait! You are not going to kill him. I'm not forgiving him or anything, but I don't think he deserves death." So Alex knows Liam is back in town now. Got it.

"Fine, I'll let him live." He looks me in the eyes briefly, and I feel it. Like a punch to the solar plexus. My toes curl and my heartbeat races. And then he turns to head out the door.

Brit is still trying to talk him down, but all I can think is: *No. It's been so long. How? He...I...didn't imagine it?* The door shutting gets my attention.

"Do you think I should call Liam and warn him?" she asks, very seriously.

I can't help it, but I laugh (to keep from crying), and say, "Absolutely not."

Brit wanders down the hall, picking at her fingers in a daze while I get lost in thought and wonder if Liam is just the latest excuse in the long line of many that Alex has used to avoid being around me.

TEN

JESS

It's hard to watch your best friend spiral. It's hard watching her flush a love like Liam's down the drain. It's hard for me to help her do it, but I try. I help her pick out clothes for a date with the other guy, I take care of her when she stops taking care of herself and gets sick, I even attempt to manipulate the situation, which ends up backfiring. (I know, I've learned my lesson, don't worry.) But no matter what I do, Brit is hellbent on going through this rather horrific train wreck full steam ahead.

I just have to take a back seat and brace for impact, vowing to help put her back together in the end. She's done it for me. I know she'll do it for me again, too. When we come out the other side of whatever it is she's going through, I'll tell her, and just like we do, the roles will swap. The caretaker will become the patient.

Her and I have that sort of symbiotic relationship. We

find equilibrium in being the other person's champion. (Yin and Yang.) And right now, I'm surviving on the fact that she needs me, her daughters need me, and Eden needs me. I can spread myself thin and let the "doing" carry me through this time, too.

A time when I haven't heard from Tommy. At all. No text messages to check on Eden. And certainly no text message responding to my "fuck you" text. It stings, and if I dwell, I'll dissolve. Can't do that. Not yet. My girls all need me.

As I finish getting Eden dressed in her jammies, Caroline pokes her head into my room. It's almost eerie how much she looks like her mom. She's just a bit taller, but has those same green eyes, same golden blonde hair, same half smile.

"What's up, babe?" I ask, snapping the buttons on Edie's onesie.

"Do you think she's okay?"

I sigh. "She's going to be okay." I look at her, trying to will some of that belief into her with a warm smile.

"I feel like they should be here by now," she says, worried.

I shake my head. "Hospitals are slow. Even if they discharge you, it could be hours before you get to leave." Brit ended up in the hospital...again. She had another fainting episode, but this time Liam was there for her. And oddly, that's a huge relief. There's no one better for the job of taking care of her. Which means I might be out of a job soon when we all move into his house at Spearhead Lake tomorrow.

Liam all but begged for us to move to his house, and reluctantly I caved.

I think I'm more curious than anything. Brit's told me her house looks like a hovel compared to his place on Spearhead.

All I said when Liam texted me to make sure it was alright that the girls and I stayed with him while Britain recovers was, "I'll help Alex burn your body if this goes south." And he said, "message received." I hope it is. For Britain and the girls, I really hope.

"Okay." Caroline's small voice betrays her. She is not okay.

"Okay, raid the pantry. Get your sister, meet me in the living room in five minutes." I instruct her.

"Okay?" Is all she says before shuffling down the hall for Elodie. I blow a couple raspberries on Eden's cheeks and listen to her giggle before sliding her on my hip and walking towards the living room. I text Damian on my way.

JESS

Where are you? Brit ended up in the hospital again.

DAMIAN

Liam is with her, right?

Yes, and?

Jess, I can't be there. With all of you. It's killing me.

Oh, Damian. He left a couple days ago for a meeting in Silicon Valley. I think it might have been a farce, though. Watching Brit do this dance with Matt and Liam, it *is* killing him. I saw it firsthand. If I know him, he'll have flown Summer out in an attempt to bury his hurt in someone else. I guess I'll leave him to it.

"What are we doing?" Elodie dumps a pile of candy onto the coffee table.

"You girls ever seen Goodfellas?" I ask. They both reply, 'No.' "Well, you heard it here first, mob wife aesthetic is gonna be big. Your education starts today." I may as well be speaking Greek, but they shrug and settle into the couch. Caroline takes Eden from me and cuddles her into her Boppy while Elodie sprawls out beside me.

Mob wife aesthetic might not *actually* go big, but at a minimum, I know I'll smile when I hear Spider say, *"Why don't you go fuck yourself, Tommy."* (See, already smiling.)

———

The first time I came to Spearhead Lake, I'll admit, I was underwhelmed. There's not a lot to it. Three businesses housed in log cabins on one side of the road, the same thing on the other side, and just dense forest all around. We never even saw the lake that day. Just these sort of drab-looking, side-of-the-road, mountain-town businesses.

But the second time, when we crested the top of the mountain road where Liam's house is, I caught a glimpse of the water, and it started clicking. Why Brit loves this place, why she feels at peace here, why she couldn't wait to get back to it all.

Then seeing Liam's house (think Arch Digest-level mountain house that could've been designed by Amber Lewis), meeting Carly (their chef) in real life, and walking around the back deck and lake front, it was even more obvious why she loved this place. (And Liam.) I'd convinced myself if Liam and Brit don't work out, I'll take a crack at it. Because *this* is the fucking dream.

It's been *a dream*, being here. Really. The girls take Eden all the time. Carly cooks. There's a staff of cleaning crew that comes every few days, and aside from hearing Brit and Liam have sex occasionally, I'm sleeping well.

I could be really happy, enjoying this break from reality. But I'm scared for when the time comes and I have to go back. To DC. To Tommy's house. To deal with...that. And it's coming, I know it.

As I sit with Eden on a blanket on the little beach area beside the dock, I think I probably look happy, pouring sand into buckets and watching Eden's eyes go wide with delight. I laugh when she squeals, and we do it over and over again. A snapshot of us would be titled, *"Mother and Daughter Enjoying Vacation."* But you know how that goes, it'd hardly be the truth.

When we head up the dock steps to reapply sunscreen and refill water bottles, I could die when I walk into the kitchen in just a bikini and see Alex sitting at the island reading a newspaper. (Who even gets newspapers anymore, you ask? Liam. Liam does, because he's old.)

I freeze (my M.O. when it comes to this guy), but he barely acknowledges me. He lifts his head, sees it's me, and then it's back to reading. *Cool.* Fucking amazing even. (I'm obviously being sarcastic.) I know my body isn't "bangin'" like it used to be. I've had a kid, and I'm in my 30s. But, like, not even a small glance? It's always like this, though. Whatever *this* is. It's one-sided.

No, it's two-sided. It's just that I like him, and he hates me, so now I have to hate him, too.

I thought for a while he didn't hate me, maybe even liked me, but turned out I was just a distraction while he was trying to get over his real love, Amy. (Also my M.O. now, being the placeholder.) Hate that that's who I am. I've never been a "poor me" type person, but fuck it. I just want to feel sorry about myself for a little bit.

One question, though: When do I get to start being the one that got away?

"Hi, Alex. Great to see you, too." I deadpan without looking at him. I put Eden in her highchair, throwing some cheerios on her tray while I refill our water bottles. All while Alex says...nothing back. I don't think he even sees me and the back of my throat burns painfully at that barb of truth.

I grab Brit's tote bag out of the mudroom, throwing the sunscreen, a couple pouches, and some snacks in it. Looking at Eden, who's still busy fingering her cheerios, then at Alex, I make the decision to leave her and run upstairs for the Pack 'n Play. If Alex is here, I won't be. We'll be on the deck or the dock all day.

I set everything by the back door and start cleaning up the mess Eden just made.

"You need help?"

I slowly turn from where I'm squatting on the floor picking up cereal to look at the man who just spoke to me for the first time in...years. (Aside from when he said my name at Brit's house. Which I don't think counts, because I'm almost positive I imagined it.)

My mouth is almost certainly hanging open, staring at this stupid man who still makes me swoon. This attraction, it doesn't even make sense. He's got light hair (sandy colored) and blue eyes, and has a body only capable of being formed by hours in a gym per day. (He's bulky, in the best way.) He's just *so* not my type. Tommy is my type. Dark hair, dark eyes, slim, dresses like a city boy, might run, but that's the extent of his exercise plan.

This Chris Hemsworth knockoff is not supposed to do it for me, for so many reasons. And I hate him for that. I hate that he ignores me, avoids me, and treats me like shit. Hate him for those reasons, too.

"Not from you," I finally manage to get out. As if I wasn't already confused as shit by what's happening here, Alex looks at me. I mean *looks* at me. Not in the eyes. He checks out my breasts, my ass, the v between my legs that's spread wide open in my squatted position. It's quick, but I see it. It makes me irrationally happy for the briefest of seconds. No clue if he liked what he saw, but he saw me. (Also glad I opted for the coral bikini, LSpace, with the low cut bottoms. It makes my olive skin and dark hair pop.)

Dropping the cereal in the trash, I wash my hands, throw my hair up in a claw clip and get ready to leave. But he stops me.

"So, where's Tommy?" He's looking right at me now and my heart stops in my chest. Alex asking about Tommy makes me feel queasy.

"Asia." That's all I say, staring back at him.

"With Jamie?"

The color drains from my face. This fucking dick. He knows. He saw my text.

"Yeah, with Jamie." I stop looking at him. "Thank you for the reminder." I dry my hands off, then head for the mudroom where I slip on the first sweatshirt I find. I suddenly feel exposed and I hate it.

"Sorry, bout *that*." He says, going back to reading his newspaper.

I scoff, "I'm sure you aren't." I roll my eyes and shake my head.

"And how would you know?" he asks back, tone even, not invested in this conversation at all.

"Because I know you, Alex. Why are you even talking to me if not to hurt me?"

"Not true," he says nonchalantly.

"Sure it is. But why? Why do *you* get to hurt me? Why would you want to? Why do you care, huh?" He pulls his head back slightly like he's surprised.

And then he gives me the most I've gotten from him in six fucking years. "Because you hurt me first."

No. I shake my head. He has it all fucking wrong.

"Not possible." I'm vehemently shaking my head back and forth. *In order to hurt someone they have to care.* "You," I accuse trying to solidify my tone, "called me a distraction, a no-body." He shrugs. He *shrugs* and it deflates me like a three day-old balloon. "You made me feel so stupid," I say, sounding (and feeling) about six inches tall. Just like I did when I overheard him talking about me.

He doesn't say a word back. Not one fucking word.

"You know what, you were right, though. I am a distraction, just a 'bump in the road,' for a lot of people. So thank you for reminding me exactly who I am to everyone here." I turn away, hiding my watery eyes, and march out the door with a baby on one arm, and the tote and Pack 'n Play on my other.

In hindsight, sending that text to "Amy" may have been a mistake. Because now that I know Alex knows, I have to tell

Brit. And then maybe it's time for me to stop being a supporting cast member, and just pack up our things and go.

———

Alex

She overheard me? I try not to think about that night. Mostly successfully. I think about *her*. A lot. Too much. But not that night.

I might have called her a distraction. I think I used the exact words calling her 'a bump in the road.' I think I said something worse, too, but it's fuzzy. Whenever I think about that night, I think about other things, and all I see is red, so yeah. I don't remember exactly what I said. Jess does, though. *Fuck.*

Soon to be in my new nightmare rotation will be Jess in that little bikini telling me I made her feel stupid. Right on cue, there it is again, that fucking pain in my chest I felt when she just told me that.

I'm practically living the nightmare now. I can see it. Jess and Eden playing on the beach, laughing together, having not a care in the world. And then it'll be fucking slow-motion torture watching her bounce up the deck stairs. I'll have to rush to the kitchen island before she spots me, and then pretend like I don't see her. Which is fucking impossible.

She's this leggy little thing with an ass that's too round, full as fuck breasts, and tan skin that doesn't come from a bottle. And that hair. That hair has haunted me from the moment I saw it. That long Disney princess-type hair that she almost never wears entirely up. It's always down and around her shoulders, a special kind of torture for someone like me.

That would be someone who's dreamed about wrapping her hair around my fist while she moves over me. *I'm so fucked.*

It's been six fucking years. And hating her, it's been fucking miserable.

But maybe, for the first time I'm seeing it like I fucked her up first. *Fuck!* This doesn't make shit better, though. It's just the sixth circle of hell. Just another way this whole situation gets even more fucked.

I walk into the great room and stand at an angle from the large picture windows so no one can see me. And I watch her struggle. To set up the Pack 'n Play with one hand. I should go down there. I'm actually itching to go because it's painful to watch. And then she drops the Pack 'n Play in defeat and uses her one free hand to wipe away tears from underneath her sunglasses. *Fucckkkk.* Alright, this might be worse than the chest pain earlier.

"Alex!" My niece Elodie exclaims from the front door.

"Hey, E." I quickly turn away from the window.

"What are you doing here?" She asks with excitement. She's just like Damian. Looks like him, too. It's funny to see my best friend reincarnated as a kid. Not both kids are like this, though. Caroline looks just like my sister. Elodie looks just like him. Acts like him, too. Just happy, and charming all the fucking time.

"Liam asked me to come over for a bit. Hey, you got a minute?" She nods with a smile. "Can you go help Jess? I think she needs a couple extra hands."

"Aye Aye, captain!" she says, then bounds out the back door and down the deck. I go back to watching, making sure Elodie helps, but what I see next wrenches my heart.

It's Elodie embracing Jess as she cries, baby still perched on her hip. I don't know if she's crying for me? Or about Tommy? But being the sick fuck I am, I hope it's for me.

They break apart a moment later, when Liam, Caroline, and some other teenager make their way down the back steps hauling paddle boards. I was trying to leave Brit alone. Liam said she had "the talk" with Matt today, which thank christ for that. But does she know her best friend is out there crying by herself?

It's not really my place to say anything, I don't think. Also feel like maybe Jess and Tommy splitting up isn't common knowledge. Damian would've told me if he knew. I think.

"Hey, man." Liam comes through the door that leads out to the deck. "Thanks for coming."

I nod. "Yeah, sure."

Liam sort of bounces his palm against a leg. *Nervous.*

"Think you could stick around a bit longer? Just have a... let's call it a...bad feeling." Wasn't really planning on staying here any longer than necessary. Not good for my mental health being around Jess, but bad feelings tend to actually mean shit to me. Whenever I've gotten one, there's usually something pretty fucking shitty on the other side.

"Yeah, I'll be here." I take a seat in the great room, in a deep club chair that gives me a clear view of the back deck and dock. I'll just burn the view of Jess in that bikini into my brain and accept that I'll never sleep again.

———

The banging on the door instantly has the hair rising on the back of my neck. I was just about ready to leave, too. Something about sitting here, watching this sort of idyllic summer day unfold in front of me was unnerving. I'm still not in it. I'm just sort of existing on the outside, looking in. I know it's my family, too, but it's not *my* family. *Make sense?*

Bang. Bang. There it is again. Seven paces to the front door and I open it, already pissed off.

Matt looks fucking drunk.

"You made her cry, didn't you?" I ask him

"If I haven't yet, I will," he spits back in a sadistic tone. For that alone, I could kill him. But I know how these things go. Can't be the first to throw a punch, can't actually kill him either. At least not right here, right now. Too many witnesses. Too many liabilities.

"Your daddy know you're here?" I ask him, and his eyes practically bulge. "Should I give him a call?" I pull my phone out of my pocket, and taunt him with it.

"Fuck you, Alex."

"Sick comeback, *bro*." *Bro.* It's a taunt. His dad treats me like the son he never had, and Matt knows it. "You about done here?" I ask. When he doesn't immediately respond, because he's moving slow, high on something, I slam the door on his face and lock it.

I hedge my bets with a quick call to the sheriffs, then send off a quick text to Constantine about his son just as the banging picks back up again. Just like I knew it would.

This time I open the door and slip outside. Could get ugly. *Kind of hope it does, need to take out the self loathing on something.* I back Matt up and away from the front porch so what I say doesn't make it onto the doorbell cam.

"I fucking dare you, Matt. You have no idea how much you'd make my goddamn day by attempting to lay a finger on me. But you won't do it...can't, can you?"

He spits on the ground. *Weak.*

"You're gonna beat the shit out of me? Just like your dad did to your mom?" His retort is a low blow.

"Nah, I won't have to hit you that many times," I say back coolly. Not letting him see how much that comment actually hits and hurts. I've tried so hard to be everything Ray couldn't be.

"What happens when my daddy finds out you hit his precious *son*?"

"He'll probably give me a pat on the back for sticking up for his *daughter*." He didn't like that one. It sounds incestuous, but I promise, it's not. Constantine just thinks of me and my sister like his kids. I don't think I'd be lying if I said he loved us more.

Liam comes flying down the front steps, looking out for blood, but I can't let him take this moment from me. I need it. Matt's close to cracking, so I get between the two of them when Matt goes off. He really loses his crap this time. Spewing shit about my mom and my sister being whores and white trash. I let it go. Most of it rolling off my back.

Before I let Liam get a word in edgewise, I respond. "The only reason you're not already unconscious is because you're too fucking weak to take a swing," I say viciously. "Your ass would be fucking toasted and you know it. But if you really wanna talk about scum of the earth, it's you, bud. I should've fucking ended you 17 years ago. You've grown to be such a big man, talking about women like this." I practically spit, "Pathetic. You are your mother's son, *Matt*."

And that's when Matt loses control and takes a swing. *Finally*.

I let him clip me, just barely on the chin, then stepping back, putting my weight into it, I slam him back and the audible crunch is almost as deeply satisfying as the view I have, looking down on him, knocked out cold on the ground.

Chances of him ending up with Britain -%100.

ELEVEN

ALEX

The thing is, spending time around Jess, it's not good for me. Every word, every look, every laugh, frown — it stays with me long after she's gone.

It's been days since I saw her, but here I am. Sitting at my kitchen table, still thinking about *her*. There's almost nothing I can do to get the mental onslaught to stop. It's just a relentless pulsing in my brain. A laugh. A scrunch of her nose. That sad look she got halfway through lunch. Then repeat it all again.

I shouldn't have stayed for lunch that day, after the Matt incident. But Brit wanted me to, Liam wanted me to, and, well...I'm trying to stick. I just wish they would've asked me to lunch on a day she wasn't there.

At lunch, though, there was something she said...and I can't fucking shake it. She said, "Who knows where I'll be this time next year." It was more *how* she said it than what she said.

Why wouldn't she be in DC? Her and Tommy have a nice row house. Capitol Hill. He makes a shit ton of money as a lawyer. She'll be okay...right? Alimony, child support, half whatever that house is worth...

She's not my problem. Yeah, no she isn't. But also sort of wish she was.

I also can't shake the fact that she overheard me talking about her *that night*. And if she hadn't heard me, would everything be different? It's not that what I said wasn't true on some level. It's just that I didn't mean any of it. I didn't want people to know Jess was Amy's cousin. I didn't want people to have any preconceived notion of who she was to me, so that someday, when she was mine, people would just say, "That's Jess, Alex's wife." *Why is that the first word I think of?*

I never wanted it to be, "That's Jess, his late wife's cousin that he sometimes texted with about his late wife and daughter and now he's fucking her." Because I sort of wanted her to be mine. Just mine. All of that is past tense, though, isn't it?

I've spent years despising her, thinking she was something, that really, *maybe*, she wasn't...

I don't really let people in. But I let Jess in. Or maybe she pushed her way in, but either way, I wanted her there.

It might have been the first time I saw her in that sundress with yellow flowers. It might have been that Christmas when she didn't reach out. It may have been the first time we talked on the phone, not just texted. It could have been when I saw her *that* night that I knew. And then kind of like my life goes, it went to shit. I saw her, I knew, and then I had that weird gut feeling, and it all went sideways.

I may have played it too cool, though. *Obviously*. I over-sold her meaning nothing to me. Clearly.

The nagging feeling about Jess' situation just won't stop, though. *Fuck*.

I tell myself I'm just playing devil's advocate, but really I'm just acting like a fool when I open my laptop and write a quick email.

Hey,

I know it's been a while, we need to catch up next time I'm in the city.

This might seem sort of out of the blue, but I'm looking to get a prenup drawn up. Keep it on the DL, please? Haven't told Damian or my sister. Just curious about your recommendations. Happy to put you on retainer if you can do it, or if you have a referral?

Thanks,

Alex Palomino

My front door swings open, and I slam my laptop shut when my sister traipses in looking like someone just pissed in her Wheaties.

"Brit? Is everything okay?"

She barely registers me and says, "I just need sleep." That's fair. I'll check on her in a couple hours. I can't keep up with the ups and downs between her and Liam. I have to disconnect from it a little bit just so I don't preemptively kill him just because he bought her the wrong coffee creamer or something. Not that he would. Pretty sure that man is thoroughly and completely pussy whipped, which is disgusting because that's my sister.

Blech.

———

Alex!

Congrats, man! Never thought I'd see the day. Do I know the lucky lady?

Happy to help. I can have my assistant reach out about billing. I'm sort of stuck in Taiwan waiting for a hearing, so this'll give me something to kill some time.

It's all about preference, but for me, I kept things fairly simple. Any property acquired prior to the marriage remains in my possession and then all alimony was waived. Which I'd probably recommend to you as well.

Let me know what I can do to help, and again, congrats!

Tommy DiAngelo

Yeah, that's sort of what I thought. Things could be different, though. I don't know every finite detail of their agreement based on this email. But he's a fucking lawyer; only an idiot would think he hasn't drawn up a tight contract that covers his ass completely, and more than likely leaves Jess hanging out to dry.

I'll have to explain all this away later. Sort of pissed at myself for sending that email, but I'm already in this deep...

Hey,

It's someone I knew a long time ago. Recently reconnected.

Can you have your assistant send over docs on proceeding?

I'm curious about your thoughts on pre-funding a divorce settlement. Would that be best in a trust?

Thanks for the advice.

Alex Palomino

———

It's easy to find her. She's slightly bent over the top deck railing, her ass sticking up and out slightly. Her tan legs looking a mile long in her short shorts. It's another mental image I sure as fuck didn't need to add to the bank.

There's a whole party going on inside the house, but she's out here alone watching the lake turn from blue to black as the sun sets behind us. It's nice out. There's flower petals all over the deck, and candles burning. It's quiet, too, just a soft hum of music leaking from inside. Can't take any credit for the setup, though. Liam proposed to Britain this afternoon. This is just the remnants of the spectacle.

I'm happy for my sister, but you know, this is the second engagement party I've been to for her in the last couple of months so...

"Hey," I say, taking a spot next to her, leaning against the rail facing her instead of the lake.

"Hey," she doesn't turn or anything. *Bad day?* That's what I want to ask, but it'd be stupid because I bet a lot of her days are bad right now.

"Something you said at lunch the other day...it's been bothering me."

"Whatever it was, I'm sorry." She doesn't look up, but oddly sounds sincere. And defeated. It's so not like her.

"No, it uh-it wasn't like that. Just, are you gonna be okay..." I don't know how to say this without insulting her, "without Tommy?" She grimaces.

"Eventually, I'm sure. Why?" She takes a swig of her clear drink on the rocks, then sets it back down beside the baby monitor perched beside her.

"Just was worried, that's all." My mouth twists a bit. I'm relearning what it's like to talk to her, but it's different now. All of it. Both of us. Maybe too much has happened.

"Again, why?" Her tone. It's so devoid of what makes Jess *Jess*. It's weird.

I shrug, and so does she. She grabs a clip that was snapped on to the hem of her button down shirt and winds her hair up tight, and for some reason that gets me hard.

"So, how long are you staying for?" Back to basics. Small talk. Hate it.

"Tonight's it." Oh. *Fuck.*

"You're leaving?" I don't know why I sound so surprised.

"Yeah, I think so."

I nod. "Back home?" She looks up at me. Something like hurt flaring in her eyes.

"Back to Tommy's house, for now, yes." Tommy's house. I see.

"You...could stay..."

She shakes her head, takes another sip of clear, and says, "It'd just be on borrowed time before I have to go, and I think the family could use some time 'just the family,' you know?" She nods towards the great room picture windows where Britain and Liam and her kids, his parents, Constantine, and his kids are all watching Damian play with their new dog. Yeah, I get it.

Pretty familiar feeling for me, outsider looking in, but this feels like new territory for Jess, maybe.

"Okay...if you ever need anything, you should call." She looks at me in disbelief. I don't want to give her a chance to come up with a dig or a comeback or say something snide, so I blurt out, "I'm sorry." It's rushed.

Her incredulous look turns to surprise. "For what?" she asks cautiously.

Don't like this feeling. "For making you feel stupid...for being a dick." I shrug to try and play it off like it's cool. This isn't a big deal, just a regular apology, and not like her accepting it will change the rest of my life.

"Okay." That's it. That's all she gives. *Fair.*

I knock my knuckles against the wood, getting ready to say goodbye, sending a vibration down the railing that, in turn, sends the baby monitor falling off the second-story deck into some bushes below. Jess let's out a little gasp while leaning over the railing to see if she can see where it landed.

"Fuck, sorry. I'll get it." I push off the ledge and jog down the dark stairs. Of course the sun has finally tucked itself behind the house and all I can see is the lit-up stair treads and not much else.

Stepping to the side, I look back up at the deck, gauging where the monitor might have landed, but Jess isn't there anymore. She's at my back, following me. Nearly colliding with me where I've stopped.

Her eyes go a bit wide, pupils blown. Could be lust, could be the low lighting. Hard to tell.

I step off the stairs and on to the inclined landscaping that slopes towards the lake. And Jess is still right behind me, a gentle hand on my arm like she might get lost if she lets go, but it's not that dark.

Judging where we were standing, I look up at the top deck. Then back down into the bushes and it should be some-where in...*here*. I lean forward and pick up the monitor. As I turn to show it to Jess, her foot gives under the slippery pine needles. *She shouldn't have come down here in those sandals.* But I reach out an arm, right around her midsection and haul her up against me before she even has a chance to fall.

Her hands find my chest, her eyes find mine, her breathing speeds up, and her heart rate does, too. It's easy to tell because my body wants to fall in sync with hers. My breath matches hers, my heart mirrors hers. And we stick together like that. *How we should have been all along.*

"Jess..." I say softly, almost a whisper. I miss hearing her name. I've dreamed of hearing her name on my lips...like this.

"Alex..." she copies in the same tone. Her tongue darts out wetting her top lip...*fuck me.* I pocket the monitor, bringing my hand up to her forearm to hold her steady. *Fine, it's so she doesn't leave.* Even though I keep a firm arm around her midsection, I let my other hand start a gentle ascent towards her neck.

Fuck me if my hand doesn't slightly tremble, and in response she gets goose bumps. She could stop me. I'm not holding her that tight.

"Alex...wh-what are we doing?" she asks, sending a zinging bolt of fire through me. She asked 'what are *we* doing?,' not 'what am *I* doing?' She's in this with me.

"What I should have done the first time I saw you." I drop my head slightly, and she reaches up. I can feel her grip deepen as she goes up on her toes, and then I slam my mouth down on hers, unable to hold back a second longer.

There's nothing gentle about what I'm doing. It's a claiming. It's a kiss that says, "This is Jess, Alex's Jess." *Do you understand?* It's an open-mouth feast, and I've come hungry. Starved, actually. Because this kiss is the shit that men go to war over, and she has not a fucking clue I would for her. I already am.

I slip a hand to the back of her skull, undoing the hair she just put up and let the clip fall. *Hope she wasn't sentimental about that.* Her hair tumbles down and I pull away from her mouth because I want to see her, memorize her.

In the low light, I can just make out her swollen lips, red from rubbing against my short beard and *fuck*. Can't wait to see her inner thighs look the same way.

Her eyes are wide and hungry, like maybe she's been starving, too. Her hair falls, framing her heart-shaped face, and my hand glides up the back of her head. The feel of her silky hair between my fingers feels like a dream. Is it a fucking dream? How does this end? Just an abrupt awakening? Does it turn into a nightmare when she pushes me away? Does it turn into more?

"It's up to you," I whisper to her, knowing she knows what I mean, leaving the ball in her court. I want this. So unequivocally. But maybe she doesn't.

She takes a step away, taking everything good in life with her. My one arm is still around her waist to keep her from slipping, but I let the hand that had been in her hair fall. *Right*. Cue nightmare.

She takes my now free hand between both of hers, running one hand over the top, while the other cradles my hand from below. There's a tenderness there as she slips her small fingers over my bruised knuckles, then threads a hand in mine and leads me back up, but just to the lower-level deck.

It's attached to the basement level that's never used. The only light comes from slivers of yellow pushing through the cracks in the deck flooring above us.

There's a couple outdoor sofas with covers still on and Jess pushes me to sit down. And, of course, I fucking do. I've fantasized, gotten myself off so many times just thinking about this. Her. Pushing me down, and having her way, because Jess isn't the type to be dominated. Not that I won't break her of that eventually, but right now, she's the boss.

She settles on top of me, her thighs straddling mine, and when she reaches for my belt buckle, I pull her face towards mine again, kissing her with my all. I run my tongue along her full lips and she opens on a sigh. It's so fucking subtle, it's beautiful. If I could record that sound, I think I could eventually be conditioned to come every time it played.

"Do you want this, Alex?" She pulls away, asking in a whisper. She doesn't know I do?

"More than anything, Jess." I grab her hips and push her down on my lap so she can feel how much I want this. *Need* this. She holds my face in both her hands and then reciprocates the claiming kiss of earlier in her own way. Her tongue seeks, her teeth nip, she sucks me in and I imagine soon she'll be sucking my cock like that and...*now*. Need her right fucking now.

"Jess...don't have any condoms." *Please, please.*

"On birth control. Clean."

"Same," I say, reaching out, undoing the top button of her jean shorts. When it doesn't immediately give way, I rip the thick denim, eliciting a raspy gasp from Jess.

"I'll buy you new ones," I say, then kiss her as I force the zipper open. She stands quickly, removing sandals, jeans, and her innocent-looking white cotton undies, but then climbs back over to finish undoing my belt, then unbuttoning and releasing my strained jeans.

I lift my hips, letting them slide down, and she pushes my briefs with them as I do. My cock springs free, and there's that little sigh again. At the sound, a bead of precum releases. I think for a second she might lean down and lick it away, but she changes direction and with a hand on my chest, she positions herself over me.

Yes, fuck.

She leans forward and starts placing kisses up my neck until eventually she's pulling my ear into her mouth. Just as the tip of my head hits the apex between her thighs, she whispers, "You're cock is so fucking beautiful." And at the same time she pushes down on me, I lift my hips thrusting into her. And my cock is nothing compared to the sight in front of me.

Jess is picture-perfect perfection. Her olive skin against her white tank top and button down that's started sliding off one shoulder, and the hair I've dreamt of bounces as she comes to a stop at the root of my dick. I'm staring at her because this...this is fucking new. It's a new feeling fueling this need to keep her. Claim her. Mark her. Maim her. Anything that says, *"Alex Palomino was here,"* when she's walking around tomorrow.

With a hand still firmly gripping her hip, I pull her towards me, dragging her clit against my lower abdominals. "Your skin is so fucking beautiful and all I want to do is ruin it." I lean forward, catching her neck and sucking her in. When I do, I feel her clench. My girl likes this, fucking wants it.

"Where do you want me to leave my mark, Jess?" I move her hips back and forth against my pelvis. The slightest of pants hits her lips when I push her back and forth again.

She immediately starts discarding her button down, then her tank, revealing brown nipples through a semi-sheer bra. *Need. Fucking need.* I continue to drag her back and forth across my dick.

"My tits, Alex. Mark me." I want so badly to tell her, *"Baby, you've made my whole fucking life."*

Instead, I say, "These perfect fucking tits? I'd be honored." Before I do, I pull her face down to mine, feasting on her sweet taste. When I release her, I keep one hand on a hip, which affords me a half handful of her ass while my other squeezes between us, palming her round globes through her bra. Then I place my hot tongue against the sheer fabric and press against her pebbled nipple.

Her head falls back and her pussy clenches.

I make quick work of unfastening her bra and then my mouth is engulfing one of her breasts, sucking her in. I'm palming one breast while I mark her other. And I go back and forth, continuing to gently thrust into her as she rides me.

The more marks I leave and the harder I go, the rougher she rides. I don't know if she's being quiet because we're out in the open, but there's nothing for show here. She's just enjoying the fuck out of my cock, and I've never been happier.

"So close," she whispers with a sigh. My dick swells and with a hand fully gripping her ass cheek, I pull her closer, I make my abdomen a fucking washboard she can ride her clit against, and she does. I only lift and swivel my hips slightly, hitting a spot and she fucking loses it. I grab her face by the chin and tilt her head down to look at me, and she does.

I watch this beautiful face turn from bliss to shock and delight, to eventually, what I think looks a lot like love. *Love.*

I slam her tight little cunt back down around me and I pulse and spill. And when I pull her body tighter against me, she comes undone again. Her eyes rolling back, her hands clenching my pecs.

"You ride me so fucking well, Jess, Uh." I thrust again, letting every ounce of what I have fill her. *Take it, baby. It's fucking yours. All of it.*

Jess shivers and her nipples turn taut against the cool breeze off the lake, and I only need 30 seconds before I'll be hard again.

I lean forward to place a kiss on my girl's mouth, but she

pulls away from me slightly, leaning back, my semi-hard cock, my seed still filling her body.

Gut feeling starts screaming at me. *Don't like this. Do not like this.*

In a quiet, gentle voice, she says, "I'm not interested in being somebody's bump in the road, Alex. No matter how much I wish I could be that for you." *Pain.* It hits deep, somewhere around the seventh or eighth rib.

I don't know how to tell her she *is* the bump in the road because she's the whole fucking road. She's my path. Always has been. Everyone else was just a fucking pit stop. She's the beginning and the end, and I'd ride her as long as my journey on earth lasts.

It didn't matter the destination. It was her. Every road led back to her.

I don't know how to tell her that, *this* just sealed it for me. How could she think that's just something I give away to anyone? It's never like this. Never face to face, mouth on mouth, leaving my marks.

"Maaaa," followed by a cry, echoes from my pants and I retract my hands from her body. She slides off me, dressing quickly while I fish the monitor out of my pants and hold it out for her. She takes it, finds her way back to the lit stairs, and leaves me sitting there with nothing but enough material to fill my nightmares until my dying day.

TWELVE

JESS

"I wish you'd stay..." Brit says as she helps me fold and pack for our flight this afternoon. I look at her and give a soft smile, but she can't talk me into staying. It doesn't feel like the right fit anymore. I'm in the way.

My departure seems to have taken her by surprise. I think Brit planned for me to move into the apartment at Liam's house as soon as we had "the talk." The one where I told her that Tommy was in love with someone else. She'd mentally already planned out the next six months of my life, tacking me alongside hers. Just another afterthought. Side character. *Supporting cast.*

"I should really start figuring my life out, you know, post-Tommy?" I exhale, "It's kind of hard when everyday's a vacation here..." I might mean that as a dig, because for all the drama Brit goes through, her life is a fucking cake walk. *Now.* It's a cake walk *now.* I know it wasn't always like this, but I'm jealous. (Okay? Yeah, I can fucking admit it.)

I put a stack of Eden's pjs in the suitcase, then take a seat beside her on the bed. "Brit, green's not my color." (Not entirely true, I've rocked emerald before.) She looks up at me, every emotion right there on her face. Sad for me. Embarrassed. A splash of pity. Don't love that, and that's why I'm leaving. Right there. That splash of pity.

"If it helps…I've been jealous of you for years. And years. Probably from the moment I met you," she says. That surprises me.

"Stahhhpp it." I bump her shoulder with mine.

"No really, Jess. You have no idea." I feel a pang of anxiety for the briefest of moments, then it subsides. "You're fucking swimsuit-model gorgeous, you're smart and stylish. Confident and witty. You don't take people's bullshit, and yet everyone still wants to be friends with you. And don't even get me started on how good of a mom you are. Sometimes I worry you're a better mom to my own kids than I am!" She's not really looking at me anymore. This, right here, is why I could never be fully honest with her.

"How about this, let's just accept that we're both equally amazing, sometimes in different ways, okay?" I don't want to sit here going back and forth about who's dick is prettier.

She nods with a smile. Good.

"Now get out of here. I don't need help packing, I'm sure your fiancé is probably wandering around like a lost puppy looking for you." She blushes, gives me a quick hug and heads out.

I probably should have left a couple days ago, but when Liam asked for help pulling off an epic proposal that would be worthy of Britain, there was no way I could say no. He knew he botched it the first time, so the second time had to be one for the books. (His words, not mine.) I'm positive we succeeded. They're sickeningly happy. And I'm happy *for* her. Not even begrudgingly, I'm just happy for her. I can be jealous and mad and disappointed while still being happy for Brit.

JESS

> Just letting you know Eden and I are flying back to DC today.

TOMMY

> Okay. How is she doing? Sleeping okay for you?

Aside from one measly text a couple days ago, I haven't spoken to Tommy since I've been here. Which was probably for the best. I needed a cool-down period. And to start coming to terms with what will be my new normal. The second part of that, is that as much as I'm dreading going back to DC and dealing with custody and divorce attorneys, I actually have to go do it. I need to know what my life is going to look like once we separate.

I'm definitely not feeling as sad about Tommy as I was. Now it's just like sadness *lite*. Last night with Alex might have had something to do with it...

Last night was...like nothing I've ever experienced before. It was need and desperation and it was like I'd been parched and I didn't even know I was thirsty...until him. And I wanted more, but you know the saying, "One is too many and 1000 is never enough?" That was *this*.

So I was honest with myself and with him. I've done the

casual sex bit before. (It's great, no shade there.) Just, it wouldn't have been casual for me and I'm done playing second fiddle. Done being a seat warmer. I'm no longer competing with dead wives and true loves. I probably could have been content with Alex at some point. (Yeah. Okay. Happy.) I could have been happy with him, but it would have been a lie just like it is with Tommy.

JESS

Yeah, she's been good. Sleeping okay most nights. Had to bring her in the bed a few times.

TOMMY

And how are you?

Fine.

How's Brit?

Happy.

And Damian?

I don't know. I assume also fine?

You do know that Summer is here. With him. Right?

Oh, okay.

———

It's small. So small. "There's a large closet that you could maybe put the crib in." My jaw practically falls open. I'm not having my daughter sleep in a closet. I know I can't afford a lot, but like, we can draw a few lines. We can share a bedroom, it's not the end of the world.

"That's um, not. No. One bedroom is fine, but it does have to be big enough to fit a bed *and* a crib." The elderly real estate agent just nods along with me.

Janet came recommended. Probably won't be seeing any more apartments with her after today.

"I'll just finish taking a look around and meet you downstairs in a few minutes." She grabs her umbrella, leaving me in one of the saddest looking buildings we've seen so far. I can work with a lot, but this one might be beyond me. Worst part is I can barely afford it.

Hiring a divorce lawyer practically drained my savings, and now I'll be using the nest egg I got from selling my dad's house to potentially buy, but probably just rent, for the next six months while I wait for the divorce to be settled. And then...I have no fucking clue. Hope I find a better paying job before then?

I pull out my phone to call May because she asked me to after I looked at places today.

"Hi, Jessie." I can tell by the tone in her voice that she's ready to console me.

"It was a bust." She's probably nodding along.

"My offer still stands." I tilt my head up to the water-stained ceiling, letting gravity do the work of keeping my tears in.

"Okay." I try to keep the reluctance and the fear out of my voice.

"Okay?!" May gets excited. At least there's that.

"Yeah, okay."

"Oh my gosh, I just got so excited!" May offered the loft

in Noho to Eden and me while we wait out the separation. Six whole months of it. It's sort of bullshit. If you decide you want to stop being married to someone, you should just be able to stop. It shouldn't take six months "without cohabitations" to then stop being married. Feels like there's some patriarchal bullcrap reasoning behind it.

"I'm going to call Ellen and let her know. She's so excited to meet you. And Eden! Okay, I've got to start cleaning. You just tell me when you plan to be here, and it'll be all set for you!"

Ellen is May's girlfriend. *Serious* girlfriend. It's still weird for me for May to be with someone who isn't Jules, but I'm happy for her. May said she'll stay at Ellen's to give me and Eden breathing room. She has no idea just how much that means to me right now.

I feel like the walls are closing in on me at Tommy's house. Like any minute the rug could be pulled out from under me. Probably because it could. He could literally tell me to leave, and I'd have to.

———

When I get back to the house, I'm surprised to find Tommy in the living room with Eden and not Glenn.

"Hey," I say hesitantly, closing the door behind me. I don't take off my rain jacket because I'm pretty sure you can still see the remnants of a fading hickey on my neck.

"Hey," he says back, sounding a bit off.

"I didn't know you'd be back so soon." I thought I had at least another week.

"Decided on a whim to come back." Decided to take a 23-hour flight on a whim?

"Okay..." I trail off, taking a seat in an arm chair across from him.

"We need to talk." We both say it at the same time. Normal people would laugh about something like that, but things are stilted right now and neither of us so much as smiles.

"You go first," I say.

"I've been offered partner." Wow. *Wow*. My eyes are probably bulging because that's amazing news. For him. Really means nothing to me. "But I have to commit to a year in Taipei." Oh. Still doesn't really mean anything for me.

"I have to take it," he resigns. I mean nobody's holding a gun to his head.

"Okay..."

"Is there any chance you'd consider moving?" Here we go.

"No." That's my final answer. Absolutely no wiggle room on this. I'm happy for him, but will absolutely not be putting my life on hold to go live in Taiwan for a year. For *him*.

Tommy drops his head, clearly distraught.

"What if we paid you?" *We?* Eww. No. Even more of a no than it was before.

"That's a hard no." I'm mentally patting myself on the back for not getting up and screaming, *"Fuck you!"*

"Okay..."

"I want a divorce." It just comes out.

"Okay..." he says again, not entirely surprised.

"I don't want anything, I won't contest the prenup, I just

want primary custody of Eden. You can come visit her whenever you want. But I can't move to Taiwan and I have to stop prioritizing other people's lives, including yours." When he doesn't immediately say anything, I add, "I deserve to be happy, too."

He eventually nods, maybe gets misty eyed, but surprisingly, I don't. The sense of relief is almost immediate. I guess I've moved into bargaining. Before you know it, Tommy will just be a memory I sometimes look back on. It feels good. Better than good.

I'm ready for my fresh start.

———

September 22, 2023

It's been ten years since the first time I came here. (Seven years since the last time.) But since we're moving to New York (today), I thought we'd say goodbye.

Eden and I would have picked up flowers if our SUV wasn't filled to the brim with suitcases and clothes. Since I didn't want to pay for movers, all we're taking is what fits in the car. Eventually I'll go back for the rest of our stuff, but since Tommy isn't there, it'll keep for a little.

In an effort to avoid being on the road too late today, Eden and I arrive at the cemetery early morning. (Definitely want to be in New York before rush hour.) So it's only a quarter past nine when we reach Amy and Tally's gravestones. (And okay, maybe I wanted to come early so there wasn't a chance of running into Alex. I'm sure he still comes here. And I'm sure the sight of him kneeling over his wife's grave would completely annihilate me.)

The weather's mild today, just a slight breeze with cool air behind it on this sunny morning. I sit down criss-cross applesauce and place Eden in my lap, hoping I've got maybe three minutes before she gets bored of sitting still.

Hey, Ames...moving back to NYC today...

I haven't had this issue before, but I'm at a loss for what to say. What to share or talk about. My mind can only think one thing, and it's like if I can't say it, I should just leave and not say anything at all.

I think I might have fallen in love with your husband. The tears form in my eyes and I don't do anything to stop them. I didn't say it out loud. (Obviously.) But I feel like I may as well have with how surprised I am at the spoken thought.

I think I might have loved him. (Past tense. I don't let myself love people who can't love me back the same way anymore.)

Even though it's only been a minute, at most, I hoist Eden back up, standing with her on my hip.

I don't think I'll come back again. I just hope wherever the two of you are, you're together and happy, or at least at peace. Goodbye, Amy. Bye, Tally.

As we walk back to the car, Eden places a hand against my damp cheek and I move her hand to my mouth and place a big kiss on her open palm.

"Just you and me, baby."

If you think moving back into your childhood bedroom after college is depressing, just wait till you're a soon-to-be divorcée in your 30s...moving back into your childhood bedroom *with* your child.

It's demoralizing.

"Oh, stop it already. It's not the end of the world. You just moved back to the greatest city on earth!" May comes in, toting Eden with her and just like she found me last time, I'm laid out on my bed staring at the ceiling where there's still tape from my Lance Bass poster.

I've never dated anyone with blonde hair before. (I never dated Alex. I think I just fell in love with him.)

Dating. *Holy shit.* I might have to do *that*...again. *No,* actually. I don't think I will. There's comfort in that thought.

"May, I need a job," I say, rolling over and propping my head up.

"Okay. Go get a job." I laugh at her overly simplistic answer. I've worked for Britain for so long, I'm worried I'm not cut out for the real workforce anymore.

"Okay. I will. Any suggestions?"

"Well, you could start at the cafe downstairs. They can't make a cappuccino for shit."

I laugh. "Okay, then. That's where I'll start."

———

BRITAIN

How you doing, babe?

JESS

Great!

Really?

Sure. I just got hired at a job that pays minimum wage, I'm sleeping in the same bed as I did at 13, and I'm pretty sure the homeless man in front of my building just hit on me.

Okay...

Why don't you just work for me full time?
You could even come back to Spearhead!

Because you don't actually have any work for me to do. You're basically paying me to be your friend and give you fashion advice. Which btw, I love you, but I quit.

Are you mad at me?

No. I'm really not. I just have to figure some stuff out on my own.

I hate this.

I wouldn't say I'm loving it either.

———

BRITAIN

Can I come visit?

JESS

When were you thinking? My schedule at the cafe is a bit wild at the moment.

Okay, just whenever you can pencil me in.

I'll let you know in a couple weeks.

Okay...

———

TOMMY

How's E doing?

JESS

Good! Took a step today. I'll send you the video.

No way! Really?!

Yup.

How are you? How's the new nanny?

Fine. New nanny is great, thanks for hiring her.

And the job?

Is great.

Cool.

Yup.

Did you hear Alex is getting married?

Plunk. I drop my phone into the cup of coffee I was pouring. Instantly there's water in my eyes. My throat gets painfully tight. A hand goes to the pulsing pain in my stomach. *Wow.*

I pinch my lips together to stop the trembling. I pinch them so hard, my teeth feel like they'll pierce through the skin at any moment.

"Jess? Your phone is in my cup." Christoph, my favorite regular, is staring at me like I've flown the coop. (Mentally that is.) (And mentally, I have.)

"Oh, shit." I reach into the scalding hot coffee, burning my fingers as I do. I hiss, then drop my phone on the ground watching the screen fracture. *Perfect.*

"Maybe you should just take the morning, doll," Christoph suggests, understanding I'm on the verge of a mental breakdown.

"Yeah, I think I might."

I pass Marc on his way to the back office, "I need to go, are you okay?" He's stoned nine times out of ten, but today he isn't. I feel like I'm leaving the cafe in moderately capable hands.

"Sure, whatever," he shrugs me off.

I walk out of the cafe in a daze. Broken phone in one hand, the other sort of just lifted up because my fingers are still stinging from the burn, and then I cry. (Snapshot title would be: *"Emotionally Unstable Woman Cries in the City."*) (It would be accurate.)

I cry the whole walk up to my mother's home to go relieve a nanny (who makes more money than me) because I might still be a little bit in love with someone who once called me a "bump in the road."

———

BRITAIN

Hi, how are you doing?

It's been a couple weeks, everything alright?

Jesssssss

THIRTEEN

JESS

At 8:30, I buzz Marian, our nanny, up. Eden's been fed and dressed so, logically, I should really think about doing the same. I look down at my coffee-stained AGOLDE jeans and shrug, throwing on a baggy Cuzco's Cafe t-shirt, socks and a pair of Birks. (That would be Birkenstocks, not Birkins.) (This is my life now.) (For the record, I could never afford a Birkin before, but it's fun to dream.)

I unlock and open the door, but instead of my 60-year-old nanny, my green-eyed, cute-as-a-button pregnant best friend stands in her place, carrying a drink holder and a Levain bag.

"Oh, thank god!" she says, sounding relieved, reaching out and hugging me, drink holder and bag still in hands. She walks past me, setting everything down on my eat-in table, then immediately picks up her phone.

"Yeah, she's here, we're good. I'll call when I'm ready to be picked up." Pause. "Love you, too." *Liam*, I'm sure.

"What are you doing here?" I turn from where I'm still standing by the door.

"Are you kidding me right now?" she asks, almost sounding pissed at me. "I thought something happened to you. And Eden's birthday is this weekend." Time flies when you're wallowing in pity, but forced to survive because you're a single mom. Thanksgiving is next week. *Fuck me.*

"My phone broke."

"And....?"

I shrug. The truth is that I just don't care. She looks around at the small kitchen. Dishes piled on the counter. Dead plants in the window. Coffee that may or may not be growing mold in the pot. "Okay. I had no idea things were this bad. *Alexa*, stop playing Sad Girl Starter Pack." Brit says into the void of the kitchen. Alexa just replies, "Okay," and the music stops.

"How'd you know it was the Sad Girl Starter Pack?" She gives me a sad, knowing smile in return.

"Because I know, Jess. You should have called me."

"My phone's broken." She rolls her eyes, picks up her phone and starts texting.

"What are you doing?" I ask.

"Sending Liam to get you a new phone." She says it so nonchalantly.

"You don't need to do that, I can get a new phone."

"Sure, maybe you *can*, but have you?" I shake my head, and she continues, "No, you haven't. So I'll do it for you." She looks down at her phone then back at me after it pings with a new message. "See, done."

Imagine just having it like *that. Hey babe, run to the store and get my friend a new phone?*

Fucking cake walk.

"I'm fine, Brit. You've come, you've seen me, you've seen Eden..." who is sitting in a Pack 'n Play in the living room while Bluey plays. "I have to go to work." She frowns at me.

"Assuming I came here and you weren't rotting on your apartment floor, I have a surprise lined up for you."

"What?" I say, a bit exasperated.

"You have an interview tomorrow." As if it isn't pitiful enough she's buying me a new phone, now she has to get me a job, too?

"You don't have to do this. I can get a different job...I'm choosing not to. This one is mindless and it's perfect. It gets me up and out of the house. It's close proximity to home, and I like the regulars."

"Are you trying to convince me or yourself?" I hate when she uses my own words against me.

I walk over to the eat-in, grabbing for a cup of coffee out of the drink holder, but Brit stops me. "Uh-uh. No coffee until you agree to go to the interview." I'm suddenly a surly teenager, pissed off and moody.

"Fine, *Mom*." I say back to her, but she just laughs. Loudly, in my face.

"Great!" she says back to me. "Call in sick and go take a shower." There's a large part of me that wants to fight back, tell her to go to hell. I'm making it just fine on my own. But then, there's the other part that's just so fucking relieved to have someone take over and take control, even if it's just temporary.

I (begrudgingly) grab a chocolate chip cookie, a coffee, text Marian to take the day off, and go sit in the tub for an hour before Brit starts yelling at me to move my ass. I can even hear her little booted foot tapping impatiently outside the bathroom door. *Fine.*

Throwing on a baggy cable knit sweater and even baggier cargo pants, I walk out of my room and see Liam playing with Eden while Brit washes my dishes.

"Hey!" Liam says, genuinely happy to see me. I give him a head nod.

"Oh, good." Brit sets down the last dry plate. "Your options are, to A. Accompany me on a bakery crawl, or to B. Let me take you shopping, aka, I need your help shopping." She stands there, dead serious, waiting for an answer.

"I'm really hoping you make the right choice because none of my clothes are fitting," she pats her belly, "and I really don't need any more croissants."

"I don't know...I could really go for a cupcake, or twelve..."

Her face falls, but then she sort of snarls her lip. (It's not really possible, she's too cute.)

"Fine. Let's go shopping."

————

When we walk into Gucci on Wooster, that's when I know this shopping trip isn't for Brit. The Great? *For sure.* Celine? *Maybe.* Gucci? *No.* I have never once seen Britain willingly reach for anything Gucci.

"Brit..." She ignores me.

"Why didn't you tell me it was this bad?" She doesn't look at me when she asks. She just starts overturning bell glasses, smelling each parfum in the apothecary section.

"Because it wasn't..." Until it was. And obviously, I can't

say: *"Oh, because I think I maybe, likely, fell in love with your brother years ago, and when I found out he's getting married, I think a little piece of me died. And I don't even really know that it's because he's getting married, but just that everyone else's lives seem to be moving forward while I regress, and I'm having a pity party."*

Instead, I say, "I was honestly okay for a bit. Not great. But okay. But yeah, things could be better, and I'm alone with Eden all the time, and it's hard single parenting. There's no breaks, I don't get to ever be 'off.' And I'm tired. I'm tired of carrying it all on my own. But I also don't want anyone's help. So I just get overwhelmed, then a little bit stressy-depressy, add in a splash of anxiety about what the hell I'm doing. Et voilà! I'm listening to Lana Del Rey on repeat while wearing socks with Birkenstocks."

Brit holds up one of the bell glasses for me to smell; it's basically the scent of money. (Not literal dollar bills, just expensive.) I nod, and she asks the sales associate for four bottles. The girls will love the Alchemist's Garden bottles.

She picks out a few different cardigans, one logo (mohair, long), one cropped (logo, cashmere). And honestly, all her picks are on point. Brit's speed is more Eileen Fisher, but here we are. She's impressing the shit out of me.

"Since when do you shop at Gucci?"

She shrugs, "Since reading *Magnolia Parks*." Makes sense.

After Gucci, we hit up Celine, The Great, and Trudon, then grab lunch at Cipriani's. She's fawned over me as I've tried things on. She's insisted on treating me at every store, and when we come back to my apartment, she has a cheesy smile on her face.

There are boxes and bags from everywhere we went today, piled around the entryway.

"Just a little gift. My way of saying good luck at your interview. Also, it's your severance...and it's me bribing you to come to Spearhead for Christmas." She gives me a tight little hug before leaving to check on Liam who's been with Eden all afternoon. I'm sort of pissed, but honestly, a bit excited. Maybe it's finally time to get back on the wagon.

If I wouldn't waste my life moving to Taipei, I shouldn't waste my life here either.

———

My new boss is wearing Crocs and a snapback. He's definitely in his 30s. Definitely loaded, but definitely dressed like a man child, and it absolutely works on him. His name is Caleb, and he's exactly what you'd expect a techy billionaire to be. (The only thing missing is a puffer vest.)

My interview lasted thirty minutes. Most of which he spent talking to me about his latest trip to Bali. The only question he really asked was, "You worked for Brit, right?" I said, "Yeah." And he said, "Good enough for me." That was it. (Classic people-with-money shit.)

I owe Brit for this. Not *just* for the new Triomphe bag, not *just* for the interview, but for pushing me and giving me exactly what I needed. What I'd needed was a day without Eden, a killer outfit, small-town gossip which is ten times better hearing about because I have no skin in that game, and not one single reminder about Tommy, or Jamie, or even Alex. For an entire day.

Was it hard not to ask about Alex's impending nuptials?

Yes. Would it have been harder to hear about it? *Also, yes.* Brit didn't bring it up either, so who was I to rock the boat?

"So, this is my office," Caleb gestures around the space that features floor to ceiling windows framed by the changing fall trees outside. It's a massive space, taking up half the second level of his townhouse in Soho. He motions over to where there's already two desks, which is nice. "You're welcome to use my partner's desk when you work here, but don't feel like you have to come here to work. We're gone so much, I imagine it's probably easiest for you to work from home."

Caleb gives me a run down of what he needs, help with travel arrangements mostly. Some light event planning. Help with organizing meetings with clients.

Aside from being independently wealthy, he runs a sort of travel/experience/extreme excursion business that caters to high-net-worth individuals and their upper-echelon crew. Definitely sounds like good ol' boy shit, but for the salary he offered, and the minimal hours required, I can look past it.

"My partner is taking a, let's call it, 'sabbatical' or a 'time out' even, and I need...help." He smiles at me, boyish charm, dimpled smile, genuinely seems like a happy person. (A billion in the bank tends to assist with that.)

"He normally does all the prep and ground work, but now that's me until I get someone else." Apparently there's some big trip to Patagonia coming up.

There's a gentle knock at the open office door and a lanky (clearly) model (looks Russian) pokes her head in. She says something in Russian, and Caleb replies, (also in Russian) and then he introduces me as his new assistant.

"Hi, I'm Jess." I extend my hand and she takes it, limply.

"Hi. Anya." That tracks. She seems nice enough. But also seems like another reason I'll end up working from home. She gives Caleb a kiss on the cheek, then says "Paka" to the both of us.

Caleb isn't wearing a wedding ring, not that that means anything, though. "Girlfriend?" I ask, and he blushes.

"I wish."

I laugh. That's how it is here. Got it. I hear Anya exit as someone enters, and then there's footsteps on the stairs. "Alright, let's get you an email set up, and some paperwork going, and then mostly everything else we can do virtually. Of course you're welcome to come in, though! Just let me know your preference." Uber accommodating, that's nice.

I smile and just say, "I'll work from home unless you need me here. I have a 1-year-old."

He looks at me with a strange look, and says, "That's awesome," but punctuates the statement with a sincere smile.

"Ahem."

(Pause.) Have you ever had that thing with a person where you can feel they're there before you know it. You can't see them, hear them, but you sense them? That's us. I probably guessed it the moment I heard a booted foot hit the first step.

Alex clears his throat from the doorway and...seeing him...looking sun-kissed, with hair that's been naturally windswept on this blustery November day makes me physically weak in the knees. Like someone took a baseball bat right to the back of my thighs.

I don't really know where we stand. There's no hate for

him from me, it's just I maybe always wanted more than he could ever give me. That's it. But does he still hate me? He sort of acted like maybe he didn't anymore, and then that night...wait, was he dating/engaged when we had sex? That definitely makes my stomach lurch then roll. Also, he's been a major dick to me, and made me look and feel stupid. (I retract what I said about not having hate for him.)

Wait...is Anya? I feel legitimately nauseated, then ten times worse because she seems like his type. They'd have gorgeous nordic-looking babies together, that's for sure. (Hmm, I don't want to think about Alex making babies with someone else. No, thank you.)

I wait for him to make the first move. Is this civil? Is it back to ignoring me? And then, why is he here?

"Pal!" Caleb calls out to Alex.

"Blanks," Alex nods back in acknowledgement. Caleb's nickname is *Blanks*?

"You probably know Jess, right? Brit's assistant?" Caleb asks him.

"Yeah, I know Jess." He smiles. (He smiles!) I blush.

"Hey, Alex," I try my best to sound absolutely, completely polite.

"Well, that saves me from having to introduce you to your other boss. Alex is my business partner." *Oh. Oh...no.* My mouth forms a little "o," but no words come out. (Shall I just step in front of a train now? Or wait till later?)

"I just hired Jess to help with logistics while you take your," Caleb uses air quotes, "'leave of absence.'" Ahh, leave for...his wedding. My heart stutters.

"That's right," I finally find my voice. "I hear congratulations are in order." Alex looks at me, giving me wide eyes.

Maybe surprised, maybe a bit scared? I try my best to keep my smile normal. Caleb is looking at me, then Alex, waiting.

Then Alex says, "Jess, can I talk to you for a minute? Outside?" I feel like I've just gotten called to the principal's office.

"Um, sure." I sort of look to Caleb first, checking if it's okay and he shrugs.

I follow Alex, but instead of going outside, he takes my hand, pulling me down the second flight of stairs to the basement. It's like a separate apartment from the rest of the townhouse. Small kitchen at one end, living space, and several doors open. One leading to a gym, maybe one to a bedroom.

"How are you doing?" Alex asks, surprising me. I thought I was going to get chastised, maybe put in my place.

"Umm, I'm okay." I fidget slightly, straightening my cardigan (the cropped one Brit bought yesterday), standing up a little straighter. No one has ever made me feel like I'm crawling in my own skin the way Alex does.

"Promise?" He tries to find my eyes. I eventually let him. I'm having a hard time lying to him. I sort of shake my head, but don't say anything more. Alex swallows and nods, I think understanding.

"There's been something I've been meaning to tell you... ask you..." He trails off.

"I heard." I say. "Congratulations, really." Good for him for being able to finally move past Amy. "I'm sure that thing that happened by the lake didn't mean anything, and I can keep a secret...if that's what this is about?" His face turns red. I can't do this.

I dig deep, steeling myself in my new Gucci slingbacks. "Brit is throwing Eden a birthday party at Serendipity this weekend. You should both come." (Look at me go!) (Alright, fine, it nearly killed me.) When he doesn't immediately say anything back, I lean up, placing a kiss on his cheek and quietly say, "I'm happy for you if you're happy." Then walk away like a queen. Head high, steady, and extra grateful I opted for the shorter skirt this morning.

FOURTEEN

JESS

The upstairs dining room at Serendipity is packed. Not necessarily because there's so many people here, it's just a small space and it's decorated to the nines. I am happy to see some familiar faces, though. Damian and the girls made it. Obviously Brit and Liam are here. May and Ellen immediately find me, taking Eden out of my arms. I spot my (no, not *my*) Tommy with Jamie, too.

Brit finds me, all smiles. "What do you think?" She motions to the pink and teal space decked out in disco balls and balloons. A cake, entirely too big for a 1-year-old on a table at the far end, pink wrapped boxes piled high beside it.

"Wow. You did this?" Since when does Brit know how to plan a party?

"No, Liam did. But I supervised!" I roll my eyes. Seriously, they're sickening. Perfect for each other. They even look like the perfect match, too. (Think like Batman and

Barbie.) Liam's gray-haired, muscly, and decked out in his signature black jeans, gray t-shirt, and Sambas. And then Brit, looks amazing in her sculpted, boat neck Bumpsuit dress with the long mohair cardigan hanging off one shoulder, and heeled midi boots.

It's like somehow the universe has flipped on its head and we've traded places. It's like I'm seeing a side of her I never knew existed because Liam brings it out in her. He gives her the space and confidence to be the best version of herself. This glammed up version, but also the baggy t-shirt, no makeup version, too. And she deserves that.

"This outfit is serving, Brit." I motion up and down her body, her bump extra bumpy today.

She leans closer, whispering, "Liam likes me in heels. This is the last time they'll see the light of day, though."

"Yessss, queen." I smile and laugh with her.

"You look great, too, by the way." She looks down at my Gucci slingbacks, Cami NYC Everly tank tucked into my ripped AGOLDEs (not the coffee-stained ones), and an old fuzzy cardigan. It's very aughts inspired.

"Hey, happy birthing day." Liam joins us, offering me a hug. I accept it.

"Babe, it's weird when you say it," Brit chastises him.

"We just had a whole talk about this. You said first birthdays are for the moms, not the kids. You said birthdays should really be called birthing days. Did you not?" He looks at her, confused.

"Yeah, no, you're right. Next time let me say it, though. Happy birthing day!" she exclaims, throwing an arm around me, hugging me tight. I laugh.

"Fuck, they're supposed to bring out the frozen hot

chocolates *after* the food, hold on." Liam leaves us to manage the party.

"How do I find one like that?" I ask Brit, both of us watching her man walk off.

"I don't have that answer...but you will find him." She squeezes my arm. "I'm going to go meet the famous Ellen. Want to come introduce me?" she asks.

I shake my head. "No, you go ahead. I have to say hi to the ex-hubs and his boy toy." She laughs, then walks off, hardly any waddle to her 8-month gait.

Don't want to do this, don't want to do this. "Hi." Jamie and Tommy both turn to me. "Glad you could both make it." It feels weird, greeting them like acquaintances.

"Hey!" Jamie says, too much overt cheer in his tone, then reaches for a hug. I allow it. Followed by a weird side hug from Tommy.

"You guys coming over after this?" I think they just got in this morning, otherwise I'm sure they would have come to see Eden before.

"Yeah, if that's okay."

"Definitely!" Now I'm the one forcing cheer. An awkward silence descends on us, but doesn't last long because the hair on the back of my neck stands up. And when I turn around, I see that Alex and...Caleb(?) have just arrived.

I use the excuse of new guests to leave the two men I could really live without being here for the other two men I'm entirely confused *about* being here.

"Hey!" Alex turns towards my voice, immediately presenting me with a gift bag from FAO Schwartz. Caleb passes me a bag from Byredo.

"I picked out the gift for Eden, Caleb picked out the gift for you. Brit said we were celebrating your accomplishment in *birthing* today." Alex's cheeks go a bit pink. (That's not fucking awkward at all.) I laugh.

"Great. Entirely unnecessary, but super thoughtful of you both. Thank you!" I take the extended bags and drop them at the gift table where I find that half the gifts are addressed to me, the other half to Eden.

It's a small party, but all the major players are there: my best friend, my mom, my soon-to-be ex-husband, the guy I might still sort of be in love with. The whole thing lasts two hours, flying by. There's lots of laughter, lots of oohing and ahhing over Eden's wobbly attempt at walking. We eat way too much cake, and then it's time to pack up.

I'm putting the cards in my diaper bag when Alex comes up to me. My heart beats a little faster in his presence, my whole body warms a few degrees, too.

"Hi," I say. He's sort of staring at me, something uncertain in his gaze. He's so beautiful. I know I've called him a Chris Hemsworth knockoff, but that's not true. He's better than him. I love seeing him not in roughs (he's always dressed like he just got back from a hike), but today he's in jeans and a long sleeve henley that's almost too tight. It's perfect.

"Do you trust me?" he asks, voice lowered and deep. I have to take a second to comprehend. And then, he does something that rocks my world. Seriously, the earth shifts on its axis. Somewhere planets align.

He takes my hand, threading our fingers together. His massive hand swallows mine, and it feels...perfect. I love the way I feel being swallowed by his presence.

"Yes," I finally manage to croak out. I look at our hands

twined together then back up at him. He squeezes my hand, gets a sad sort of smile on his face, then takes my face in his other hand and places a kiss on my forehead. When he pulls back, I wonder if I've died. Why does a forehead kiss from Alex Palomino feel like an instant hit of dopamine?

"Excuse me?" Alex raises his voice, turning me towards the rest of the small dining room to face everyone. "I just wanted to say thanks for coming today, and to my sister and Liam for planning it." He looks down at me, and I look at him confused. He pulls me into his side, fingers still threaded together.

The natural instinct here would be to look at the faces of the people gathered around, likely all staring at Alex and me now. But I don't. I'm staring at Alex not knowing what's coming, but also not caring because he's acting a certain way towards me that I've only dreamed of for years.

"We were going to wait till Christmas, but with everyone here, I think it's the right time." He looks at me, then back to everyone else. "Jess and I are getting married." There's a collective gasp from the room (and me) and my stomach falls 40 stories. Alex's hand squeezes around mine. My mouth falls slightly open, but before I can speak — question — anything, he lowers his mouth, placing a sensual kiss on my lips. There's just a small brush of tongue across my lips, and it finishes with a hand cupping my cheek as he drops one last kiss on the corner of my mouth.

It's not the passionate, NSFW kiss of last time, but the effect is the same. I'm fucking soaked.

"Alex..." I say softly, surprised to find I've absentmindedly placed a hand on his arm that's holding my cheek. He sort of shushes me.

Talking to everyone else, he says, "Jess wanted to wait," he redirects his eyes to mine, searing my soul with his next words, "but I don't want to wait anymore." The smile that forms on my face is involuntary. (Snapshot title: *"Dreams Come True Serendipitously."*)

———

Alex

She's good. Not sure how she caught on so quickly, but this is believable. I fucking believe it, and for a moment that scares the shit out of me.

She's giving me a smile and looking at me like she loves me. Fuck, I wish she did.

I look down at where our hands are threaded together and make a vow to not let her go until we're walking out of this place together. She wants to talk to her mom? Great, me too. Brit wants a hug? Same. Tommy wants to have a chat? He can go fuck himself.

Before my impromptu announcement, I'd stepped outside for some air because, well, little kid birthday parties still get to me. *I know it's been 13 years, but it's never gone away completely. Still think about Tally at times like this.* But when I entered the vestibule, I overheard Tommy and Jamie standing outside the entrance.

"Hey, just a few more months." Jamie was consoling Tommy. *"Just a few more and then we'll file a modification to the custody arrangement, and this time next year, Eden will be living with us full time. Second birthday party will be at our*

house, okay? Eden isn't even going to remember this time in her life. She'll remember her life with us, okay?"

I got fucking chills. It was a declaration of war. It felt obvious what needed to happen. It was time. Jess needed top cover, and that's something I can do for her.

I look at the faces all staring at us in varying arrays of shock. Her mom, May, looks confused. Damian is smiling, but not meeting my eyes. My nieces are clapping their hands together in excitement. My sister looks sad. Her fiancé isn't looking at us, but instead at her. Then there's Blanks who's staring at me in a weird sort of awe, like when the last piece of a puzzle gets snapped into place. He's figuring it out.

And then there's Tommy, looking red-faced and pissed, hands clenched tight while Jamie is looking between Tommy and Jess trying to understand how this could've happened while they were busy playing house in Taiwan. I fucking love that I've just thrown their little plan into chaos.

They think they've got a lock on custody because they look good on paper. Fuck them. Jess and I will look better. It's amazing what money can do. I'll hire the best. I'll bury them in litigation because my pockets are deeper than theirs. They think they can pick on Jess? They've thought wrong.

With our hands still linked, Jess pulls me so that my back is to everyone else and I'm facing her alone.

She whispers, "What is this?"

I whisper back, "Trust me, okay?" I can see her thinking. She searches my face trying to fully understand if she can.

"Okay." The smallest of smiles shows on her face. *That's my girl.* I reward her with a gentle kiss.

May is the first to approach. "Well, *this*," she motions between us, "is a surprise. JJ, care to explain?" *JJ?*

Jess looks to me, unsure what to say. Top cover, got it. "When we caught up in Spearhead this summer, it all sort of clicked for us." I brush a nonexistent piece of hair off her face, noting the way her cheeks splash pink when I do. It makes the blood rush to my groin. "I don't know if you know, but Jess and I were together. A long time ago. This time it just felt like we were both in the right place at the right time. Finally past all the pit stops and land mines that we've been navigating the last five or so years." I know Tommy can hear me. Felt him moving closer, and that last bit was for him.

You're a fucking pit stop, bud.

"Well, Jessie, if you're happy...I'll be happy for you?" May looks at Jess.

Jess puts on a smile and says, "I'm actually really happy." She sounds almost surprised. Like she might possibly be quite happy.

"You guys used to be together?" Tommy asks, voice laced with disbelief. His question is directed at Jess, but he needs to get used to going through me now. I position myself slightly in front of her.

"Yeah." I give him a shit-eating grin. "She's the love of my life, and I let her go foolishly. Won't make the mistake again, Tom." He hates that. *Tom.* I can feel Jess holding back a laugh, and the warmth I get from pleasing her snakes up my spine, hitting me in the chest.

I won't give him the satisfaction of having this conversation here, in front of all the people she cares about. Never had any sort of beef with Tommy until he started fucking with Jess. Now it's easy to spar with him. It'll be even easier for me to crush him.

"We should probably get a move on. Car's waiting for us, baby." Her cheeks turn from pink to crimson. Would have loved having her alone the first time I called her baby. To see what it does to her. Does she turn pink all over? Is she wet? *Fuck me.*

The car *is* waiting. I planned and waited till the party was almost over to drop the bomb, then planned for a quick escape. Tactics I can absolutely do. We might not be in a knife fight *yet*, but psychological warfare, yes. And I can excel here.

I motion for Blanks to start taking gifts and bags down to the car, then look at Jess. I have to let her go so I can get everything in the car, but I squeeze her hand tight for just a second, telling her with my eyes, *"Be strong, don't take any shit."* She nods even though I'm certain she has no idea what just passed between us.

Her mom's girlfriend moves in, carrying Eden over and when I pass my sister she gives me the cold shoulder. *Fuck.* I grab a pile of boxes and quickly move them into the trunk of Blanks' Escalade waiting at the curb.

He's waiting for me by the trunk.

"So that's *her*?"

"Yeah."

"You know how to pick em'." I give him a murderous look. I know he thinks Jess is attractive. Probably hired her on looks alone.

"Find your own ride home," I tell him, and he scoffs at me.

"That's fine. I'll just go to Anya's. You good here?" He throws a thumb over his shoulder, asking permission.

"Yeah."

"K," Blanks says, then walks away. Don't do goodbyes. Still.

When I get back to the upstairs dining room, Brit is talking to Jess in a hushed tone. I don't hear all of it, but I do catch the last part.

"You're either lying to me, or to yourself, or to my brother. Or all three." Brit shakes her head, then turns around, her bump bumping into me. She has tears in her eyes and Liam shoulder checks me to get around to her. He pulls her into his side and they leave without a word to anyone else.

Jess looks stricken.

It'll be alright. Eventually.

May and Ellen pass off Eden, giving quick cheek kisses, and it appears that Damian and the girls have left as well.

That leaves us...and the dads.

"Still coming over?" Jess asks the two of them.

Jamie answers for them both, "Yup."

"Great," I say. "We'll see you there. I'd offer a ride, but we're overflowing at the moment." I don't let Jess make any apologies and they follow us downstairs. We part on the sidewalk as Blanks' driver starts installing Eden's carseat into the idling SUV.

"Explain yourself," Jess demands as soon as Tommy is out of ear shot.

"We'll talk in the car, okay?" She nods.

While I put the stroller in the trunk, Jess buckles Eden in. As soon as we're both seated, I ask Jess to tell the driver her address, then I add, "But take the long way, get us lost." Ari nods in understanding.

Once Eden falls asleep (*only took about two minutes*), Jess turns to face me. We're seated next to each other and with the carseat on the other side, her body is forced up against mine. Love it. Her thigh against mine. *What I really want is her thighs straddling mine...*

"Tommy and Jamie are going after full custody when they move back in a couple months." Her face falls. I reach out for her hand. "But fuck them. Listen, I can help. I'm *going* to help." I inhale, preparing for this next question. "Marry me." It comes out more a statement than a question, though.

She takes a sharp inhale, but doesn't say anything.

"Tommy and Jamie might look great on paper in court, but we'll look better." She's still quiet. Her hand is still in mine and it's not limp.

"Aren't you engaged?"

"Well, to you, yes."

"No!" She drops my hand. "To Anya or someone else. Tommy told me like two months ago you were getting married." She seems slightly upset. That makes me feel some sort of way knowing she was...jealous?

"That's a long story, but no, he misunderstood." There's some understanding dawning on her face.

"Why?" She shakes her head. "Why would you do this... for me? What's in it for you?" If I'm honest, I'm in it for Jess. To be with her. To get her to finally understand I don't see her as the runner up, I see her as the championship prize. I see her above all else. If I never loved her, I never could have hated her. *How doesn't she see that?*

Instead, what I say is, "Atonement." She can parse out the meaning from that however she chooses.

She doesn't love that. Can see it written all over her face.

She turns away from me, facing the windshield, but I

don't. I continue watching her. The further downtown we drive, the more my blood pressure increases. *She's going to say no.* She doesn't understand what I can offer, does she?

"Jess, I have a lot to offer. I know you probably think I'm just some fucking hiker that lives out of his 35-year-old Jeep, or his buddy's basement—"

"Stop," she interrupts me. "I don't care. Okay? I'll do it." She doesn't look at me once. "They don't get to take Eden away from me." Still staring straight ahead, she says, "We need some rules, but let's do it."

All I want is to take her face in my hands and kiss the shit out of her, but I can read the fucking room. Her mind is somewhere else right now. She looks like she's trying to figure out the quadratic formula while eating a bowl of cereal upside down. There's that little crease between her eyebrows. Definitely something going on behind the scenes.

"I'm not gonna fuck you over. I promise. Whenever this ends, however it ends, you'll be better off. I promise." She will. She can take her trust and do whatever the fuck she wants with it. And in the off chance this works out, I'll make her the happiest, most well-loved woman on earth.

FIFTEEN

JESS

"Marry me."

It was a command, and like one of Pavlov's dogs hearing a bell, my mind immediately said *"Yes."* No explanation needed, I was in. But that's the thing with Alex and me, I tend to act first, think later. I try to think in the car, but all I can think about is his hand intertwined with mine, that first sensual kiss, then the tender one that followed. *Fuck.* The sound of his voice calling me *baby*.

I could've died happily right then. Alex 'Cold-Hearted-Prick' Palomino called me *baby*. Call it, Jessica DiAngelo (could have been Palomino) died in Serendipity at 3:58 on a Saturday afternoon. All my headstone would read under my name is *"baby."*

I mean, it was that fucking amazing.

And that's the problem. I'm hearing *"I don't want to wait*

any longer," "baby," and *"she's the love of my life,"* and I believe him. I believe all of it, but it's just another lie, right?

Dangerous territory. That's where I'm headed, but what's the alternative? Continue managing on my own? I can't even afford my own place. What judge is going to look at me and think I should get primary custody? No judge, that's who.

He wants atonement and I want to keep custody of my daughter. That's where we're at. And it sucks because I'm yet again another pawn in some sort of redemption scheme. But beggars can't be choosers. No one else is going to swoop in and save me, and I don't think I have it in me to fight to save myself.

"What's the plan of attack? When we get in there?" I ask Alex. He's the mastermind here, the tactical warrior.

"Just follow my lead. I'll do most of the talking, if that's okay with you?" He's genuinely asking me. Not used to it. I'm used to bossy Alex, short-tempered Alex, not-a-care-for-anyone-or-anything-else Alex. I'd love nothing more than to let someone else carry the weight for a bit, though.

"Yep. And..." *Fuck me*, I don't know how to ask, "Are we touching? Are we coupley?"

He looks at me, a sort of darkness filtering over his eyes before he replies resolutely, "Yes."

Okay. I nod. He picks my hand back up as we make the turn onto my street, then places a kiss on the back of my palm. He slips into his new role with ease. Carelessly. (If I'm not careful, I'll be begging him to slip into me.)

My cheeks flame.

Tommy and Jamie are waiting on the sidewalk in front of my (our?) building, and before we get too close, Alex slides a hand around my neck and pulls me in. He places his mouth on mine and it's instant heat filling my panties. His lips move across mine softly, his short beard bristling against my skin before he strengthens his grip, his pressure, his ferocity and sucks my tongue into his mouth, making me clench my thighs together. *Fuck.*

I don't realize we're stopped because all I can think about, all I want is more. *Touch me. Feel me. Fuck me. Please.* I've never begged for anything from a man before, yet somehow I know I'll be begging this one.

Ari (I think it's Ari. I heard Alex say thank you to him earlier) opens our door, and the cold wind whips into the cab. I don't get goosebumps. I can't. I already have them.

When I remove my hands from Alex's henley that I've unconsciously been clutching on to, Alex starts to slowly release me in turn. And when he opens his eyes, there's something I've never seen there before. It's a change.

"You get E, I'll get everything else, okay?" he says as he gets out of the car, holding a hand out for me.

"Thanks, babe." I go up on my tiptoes to give him a kiss on the cheek. My lips and chin tingle in the cool air and I know without looking in a mirror I've got beard burn from *him.* I like the way it feels on me. I like the look it's putting on my ex's face almost as much.

Ari brings a sleeping Eden, still in her carrier, around to me, and Tommy immediately steps forward to take her so I can unlock the door. I don't miss that neither he nor Jamie speak a word.

Alex is right behind us, passing an armload of bags to Jamie, then picking up another load for the short elevator ride.

As soon as I have the front door unlocked, I wonder if it'll be obvious that Alex has never been here before. But it's not. He sets everything he was carrying in May's office, then comes back to the entryway where he puts his wallet, keys, and phone in the same wood bowl as I normally would. He even offers Tommy and Jamie something to drink, which they, thankfully, decline because I have nothing but baby food and milk for Eden in the place.

We let Eden continue napping in her carrier for a little bit, all of us finding a seat in the living room. Tommy takes a club chair, and I choose the sofa. Then Alex sits right next to me, draping an arm across the back of the sofa around me. Love the subtlety of that. And Jamie stays standing by the fireplace. Arms crossed over his chest, deep in thought.

"You expect me to believe you're deeply in love and happy with *this guy*?" Tommy is sitting on the edge of his seat as he motions to Alex. "The guy you couldn't even stand to be around for the last five years?"

"That's my fault, Tom. I was just jealous she ended up with you." Alex smiles, I smile, and giggle internally. Love that he calls him Tom. No one has ever called him Tom. It's not an endearing nickname.

"How come Jess never even mentioned *you* then?"

Alex goes to respond, but I stop him with a hand on his chest. I nod, telling him without words, *"It's fine, I got this."*

Then, without even looking at Tom (officially his new nickname), I say, "Alex hurt me, and then we hurt each other, but I think, after some time, we can both look back and say neither of us meant it. I know I didn't." I look into his eyes, sincerely telling him I didn't mean it. I even run my hand down his chest in a warm gesture. "But when you love someone as much as I loved him, love him still, it was too painful and raw to explain. So I didn't." I wish Alex knew that everything I just said was the truth.

"How did you two even meet?" Jamie finally asks, the lawyer looking for holes in our story.

"Well, believe it or not, it was at a cemetery," Alex says with not an ounce of defense to his tone, just pure nonchalance.

"What the fuck?" Tommy asks, his face showing the confusion.

"You can't make this stuff up," Alex says in response.

"Which cemetery?" Jamie, again.

"Fairfax Memorial," Alex and I say at the same exact time, sealing our story with gentle knowing smiles at one another.

This sends Tommy out of his seat and pacing in the living room. *Good.* He should be worried.

"Why don't you live here then?" Jamie's question is directed at Alex. I immediately go to pipe up that he does, but Alex beats me to it.

Rubbing a hand up and down my forearm, he says, "I've been supervising the build of our dream house, in California. It'll be ready by Christmas. You two should join us," he poses back to the two men. I can't tell fiction from fact anymore, but I assume there's an actual house in California, otherwise he wouldn't have invited them, right? Either that or he is the best bluffer I've ever met.

"We'd love to," Jamie says sort of smugly.

"Great!" Alex replies, "Pack your snow boots!"

"Wait, were you talking about Jess when you emailed me about doing your prenup?" Tom's mouth is hanging slightly open, a hand in his hair. He's definitely shitting bricks now.

"I was," Alex says, no bullshit.

"That was in July! Before Jess even asked me for a divorce!" I look at Alex, astounded.

"I didn't know you did that," I say quietly, genuinely surprised.

"When you know, you know," Alex says then shrugs, but I don't miss his pink cheeks when he leans forward and gives me a soft kiss.

———

Tommy and Jamie finally leave around 8:00 and I immediately move into bedtime routine for Eden. I bathe her, lather her up, brush her hair, and read two books. I'm singing her our nightly lullaby when I sense him at the doorway.

"Sleep, pretty darling, do not cry, and I will sing a lullaby." Suddenly, I'm feeling very self-conscious about my singing voice.

I close the door to May's room, where Eden's been sleeping, and he moves slightly out of the way to make room for me in the hall. I whisper to him, "Let's talk," then motion for him to follow me into my bedroom.

Why? Why do I do this? (Well, that's where the monitor is. Duh.)

After I get the monitor off my bedside table, I find Alex has shut the door behind us and is perusing my space. The books on my shelves, the photos on the pinboard. I'm embarrassed to admit I never got around to updating the space too much. (Yes, I took down the Eminem poster. No, I didn't take down my prom pics.)

I'm kicking myself for that when I catch him stuck on one

photo in particular, the photo of Amy and me. She was probably 16 and I was 13. I feel a flush of heat and my throat goes bone dry. It's still Amy for him, isn't it? *It'll always be Amy.* My chest aches. A snapshot of him staring at that photo would be titled, *"Nostalgic Man Longs for Something He'll Never Have Again."*

It's a good reminder. My instinct was to wrap my arms around him and then push him down on my bed, but that would be misguided. The words, the touches, the feelings I felt today, those were all Amy's.

"She was the only friend I ever had when I went to my Dad's house during the summers." He simply nods and starts looking at the other items on the pinboard like I didn't just catch him in the act of staring for too long at his late wife's photo.

"She was really great, Alex. You were incredibly lucky." *She* was incredibly lucky. That's what I really want to say.

"Let's talk about next steps," he says, still not looking at me. Now he's standing, looking too intently at my collection of snow globes that are completely unremarkable.

"Okay."

"Would you consider moving to California?" He turns around. The top button of his henley has finally popped under the strain of his muscles and I can't help but stare at the definition of his pecs now on display. "I think it makes sense and it makes us look good. We have a community there, family. New house is pretty amazing, though I'll leave that to you to judge..."

"Umm," I try to think of all the reasons to stay in NYC, but aside from May and my pride, I don't know that I have one. "I'm worried...last time I put my trust in someone, depended on someone, I was left with absolutely nothing. I know at the end of the day all I need is custody of Eden, but I need a job. *I need a life, too.*"

"You can keep working for Caleb. He said you'd want to work from home anyways. But what specifically do you need? Tell me, because if you're worried about finances, I'm going to stop you right there. That will never be a worry for you, us, or Eden. Ever."

I look at him, a bit confused.

"I'll send over the prenup tomorrow, but I think it's pretty fair and satisfactory. I may have had Tom do the first draft, mostly as a fuck you, but I've had it amended since and I think the guaranteed settlement is sufficient. Again, I'll let you be the judge."

"Why would you give me a guaranteed settlement when you're the one doing *me* a favor?"

He shrugs, "Because I can. Amy would've wanted this." Right, Amy. *Just a jab, a quick uppercut. Why not just remove my fingernails while we're at it?*

"I'll have to think about California." Alex nods. He's leaned up against my pitifully small desk, arms crossed over his chest making the expanse of his shoulders even more protruding. "But as for rules..." I trail off hoping he'll come up with some...but then he doesn't. *Okay.*

"We probably shouldn't have sex," I say. It's better if I say it. If he says it, I'll know he really doesn't want me like that. And if he doesn't say that, I'll be wondering if that's all he wants out of this. Both are equally agonizing thoughts.

But like he just reminded me again, he's doing this for Amy. To atone. To protect me and Eden when maybe he couldn't do the same for Amy and Tally. I'm a pet project to him. One with the potential for a lot of orgasms, but that's still all it'd be and I can't let myself go there. Can't get confused when the sex makes me think we're real.

Having sex with Alex once was one too many for this exact reason. *1000 times would never be enough.*

He doesn't say anything about that rule, but he does say, "Well, we should probably live together. So whether that's California or here, I guess just let me know. Though, if it's here, your place doesn't exactly have enough beds for us to sleep separately..."

And that's one point for moving to California.

"Well, when would we go?" I ask.

"The plan is to be moved into the new house by Thanksgiving, and then, Brit is hosting..." *Fuck.* My best friend who probably hates me. Who knows there's no way I'm happy with Alex after she just saw the ruins of my life this past week. Which, ironically, was because of Alex and I lied to her about it then, too.

"I have to tell Brit...about this arrangement."

"No."

"What? Why? She already knows something's not right. She showed up this week, and I was a mess. The house was a mess and she knew I wasn't happily engaged."

"Tell her you just missed me, but that we were planning to tell her when you came out for Christmas."

This is so easy for him. "I hate not being honest with her..."

He gives me a look. It's a reminder that I haven't been honest with Brit in a very, very long time. I hate that. I hate that he's also reminding me that he knows. That he still thinks of me as *that girl.*

I look down at my hands that are naked. Haven't worn my wedding ring from Tommy in months. Not since the night I hooked up with Alex actually.

"I'll get you a ring." Alex moves to sit beside me on the bed. "Any requests?" Who knew *this* would be the most painful part of it all. A fake wedding ring. He'll give it to me. And I'll wear it. And it'll mean nothing. *To him.* (And everything to me.)

"You don't have to. That's an unnecessary expense."

"Okay." *Okay.* I'm surprised how disappointed I feel at his response. But then he just stands to leave. "I'll send you the prenup and call you tomorrow to talk about it, okay?"

"Yeah." I give him a gentle smile. "I guess, also, thank you. For doing this and helping. I can't lose Eden, I just can't." He just sort of makes a gruff sound and heads for the door.

He calls out, "Lock this behind me, okay?" And then the door clicks shut. I make my way to the front door, going on tip toes to look through the peephole, and he's still standing there. I slide the deadbolt into place, but he's still there, deep in thought. Regretting this whole day already, I'm sure.

———

There's too many zeros. That's the first issue I notice with the prenup. The second is the time commitment. The third is that the contract goes into effect as soon as I sign this, regardless of when or *if* we marry.

My phone vibrates, and I'm honestly expecting Alex, but instead see it's his sister.

I swipe to answer the call.

"Hi."

"Hey." Brit sounds slightly uneasy.

"I was planning to call you today to say thanks for everything you and Liam did for Eden's birthday, and all the gifts."

"Okay, you're welcome."

"Listen, Brit, you're right that I haven't been honest with you." She stays silent on her end of the line. "Before I ever even met you, I met your brother. And I may have developed feelings that went unrequited and so I buried it deep. Especially because I didn't know Alex was your brother when I took the job working for you." (So far, all this is true.) "Then when Alex and I saw each other in Spearhead over the summer, things just clicked, and I didn't want to get my hopes up, okay? I didn't say anything because I really thought it might not work out." (Skirting the truth now.)

"And, I may have fallen into a bit of depression when I moved to New York, but once the dust settled around Tommy and me, Alex asked me to marry him and I said yes. And I'm really, really happy about it. And I don't want you to think I'd ever lie to you about something like this because I wanted to tell you, so many times." (Still some truth to what I'm saying.)

"Jess?" Britain asks.

"Yeah?"

"Don't hurt my brother." My stomach sinks. "Whatever *is* going on here, whatever happens with all of this, just don't hurt him. He doesn't deserve it. He doesn't deserve to be used or not loved absolutely."

"Okay." I say it far too quietly. It's obvious how much her threat is hitting.

"Will I see you at Thanksgiving?"

"Yes." That's my decision then, isn't it?

"Okay, safe travels. And if Alex asks you not to fly or drive at certain times, just humor him?"

"I will."

"Okay." She hangs up. She didn't say goodbye. Didn't say I love you. Hated that. I feel like a complete sleazeball. A shitty fucking human. Worst best friend in the history of best friends.

"Glaaahhhh!" Eden screams at me from her high chair, forcing me to table my self-hate fest until later.

"Yessss! I see you ran out of blueberries. The world isn't ending, my love."

I get the blueberries out, dumping another handful on her tray, then keep reading through the document on my phone. *12 months of being married to Alexander Palomino and no extramarital affairs.* And I'll receive a settlement that would afford me my own townhouse in Soho... (I mean, really, I'm not that strong, guys.)

Fuck me. He's made it impossible to say no.

Without a second thought, I DocuSign the next year of my life over to Alex Palomino.

SIXTEEN

ALEX

J

I'll come with you. Just for Thanksgiving.
I'm not sure I can commit to moving there.

A

Just emailed plane tickets. I'll pick you up
from the airport.

K.

K. That was it. *Fuck.* I should've called. I probably should've gone up when I walked past her building yesterday afternoon, too. Just felt like if I pushed her, the answer would have been no. To be honest, I don't know that Jess is going to love living in Spearhead. But sort of like I hope she tries on being married to me and loves it, I'm hoping she'll do the same here.

Liam's truck pulls around to the front of the drive at the

new house, so I set my to-go coffee on the porch rail and walk out to meet him.

"Your sister's pissed at you," he states grimly. I shrug.

"She'll get over it." He raises his eyebrows at me, then laughs.

"Better you than me," he slaps a hand down on my back. "Anyway, you ready to do this? They'll be here any minute."

"Yep. Ready as I'll ever be." Moving into my first house today. I'm 42 and this is my first house. Hoping it'll be my home. Moments like this are always a bit bittersweet. I'm not a monster. I still think about Tally. Sometimes about Amy. But it's not how you think.

It always happens when I move into a new phase of life. With Tally, I wonder if she would've liked this house. Would she like Jess? And with Amy, it's always, she'll never get to have this. She never got to move into the house of her dreams with the man of her dreams. She never got the Alex who's settled more with age and isn't living on the outside. Would she have ever gotten there with me? Or were we always destined to end that day?

I feel like I was always destined to be here with Jess. And I do believe in destiny, in fate, in all that shit. As an operator, most of us have an air of untouchability. Nothing bad can happen. "I can't die" shit. But inevitably one of you does. And the longer you do the job, the fewer peers you have.

Why am I the one that survived, huh? In some of the instances, it should have been me. I sometimes wonder if the whole reason I joined the Army in the first place was because I'd *hoped* it'd be me.

Three massive moving trucks descend on my house and I

can't believe it, but I actually get chills. Feels like this is the precipice. The start of my life. *Our* life, maybe?

Never thought I'd be here. *Never.*

———

Jess

If you ever want to be humbled (and quickly), fly cross country with a one year old — alone. With the connecting flight, it was 8 hours of anxious misery. So as soon as we cleared the gate after landing, I burst into tears. (Eden was already crying.)

When she refused her pacifier at take off, I knew it. Right then, I was fucked. And then from there, it was all downhill, just like I thought it would be. She cried the entire first flight while I *wanted* to cry the entire flight.

People stared, some people complained, but seriously, what do you want me to do? Alex booked us first class, and in this instance, we might have been worse for it. In economy, there's probably other kids, but in first class, Eden was the only baby. And certainly the only one crying. I tried to reset during the layover (because there's no direct flights to Hicktown, USA), but nothing did it. We strolled. I rocked her. We tried a bottle. We tried the paci. We changed diapers. Nothing.

One year might be the worst age to fly with. (Yeah, I said it.)

When we finally make it to baggage claim, Eden loses her

shit completely. She screams bloody murder, and I have the urge to scream with her, but instead, I cry.

"Baby girl, pleaseee." I'm fucking begging my one-year-old while I try to shush her in between my own tears. I drop my purse on the ground next to the stroller and pick her up. It doesn't help. She squirms and fights me, all while continuing to scream.

People watch — some with sympathy, some with disdain, some who recognize us from the flight and look like they might give me a piece of their mind. I feel like my chest is on fire, my hands tremble. Sweat rolls down my spine even though it's probably 65 degrees inside the terminal. It makes me want to give up. It makes me furious. It makes me want to walk off the edge of a cliff and never look back. (I'm just being honest.)

"Whoa," a deep rumbling voice says. "Hey." Then a warm hand finds the small of my back. He shushes both of us, "Come here." And then we're enveloped in a warm embrace. Eden is still squirming, but she stops screaming.

Have you ever hugged someone and rested all your weight on them in that hug? Your body, your problems, your responsibilities and you just trust that person has you? That's what this hug with Alex is like. I said I'd never depend on anyone. Ever again. But if I did, if I could, it'd be him.

He runs one of his dinner plate-sized hands down my hair and to my back, eventually stopping just below the curve of my ass. I inhale his warm scent. It's woodsy and musky, but classic. Like this is what I imagine Tom Selleck smells like. My one free hand has absentmindedly found his chest, and he keeps stroking my head, shushing me lightly. (Snapshot title: *"Heart-Wrenching Family Reunion."*) My heart sinks at the thought. *I wish.*

"Shhhhh. It's okay," Alex says nice and low.

"Our suitcases," I hiccup on a sob and Eden does the same.

"They're not going anywhere, let 'em take a lap," he says in response. "Give me the baby, Jess." I pass over Eden and he lets me go in the process.

He puts her over his shoulder and starts rubbing her back and within seconds the little traitor falls asleep. It's so relieving, I can't even be pissed about it. Instead, I take a deep inhale and try to catch my breath. Alex is looking at me as he continues to rock Eden against his shoulder. (And my ovaries start to hurt.) *Fuck me.*

He's wearing jeans and a plain long-sleeved t-shirt. His hair is about the same length, but he shaved his beard. Suddenly I have the most insane urge to rush him and run my hands along his face in awe. He was handsome before, but now he's approaching sex-symbol status.

"You shaved," I say, mouth probably hanging open.

He blushes. "Yeah, figured it was time for a new look." There's that little voice at the back of my head wondering: Did he do this...for me? And why does that make me giddy?

It's a war right now. My body is yearning to throw myself at him, kiss him, love him, but my mind is being rational. It's thinking cautiously, pragmatically. *This is a means to an end. If I have any hope of lasting 12 months without falling (even more) desperately in love with this man, I have to have boundaries. And stick to them.*

"Do you mind if I use the bathroom?" I ask. He nods back reassuringly, continuing to rock the sleeping monster.

Picking up my purse off the terminal floor, I walk briskly to the bathroom. I have the most insane urge to rub one out to take the edge off the ache that's already started in my pelvis. Alex plus babies equals danger zone.

I don't rub one out, but when I go to the bathroom, I actually laugh when I pull down my underwear revealing what can only be described as something similar to slick. (If you know, you know, my friend.)

I check myself in the mirror after. Face is red and puffy, but at least I refrained from makeup today, meaning I'm not fighting what would surely be a losing battle with mascara. I splash cold water on my face, redo my hair that's fallen out of its half-up-half-down clip. I dab on a little solid perfume and just accept my leggings, t-shirt, and Converse are entirely basic, and that is entirely fine. Think of it like a boundary holder, I tell myself. The less overt I am at trying for his attention, then maybe he won't give it. And we can ride this thing out. (I'm now picturing myself riding him.) *Mistake.*

When I get back to the baggage claim, Alex already has all our bags loaded on a cart and is still holding Eden.

"How'd you do all that one-handed?" I ask in awe.

He shrugs. "An older couple saw you and Eden break down and asked if they could help. Said they should have offered sooner." Of course, the hot single dad gets help, but the single mother? I hate this fucking world sometimes.

I reach for Eden, but he shakes me off. "Don't want to wake her up again when we have to put her in the car. You push the suitcases, I'll get the stroller." (*We.* He said we.) I don't argue, I just follow him out into the moderate, November, California sun. *Okay.* Taking a deep breath in. *Okay. We can do this, Jess.*

This weather is giving me life. It's maybe 68 degrees, sunny, and Thanksgiving is in two days. I'm starting to under-stand the West Coast hype.

The airport isn't huge. There's not even a parking garage, you just walk out to the parking lot and find your car. I keep following Alex, but don't see his Jeep anywhere. We come to a stop and the lights flash on a Volvo SUV with 30-day tags.

"You got a new car?" I ask, astonished. He's always had his Jeep. It's a matte green, *old* Jeep. I mean, really old. Like he's had it for decades and it was old when he got it. There's a story to it, he told me once, but that's neither here nor there.

He smiles at me. "No, but *you* did." *Oh.* I immediately want to tell him it's too much, but he stops me. "It's a safety thing. I can't have the two of you in the Jeep, okay?" It imme-diately shuts me up. *Understood.*

"Thank you. I appreciate that." I just accept it because he's right.

"Go get in the car, I've got this."

I look at the baby on his shoulder, the stroller and car seat, the three suitcases. "Don't be ridiculous. Give me Eden while you install the carseat."

"I've got a car seat already installed. Let me get this, okay?" Alex moves towards me. He puts a hand on my hip and drags me a little closer. My breathing halts at his touch. "I'm sorry I didn't fly with you. I should have been there. Won't happen again." And then he leans down and kisses me. On the lips. He kisses me, and...and it's not for show. My heart thunders, heat floods my panties, and my tongue slips into his mouth. He pulls away with a gentle chuckle. "At least let me get E down first, okay?"

I nod and stand there like an idiot when he moves around

to the backseat to put Eden in her rear-facing car seat. It's a Nuna, a good one, too. *He researched it.* Fuck. How am I not supposed to fall head over heels for him? How am I supposed to not *throw* myself at him? I mean, what's the worst that could happen right? I fall in love with my soon-to-be husband? (Can't fall in love when you already are, though.) A husband I have to be with for at least a year. I might as well enjoy it...right?

I slide the two smaller suitcases in the trunk, break down the stroller and old car seat. I put my purse in the front seat and open the backseat to set the diaper bag down. As I do, I see Alex gently tucking Eden into her seat. He slowly moves her arms through the straps and clips everything in silently. It's so stealthy, and a miracle Eden has remained asleep. And that's when it grips me.

I might as well enjoy it, right? Wrong. You only reach stealth level of parenthood through doing. He's done all this before — for his own daughter. And with his actual wife. I'm just a cheap knockoff.

I take a deep breath, shut the backseat door quietly, and climb into the front passenger seat to wait.

"You're being quiet," Alex says as we drive out of town (past The Boot Barn) and weave through the foothills.

"Just tired." I give him a weak smile, then look back at the road. "It's been a long day." It's the truth. I was up at 4:00 A.M. and that was Eastern time. It's now 4:00 P.M. Pacific. I just want to get to the house and sleep, but that's doubtful. I'll still need to get everything set up. Get a changing station ready. Sheets on the Pack 'n Play. (I asked him to pick one up.) Feed Eden dinner. Set up the monitor.

I've tried to have no expectations of his house. He's told

me almost nothing about it except it's in Spearhead. *How many beds does it have?* No clue. (Hopefully more than one, though). *Is there a bathtub?* I dunno. This could be a really short trial stay, in which case I'll be back in New York by next week where I think it'll be a lot easier to pretend to be married. (Well, soon-to-be married.)

"Okay," Alex says after a little, but I notice the furrow in his brows. "Feel free to nap then. We have about 40 more minutes."

"Okay." I recline my seat and close my eyes, turning on my side, but I can't sleep. Not possible when I keep getting whiffs of his cologne, and then he reaches over and gently pushes a lock of hair off my face. Then the back of his thumb strokes my cheek. (You know, just for good measure.)

I sort of want to open my eyes and beg him not to do that. *Please don't make me love you anymore, please!* But I don't. I keep pretending to sleep and for the rest of the drive he reaches over to touch me in some way every few minutes. There's one of his bear paws settled gently on my hip. Then there's a thumb that strokes my open hand. There's fingers that trace my hairline softly. Until eventually, I do actually drift away where I dream of large hands spreading my legs wide and a warm tongue laving at my clit. I moan and wake myself up. *Fuck.*

My eyes stutter open and I see Alex adjusting his jeans to accommodate his growing cock. Fuck *me*. Now I'm thinking about his cock. It's beautiful. Really. It has this curve — (no, you're right.) This train of thought isn't going to help me with boundaries.

"Almost home," he says to me quietly because Eden is still racked.

I increase the incline of my seat so I'm sitting up just as we drive through the main strip of town. Every time I've been here before, it's been as a visitor. Didn't have much skin in the game as far as the town of Spearhead goes, or what it offers. But now that I might actually live here, I'm staring at the businesses, examining them intently with a new lens.

On the right, we have a small grocery store, Bob's Grocery. (I swear to god that's the name. You can't make this shit up.) And I mean it's really small. *That's not gonna work.* Next, a gas station with a convenience/liquor store attached. *Gonna need that.* And there's a diner...that's not open. *Okay.*

On the other side of the road is a restaurant and bar (Colton's). Still haven't been, still want to. Brit has stories about that place. (Bonus, the owner is a hottie.) (Brit's words, not mine.) Then the coffee shop that Brit's in-laws (Liam's parents) own. And honestly, their cappuccinos aren't shit. So, really, for this zero-stoplight town, it's impressive. And then there's Maggios, the pizza place. Never eaten at the restaurant, but Liam picked it up on one of Carly's days off and it was surprisingly good. It's not New York style, but still good.

Each of the businesses is practically a carbon copy of the others. It looks like someone ordered six log-cabin kits from a Sears catalog, thus founding the town of Spearhead. (Not joking.)

This place doesn't make me feel claustrophobic like Brit's place on Robles did. (Or what's the opposite of claustrophobia? Fear of wide open spaces. That's what I have.) The evergreens tower and shade every spare inch of space. They crowd you in, sort of like the skyscrapers do. And so, if I just close my eyes and play a track of the city, I could pretend I'm home. Except instead of the smell of methane and sulfur, there's a distinct earthy smell to this place. It doesn't smell like a Christmas tree. It just smells damp, but also fresh. It's astringent, but in a soothing way. Hard to describe, but...I don't *hate* it.

Alex looks over, a smile on his face. "Almost there." If I didn't know better, I'd think he actually looked...excited. It makes me excited. I bite down on my lip to hide a smile and wonder what this next chapter of my life will look like.

SEVENTEEN

JESS

Wow. Just...wow. I don't know that this is *my* dream house, but it is certainly somebody's. I mean *wow*. We pull up to a gated entrance where Alex keys in a code and then we wait for the black iron gate to swing in.

You can see the house (small mansion or moderate-sized lodge) from the main entrance, and it's beautiful. It feels more Cape Cod than log cabin, but has hints of modern, mountain-esque bits of inspiration. Like exposed wood beams and gray stone columns. (This has Liam written all over it.)

I look over at Alex and he's looking at me, seeming to try and read my reactions. So I tell him, "This is beautiful." He sort of smirks and pulls up to a three-car garage. His Jeep is parked out front, but so are a few other vehicles. None of them belonging to Brit, though. My stomach sinks. I didn't think she'd be here to welcome me, but I'd be lying if I said I hadn't hoped. *Right.*

One of the cars parked out front is a white sprinter van, but then there's also a Porsche SUV. Doesn't really seem like Alex's speed.

From the front of the house, you can't really tell where we are in relation to the lake. Is this lake front? Lake view? Lake adjacent? Even if it's none of those, it's still an impressive and beautiful home.

As I unbuckle my seat and look up at the multistory house, Alex reaches a hand over, taking my own hand in his. I look down at where they're joined. There's a tenderness Alex shows me that feels almost out of character. And each time he does, it's like my brain chemistry is altered. How can someone I thought could only ever be one thing also be this man who rubs my head and hugs me and kisses me with a gentleness that makes my heart crack?

It hurts not knowing what's real and what's not.

If this were a book, I'd start to wonder at what point this turns into some psychological thriller where Alex is just a man mad with grief, trying to replicate a life he used to have. It would end with him killing me, I'm sure of it. But this isn't a book. Hopefully won't be some psychological thriller, and with any luck, when he divorces me, it doesn't kill me.

He pulls away and I immediately do the same, opening my door and moving to the backseat to unbuckle Eden who is starting to rouse awake.

I grab my purse and diaper bag, then walk towards the front door. When I turn to check if Alex is behind me, I get a chill and visibly shiver. It's probably from the cooler temperature up in the mountains coupled with the setting sun. But, if I'm being honest, it's the sight of this domesticated Alex. The Alex rolling two suitcases up the front path of our home.

The Alex who comes around me to open the front door. The Alex who gets a smile on his face and says, "Hope you like it," like he did this for me. "I'll come back out in a few for the rest." He motions to the car, then pushes the large front door open.

It's light wide-plank oak floors. It's cream walls and organic lighting. It's airy, but cozy. Cream and white furs thrown over the backs of vintage leather arm chairs. There's a linen slipcovered sofa, and a boucle coffee table against the backdrop of large windows that look out over Spearhead Lake. It takes my breath away. It's dreamy. It's *a* dream. (Fuck, this *might be* my dream.)

A few voices sound from the kitchen, so I wander towards the sound with Alex still following behind me.

The kitchen is light oak, custom cabinetry with marble counters and a six-burner commercial range. There's cognac leather and rattan stools at the island, and an eat-in kitchen with a built-in bench and a highchair already pulled up to the round marble and iron table.

I sort of turn to look at Alex and he's looking...shy?

"So, how'd we do?" he asks.

"It's, I mean, unbelievable."

When I turn back, I see a few familiar faces make their way out of the oversized walk-in pantry.

"Jess!" Constantine exclaims, making his way over to Eden and myself. I've met him once before at Britain's Sunday-dinner-turned-engagement party. The same night... you know...with Alex.

"Hi, Constantine," I go to reach out a hand to shake his, but he swats it away and opens his arms for a hug.

"We're family now." Oh. Right, because of Alex.

He gives Eden and me a quick squeeze, then embraces Alex.

"Liam let me in," Constantine says, giving Alex a firm pat on the back. "Said he needed to get home to Brit and couldn't stay longer."

Alex shrugs, and then starts talking to Connie so I move to the side and wave a bit weakly saying, "Hey, Niko," to the tall, dark, and handsome man eating a handful of M&Ms in my kitchen. (*My?* Whoa, pump the brakes, Jess.) Niko is one of Constantine's kids, and sort of like a pseudo sibling to Alex and Brit. It's convoluted. It's confusing. (Honestly I can't keep track of their messy family tree.)

"Hey, Jess." He nods in acknowledgement towards me. "Dad wanted to come see Brit. And also Alex's new house. I'm just the driver." He says by way of explanation. "Nice house, by the way." He punctuates with a wink. It dawns on me I'm supposed to say thank you, because this is supposed to be my house with Alex.

"Yeah, thanks. Can't take any credit for it, though." Really, I can't.

Alex says hey to Niko, too, then coming up behind me, he places both hands on my shoulders and rubs gently, easing the tension from the long day of travel while he continues to talk to his (I don't know what the fuck to call them) people. (Dad and brother isn't right, even though I'm pretty sure that's the most accurate term for them.)

Oh gawd, though. His strong thumbs dig into my aching shoulders and my eyes roll back slightly. He notices I'm practically asleep, and clears his throat. He throws an arm around my waist and pulls me so I'm flush against his back. (Love that.)

"Well, I really want to show my fiancé her new house." (My fiancé!) "You two won't mind showing yourselves out?" Connie practically beams, a genuine, happy look on his face at this version of Alex. It is amazing, it's like he's someone else entirely.

"Alright, kids," Niko dusts off his hands, picking up the Porsche keys sitting on the island. Niko pats Alex on the back before hauling his dad with him out the front door.

As soon as I know they're gone, I expect Alex to release me. *Show's over.* But he doesn't, he nestles his chin against my shoulder, opposite to where I have Eden perched on my hip, thankfully with a pacifier securely in her mouth.

"Do you like it?" he asks softly, while his arm around my waist tightens slightly to pull me closer.

"I love it, Alex. Who wouldn't want to live here?" He nods against my shoulder then releases me, but takes my hand leading me on a real tour.

Off the kitchen is a surprisingly well-stocked pantry, the mudroom, and a stairwell to the basement. Also on the first floor is a guest suite and an office. And then we head upstairs where he shows me two guest suites before opening a third hall door to a room that has a very obvious purpose.

There's a lilac, slipcovered daybed, and a light oak crib. There's subtle floral wallpaper and the light fixture is a small crystal chandelier. It's a room for Eden. *How...when?* The question is written on my face as I look to him.

"It's the daybed from Brit's old house, and then I had Constantine pick up a crib in town." Like that explains away the floral wallpaper or the lilac daybed cover. This room, it does something to me. It plants a seed, a hope, a dream, that he's been planning this for longer than I've known. He wanted this before he knew anything about my future custody woes. (Alright, maybe that's a stretch. Calm down.)

"Well, it's beautiful." I walk further into the room to see a large painting of a swan above a dresser that has a changing station set up and stocked. I mean, literally diapers and wipes already here. I motion and look at him.

"Yeah, there's a service. Apparently. When you move into a new house, they come and stock it for you with...everything. From toilet paper to tampons. Liam suggested it. They're still here, actually." It's like he's thought of everything. I look over the crib, and yep, there's a monitor hooked up and ready.

"Alright, one more room." He leads me to the set of double doors at the very end of the hall that open to the primary suite. My palms get clammy. My pelvic floor clenches. This could be our room. Our bed. It's beautiful with an upholstered headboard, white bedding, and about 50 fluffy pillows on top.

"Wow." It's all I can say. There's noise from the bathroom so we head there next, past the dueling his-and-hers closets.

"Hi there!" A woman in her mid-forties greets me. "We're almost done, I promise!" She has a box of lotion bottles in her hand that she's using to stock the cabinets underneath the sinks that are already pretty full with feminine care and women's shaving products.

Wait. Does Alex want me to be in here? With him? Or is this just a generic stocking thing? My cheeks flame at the thought. I'll never be able to resist him if we're in the same bed. (I can barely resist him now.)

"Hi," I say, remembering my manners. "No worries!" Alex places a hand on my shoulder. (So touchy-feely!)

Ignoring the third party, he asks, "Where do you want your bags?" My heart beats loudly in my ears. If it wasn't for the fact I'm still holding Eden, I'd be fidgeting.

"Um, well." I turn and start walking out of the bathroom so we don't have an audience. "I'd prefer the guest room closest to Eden's room, if that's okay." What I want to say is, "Where are you sleeping and how can I sleep there, too?" But I don't. Because that would be crazy. (Right?)

He gives a quick, thin smile and lets go of my shoulder. Without a word, he turns, leaving me in his bedroom alone.

Yeah, I might be a bit despicable for what I'm about to do, but I'm curious. Walking over to the bedside table closest to me, I slide it open to see a fresh box of condoms and a bottle of lube. *Oh.* (Do we think the stockist did that?) I close the drawer and head to the other side.

I open it and my heart flat lines. A single photo sits in the drawer. It's of Amy, and Alex, and Tally in the hospital, probably right after she was born. *He's still Amy's,* the mean little twat of a voice inside my head tells me. (I know, thank you!)

I shut the drawer and take Eden to her room where we sit on the carpet. (I sit, Eden crawls around exploring.) And I let a few tears fall. Just a few. How does anyone compete? How do you compare to *that*? A goddamn idol? *He'll always belong to someone else.*

I wipe away the tears, then stand up and start familiarizing myself with the setup. Then I take Eden with me to my room where I check out the bathroom and bedroom. It's nice, albeit decorated rather generically, though there's literally nothing wrong with it.

When I open the cabinet below the bathroom sink, I find menstrual products and women's shaving supplies here, too. He definitely wasn't planning on me staying in his room then. Glad I made the right call there. That would have been fucking embarrassing.

I do check the nightstands in this room, but don't find any condoms. Or lube. So maybe those were Alex's doing. You know what? good for him, I guess. Though I'm not allowed to have extramarital affairs, but he can? *Bullshit.* Umm, I think not.

JESS

Hi. We just got here. Can I come over?

BRIT

Glad to hear. I'm a bit under the weather. Hoping to be better by Thanksgiving. I'll let you know if I feel up to visitors before then.

I've literally taken care of her when she's been sick. Multiple times. I've peeled her sick ass off bathroom floors. Since when does that mean I can't come visit?

I can feel us drifting. The wedge of the "engagement" to Alex is pushing her further away because she knows what I won't admit. That I'm lying. I've been lying to her. And she doesn't trust that I'm with Alex for the right reasons. And she's right. About all of it. I can't even fault her for giving me the cold shoulder. It's deserved. I've deserved this for a long time.

Okay, let me know if you need anything. Happy to help.

Liam and Carly have it covered, but thanks.

A weird feeling starts to settle over me. It's loneliness and guilt and a longing. It's all the things weighing me down. It's loving people who'll always love someone else more. It's about keeping secrets from your best friend. It's about keeping secrets from everyone. With a sigh, I open my messages back up.

JESS

Eden and I made it. Just wanted to let you know.

TOM

Okay. Have a good holiday.

Wasn't really expecting more, but I'd hoped. I just want someone to talk to...

JESS

Hey, are you going to be at Brit's for Thanksgiving?

DAMIAN

Nope, you're on your own. Well, I guess not anymore, huh? Your fiancé will be there...
😏

Right.

How come you didn't say anything?

Did you think I'd be mad?

No

Just didn't feel right to tell anyone until Brit knew.

Don't love the direction that's going. I slip my phone in my pocket, grab my daughter, and head downstairs to figure out what the hell there is to eat here.

EIGHTEEN

ALEX

You know when you get that new toy/bike/expensive gadget for Christmas, and it's the one thing you've had on your list for like five years? And you finally get it? And you're just fucking obsessed with it? You don't want to put it down. You want to be with/around/doing the thing just constantly, right?

Right.

I can't fucking keep my hands to myself. I think it's confusing her. I know I'm confused. She practically sticks her tongue down my throat, but then ices me out on the drive home. She leans into me when I wrap an arm around her waist, but then she avoids me while we eat dinner. Which, to be fair, she's busy feeding E...

Her phone starts vibrating against the kitchen counter, and I look down to see new texts from Damian. *What the fuck?*

"Hey, your phone," I point down at it when she looks over at me from the eat-in table.

She walks over to get it, and when she looks at the messages she sort of gets this weird look. *Here we go again.* I drop my plate in the sink, grab a beer and walk away.

I don't really drink, to be honest. At least not to *just* drink. Which I guess I'm not really just drinking to drink right now. I'm drinking because I'm pissed. Probably not healthy.

I walk out to the back deck, down the nearly 50 stairs to the lake and just stand at the edge of the empty dock looking at the dark water. It's cold. Not snow cold, but cold enough I'm regretting not grabbing a jacket.

A strong gust kicks up along the lake, blowing loose pine needles out and swirling into the water. *Georgia.*

Whenever it gets windy now, I think of my mom. Spread her ashes in Spearhead Lake this past summer. I can still see her ashes slip into the breeze and blow away. A life half lived, just dust in the wind. That'd be me, too.

Half lived.

When it's Jess, though...nothing feels half measured. I feel like I'm all in. I feel like...I need to just tell her the truth and how I feel, and see if she still wants to stick around. But maybe she won't, and maybe that's what I deserve. Maybe *this*, living in my dream home with my dream woman who's not really mine and is texting my best friend, is all I deserve.

B

Has the eagle landed?

A

Yeah

Coooooool

You could be here right now…

Maybe

?

I mean, Anya's ghosting me, so…

In a fucked up way, I hope Blanks does come. It'd force Jess into my bed because fiancés who live together don't sleep in separate beds.

Then you should definitely come.

I even think Brit and her man are fighting

REALLY?

No.

I don't know, man, things seemed off.

Don't fuck with me.

They might not be fighting, but if you want to be the backup, you gotta start socializing the idea now.

Yeah, you just really wanna see me, huh?

Sure.

I'll be there tomorrow.

Perfect.

———

It's not until my fingers and the tip of my nose turn numb that I finally turn in for the night. I decided to give Jess a little bit of space, to get acclimated on her own terms. *And I also needed to calm the fuck down.* I want to be there to help her, but it's a fine line between hovering and helping for me.

I know I'm a little out of practice, but I still remember how to hold a toddler. Bathe one, change a diaper. But I don't think Jess sees me that way. I don't know if she's forgotten I was a father once, or if she genuinely doesn't want my help because every time I've been holding or helping with Eden, she always asks me to give her back.

I hear "space" when she does that, but maybe it's that she doesn't know how to accept help. I do know that pushing her the first night, after a long day, is a mistake. I know that. I can read a fucking room.

When I get back upstairs and inside, all the lights on the first level have been turned off. There's no dishes in the sink, all the takeaway containers from Colton's have been put away in the fridge. I can even see where she wiped down the floor where E made a mess with her pasta. She doesn't need to do that. She's not on her own anymore. *You literally just left her alone tonight.* Right.

In order to get to the primary bedroom, I have to walk past all the guest suites first. I stop at her door and listen, but after a few beats and no sound, I walk a door down to the nursery. When I stop, I can hear her singing her lullaby again. It's sweet. How Jess is with Eden is different then maybe I expected.

Jess is a bit sharp-tongued, rough around the edges even, but with Eden she's vulnerable and caring. Nurturing.

It hits me in the chest. This craving. For this. With her. I can't put my finger on exactly what it is I want, though.

As I hear her start to finish up, I walk to the end of the hall and wait a couple beats before walking back out of my room as she walks out of Eden's. She's dressed in the cutest fucking pjs. Baby pink with little flowers, shorts, with a button-up top. *No bra either*.

"Hey," I say softly as the door clicks shut.

"Hey, I'm pretty exhausted. I'm heading to bed."

"Of course. I just wanted to make sure you've got every-thing you need." There's an almost sad look to her expression.

"Yeah, I'm fine." Definitely not fine.

"Are you sure?"

"Yup," her voice trembles. Definitely not sure. I advance a couple steps and pull her into my arms before she gets a chance to protest.

"Come here," I whisper gently over her head. I feel her shoulders start to quietly shake. I don't shush her, or really try to calm her. I just let her cry while I hold her. And then, I'm walking her to my bedroom, and away from hers.

I sit down on the bed, and pull her to stand between my legs. I run my hands up and down her back as she continues to hang her head against my shoulder.

"Do you want to talk about it?" I ask after a couple minutes. She shakes her head and I pull her up, into my lap in return. She comes easily, so I scoot back and make room for her. With her in my lap, her head on my chest, I rub her back. Long strokes up and down. She still has the monitor in her hand so I take it from her, putting it on my bedside table.

"Do you want to shower or take a bath?" I offer.

"No," she says quietly. I want to ask if she wants to stay here, but then if I ask, she might say no. So I won't ask again. I just continue stroking her back, and eventually the silent crying ceases. Her breathing evens out and her body feels lax in my arms. She fell asleep. On me. In our bed. I get a little bit hard at the thought.

I hold her just a little bit longer, making sure she's deep asleep, and then I lay her out on the bed. I adjust the pillows and pull the covers out from under her body, covering her.

Obviously the gentlemanly thing to do would be to go sleep in a different room. But I won't be doing that. Instead, I turn off her bedside lamp, use the restroom and get ready for sleep. And then I'm crawling into bed beside her in nothing but my boxers.

I pull her body up against mine and settle into the perfect feeling of her entwined with me. Her limbs — *her life* — tangled with mine. It's fucking perfect. *We're* fucking perfect.

———

The sound of whimpering wakes me and I look over, checking the clock, 3:00 A.M. It's 6:00 Eastern, though. I hope this doesn't mean she's up for the day. I was planning to get up with her when she is, but saying I slept great would be a flat-out lie. I was so damn excited to have her in my arms, I couldn't fall asleep.

Turning on the screen for the monitor, I can see E is standing up in her crib with her paci on the floor beside her. Jess starts to stir at the sound, so I lean over and soothe her back to sleep. Dropping a kiss on her temple, I let her know I'll go check on Eden. She gives a small "uh huh" in affirmation, then resettles.

As I walk to Eden's room, I throw on a shirt, then pick up the thrown paci off the ground, giving it a quick wipe. She's wearing a sleep sack, and her dark brown eyes are wide and watery when I approach.

"Hey, E," I say gently. "Here we go. Let's go back to sleep, babe." She takes the paci from me, shoves it in her mouth, then plops her butt back down on the bed. I watch for a couple moments, making sure she rolls over and goes back to sleep, and when she does, I silently tip toe out of the room and back to my own.

I slip my shirt back off and climb back in bed, cementing myself against Jess, her back to my chest, my hand splayed across her abdomen, holding her. I close my eyes, willing myself to settle back to sleep, but it feels fucking impossible. And then Jess gives a subtle roll of her hips against my groin and, yeah, there's no fucking way I'm going back to sleep.

I try not to read into it, but then she does it again, and this time, she moves her arm up, placing a hand over mine. And all the blood in my body rushes to my cock. As if she could get any closer, I pull her tighter and my dick wedges up against her ass.

Her fingers splay then thread with mine, and she rolls her hips again. "Jess..." I whisper out wantonly.

"Yes?" she asks back in a whisper.

I nudge closer to her ear, and whisper, "Tell me what you want." *Please be me.* It's a silent prayer to the gods. God. The universe.

She nods against me, "Please, Alex." In one quick maneuver, I have her splayed out beneath me.

If I thought the view of her moving over me was the end all be all, I was wrong. This, the view of her laid out beneath me with rosy cheeks and a look of desire, is everything. My fucking Roman Empire. The hill I'll die on. My very own Helen of Troy.

She starts unbuttoning her pajama top while I admire her. As she does, I slide her shorts down, revealing she's not wearing any panties underneath. I groan at the sight of her pink lips, already wet and swollen for me.

While she works her top off, I scoot down and spread her legs. I slip my arms under her thighs and kiss my way way down her tan skin until I'm inches from her wet heat that smells so fucking delicious my dick is pained from the strain.

I look up at her while running a long lick across her soaking wet slit. Her head tips and falls back in response, her perfect tits and dusky brown nipples bouncing with her. Fuck. *Fucked with a capital F.* That's what I am. Who the fuck could ever compare to this. *This.*

I settle in, feasting on her clit, sending her into an orgasm that has her hands clutching my hair and crying out my name. My name leaving her lips on an orgasm as she floods my mouth is a special kind of high. One I hope to experience time and time again.

"Baby..." I wipe my face off on the sheets. If that's all this amounts to, I'll be okay. I'll have to go take a cold shower or get myself off later, but it'll be fine.

"Come here," she commands. Her hands reach up, grabbing at my shoulders, trying to get me over her again. I comply. She takes my chin in her hand and brings my mouth down to hers. With one hand on my chin, her other goes down, gripping my painfully hard cock in her hand. *Don't come, don't come.*

I've thought of almost nothing else, but her tight little cunt she let me feel in July. It's November now. The way I need her is insatiable. I need her daily. I need her. That's this feeling. It goes beyond want. It's a necessity. *Now.* She's fucking hooked me, and I've never been happier than at that fact. She could be leading me to a cold grave, and I'd follow. I'm merciless against her.

"Need this," she says, her fist moving along my smooth skin under my boxers. She releases me, scoots my boxers down, and then with a slight movement of her hips, she's lining me up and pulling my hips closer.

No, she had her chance to ride me how she wanted to, now it's my turn to fuck her like I've been dying to. At first I move slowly, relishing the way her body pulls me in, makes me wet, and gets me comfortable in its new home. Being here is new, but I'm pretty sure she's always been my home.

She's the light left on.

She's the warm blanket.

She's the calm to my storm.

Once I'm fully seated inside her, she grinds against me. With her hands on my glutes, she pulls me, trying to get me deeper like I'm not already practically touching her fucking belly button. She lets out one of those little sighs and as much as I'd love to be gentle and really make love to her, I can't.

I need to claim this pussy. I need to let her know it's mine. So with a slow pull out, I quickly thrust back in. I pull her arms above her head, and with one hand I pin them down at the wrists. And then I'm rutting her. It's a pounding. If I thought she didn't like it, I'd stop, but her breathing quickens and her cheeks flush, her nipples drag back and forth across my chest, and I can feel her bearing down. I can feel her muscles clench and contract.

Placing a large palm on her pelvis, I apply pressure when she bears down on me again, and with the combination of our pressure together, she spasms and shakes beneath me. The sight, the feeling, sends a new-to-me warmth and thrill rolling through my body. My balls grow tight and the lightning flys up my spine as I release my cum into her perfect cunt.

"Fuck, Jess," I pant out as she says my name over and over, softly. I release her arms and she immediately brings them to my back, dragging her fingernails gently across my skin. My body is still pulsing, still spilling, and I drop my forehead to hers.

"You're fucking amazing, Jess." I say it, to stop myself from saying what I really want, which is, "You're never not sleeping in my bed again." I want to tell her so much more. How she's perfect. How I love the way she fits against me, how I fit inside her. How I never want to go another day without her here.

She runs a hand across my newly bare cheek and sighs in contentment. A simple smile spreads across her face and I wonder if there are things she wishes she could say, too, but it all feels too fragile. One wrong move and everything goes flying out the window.

I lower my mouth to hers and she opens for me, our tongues gliding against one another in perfect synchronization. I don't want to leave her. Not her body, not her space, but I know I need to. I just hope she'll still be here on the other side of it.

I slide out of her, leaving a trail of cum across her pink lips and I have to fight the urge to finger it back in place. Not sure she'd love that. Instead I just stare at where she and I are combined for a second too long. I look up and give her a smile.

"We're fucking good together, baby," I say, then watch as her cheeks turn crimson.

I reluctantly get up and head for the bathroom for a quick cleanup. She follows behind to do the same, so I watch her naked ass sway as she walks into the toilet room, thinking any man who doesn't want that ass must be out of his goddamn mind.

I don't want any other man to want that ass, though. I want it to be mine. Mine for more than twelve months. Mine forever.

I wait back in bed, hopeful. Will she put her pjs on and slink back to her room? Or does she crawl back in bed? Does she want to cuddle? Will she just roll over and go back to sleep? Last time she eviscerated me by walking away.

When she comes back, she avoids putting any clothes back on, just crawling back into bed and rolling towards me with closed eyes. I won't rock that boat. At all. I settle in, facing her too, but can't help but lean over to give her a soft kiss. I can tell it surprises her, but I'm just so fucking glad she's here.

"Get some rest, Jess." I give her one more kiss now that her eyes are open, and she returns it, then settles in with a hand over my arm.

This time, I immediately slip into a deep sleep where I dream of her. In a long white gown and a ring on her finger.

NINETEEN

JESS

There's a warm soreness emanating from in between my legs as I come to consciousness. It's aching to be soothed. I want him to kiss it and make it better. I scrunch my nose and smile against the sheets of his bed.

A warm hand on my abdomen. His hands holding my wrists. The view of him hovering over me. The look on his face as he enters me. I replay the night in my mind, letting the memory warm me, making me clench my thighs together.

Rolling over, I expect to see him there. Honestly, I expected to feel him at my back, cuddling me, but he's gone. Panicked, I sit up wondering the time, knowing I feel way too rested and freaking out about how, or better yet, *why* Eden has slept in. She just doesn't sleep in.

I quickly throw on the pjs that were folded neatly on top of the nightstand and rush over to Eden's bedroom, finding the door open and the room empty. The sound of *Arthur* drifts up the stairs along with some light baby laughter, so I grab my phone out of my room, then quickly descend down the stairs.

At the foot of the stairs, you can see into the large great room and part of the eat-in kitchen where Eden is sitting in her high chair with Cheerios all over the floor watching *Arthur* on the large screen over the fireplace. Relief hits me, but then, so does something else. *He got up with her?*

Alex lazily glides over to the eat-in, cup of coffee in hand, and pulls out a chair beside Eden, a pouch of strawberry beet yogurt in hand.

"Alright, kiddo." He takes a sip of coffee, then snaps open the seal on the pouched yogurt. "You eating with a spoon yet? Or just taking it straight to the face?"

Eden squeals, and says "Maa!" when she sees me, drawing Alex's attention with hers.

"Hi," Alex says, looking sleep-worn and completely adorable. His hair is tousled, he's got on gray lounge pants and a black t-shirt, and I have this urge to snap a photo of this moment. I don't want to forget it.

"Hi!" Eden mimics him and I look at her, then back at him. It's really her first word. Aside from Ma.

My eyes get a bit misty. I walk over and say, "Hi, sweet girl! You said hi!" I laugh. "Hi!" I say it again.

She replies with a "hi" back. Wow. Amazing. I hold up my phone and start a video.

"Hi, baby!" I say in the background and she responds.

"Hi!" She throws her fists down on her tray, sending Cheerios flying off and scattering the floor. I end the recording.

"That's her first real word," I say to Alex in awe.

"Wow," he says with a smile beaming at me, and then back at Eden. "Looks like I'm a good influence already." He laughs then offers the pouch to the babe. "Didn't know if she still did bottles or milk now, so all she's had is some cereal and a pouch you left in the fridge."

"Thanks, you didn't have to get up with her."

"Yeah, I know," he says as he helps her squeeze the bottom of the pouch.

Grabbing a bottle from the diaper bag, I find milk in the fridge and start filling it. Before I can even finish, Alex is at my back, wrapping his arms around me with his hands coming to rest on my hips. He places a soft kiss on my neck, making me break out into goosebumps.

"Morning."

"Good morning," I respond while screwing the bottle cap on. He pushes my hair over one shoulder and settles in. It's these moments of vulnerability that I can't shake. He can be so tender...and loving. It's not what I pictured him to be like.

"Can I make you a coffee? Need to start learning how you take it..." *I take it well. I'd like to take it nightly from now on, preferably from you, and in any hole.* (Stahp it, Jessica.)

"Would love that. Splash of cream, please?" *I'll take him with a splash of cream.* (I'm like a pubescent teen.)

He releases me so I can give Eden her bottle.

"When'd she get up?"

"About 5." I check the clock to see it's 7:30. Crap, they've been up for a while and I never even heard them. I must have actually slept like the dead. "So I wanted to talk to you about it last night, but didn't get the chance," Alex keeps talking while he puts a fresh pod in the Nespresso. I watch him, noting where the pods are at, and the coffee cups.

"Caleb's coming for Thanksgiving and he'll be staying here. So..."

I wait, not sure where this is headed. I push what little yogurt is left to the top of the pouch for Eden. "Sooo...." I giggle back, "Out with it."

"You should probably just unpack in my room since you'll be staying in there."

Heat invades my cheeks, my stomach, and my panties. Yes, because people who are engaged and living together likely share a bedroom. Not mad about it. (Forced proximity for the win.)

"Okay, I will." I shoot him a smile, all confidence to hide the fact that I want to ask him if he wants me there. Is this okay with him? Does he need some space? I'm starting to feel like he really wants me. Wants *me*. But I also wonder if we're falling together like this because of the circumstances.

Don't know. And maybe, I don't care.

He gives me a genuine looking smile back. "Also, I need you to make a grocery list. Things you and Eden will eat. I have to run out today, and I'll pick up whatever we need." I nod. "And then Brit wants us to bring a dish for Thanksgiving. Any thoughts? Requests?"

She texted Alex that, but not me. Things are worse than I imagined.

"Oh, sure. Let's make sweet potato casserole."

"Great. Just need the list of ingredients."

"Can we come with you?" He gets a little look of surprise.

"You want to?"

"Yeah. Need to get a feel for the place. Start learning the area."

"Okay." He smiles. "I have to pick up some stuff from my old house, and then I could take you to lunch? There's this old Italian deli near downtown that my mom used to take me to. I think you'd love it."

"Yes! That sounds amazing." I don't have high hopes for an Italian deli in that dusty town at the bottom of the mountain, but getting out (spending time with Alex) and distracting me from everything with Brit sounds amazing.

———

It's the smell that's a dead giveaway. This place is legit.

All authentic Italian delis have a specific smell. It's the combination of cured meats, oregano, and a hint of garlic. It smells like home. I inhale and take in the wire racks filled with dried pasta, canned tomatoes, crackers and biscuits. I take another big inhale. *Oh my gawd, yes.* I'm salivating.

In the car, Alex explained he hadn't been in years, so he hoped he wasn't setting us up for disappointment, but I know just based on the smell of this place, it won't disappoint.

We stopped by Georgia's old house on the way in. He loaded up a cooler and a couple boxes, and then we left. I didn't even go inside, but I wanted to. Kind of want to see Brit's childhood bedroom. Want to see Alex's bedroom, too, because he's still an enigma to me. There's a lot of gray area around Alex, and I want to reveal it.

I immediately grab a shopping basket and start loading up with ingredients to make my marinara. (I'll get pesto ingredients at the grocery later.) I throw some good pasta in, then head to the back wall of refrigerated goods. I grab fresh parm, meatballs, and a couple trays of premade stuffed shells. (I'm starving, can you tell?)

Alex is pushing Eden in her stroller, following me around the tight space, but when we get to the deli counter, he steps up beside me.

When a woman with an old-school guest check pad asks for our order, I let Alex do the ordering for us. (A Marco Polo and a Piedmont Special, two servings of pasta salad, two bags of chips, and two root beers.) And then we trade and he takes the shopping basket from me to go pay while I handle the stroller. It's oddly fluid how we work together. There's a give and take. *"We're fucking good together, baby,"* replays in my mind and I try to hide the smile that works it's way on to my face.

After he's finished paying, Alex finds me perusing the stacks of Toblerone. "Do you want to wait outside? I was thinking we could actually head over to a nearby park to eat." There's no eating area at the deli, also typical and legit.

"Sure." I smile, and wheel the stroller out while Alex holds the door. We're sort of downtown *adjacent*. The area is older, a bit rundown, but in a hip way. There's vintage stores, an old theater that's playing some indie films, (probably a few tattoo parlors around), and small restaurants littering the main street.

"Georgia used to bring you here?" I ask as we wait together under the fading orange, white, and green striped awning.

"Yeah. Don't know why, this place just always stuck with me." It's the smell. I bet it's the smell.

"I literally can't wait to try it. This place looks legit." I look over and give him a smile. "Thanks for bringing me here." He reaches a hand out, running it across my shoulders and a warmth runs through me.

"I'm gonna go put this stuff in the cooler," he holds up the plastic bag with my pasta goods. "I'll be right back."

Before he leaves, though, he places a kiss on my cheek. But there's no one around, there's nothing to show off. It's starting to all add up, the number of times he's shown me affection when no one's been around to see. He's either method acting...or he likes touching me as much as I like him touching me.

My phone pings and I look down at the text from Damian. I want to be there for him, but it's a tightrope to walk between Brit and Alex. He's Brit's ex and Alex's best friend. (*Was* Alex's best friend?) I make the call not to respond, which is good because Alex is rounding the corner of the building just as I slip the phone back in my pocket. He got all weird last night when he looked at my phone and presumably saw the texts from Damian, and I definitely don't want a repeat of that.

I don't get a chance to greet Alex when the bell above the door rings as a customer comes out, and I can hear them calling our number. He quickly passes me to get the food, then is back out, bags in hand. "You okay to walk? Or we could drive."

"Walk is good." It's nice out again today. Nicer down in the valley than it is in the mountains. It's sunny in Spearhead, but cold. Down here, it's sunny and slightly warm. It feels more like a spring day on the East Coast than late November.

It's just a few minutes walk until we sit down at a bench in an expansive park. He points to the road winding through it and says, "That leads to the zoo."

My eyes go wide, "There's a zoo here?" (I know, I'm acting a bit brand new. I'm just still surprised this place even has a deli.)

He laughs at me. "Yeah, I hear they just got electricity, too."

I gently shove his shoulder and laugh. "Shut up. I didn't mean it like that. Just...this place is surprising me. That's all."

Alex nods and starts unpacking the bag, laying out my food for me. It's that orange peel theory, he knows I can do it, but he wants to do it for me. He unrolls the sandwiches, then trades half of mine with half of his so I can try both. (Love that.)

Eden starts squirming and squealing seeing us eat, so I pull her out of the stroller, set her in my lap and feed her bites of pasta.

"So, correct me if I'm wrong, but this," I motion with my hands around us, "feels like a first date." I smile at him and he smiles back.

"Yeah, but it wouldn't be *our* first date." I'm sort of taken aback by his comment. Yes, it would be our first date.

"How so?" I ask incredulously.

"At the bar that night. I thought I was meeting you for a date." I thought he was, too, until I overheard him saying it was just an obligatory courtesy call for an old acquaintance. He said, *"She's nobody. Just need to check the box so I can leave."*

"I thought so, too..." I say, maybe a bit sadly because all I can think about is the hours I poured into getting ready in my hotel that night. The anticipation that kept me from being able to eat anything at lunch. The agonizing choice of what to wear. (Ended up in a slip dress with a blazer over and Prada heels.) I'd felt fucking amazing, on a natural high. Alex, the man I'd been talking to on the phone daily for the past month was finally going to be face-to-face, in person, with me, and we weren't going to be hovering over a pair gravestones.

"I said I'm sorry," Alex breaks through the mental fog I obviously slipped into.

"Okay." That's all I say back, then refocus on eating. *Well, that took a turn.* (Note: Avoid the past at all costs.)

"We should probably get our stories straight. With the holiday tomorrow. I'm sure people will ask questions."

I say, "Okay, " but continue to focus on feeding the baby.

"We met while we were visiting graves at the cemetery. I asked you for coffee and we talked and went on a couple dates prior to your move to DC, but we couldn't make the distance work."

I reply with, "Sure," not looking at him.

"When I saw you in Spearhead this summer, none of my feelings for you had changed." (Dagger. I imagine what he's saying is true and it hurts because it's not.) "And after we sort of cleared the air that day in the kitchen, we reconnected and haven't spent a day not talking since. Does that work?"

"Definitely." I cover my mouth to hide the massive bite of mortadella I'm chewing on. I swallow. "How did you ask me to marry you?"

When I look up at him, I don't love it. We were in this little cocoon of playing house all morning. But just like when you have to stop playing pretend to figure out how to keep going, it's the same now, and I can practically see the magic fading. Reality sneaks back in, reminding me that he doesn't actually love me. He never actually proposed. He didn't really build me our dream house. *He loves Amy. He proposed to Amy. Is that Amy's and his dream house?* (It's honestly pathetic being jealous of a dead woman.)

What was quickly becoming my dream feels dirty now. *Placeholder. Replaceable. Pawn.* (Shut up, little voice!)

He shrugs and puts on a small smile, (which means I'm doing a good job at hiding what I'm thinking) then poses the question back to me, "How would you want to be proposed to?"

I know, you're probably thinking gallantly. Big. Over-the-top. Extreme. But I'm not. I think those are beautiful, but what would be better is if the person proposing actually meant it. (Depressing, right?)

"Simply. Just at home. Laying on the couch, while watching our favorite movie together. Which is *Casino*, by the way." He laughs at that. I was being serious. "And the person proposing," (notice I don't say him, though obviously I'm imagining him) "would take my hand in theirs and slide the ring on my finger. It wouldn't even be a question because we'd already know we belonged together." I shrug, then help Eden who's grappling to pick up a bite of rotini pasta.

"Well, we can't use that then." I'm wondering why, when he says, "You don't have a ring." Right. Obviously.

"Okay, then you come up with it, I don't care." I try to keep my tone light and neutral, because that's what we're supposed to be doing, right? But I think a hint of agitation makes itself known.

"Okay, then I came to your work at the coffee shop, and wrote on my receipt asking you to marry me." That's honestly lame. But I said I didn't care, so I have to actually not care.

"Fine. How'd you know I was working at the coffee shop, though?"

"Brit told me." Right she did.

"Okay. We should probably wrap this up. The cooler needs ice and my grocery list is kind of massive." I start wrapping up the leftovers and rebagging them, then grab the wipes to clean off Eden.

Alex starts moving, too, and in synchronization we clean up and head for the car. He pushes the stroller with one hand, then reaches down, sliding his other into mine. We hold hands while we walk, and when I look up at him, he looks down on me with a smile.

But I'm wondering, is the smile for me? Or the idea of me?

TWENTY

ALEX

I like this. *Okay fine.* I more than like this. We're roaming the aisles of the Robles Safeway, two carts deep. His and hers. Each aisle we go down inevitably leads to questions and then often devolves into laughter. I haven't even consciously thought of how many exits there are or counted windows once today.

"What's your favorite movie snack?" I ask her in the candy aisle.

"Sno-Caps."

I look at her incredulously. "So basically just chocolate chips?"

"They are not just chocolate chips!"

I open my phone and google "are Sno-Caps basically chocolate chips?" The answer is overwhelmingly yes. I hold my phone up for her.

"Fine, what's yours? And if it's Jujubes, the wedding's off."

I laugh. "Fuck no. It's just Red Vines. Like a *normal* human being." I grab a couple packs of Red Vines...and a couple boxes of Sno-Caps, and she smiles when she sees them in the cart.

"Do you know what time Caleb is coming tonight?" she asks. "Should I cook dinner?" Blanks will be here when Blanks will be here. I stopped asking about estimated arrival times years ago.

"No clue, but I was planning to cook." I motion down at the wrapped steaks in my cart.

"You're cooking?" She's shocked.

"Yeah?" She comes to a full stop mid-aisle. "What?" I ask again.

"You, just...you surprise me. A lot, actually." I hope it's in the good way, but I don't ask. Instead, I pull her into me and drop a kiss on her pillow-soft lips.

Eden squeals at the lack of attention, and I separate her body from mine. It's hard to do.

"Why do you call Caleb 'Blanks'?" That's what she's thinking about? After I kiss her?

"It's an old Army nickname."

"Yeah, but why Blanks?"

"Because he's shooting blanks, and it was when he was like 20 years old, and the nickname just stuck."

"Oh, like...he can't have kids?" Not a fan of this conversation. Feels like a betrayal to talk about this behind his back.

"Yeah." I clear my throat. I can't remember how he found out, something about a delayed growth spurt in his teenage years and his parents took him for testing. It didn't bother him then. I think it bothers him now, which is why I don't like talking about it. Also feel like maybe the nickname doesn't hit like it used to.

"Oh." She says a bit sadly. It makes me wonder, though.

"Do you want more kids?" We turn onto the frozen aisle, our trip almost complete.

"I don't know, honestly. I think it could go either way at this point, but if I had to choose right this minute, I'd say no." *Hmm.* Okay.

"Do you? Want more kids?" She doesn't look at me when she asks. She's busy taking in the frozen fruit. *More kids, as in addition to Eden? Or as in addition to Tally?* I don't get the nerve to ask.

"Maybe. Haven't decided yet."

She nods, and then we don't talk the rest of the time. Not until we're in the car and headed back home.

"Hey," we both start at the same time, then laugh.

"You go first," again it comes out at the same time. Jess smiles then uses her hand to zip her lips shut.

I nod. "I just wanted to say, I had fun. Being with you today." I reach over and place my hand on her thigh, giving her a squeeze. I'm fucking trying. My natural instinct is to not say anything, but I want Jess to know I like this. Because I more than like this. I like *this* more than anything.

"Oh, yeah. Same. It was nice."

"Okay. Now what were you going to say?"

She gets a shy smile and says, "I forgot." *Bullshit.* But when she lets my hand stay on her leg, slides her fingers in between mine and holds on tight, I don't push it. I relish the feel of her wanting me.

Eden is still racked out when we pull into the drive at the house, so while she gets E, I work on unloading the groceries, putting some in the outside fridge and freezer and taking things for dinner inside. I'd done a basics run before Jess got here. Flour, ketchup, milk, bread — that sort of shit. But now, without the extra storage, we'd be out of room. There's a whole flat of yogurt pouches and applesauce taking over shelves, and it's weird to think this is my life now. This is my life...again.

I get everything put away, but when Jess doesn't come down, I go in search of her. I listen outside her door for a minute, and I can tell she's on the phone. I should just keep walking, but call it spidey senses, a gut feeling, I stand at her door and lean closer.

"I'm so sorry, Damian." The fuck? *"Can you come for Thanksgiving? Please?"*

"We could probably sneak off for a little bit, at some point. Or maybe you could just stay with us?" I feel like I could light a match and let this whole fucking place burn without an ounce of remorse. There'd just be more rage.

My hands shake as I walk to my room. *Are him and her...?* I can't even fucking think it without wanting to send a fist through the wall.

Instead of annihilating the freshly painted walls, I head back downstairs and out the side of the garage to the area where I've been splitting and storing firewood. I set a log down and rear back, letting the ax fall far more forcefully than necessary, channeling the frustration I'm feeling into the act of chopping wood.

Thwack. The sound of the ax splitting down the log and ending with a loud *crack* feels slightly satisfying.

She's still the same Jess. I might be different. She makes me different, but she's still exactly the same.

You think you deserve more than this? Ray's voice echoes in my mind, bouncing off my skull painfully. I raise the ax, mirroring the mental image in my mind of Ray raising a hand to me. *This is exactly what you deserve.* And as the ax falls, so does the back of his hand. *Thwack. Crack.*

I've worked hard to keep that voice at bay. The one that tells me I'm nothing. I'm worthless. I'm deserving of the hurt and pain. Once the memory finds me, though, it's not enough for it to play just once through my mind. It'll be stuck on replay until I can work it out of my system. So I commit to working through the wood before me. It's a lot. That's okay. Perfect even.

I raise my ax, I see a hand. I fell a log, I see 8-year-old Alex fall back. Again and again and again. I hear the voice: *You're stupid. You're a fool.* Again and again.

The memories would come when I was with Amy, too. Except back then it was near constant. The only way to get it to stop would be to disengage with the outside world, or to be engaged at work. On occasion she could pull me out of it, but then something would trigger me, and I'd retreat again.

When my long-sleeved shirt gets soaked, I shed it. When my hair won't stay out of my eyes, I walk and get my hat out of my Jeep.

She's gonna make a fool of you. Thwack. Crack. The voice is still there.

You think someone like her could ever love you? Thwack. Crack.

Shoot, boy, she seems pretty shitty herself. Maybe the two of you actually deserve each other. Thwack. Crack.

I yell out at the last words that are a blend of Ray's voice and my own. And I hate that. I fucking hate that I could ever think something he would. That I could ever be like him. I slam the ax down with a massive crack, lodging it deep into the stump.

"You wanna talk this out?" Blanks says from where he's leaned up against the garage. My face softens slightly. When he's out of New York, he's the Blanks I've always known. Humble. Small town boy. Orphaned at 17. Only child, but still a positive outlook on life. He also stops dressing like a tool bag, too. He's got on a plain sweatshirt, jeans, and boots. Normal shit.

I nod over at him, but don't say anything. He knows the drill.

"Alright, then." He pushes up his sleeves. "You wanna fight?" *Yes.*

"No."

"You sure?"

"No."

"Alright," Blanks says, meeting me in the semi-clear area where I chop. We circle each other like we used to, trying to take one another down. "Is it family drama?" He circles me and makes a swipe that I lean away from to avoid.

"No," I say, circling him, then taking my own swipe that he escapes.

"Ahh, woman drama." I don't say anything, and he swipes my leg out from underneath me, laying me out. Instead of advancing, he hovers over me. He doesn't have to say it, it's there in his look. *Man the fuck up. Whatever it is, it's been long enough that you need to get over it so you don't fuck this up.*

253

He offers me a hand as he says, "Don't fuck it up." Echoing the already clear sentiment. If I were in a better mood, I'd pull his ass to the ground and get him in a headlock, but I don't.

As I'm standing up, I realize the chatter in my mind has quieted back down. My blood has lowered from a boil to a simmer, and I'm ready to go have a conversation with the woman who officially owns me completely.

———

"Hey." I nod at her from the bathroom entrance, then throw on a fresh t-shirt from my closet. She's unpacking her toiletries, setting her toothbrush on *my* bathroom counter. She's wearing the same baggy jeans and sweater as she was at lunch, but seeing her barefoot, in our bathroom, looking entirely at home, comfortable and happy — it makes me want to curl in on myself and die.

"Hi," she smiles back at me. A smile that damn near brings me to my knees.

"I need you to be honest with me, Jess. You're about to come to *my* family's Thanksgiving tomorrow. We're either doing this or we aren't, but you have to be honest with me." I can see she's surprised by my tone. I'm not saying it harshly, though a part of me wants to. It's just that the subtleness of the Alex I am with Jess has sloughed off. This is the voice of the man who's hated her for years. And that's what surprises her, I think. That that person who's been tucked away is still here. I don't want this version of me to exist at all, but then I overhear her talking to Damian a certain way and I revert easily.

"I'm here, aren't I?" Her smile falls, and her tone chills. It's in the same tone as the woman who has hated me back, and not the woman I'm probably completely in love with now.

"You don't have to be, is the point. Do you want to be here? With me?" My tone is even harder than it was before.

"I mean, no one else is offering to help..."

Ouch. That's all this is then? I knew that's probably all this was.

"Are you fucking Damian? Because if you are, honestly, ask him for help." I don't wait for her to answer, I just turn around and leave. My chest feels like it's being ripped apart. All over again.

Blanks is waiting for me at the bottom of the stairs, hands in pockets, a sorry look on his face that I'm back so soon.

"Let's head to Brit's. She'll be excited to see you." My hands fucking tremble as I grab my keys to the Jeep. Blanks doesn't say a thing. He just follows behind me looking slightly sorry he ever came here. *Same, bro.*

———

They never lock their fucking doors.

"Hello!" I push open the large front door to a house that looks like a modern-day Norman Rockwell scene. Liam's in the living room reading the newspaper and Brit is trimming an oversized Christmas tree. Elodie is playing with their puppy while Caroline threads popcorn onto string to hang on the tree.

The sight makes my jaw clench. Hate this fucking feeling. It's jealousy.

"Hey!" Brit says, looking briefly over her shoulder, then back again in a quick double take. "Alex! You didn't tell me Caleb was coming! Oh my god!" She gets off her step stool and rushes over.

"Caleb!" she squeals, hugging him. Or trying to hug him as best she can with her pregnant belly. Blanks pulls her in tight, picking her feet up off the ground, a stupid grin on his face. Liam sees the exchange and sets down his newspaper to stare at the new guy.

I clear my throat. "That's enough, Caleb," I say under my breath and he releases her.

"It's been like eight years since the last time I saw you." Brit looks at him the same way you would a long lost friend. He looks back on her the same.

"Seven years, actually. Almost to the day," Blanks says, giving her a wink. Then Liam is standing up from his chair. Here we go.

"Cough—cool it—cough," I get out under my breath and Brit laughs at me.

"Hey, aren't you sick or something?" I ask Brit and her cheeks turn rosy.

"Yeah, I'm better now." My ass.

"Still pissed then?" I ask.

She shrugs, but brushes it under the rug by grabbing Blanks' hand. She quickly introduces him to Liam and the girls, then drags him to the kitchen.

"You have to meet Carly."

"Why's that?" Blanks follows her like a puppy.

"Well, for one, she's hot. Two, she's probably the best chef in the world. And three, she's gonna love you."

Blanks laughs at Brit. "Well, alright then." And with the

southern twang he only lets out when he's with his people, he sounds and looks like a dark-haired Matthew McCounaghey.

Liam glares at me. "Who the fuck's that?"

"Best friend from the Army. Also my business partner."

Liam nods, then grunts. "He's a handsy little shit."

I actually laugh. It was the right call coming here. I can decompress. I can help the girls with something and feel useful. Liam will probably pour me a drink.

"Happy early Thanksgiving! You want a glass?" he asks me right on schedule with a pat on the back, and I nod.

"Hey, C." I ruffle her hair as I pass her in the living room to take a seat by Elodie who's playing fetch with their golden, Luna. "Hey, kiddo."

"Hey, Al. Look what Luna just learned!" Elodie proceeds to show me the dog's astounding capability to roll over on command.

"Wow, would you look at that?"

"Where's Jess? And Eden?" Caroline looks up from her threading project to ask.

There's that guilty feeling. I didn't even tell her where I was going, but she also didn't say anything when I asked if she was fucking their dad. Not that I gave her a ton of time to answer...

"Eden's napping."

Caroline nods like she doesn't believe me. And she shouldn't, so I'm oddly proud of her for that.

"Where's your dad?" I ask both girls and they exchange strange glances. "Girls?" I ask again when they don't say anything.

"Summer dumped him." Elodie whispers it like it isn't

widely known. Well, of course Summer did. And fucking of course he's single.

"Why are we whispering?" I ask back.

"Because mom doesn't know and Dad said not to tell her. He wants to do it." I roll my eyes. The Damian ship sailed a long time ago for Brit. I don't know what the fuck he's playing at other than maybe he's ashamed at how it all turned out. He left Brit for Summer. So Brit went out and found the love of her life. And now she's having Liam's baby, and Summer is dumping him. I don't want to say karma, but... if the shoe fucking fits, you know?

Caroline notices my eye roll and says, "I know, right?" Then rolls her own eyes. I think Caroline tolerated Summer. At best.

Liam sets a pair of glasses down on the coffee table, sliding one in front of me, then clinking his glass against mine in a cheers.

"Cheers, brother." Liam and the Scala clan have folded me into their BRO-therhood. Well, most of the Scala clan. Last I heard Matt still has a chip on his shoulder about his broken nose.

"Cheers," I say back.

"She love the house?" *Jess.* Pang of guilt. Again, fucking hate this.

"Yeah, man. I owe you."

He shakes his head. "It's what family's for...but also if you could not bring over your centerfold, billionaire best friend to regale my wife with tales of his latest excursion to Everest, that'd be great, k?"

"Wife?" I ask, raising an eyebrow.

"Wife," he says smugly, holding up his left hand, showing

me the gold band. Jess is gonna be pissed. *And hurt.* Me, on the other hand, nothing but happy for Brit. Hate that I think about Jess's reaction first, though. *Huh.*

"Well, congrats." I say it sincerely and we clink glasses once more. I look at my nieces wondering if they're good with it, and Elodie takes it as permission to launch into a spiel about how she got to be a maiden of honor with Caroline. I'll ask Caroline later if she's fine because she's still just working away at her popcorn garland like the rest of us don't even exist.

I stand up once Elodie is finished, and sit beside Caro.

"Teach me?" She nods, then pulls out another string and a needle and we sit in total silence, both of us getting lost in the monotony of stringing popcorn. It's exactly the thing I need to take my mind off the fact that I'll probably go home to an empty house later. And maybe this was my last chance at a family and I still can't make it work. Probably didn't deserve the last 24 hours, let alone a happily ever after.

Tally would be almost the same age as Caroline. They'd look similar, too, because Tally looked like Brit. It's the exact reason I stayed away for so many years. Fucking painful to see what could have been.

Could have been *my* Norman Rockwell Thanksgiving.

TWENTY-ONE

JESS

It's fucking laughable. I actually laugh. As Alex walks out the bathroom door, I think I'm stunned silent for the briefest of moments, and then I'm laughing. (Fine, and crying.) But mostly laughing, and then there's this heat that sort of forms somewhere behind my ribs because he's jealous. Alex is jealous. Of me...and someone else.

The way he spoke to me, like I was fucking scum, *that* pissed me off. But if I go back and think about it, it was also kind of hot. Which makes me pretty fucked up, but we already knew that. (Didn't we?)

My hands shake slightly as I finish placing my skincare products on the sink beside his. Maybe I shouldn't be unpacking in his room, but if he's worried about me not wanting to be here...maybe that means he really wants me here. And I want to be here. Really. Just as long as he wants the same.

So yeah, fuck it. I go to the guest room (my old room) and get the suitcases that I never unpacked in the first place and wheel them into the empty closet across from Alex's in the primary suite. I won't brush off what happened today, but I won't let it ruin what was one of the best days I've had in years. It was easy, and comfortable. Like throwing on the perfect pair of worn jeans and a favorite sweatshirt. There's a comfort and even a feeling of safety that comes with spending time with him. It eases and relaxes me.

I almost ruined it, too, in the car. I almost asked if he would ever marry again (as in real marriage), aside from me. But then he said he had fun with me and it was in the nicest voice I've ever heard Alex use. It fucking melted me. And I figured there was no quicker way to ruin said fun than for me to ask (and think) about him being with someone else. So I shut the fuck up.

Eden's little grunts and whimpers start echoing throughout the cavernous primary bathroom where the monitor is on the counter. So abandoning the opened, half-empty suitcases, I go get the baby. When I open the door, her hair is mussed and slightly damp, her eyes still heavy with sleep.

"Hi, babes," I say gently, walking over to her.

"Hi," she says back around her paci that she lets hang out the corner of her mouth. The sound of her talking back is still amazing. I want to cry every time I hear it. I know that'll fade, but it's just so fucking amazing that some day this little being is going to be having a full-on conversation with me.

"Alright, let's go up." Eden lifts her arms up in response and I lift her out of the crib. We do a quick diaper change and straighten out her hair, then head downstairs.

It's quiet. Obviously he's not in here, but I double check outside. Jeep is gone and he's not at his wood-chopping station. (Which, guys, wood chopping, 100% an aphrodisiac. Good lord. I watched him from the bedroom window and ended up needing to change underwear.) (Yeah, that fucking good.)

I hope he comes back. Don't love that thought. Don't love that he *might not* come back, or the fact that I sound a bit desperate.

Walking back into the house, barefoot and with Eden still on my hip, I pull out my phone and hit Britain's contact. It rings and rings until I end up in her voicemail, so changing course, I call Caroline instead.

"Hi." She answers on the second ring.

"Hi. How's your mom feeling?" It's silent for a beat.

"Yeah, I think she's all better now." There's that sour feeling in the pit of my stomach. "Your fiancé is here." Oh.

"Oh really? Would you ask him what time he's planning to be home so I know when to start dinner?" I ask in the sweetest voice possible.

Caroline's voice only dims slightly like he's right beside her. "Jess wants to know when to start dinner, so when are you leaving?" Again, it's silent for more than a beat.

"Um, I'll be home in 15 minutes," I can hear Alex eventually say, maybe sounding a bit surprised. Good.

"Did you hear that?" Caroline asks.

"Yep. Thanks, babe. Now, your mom though..." That's not for Caroline to deal with. "You know what? Nevermind. I'll see you tomorrow, sweets. Tell Elodie I said hi."

"Okay, love you," is all she says back.

"Love you, too. Bye." And then she hangs up.

I send a quick text.

JESS

> Hi, heard you're feeling better. Can't wait to hang out tomorrow. Can I come early and help? Or just hang out?

Ten minutes later, a text comes through.

BRITAIN

Do you want to meet me at The Grounds for coffee around 9?

Why do I feel like she's breaking up with me?

> Yeah, I'd love that.

Great, see you then.

Great.

————

Steaks are on the counter coming to room temp, arugula salad is tossed, and the Prince playlist is hitting.

"I would," *pause*, "die for," *pause*, "you." I sing with his highness into my wooden spoon while pointing to Eden who claps for me.

"Ahem." *Right.* Alex clears his throat from the entrance to the mudroom. I smile and he doesn't return it. A second later, Caleb is right behind him. I immediately kill the music playing on my phone and set down the wooden spoon.

"Hi," I say generically to both of them. "Do you think we could talk for a quick minute?" My question is directed at

Alex. He nods, and Caleb grabs a beer from the fridge and heads out to the back deck. Alex leans against the entryway, arms crossed over his chest, looking closed off.

Once I hear the back door click shut, I immediately launch in. "I'm not fucking Damian. Not even remotely. We're friends. Just friends."

"Friends don't normally have to sneak off together." So he was eavesdropping.

"No, you're right, but when it's your best friend's ex, things get trickier..." He doesn't nod in understanding. He just stands there stoically. Still. "He's my friend. I don't know what you want me to say or do about that, but I'm not fucking him, don't intend to, and don't have those kinds of feelings for him."

Nothing back. Still.

"He called because Summer moved out. Gave back his ring, and he's feeling a little out of pocket this holiday. I invited him to stay with us to take the pressure off being around Brit and Liam. That's all."

Nothing.

"And I told him we could probably sneak off to grab a drink and talk because Brit doesn't know that we're friends like that because I don't know that she would understand. But if it's important to you, I will tell her."

"Okay, great." I'm surprised when he finally says something back.

"Okay, you want me...to tell Brit that I'm friends with her ex-husband?"

"Yes, honesty is important to me." Ahh, there it is.

"Okay, then I will," I say back with resolve. When he doesn't say anything more, I turn around to pull the food

264

processor off its stand, where the pesto is still sitting. Avoiding looking at him, I say, "And I want to be here, too, Alex." But when I turn back to look at him, he's gone, and so are the steaks off the counter. He's fucking stealthy.

———

"So, how'd you two meet?" Caleb and I ask at the same time. Both of us were probably desperate to break the icy tension that's settled over the dinner table from the moment we all sat down. I smile, and so does Caleb, but Alex just glares off distantly.

It's such a stark contrast to the man who took care of me last night, or fucked me in the early morning hours. So different from the man who fed my daughter breakfast or took me to a place he used to go with his mom. This man is night and day from the one who kissed me in the middle of Safeway because he wanted to. It's a reminder, I guess. The man still mostly hates me.

I motion to Alex. "Go ahead, sweetheart. Tell him how we met." I place my fork down and lean back in my chair slightly.

"She's Amy's cousin," he says coldly, if not dismissively. And *wow*, does it fucking hurt. The way he says it detaches any sentiment towards me. I'm just here *because* of Amy. Another reminder. Caleb makes a snorting sound when he lightly chokes on his pesto pasta. (Kale and walnut pesto. Honestly, it's my signature dish and I've wasted it on this shitty night. Nobody's appreciating it at this meal except Eden.)

"Yep, I'm just the next best thing to the original." I say

back just as cooly, looking Alex in the eyes as my own turn watery. I've taken, at most, one bite of food, so setting my napkin on the table, I stand calmly and start undoing the straps on Eden's highchair. I dust a couple pieces of pasta onto the floor, then grab her diaper bag and my purse, and head to go find dinner somewhere else. Anywhere the fuck else.

———

This car is nice. If I could ever afford this in the future, I'd absolutely buy it again. (The chances of me lasting a year with Alex to get the settlement are dwindling by the second.) As of now, I'm just praying to win custody, and nothing else.

"Maaaa!" Eden screams. She's getting fussy regardless of the smooth Volvo handling the mountain roads. She's probably starved.

I so badly want to drive to Brit's, but I'm not sure I'm welcome anymore, so instead we head to the main strip of town. I've got two options, Maggio's or Colton's. Pizza or the bar.

The parking lot is surprisingly crowded at Colton's, but a massive truck vacates as we pull in, luckily, so I make the split-second decision and park at Colton's. While I'm unbuckling Eden, I check out the exterior of the place. It looks like a big log cabin except for the sign out front that says "Coltons." That and the neon I can see glowing through the windows.

We walk up the front steps where there's a porch with rocking chairs, one occupied by a man in a cowboy hat smoking a cigar. I swear, you can't make this stuff up.

Inside, the place is just wood. Everywhere and every surface is just...wood. Bright, yellowy pine screaming at you behind lit-up neon. It smells slightly musty, with a hint of beer and fried food. *"Brit said this place was good. Give it a chance. Our takeaway last night was decent,"* I repeat to myself over and over.

There's a sign that says "Seat Yourself, Folks!" so I do. Not that there are many options, but I choose a table that's as far away from the rest of the locals as possible. There's a stack of highchairs in a corner by a jukebox, so setting down our bag, we head over to get one.

Mid-lift (mid-attempt) to unstack the chairs, a gentleman swings over to help me. He's got tattoos running up and down his arms and longish sandy colored hair thrown up into a man bun. Bet this is the hot owner. He has a bar rag hanging out the back pocket of his tight black jeans, and his flannel shirt is unbuttoned one too many, revealing more tats on his chest.

"I got it, take a seat. I'll be right over," the man says to me kindly.

He follows us back to our table, carrying the chair like it isn't made of solid wood and weighs nothing more than a feather. I get Eden strapped in, but she's already reaching for the caddy of sugar packets. The man that brought over the highchair notices. He leaves, but is back in a flash with some packets of crackers.

"She looks 'bout ready to eat," he says jokingly and I look at him with genuine gratefulness, unwrapping a packet and letting Eden go to town on the saltine.

"What can I get you to drink, darling?" I let him calling me darling slide. (Just this once.)

"A beer, any kind, and an apple juice for her?" I ask,

sounding more tired than I thought I was. He gives an almost sad smile back and leaves.

I pull out my phone, but this should come as no surprise, there are no new notifications. I grab the menu from where it's slid up against the wall and look for something that I know can be cooked well-done and I can split with Eden.

Hot bartender comes back with drinks and tells me the special. (A wagyu burger with bacon jam and tomato confit.) *Umm, say less, my friend.*

I order that and a grilled cheese. Then, mostly kidding, I toast my beer against Eden's apple juice. "Just you and me, baby."

I suck the tears back in, cue up *Bluey* on my phone, and sit back to people watch while we wait for our food. I should feel out of place. These people are not my people. Not a single city person, at least from what I can tell. But tonight, it doesn't bother me. It's like I've shed the last of my fucks, and now I'm just doing the damn thing. Which is surviving.

No one looks at me oddly. No one stares unkindly. In fact, a family with a small toddler also in a highchair occasionally glances over and makes heart eyes at Eden for her good behavior. I want to lean over and tell them I just got lucky tonight to make them feel better about their kid who's dumping salt all over the ground, but I don't.

I don't recognize a single soul, not that I should, and I think that's what makes me feel okay. I can get lost in the crowd again. In that way it feels like New York. No one sees me and thinks, "Oh, here's this woman whose life is mostly falling apart. Whose heart has been trampled on." I'm just a random person who showed up in their bar, and they'll never see me again.

"Jess, honey! What're you doing here all by yourself?" Sandy's twang has me sitting up straighter. I guess I spoke too soon.

"Hi, Sandy." I set my beer down and stand to give her a hug. (Sandy is Liam's mom. Probably the coolest member of their family, too.)

"We missed you the other day!" I tilt my head, confused. "At the ceremony. Brit said you were busy moving into the new house. Which I hear is fabulous, by the way." Her tone is utter kindness and positivity. I know she's not saying any of it to hurt me, but hurts nonetheless it does.

"Wedding ceremony?" Because what other ceremony would she mean?

"Yes...Brit didn't tell you?" Now she's looking confused.

"No, I had no idea." I try to sound unafflicted, but don't think it's possible. Sandy does this tight-lipped smile thing, then automatically slides into the chair opposite Eden, and I sit, too, because what the hell else am I supposed to do?

She sets her Kelly handbag down on the open chair beside her and I stare at it a bit wildly. Sandy looks like she could be a rancher's wife, plucked right out of *Yellowstone* or something. She's wearing cowboy boots, bootcut jeans, and a flannel shirt. Her white (not so blonde) hair is styled to perfection and she's rocking a diamond ring big enough to cut glass and a Hermes Kelly. *Good for her.*

She settles in and pulls out a menu. I almost ask what she's doing, but I know what she's doing, and so does she.

The hot bartender (should really find out his name so I stop objectifying him) comes back over when he sees the additional guest at our table.

"Hey, Sandy," H.B. (hot bartender) drawls out.

"Hey, Rick baby." (H.B. is now Rick. I think Sandy just added 'baby.' 'Rick baby' would be quite the mouthful.) (For some ladies, I'm sure it is.)

"You want your usual?" I swear he sounds more country than he did when he took my order. It's funny how people do that. New Yorkers sound more New York when they talk to each other, too.

"Yes, sir. And I'll take the cod in caper sauce. And then a special to go in a bit for Jim." *Cod?* From this place? Bold. Rick just knocks his knuckles against the edge of our table and disappears.

"Alright, sugar, who licked the red off your candy?" I shrug. Like I don't know when I absolutely know. "Alright well, how 'bout where's your fiancé?" Sandy asks.

"Probably sitting at the dinner table where I left him." Sandy breaks out in a gregarious laugh.

"I'm sure rightfully so, too!" A small smile breaks out on my face at her response. "And why, pray tell, aren't you at Britain's then?"

"She's mad at me." I shrug like I have no clue why, when I have absolutely every clue why.

"Hmm," Sandy says, mulling it over. Rick sets down what looks like a negroni in front of her before whisking away again.

Sandy picks up her drink and holds it up to me in cheers, "To absent friends." I clink my glass against hers and swallow my beer (and the lump in my throat.)

"You're gonna be there tomorrow, right?" Sandy asks after taking a drink. Honestly, am I? I might meet with Brit, tell her I'm friends with Damian, add that to the fact that I'm engaged to Alex, and she just might write me off.

"I was supposed to be. She asked me to meet for coffee tomorrow morning."

"You wanna talk about it?" The thing you have to understand about Sandy is the investment to her friendship is low. If I say no, she's gonna move on. She'll leave it alone. She'll start telling me gossip about townspeople I've never met. But if I say yes, she'll be all in, completely devoted.

"Sort of." I give her a small smile and she settles into her seat with a nod. I take a deep breath and dive in. I actually tell her all of it. ALL of it. (Things I haven't even told y'all.) Things I haven't talked about in years. Things I literally black out from my memory.

But I tell her about meeting Alex, the real story. The weird text messages. The weirder time we met in a bar. I tell her about Amy. I tell her about how I came to work for Brit (through Alex), and how I'll never understand why she hired me after everything that happened.

I tell her about Tommy (and Jamie), about how I can't be their third, about how I'm scared I'll always be the second-string quarterback. The B team. The practice squad. Whatever you want to call it.

And then I tell her about Alex and me now, the arrangement. She doesn't say anything, but her eyes go a bit wide at the truth. I tell her how I'm pretty sure I'm just some sort of weird consolation prize to Alex. The wife and daughter he could've had. It's fucked up, and it's weird, and I accept it because I want so badly for him to want me because I loved him the moment I saw him crouched over two headstones. And what kind of person does that make me?

Sandy leans forward, wiping a tear off my face. "Oh, sugar."

"Alright, ladies," Rick says, setting plates in front of Sandy and myself. In front of Eden, he sets down a grilled cheese already cut up into bite-sized pieces and an applesauce. Bless him.

"Thank you, so much. Really. You have no idea," I say to him, almost certain I'm still crying.

"Thank ya, baby." Sandy echoes me.

"Holler if you need something," Rick just barely gets out before backing off quickly. (Doesn't like tears, does he?)

"Well, honey, they say honesty is the best policy for a reason," Sandy says. It doesn't come off condescending like one might think. "You just gotta be brave enough to make that jump. And you will." She sounds so sure. Like everything will just be alright.

"And everything will be fine then?" I ask her, hoping she says yes. Because if Sandy says yes, I think I could really believe her.

"Oh heavens, no!" she laughs. "But at least you'll be able to sleep at night." *Fuck me.*

TWENTY-TWO

JESS

When we get back to the house. It's not even 8:00 P.M. but all the lights are off, casting the glow from the lights on the back deck into the house. Alex and Caleb are sitting around some sort of tubular fire pit thing.

The kitchen has been cleaned at least. Food processor has been disassembled and laid out to dry, and my stomach sinks. It was my first time cooking for him and it was shit. (Not my food, the night. The night was shit.) It's stupid stuff like that that sends me into a tailspin because it means a lot to me. And nothing to him. The only other man I've ever cooked for was Tommy.

I drop the diaper bag in the mudroom and head upstairs, grateful Alex is outside. This way I can grab pjs and wash my face without him here. As soon as I'm changed, I pull my hair up into a high pony and head to Eden's room for her nightly routine.

As we walk, Eden pulls on my hair and for the first time, I have this insane desire to chop it off. Like that's what's weighing me down. (Not the fact that I'm lying to people.) Maybe I'll do both, though. I'll tell the truth, cut off all my hair, and just live that villainous lifestyle. I'm hardly the princess in the tower. I need to stop acting like it.

We do bath, pjs, lather on lotion, read two books, and I sing. Eden goes down relatively easily, allowing me to plug my phone into the charger, hit the lights, and crawl into the daybed in her room to (hopefully) fall asleep.

The sleep will not come. I refuse to look at my phone, lest the time will taunt me, but I'm awake when I hear footsteps. Footsteps that stop outside the bedroom where I was supposed to sleep last night, but didn't. Then they resume and stop outside Eden's room.

My pulse quickens and my palms sweat, worried he'll poke his head in or something, but he doesn't. Then the footsteps fade when he enters his bedroom before coming back out into the hall again. The sound of footsteps grows nearer, but then they stop, and retreat again. And I let loose the breath I didn't know I was holding.

———

"Hey," his deep, raspy whisper rouses me.

"Hmm," I stretch my legs and yawn, but don't open my eyes.

"Come to bed?" I think it's a question, but then he's lifting me out of the daybed and my half-awake body betrays me by slipping my arms around his neck. My head falling a bit slack against his hard chest.

I open my eyes briefly, then take one slow blink, and he's lowering me onto my side of his bed. I immediately pull the pillow tighter and roll to face away from him, praying to just fall back asleep, but he doesn't let me. He pushes his large, warm (mostly naked) body against my back, and my fucking traitor body sighs out and relaxes. I try not to focus on it, otherwise I'll get pissed and that'll wake me up. And I'm pretty sure if I'm awake in a bed with Alex, it will eventually lead to fucking. And my heart can't take much more of that.

———

"Jess..." It's whispered, feather-soft across my temple as I feel his engorged cock slide against my ass while his fingers hold a biting grip on my hip. I instinctively grind my hips back before I can even tell my body not to. It just feels so fucking good. His cock, but also this feeling that he wants me.

His hand leaves my hip and slides into my pajama bottoms, finding me hot and ready for him and he growls in my hair. I go to turn towards him, but he stops me, flipping me onto my stomach.

It's so fast, I feel like the winds have been sucked out of my sails. I gasp slightly at the roughness, but then he's at my back pulling me up on all fours, and the asshole asks, "Do you want this?" His dick is there, pushing against the fabric of my pajamas.

I moan when he slides his dick forward, pushing it up so it strokes my clit through the thin fabric.

"Yes," I whisper back. And he slides my pajama pants down to my knees, letting them stay there. Then he lines himself up and pushes in. *Fuck*. Fucking hell. His cock has this curve to it that makes the most delicious sensation when he rubs against my inner walls. With him behind me and my ass up, the sensation is doubled.

My hands clench at the sheets, my toes curl, my walls tighten, and when he slams into me, I let out a quiet huff. And then his hands are at my scalp. I don't know if he's aware he does this, but each time we've had sex, his hand always finds its way into my hair. He tangles it. He tugs it. He lets his fingers glide through it. It feels amazing. I love this feeling that he has something about me that he loves.

"Louder." The command takes me by surprise. I'm not a moaner, a screamer, never have been, but the fact that he wants to hear me makes me swell with pride a little.

He slams into me from behind harder, and this time I let the pant leave my mouth with a little more gusto.

"More." The hand in my hair tightens. The hand gripping my hip grows stronger. "Tell me who's fucking you." He slams against me again, rocking the upholstered headboard against the wall. *Knock.*

"Alex," I reply.

"Louder." His voice is commanding and brash as he slams into me harder. *Knock* goes the bed.

"Alex!" I say louder. Slam. *Knock.* Grip tightens.

"One more time," he says gruffly. Slam. *Knock.* Hair gets pulled.

"Alex!" I practically scream. Slam. *Knock.* He lets go of my hair and pounds into me relentlessly. It still feels amazing, but there's another feeling that starts to come over me, and all of a sudden I want to vomit. *Is-Is this for show?* My walls are no longer clenching him tight. My toes slowly unfurl.

When I turn my head to look back at him, his eyes are

closed. *Spear, right through the abdomen.* Wind knocked straight from me. Searing pain slices at my insides and after I inhale deeply, I bury my face in the pillow with a cry.

He's just using me right now. *That's* this feeling. He's somewhere else and I could be anyone.

Slam. *Knock.* I feel like dying. My body is only being held up by the hands that are holding my hips.

Slam. *Knock.* My chest heaves at the pain. He hates me. Still. I'll always be less-than in his eyes.

Why am I here? I turn to look back once more, hoping he'll have eyes wide open that see me. That see how much he's hurting me, but when I look back, his eyes are still clenched.

"Alex," I say softly, same as my body. There's nothing taut about this. My body isn't straining, clenching, racing to the other side like his is. He eases up at my voice. His pace slows, his grip loosens, and he eventually comes to a complete stop.

I stare back down at the pillowcase, tears streaming down my face. "If you're gonna use me, at least be a man about it and look me in the eyes." Goosebumps break out all over my body and then he's pulling out of me.

He practically stumbles out of bed, pushing away from me. Like he was fucking sleepwalking and ended up fucking me instead. (Maybe he was.)

My hips slowly slide down to the bed and my chest heaves with a sob. I pull my pants back on and sit up. But Alex is just standing a few feet back from the bed looking stricken.

"I know you think I'm a shitty person, but what you're doing is worse," I say. I slip out of bed, and when my feet hit the soft rug, I have to fight to stay standing after the unrelenting way he was using my body.

I don't look him in the eyes as I get up and walk to the guest room down the hall. I use the bathroom, then crawl into the bed and cry because I let him use me. I want him more than the pain bothers me. (I know I'm a masochist.) But I can't do it. I can't be Amy. I'm not loud when I'm having sex. I don't need some bro to hear it in the middle of the night. I'm not some show pony you can just buy, which is exactly what he thinks of me, isn't it?

Well, fuck him.

Fuck this house.

Fuck this town.

Fuck all of it.

———

I pull out the card that's for emergencies only and press the purchase button. I wait till six, and then text my old contact, James, to ask if he'll drive me to the airport after I meet with Britain. I know it's Thanksgiving and all, but hopefully it's early enough it doesn't deter his day.

I don't want to make a big thing out of this. I want to just slink away as quickly and as tacitly as possible. (Does that make me a coward? Yeah, so what?)

I was in Eden's room at four, quietly packing her suitcase. I carried it down the steps as silently as possible and put it by the door in the mudroom for when we leave later to go talk to Brit. It sounds shady. It probably is. But I don't want to see him look at me in the light of day…maybe ever. Every time I start to think about his eyes clenched shut (picturing Amy probably), I want to vomit.

The soreness between my legs physically and emotionally hurts every time I take a step. And I want to take so many steps. Away from this place, away from these people, away from my life...

When Eden wakes up at 7:00, I try my best to get her to go back to sleep. We have a long day ahead of us and the more time I spend in her room, the less time I have to spend out there, potentially running into people I have no desire to see.

By 7:30, there's no holding her back. She's hungry, so I take her downstairs to feed her, trying to act as casually as possible, but my body locks up when I find him in the kitchen. Making pancakes. *Fucking psychopath.*

He looks over and stares at me, almost vacantly. He still doesn't see me. *He never will, Jess.*

I strap Eden into the highchair, pour her a bottle of milk, and drop Cheerios on her tray. Still not looking at him, I ask, "I need to change really quick. Would you watch her for just a moment?"

His voice is barely audible, but eventually he says, "Yeah." I run upstairs quickly and try to think about the best way to do this. But unless I haul down a suitcase which will inevitably draw questions, there's no way I'm getting any of my clothes or belongings. And honestly, you know what? That's fine.

I throw on my best bra, I double up on underwear (because apparently I'm a psychopath, too), and then layer thoughtfully. (Tank top, long-sleeved shirt, sweatshirt, and a jacket over top. And leggings under jeans.) I'm no mathematician, but I just made at least six outfits out of one. (Feel free to do the actual math and then shame me with it.)

I grab my toothbrush before heading back downstairs. I'll have to buy toiletries and a bag at the airport.

When I get to the kitchen, Alex is sitting beside Eden absentmindedly feeding her pancakes. I want to say or do something that'll make him go away, but again, that would lead to attention which would lead to talking which would lead to me crying. Because I'm coming to see that every time I think Alex and I could be something, it'll end. With me crying. And I'm not even a crier.

"I can do that," I say to his back and when he doesn't put up a fight, just stands and moves over, I don't know if I feel relief or misery. Relief he got up, miserable because he caved so easily.

I feed Eden until I'm certain she can't take any more, change her one last time, and then make my way to the mudroom for our bags and keys.

"Do you need help?" Alex asks me from the kitchen.

"No, just going to meet your sister for coffee at The Grounds."

"Okay."

I don't say anything back. I don't say goodbye. I just open the side door and wheel the little suitcase out to a car that doesn't belong to me so I can go play family in someone else's life. Again.

―――――

I'm early. I knew I would be. But still, a part of me is surprised to see this place is actually open.

When I walk into The Grounds, a bell rings over the door and Sandy greets me. "Happy Thanksgiving!" she says merrily, wearing a brown turtleneck that's the same color as her boots under a floral apron. She's the picture of matronly charm.

"Hey, Sandy." She looks me over, reading me like a large-print book.

"Honey, it's not that cold out." Yeah, I know.

"Just can't shake a chill, might be coming down with something," I lie, then say a small prayer willing Brit to get here already. She's a punctual person. She'll be here soon.

"You want a medicine ball? A coffee?" The only thing I think I could actually stomach would be ginger tea so I decline.

"No, thanks. I'll just wait for Brit over here." I point to a table off to the side, away from the other customers enjoying their normal lives.

I take a seat and my leg bounces. My phone vibrates, but I don't take it out of my pocket to check. Too nervous.

At 8:55, Brit walks in looking like a goddess compared to me. Fresh blowout, fresh-faced, like she woke up naturally rosy cheeked and happy. I bet she did, actually.

"Hi," I say first, getting her attention, but I don't stand up to hug her and she doesn't stand there expectantly waiting for more either.

"Hey," she says with a sad smile.

"Heard you got married. Congrats."

Her cheeks go pink. "Thanks. It was just parents and kids," she says as an explanation.

I shake my head like it's no big deal because it isn't. The

biggest deal now is that I unload and confess my sins, then blow this town.

"That's okay. Sounds perfect." I try to reassure her with a smile, but she frowns. That's not the answer normal Jess would give. She knows it. Well, guess what? Normal Jess doesn't exist anymore. Desperate Jess? Oh yeah, she's present and accounted for. Soul-crushed Jess? Also here.

"Listen, I want to tell you the truth...about everything. I just need you to listen, okay?" She nods. And I unleash.

Much like it was with Sandy last night, I tell her how I first met Alex. I even tell her when I fell in love with him. I tell her that we hurt each other and that I'd circle back to that in the end. I tell her about my potential custody issues, and my inability to be a functioning responsible adult who can care for my own child independently. And she listens to all of it, wholeheartedly.

I tell her about Alex's offer and how I jumped and how I thought maybe things between us could be real, but they're not because we still have too many issues and he still hates me.

"So, I guess the first thing to tell you is I've been keeping something from you, and I don't want any of this to hurt you. I really don't. You always came first to me." Brit takes a deep inhale, bracing herself. "Damian and I are friends." I let out a little exhale, feeling the weight of some of the lies lifted. Though certainly not all of them...

"Oh...really?" she asks confusedly, but sincerely. "I thought maybe you guys were...you know..."

I look at her crazy. "Were you know...what?!"

"Knocking boots." She shrugs.

"No! That is not at all how I see him." My stomach sinks

because I have to unload this final bomb. I feel like I could throw up again, and not because Alex anger-banged me, but because I can see the end of our friendship right here, right now.

With Eden still perched on my leg, I lean forward and hug Brit. (Snapshot title: *"Heartwarming Embrace Between Best Friends."*) (That would be a lie.) It's like the opposite of the kiss of death. It's Judas giving Jesus a kiss goodbye. You know it's the last time.

"Brit, you've been my best friend for so many years, and you've been so good to me, really. Way better than I ever deserved." I sniffle because I'm crying now, and she extends her arm, taking my hand in hers.

"It was a lot of years ago..."

"What was?" Brit asks.

The sound of the door swinging open forcefully draws our attention. (Well, everyone's attention.)

Alex takes a step in and scans the place frantically, eyes landing on me. Hate it immediately. Don't like it. I wish he'd look away.

"You're leaving?" he asks brusquely. Only having taken three steps, he comes to stand in front of me.

I straighten my spine and fidget under his gaze. With me sitting down and him towering over me like this, I've never felt so uncomfortable. My pits start sweating, either from the heat of his temper or the fact that I'm dressed for the frozen tundra. I don't know.

"Yes." It doesn't come out as strong as I would have hoped.

"And you weren't going to tell me?" He sounds genuinely

pissed. Maybe even a bit hurt. But you know what? Fuck him. I'm the one he hurt. *Me!* Don't I matter?

"No!" I shout back. "So you could pretend to feel some sort of way about it? Guess what, Alex? You're the only one pretending! It's real for me, all of it, and it's *fucking* killing me." I look at where I'm bouncing my child on my leg. Fucking terrible mother, I know. Add it to the list. "I'm not *her*. I'll never be *her*. And trust me, I'll walk away and it won't be like her leaving because I'm. Not. Her. The end."

He scoffs at me. "No, you certainly aren't her. She would never leave without saying goodbye. You know what? I'm sorry I tried to help." He looks at me, then looks at Brit. "It's not real for her either. She wouldn't know the truth if it smacked her in the face." I look at him like he actually did just slap me. He might as well have. "She tell you yet?" he asks Brit.

"Yes, now shut the fuck up before you ruin everything," Brit says to Alex in my defense, surprising me.

"Well, just in case, let me fast forward the process for you. That best friend of yours," he nods towards me.

"Alex, stop—" I try, but he talks over me.

"Yeah, her. Well, she fucked your husband." Brit and I both gasp in shock.

TWENTY-THREE

September 23, 2017

Jess

I pull up the one and only picture I have on my phone of Alex. It's a bit grainy. Phone cameras weren't as amazing then as they are now. But there he is, squatting down, baseball hat worried between his hands, focus intense. *My heart.* This man has my heart and I haven't even kissed him. I haven't even been on a date with him yet!

It's so crazy. The feelings I have for him are tenfold anything I've ever felt before and all we've done is talk. It started out after he texted me about the job opening. At first, it was little things. Like things I should see or do or eat once I move to DC.

ALEX

Pandas, gotta go see the pandas.

That text was followed by a photo of a panda lazing about.

The best view of the city is from the Old Post Office, don't let anyone try to tell you differently.

I know everyone says you have to eat at Ben's Chili Bowl...and I'll tell you the same. It's practically mandatory to get a DC driver's license. Or so I've heard.

And then it shifted.

ALEX

What are you doing?

JESS

With my life? Right now? Tomorrow?

Right now.

Right, of course. I'm watching a movie.

Which one?

Don't laugh.

???

The Parent Trap.

Like the Lindsay Lohan one?

...yeah.

Why?

It's my comfort movie.

What's yours?

Top Gun

Ha!

Wait srsly?

And you told me not to laugh...

And then there were hundreds. And it was books, and things we saw throughout the day. And what we were eating until I realized I hadn't gone out once the entire month of July, and I'd never been happier. I had unconsciously made myself exclusive to this man. A man I wasn't entirely sure was feeling the same way about me as I was about him, but I figured you don't text someone upwards of fifty times a day without being interested.

And then September came, and I applied for the job when he sent me the rec. I might not have had all the qualifications, but I had enough, and I could fake the funk if needed. But I was still surprised when I got a call to schedule an interview. *September 25th.* In a sick way, I was glad because I knew Alex would be in town for Amy and Tally.

JESS

My interview is the 25th. Was wondering if you'd want to meet up the weekend before?

ALEX

Sure.

The response was maybe lukewarm, but I think he was just playing it cool. Because he then proceeded to text me a list of bars and restaurants we could potentially meet at. All the locations were near my hotel and the office where I'd be interviewing. It was cute.

And then he called me for the first time on September 16th. At first I thought he butt dialed me. So when I answered, I didn't say anything for the first couple of moments.

"Jess?"

"Oh, yeah. Hi."

He laughed. "Just checking that I haven't been messaging with some rando for the last month or so." Then I laughed.

"Nope, it's me." Though I'm probably still a rando.

"Haha, alright. So...what are you doing?"

It lasted 39 minutes. And then he was calling me every night. We talked about childhoods. (Mostly me talking about that bit.) We talked about our favorite everythings. Favorite season, favorite vacation. We talked big and small. And I'd never shared as many things with anyone as I did with him.

So standing in my hotel room tonight, getting ready to go on a first date with the person I think might be *my person*, I can't sit still. I'm up, I'm down. I'm changing my shoes. *Loafers. That seems like a DC thing. But I'm not a DC girl. Prada pumps are the right call. But what if I over exaggerated his height in my mind and I tower over him? You will not tower over Alexander Palomino. Probably ever.*

The inner monologue goes on for far too long when I finally allow myself to look at the clock and realize I'm going to be late. *Fuck!* I purposefully wouldn't let myself look because time was ticking by so slowly. Until it wasn't. Prada heels it is because I'm grabbing my clutch and walking out the door like this is the moment that starts the rest of my life.

It feels like one of those nights when the stars align. When everything feels transcendent. And when I step into the loud and crowded bar, even though I'm nervous, I feel... sublime. Otherworldly. I'm about to have my real-life meet cute. Just like in *Serendipity*.

I spot him easily, standing at a high-top table. He's definitely just as big as I remember, if not bigger. And he's even sexier without the beard. (Don't get me wrong — Alex plus facial hair is fucking delectable) But now I can see his face. *Love that face.*

I did not just think that.

I start moving towards him and it feels like it's all in slow motion. I watch as some other guy joins him at his table and they start talking. They're obviously familiar with one another, the way the other guy places a hand on Alex's shoulder. Their backs are towards me, but the other guy is just a hair shorter, and with shoulders that aren't nearly wide enough to be considered linebacker status like Alex's.

They're still talking when I finally get close, so I wait for the server carrying a large tray of drinks to walk between the tight tables in the crowded oyster bar so that I can pass around to be in front of them. And while I'm waiting, I hear...

"It's not like that. She's a nobody. Just need to check the box so I can leave. She's just a fucking bump in the road. Fucking hate distractions like this." Alex pauses to audibly scoff, *"And she's late."*

Wow. I actually take a step back. And then another. Honestly, it's miraculous that I didn't keel over and die because that's exactly how I feel. Like I'm dying. This is worse than being catfished. He's fucking amazing and gorgeous and funny, but he's not actually interested? Fucking wasting my time, stringing me along? I turn and head back towards one of the other bars on the other side of the restaurant.

(Why does a restaurant have four different bars? Because when you live in DC, apparently it's necessary to be drunk. Message received. Plus this place is fucking ancient. Literally the word "old" is in the name.)

"Excuse me!" I lean forward on the bar to get the bartender's attention. When they notice me, I ask, "Shot of Don Julio?" *Por favor. Rápido.* I say that part in my head.

I can't remember the last time my soul has been crushed like this. Not when Donny got Nicole pregnant (while we were together). Not when my mom died even. I want to cry so bad, but like fuck am I ruining how good I look for that man.

The bartender brings me the shot and a check, and I drop a couple twenties down. I slam back the shot, no lime or salt needed here. I throw my hair back over my shoulders and strut back to the oyster bar to make him regret making a fool out of me.

This time, the world doesn't move in slow motion when I approach. This time he sees me coming, but there's no glimmer in his eye, there's hardly even an ounce of recognition. It's not like the movies at all. It's like meeting your distant cousin twice removed because your mom made you or something.

I give a sort of sickly sweet, fake smile (probably the same one I'll use at my interview on Monday) and the fucker doesn't even smile back. But his friend does. Well, okay then.

I flash the friend a genuine smile and my cheeks heat because I want to cry that Alex wasn't real.

"Hey!" *Too much, tone it down.* "Glad we could catch up." I extend a hand to Alex. Business like. When he takes it, I make sure to firm up my grip. No limp hands here. Back straight, head high, nose up.

"Hey." His tone is monotonous. Like this is just very much a generic acquaintanceship and not like I've spent more quality time connecting with him than I have with any other human being. Ever.

I turn my attention to the friend instead. "Hi, I'm Jess." I extend my hand to him and he takes it, returning my genuine smile.

"I'm Damian, nice to meet you." I notice a dimple pops when his smile finally breaks. That's cute.

He's cute. (The friend.) He has sort of moppish, reddish hair. I wouldn't call it red, and I definitely wouldn't call it orange, but also wouldn't call it brown. And he's tall, with a charming smile and a nice body. Wearing a suit that probably costs more than most people's first car.

I walk around to stand on the side of the table closest to Damian, and set my clutch between Alex and myself. A physical barrier of sorts.

"First night in DC and I'm already meeting a cute local?" I lay it on thick. I can see Alex's eye twitch out of the corner of my eye, but he says nothing.

"Nah, I wouldn't call myself a local. I live across the border in Virginia. But cute, yes, I will accept that," he says with a bit of a bashful chuckle.

As soon as Alex goes to interject, his phone starts ringing. Damian and I both look at him. There's some sort of internal debate going on. Because he's looking at his phone and looking at us, then the phone.

"You should take it. I'd hate to keep you from anything important!" I'm overselling it.

Alex just clears his throat, "I'll be right back." And as he walks away, I admire his ass in his jeans. *Stop it.*

"So..." I laugh awkwardly turning to face Damian. "Sorry I just got dumped on you."

"Ha, no, I wasn't thinking that at all, Jess." There's something about the way he just said my name. Like he remembered it, like I'm not forgettable. Like I'm not a nobody. I give him a wan smile.

"It does sort of feel like we just got set up on some weird blind date, though, doesn't it?"

Damian chokes on his beer in response, then eventually starts laughing.

"Yeah," he chuckles, "the, uh, setup," then shakes his head, "it was all wrong. Alex wasn't smooth about it. At all."

"Is he usually so emotionally stunted, your friend?" I ask him.

"Yes, actually. But it's what endears him to me." I laugh at that. Right, maybe that's what I need. A friend.

"Okay. Are you suggesting I go out and find a friend who's a bigger mess than myself to make me feel better?" Damian raises both eyebrows and sort of nods like I couldn't have hit the nail on the head any harder.

"That's not what I was saying *exactly*, but don't think it could hurt," he answers with a cheeky smile that makes me take a second look at him.

"Okay, great. Are you a mess? If yes, would you like to be friends?" I ask him, completely straight faced. He laughs this big warm laugh. For a second, when he laughs, it snuffs out the pain of earlier.

"Check yes or no? Huh?" I shrug at his question. "What happens if I check yes?" He asks with a smile. *I think* — yes, definitely — he's flirting with me.

"If you check yes, we're going to have an amazing night. If you check no, we'll stand here and blindly watch this UFC fight playing in this fine establishment until someone gets knocked unconscious." I wonder if some of our country's greatest politicians ever stood in this exact spot and had money on our society devolving to watching people get pummeled nearly to death on tv.

"And also, do you like this?" I motion to the tv.

"No, but I like the distraction," he says a bit solemnly. Okay, I can agree with that.

He stealthily pulls a pen out of his jacket pocket and draws a square on his cocktail napkin. He writes yes beside it, then checks the box. He slides the napkin over to me and I give him a smile.

"Alright then, drink up. Big night ahead of us." He downs what's left of his beer and then I take his hand and lead him out to an atrium that leads to the other side of the building. *Fuck you, Alex. And goodbye.*

———

"I haven't eaten, so if there's any chance of me lasting till 2:00 A.M. for dancing, this girl has gotta eat. So Jumbo Slice or Ben's? Your choice."

Damian stares at me like he might be in love before eventually saying, "Jumbo Slice." That's what I was thinking, too.

"Great!" After the shot at the other place and the three beers we drank playing pool and skee ball at a very seedy establishment, I'm feeling warm and nice and not at all like an epic failure for putting all my hopes and dreams into a man who turned out to be a farce.

Damian leans forward and tells our cab driver where to go while I quickly kick my heels off and stretch my toes before sliding them back on. I notice Damian watching me as I do, a sort of heat in his eyes.

"I mean, foot fetishes aren't really my thing...but I could be open." I say it semi-jokingly and he starts laughing his ass off. When he settles back in his seat, heaving a deep breath, I slip a hand on his leg and whisper, "Really this is a judgment-free zone here, D." His cheeks turn bright pink. And he blinks a couple times, looking down at my hand and then back at me.

"Has anyone ever told you you're beautiful?" I laugh at his *corny* fucking line. But honestly, for as corny as it is, not that many people have when I actually think about it. People always say "pretty." Or "hot." The word "beautiful" doesn't get tossed around nearly enough.

"Yeah, I think a gay guy at the subway once said it in passing, but I think he also said it to the 90-year-old woman standing beside me. Not that she's not beautiful, too! Because beauty comes in a lot of different—"

His mouth over mine shuts me up. My stomach sinks. *Not Alex.* But then my heart soars because this man has been a *fucking* pleasure to be with. All night.

I slip my tongue into his mouth and he groans, sending a sort of pride and need pulsing through my veins. He bites my lip, and I fucking love it. And yeah, maybe I'm just throwing my problems at this situation. Maybe I'm throwing caution to the wind. My question here is: Why? The fuck? Not?

He finally releases my face when the cab comes to a stop, but not before gazing down on me first. There's something he leaves unsaid, but I have the strangest feeling. I want to know what he's thinking...

"Ahem"...and the cab driver is less than enthused with the wait for us to vacate.

We both sort of stumble onto the sidewalk laughing, and yeah, this is nice, too. Damian might not know everything about me. He doesn't know my favorite movie or song, but he doesn't have to. We can still have a good time. This still gives me hope that my person is out there. And maybe, just maybe, they won't know a single thing about me, and they'll still want me, regardless.

When I refuse to share a slice of pizza with the man, he actually pulls me into his side and wraps a hand around my hip.

And I like it.

He promptly orders two slices. Then, like a gentleman, says nothing when I only eat half of mine. But he does smile aggressively when he watches me try and sneak it into the trash can.

"Okay, where to now?" I dust my hands off as Damian throws his greasy, very empty plate away. "Look! See," I point to the empty plate, "this is why we didn't share. You wanted a whole slice!" He laughs, and we start walking.

"Well, just for that, we're walking instead of cabbing." *Fuck.* I gently push him in fake annoyance, but he grabs my hand and pulls me back. Then he just holds my hand. And it feels fine. Normal even. Maybe even more than fine.

"So, you know where we're going then?" I ask.

"Yup. You said dancing. This place does dancing."

———

So this place is really good for dancing. There are four floors and a rooftop. Each floor is a dance floor and is playing a specific kind of music.

First floor is for smooth jams. It's an older crowd. Very cool, but not tonight. Second floor: hard rock. Very goth. Love it, but also not tonight. Third floor is a mixture and I immediately recognize the song playing. It's Mac Miller, but also this indie song that's hot right now.

"Ahh, I love this song!" I exclaim loudly to Damian, pulling on his suit coat to get him to stop walking toward the stairs.

"Really?" he shouts back. I nod enthusiastically, then dance the two of us over to the main floor.

I take a deep breath, looking at Damian's blue eyes, and then I just let loose. I let the music guide me, take *us*, and it feels good. The rest of the world sort of just...fades away around us. And it's just him, and me, and I'm not thinking of what was, I'm just here. Right now. And it feels better than good that he has a hand on my hip and he's dancing with *me*.

At one point he even breaks away and dances on his own, and there's just something so disarming about watching this man. Clearly a serious businessman, who is a fucking joy to be around, get down in this bar and let loose. He's a mess, clearly, but then so am I.

"Hey," I walk up to him and grab his chin with my hand. He smiles back at the touch, pulling my body into his. "Let's be messy together, yeah?" I ask and he nods, threading his hands around my waist and pulling us together flush.

And with that, he sinks his mouth onto mine and we get lost, this time together. We're swaying and moving and then we're moving away.

We're in the hall, my back against the wall, his tongue on my neck when I whisper out, "I want you."

He gives me a look in return that does something to me. "I needed you," he whispers back.

That simple admission has me throwing in the towel. I'm done fighting. I'm done pretending. Maybe casual sex is all there is for me in this world. This man needs me. I want him. *Fuck it.* I drag him to the bathroom, shut the door, lock it, and hop on the sink.

The man doesn't need any instructions. He's between my legs, sliding my dress up with a hand gripping my thigh. His mouth is on mine in a way that makes me feel fucking worshiped. And then my hands are pushing his suit jacket down.

When he releases my mouth to trail down my chest to where my nipples are taught through the thin slip dress, I tell him again, "I want you."

He nods against me preparing to go to his knees as he says, "No condom, though, Jess." But I stop him, opening my clutch to pull one out and he stares at it like it's a precipice.

"I think it's pretty clear we need each other," I say at last. And then like a dam breaks, he's unleashed and it's the best kind of consuming. He can't get close enough to me, he can't get his kiss deep enough. I've become his greatest desire and I have his complete focus. Damian is focused on me. Just me.

"God, Jess, you...fuck." There's so much desperation, on

both sides, words die before a coherent thought forms. I'm grasping and unbuckling his belt, and then we're both pushing his pants down. My underwear is pulled to the side. He pulls me to the edge of the sink and drives his rock-hard cock into me at the same time as he sinks his tongue into my mouth.

I grab at him from behind and grind as he thrusts. It's messy, but beyond satisfying. The sounds of skin slapping, his smooth shoes squeaking against the dirty tile floor, his groans, my pants; it's a cacophony of indiscretion and I love it. It's a symphony of desperation and I fucking *love* this feeling. This high.

It's like when the beat drops and you just *need*. You need to move. To bang your head. To thrust. To ride.

"Jess...I..." Damian stutters. I clench a little harder and ride against him, my back arching, my hands clutching at his ass, and then I'm coming, and so is he.

The explosion that rocks me, starting at my pelvis and expanding, is nothing like what I expected. It's more. *This man* is so much more than I expected. And I smile through the fight to catch my breath.

"I needed this so bad," he practically cries onto my shoulder as he releases into me. We both take a moment to look down at where he's continuing to thrust against me as I ride out the orgasm I didn't know I needed either. And suddenly, the casualness of it all fades and this feels like something else...

There's this kindred intimacy we're sharing that I haven't had with anyone else before. The chemistry, the connection feels tangible, like a blanket thrown over your lap on a cool day. Like the first ice cream cone on the first hot day of summer. Like this, all of it just makes sense. It belongs.

I stroke his neck softly as we both start to come down. I run my hands through his hair, appreciating him, thankful that we could give each other something we both needed. I no longer just feel what's happening right now in my pelvis, now there's that tightening in my chest. *I like him.*

And then I realize he actually is crying. "Oh my god, Damian. Are you okay?!" I'm pushing his face up off my shoulder so I can look at him. With his cock still twitching in my body, he kisses me and the pressure in my chest increases. *Oh.* I *like him* like him.

He pulls out a second later and looks me in the eyes. "This *was* an amazing night, and one I'll never forget. Thank you. For wanting me." He runs a thumb across my cheek, but there's something so fucking sad in his words. I want to ask more, but then there's banging on the door. *Shit.*

He trashes the condom and I pee, then wash hands expeditiously. I'm still straightening my dress when Damian opens the door and is met with a fist to the face. *The fuck?*

"What the fuck?!" I yell, then turn around to move to Damian's side where he's clutching his nose.

When I look up, there's Alex. He's fucking fuming and I'm hit with the overwhelming urge to cry. I never once felt like I was doing anything wrong all night long...except now. He's looking at me like I'm trash and I want to scream at him, *"Well, you didn't want me, what do you expect me to do!?"* But then he's yelling at Damian.

"You fucking piece of shit! If you don't tell *her*, I fucking will," he yells at Damian with a finger pointed in his face.

He looks at me, and my chest caves inward.

"*You*," his chilling malice slices me open, "were a mistake. You coming *here* was a mistake." And then he's storming out, pushing through the crowd to get the fuck away from us as quickly as possible.

"Who is *her?*" I ask Damian, a bit bewildered.

He looks at me a bit oddly and says, "I'm sorry." And then security guards are escorting us out, and Damian goes out the back and I get taken out the front where I stand like a fucking idiot for far too long looking around at the rest of the world just taking place. How can the world just keep going when I feel like my soul has been ripped from my body, wrung out, then hung up to be stoned to death while a 12th-century woman yells "Shame!" at me over and over?

TWENTY-FOUR

THEN

Alex

I pick up the call as soon as I clear the door. It's a recording like it always is with a code at the end. The code tells me where I'm supposed to be and when. *Not now.* I hang up and immediately call Blanks. It rings four times, and I'm about to give up and start calling the others when he finally picks up.

It's loud. He's out. *Fuck.* He never goes out.

"Let me guess, you just got a call?" I'd ask how he knows, but I'm guessing he's with other unit members who also just got a call.

"Yeah, but I'm in DC. Can you cover down?" I can hear some girl talking in the background. *Fuck me.* He never goes out to meet girls.

"You're killing me, Pal," Blanks groans. I can picture him in the bar, beer in hand, head tilted back in annoyance.

"I'll owe you."

He groans again. "How big a deal is this, really?"

"I'm meeting her. I-I'm with *her* now. I just fucking walked out of the bar to take the call, and now I'm out here talking to you while Damian charms the pants off of her as we speak probably!" Might be too loud.

"Whoa whoa, calm down. Who is *her*?"

I pace in front of the Old Ebbitt Grill and run a hand down my mouth and over my chin, preparing for the shock that comes with admitting this.

"I know I said I'd never get married. Ever again. But if I did, it would be with her." There's a sound of a bottle crashing over the line.

"Wow," is all Blanks says back.

"Yeah." I'm still pacing, running my hand through my hair because every minute I spend out here talking is one less minute I've had with her. "Come on, man, please?" I'm fucking begging, for this woman. Never thought I'd see the day. But here I am, fucking ten minutes from getting down on one knee. Not that I plan on doing that tonight, but I could see it soon. Sooner than later. Just need to get off this call and get Damian to go the fuck home to his wife instead of moping around some oyster bar like a fucking loaner.

"Alright. But I'm the best man at your wedding. Fucking promise it. It's not Damian, it's me." He's being one thousand percent serious.

"Done."

"Deal." We both hang up at the same time. Don't like goodbyes.

I walk back into the restaurant like this is the start of a new chapter or some shit. People like me don't get second chances. I won't fuck it up this time.

I walk into the oyster bar and find our table has been turned over to a group of interns. Heart rate spikes. *There are seven exits and twelve windows, not including the ones that open to the atrium.* And there are four bars. Maybe they moved? I know they didn't fucking move, but I still check each bar before walking out to the atrium to see if they're there, too. They're not.

What started as an off feeling when Jess showed up has turned into an all-out infestation growing rapidly, seizing my lungs. It's the start of a panic attack. So I quickly find an empty hallway in the business side of the building and I box breathe. And focus. I pull out my phone and call Damian. No avail. I call Jess. Nothing.

Calm down. It's not like they've been taken. It's fucking DC for christ's sake.

I break out the big guns and call Brit. But she doesn't fucking answer either, probably because it's bed time. I pace the hallways, and when no one calls me back, I just start walking. Head on a swivel, I walk the streets of DC in hopes I might find her. All while the gut feeling is telling me I won't.

———

I walk down U Street on a fucking hunch, but nothing. When my phone vibrates, I immediately slide to answer without even checking to see who it is.

"Hello?" I sound like I'm out to kill. Probably am.

"Oh my, are we in a bad mood, too?" Britain.

"Just annoyed."

"Yeah, you and Elodie both. I just spent two hours helping her construct a model replica of a pyramid just for her to tell me Cambri's mom did it better."

"Little shit. Hey, don't mean to cut you off, but I'm supposed to meet Damian, but he's not answering his cell. Can you Find-My-Phone him?" This might be a slightly unethical ask, but fuck it. Also, there's no guarantee that Jess is with him, but I get the feeling she is.

"Ugh, fine." I wait a couple moments and Brit reads off an address to me. She doesn't care what it's to or where it's at. It's almost like she doesn't care at all.

"Thanks. Gotta go."

"Okay! By-" I hang up on her before she even gets to fully say goodbye. I quickly hail a cab and head for Adams Morgan where Damian has exactly zero fucking business being at tonight.

———

I check each floor and then I check again when I see what looks like the back of my friend's reddish head entering a bathroom. Slight relief at that. I double check the floor again, for Jess, but don't find her, so I go to the bathroom and wait.

And I fucking wait.

It's fucking loud in the club, but I get closer to the door, and I hear....*no*.

Don't want to believe it, but I put my ear back to the door again. *And fuck*. It's people having sex. It's not loud and overt, but it's there.

I roll up my sleeves and bang on the door. And then there's a decidedly female voice, that I instinctively know is Jess' and my stomach turns. I actually have to bow over to fight down the nausea. It feels like taking a meat cleaver straight to the chest. The pain is so intense.

I hesitate to push in when I hear the door unlock, but as soon as it's open and I see Damian's face and those eyes that tell me everything without telling me, I know.

I throw the punch and he takes it standing. He sees it coming and takes it. He doesn't block or duck. He just stands there, and then he's the one bowed over. I look at Jess who rushes to him, screaming something, but I don't hear her over the buzzing in my ears. I've never been so angry in my entire fucking life. Never. I want to scream at her. I want to shake her and ask why, but that's shit Ray would do. And I am not him. I'll never be him.

Instead I yell at my best friend that if he doesn't tell my sister what he's done, I will.

I have everything and nothing to say to her, so I tell her she's a mistake. All of it was.

And then I have to get away. The pain in my chest pulls tight. My vision tunnels, I'm running down the stairs and out into the street searching for an alley, a darkened stairwell, *anything* where I can push myself against a wall and calm down before I die. But really what's left? What the fuck am I scared of dying for? I've got nothing left to lose. The pain eases slightly.

Fuck it all. Honestly.

———

Jess

I don't call Alex. He doesn't call me. We don't text. It's just cold turkey.

I got the job. Nice woman. She's about my age. Pretty, but dresses like she's 55 and not 29.

It's October 2nd and the first day at my new job in the city I just moved to. Admittedly, it's been a bit of a tumultuous start, but at the end of the day, we all make mistakes. That whole night was mine. Meeting Alex. Leaving with his friend, who very clearly is in some sort of serious relationship. It's not like he told me, but even if he had, I don't know that it would have made a difference. Because that's just me. (I can be honest and accept that I'm not a model human being, okay?) (It's freeing, honestly. You should try it, too.)

I'm meeting my new boss in her office today, and this is good. I'm feeling great in my pencil skirt, Prada heels, and fitted white blouse. Classic, chic. Ready for the new Jess.

When the elevator opens, my new boss is standing right outside waiting for me.

"Great! You're punctual, love it!" She high fives me, and then leads me to a back corner office.

"So my office is up here at the end. You'll have the cubicle right outside of it, though honestly, if I'm here, expect to spend most of your time in mine." As we walk, she talks. About the perks of the company. (Onsite masseuse sounds lovely.)

"And this is it!" Her office is large. I mean way bigger than I expected. There's a seating area with a large leather sofa and two upholstered lounge chairs. There's bookshelves covered in kid's art and family photos. And then her desk is a monster, complete with three monitors.

I look through the family photos as she sits at her desk to settle. But I freeze where I'm at when I spot a very familiar face staring back at me. Two of them, actually.

"How do you know Alex?" I ask, trying my best to be completely nonchalant.

"That doofus is my brother." If I were drinking coffee I'd have spit it out. All over this Tiffany's framed family photo.

Britain joins me and holds up the photo in hand. "And that's my husband, and our two girls." *Do not vomit on this woman's carpet. Don't do it. Hold it.*

Instinctively I look down at my shoes. The shoes I wore when I fucked her husband this weekend.

I take it all back. I am a shit human being.

TWENTY-FIVE

NOW

Alex

The first clue should have been what she was wearing. The second clue was the look on her face. The nervousness she exuded. The slight tremble to her hand as she fed Eden. All of the hundreds of clues were there, though none of them more pervasive than that fucking gut feeling.

I didn't know how to do it, though. I didn't know how to throw myself at her and beg forgiveness because yes, I'm fucking angry at her. Still. And yes, I fucking took it out on her. But I wasn't using her. Never. I didn't know anything was wrong until she said something.

The fucking sound of her voice. And the tears in her eyes. I wanted to kick my own ass. But I was only ever thinking of her. I was thinking about how much I loved her in the deli, how much I loved her singing lullabies to Eden. I was thinking about how I love her so much, she shouldn't be anyone else's, let alone two other fuckers. Both of whom I know personally.

The fact that Damian had her first... I can barely stand the thought of it now. But then Tommy, too? It's like she did it just to spite me. And I'm fucking pissed. As I should be because she robbed us of six fucking years. And when she was saying my name last night, I was creating a new fucking memory over the one of her muffled moan through a closed door at the hand of someone else. At the hand of my best friend. When it should have been me.

I would have fucked her that night. I would have fucked her publicly at the goddamn oyster bar and gladly gone to jail. That's how fucking sure I was about her. And I lied to Damian to get him off my fucking scent, and it backfired. Yeah, I fucking know.

I throw down the kitchen towel once the last pancake is pulled off the griddle and head upstairs. I check her closet, but nothing looks amiss. I check the bathroom and nothing. No, her toothbrush is gone. I walk into Eden's room and find that all the drawers have been emptied. The suitcase is missing from her closet, too.

She just wasn't going to say goodbye?

I practically fly down the stairs, grabbing the Jeep keys and a baseball hat.

She just fucking left?

I'm doing 70 in a 40, definitely going to jail if I get caught.

She doesn't fucking love you. Obviously.

I slam on the breaks when a raccoon scurries out in front of me. *You're supposed to be nocturnal!* I want to scream at the little shit.

She's just using you.

And then I'm driving way too fast again.

She'd never want you.

"Shut the fuck up!" I yell at myself. At the voice that makes me feel like I am the son of Ray, and that's all I'll ever be.

At The Grounds, her car is parked out front and I double park right behind her. Though it's not like I'm really gonna stop her if she wants to leave. Which obviously, she does.

I throw open the door, and the cold wind whips around the cafe and shop, blowing napkins and scattering disposable utensils.

Three strides. .8 seconds. That's all it takes for me to get to her. I feel like shit because she actually looks scared.

"You're leaving?" I try to temper my voice, but it's fucking impossible. It's just raw fear gnawing at words. She fidgets as I hover over her, and it must be domineering because she has to straighten her spine in order to find her resolve.

"Yes." White-hot rage races against my spine.

"And you weren't going to tell me?" Why does Jess walking away from me feel like the actual end of the world all over again?

"No!" she shouts back. "So you could pretend to feel some sort of way about it? Guess what, Alex? You're the only one pretending! It's real for me, all of it, and it's fucking *killing* me." She looks like she might fucking cry. "I'm not *her*.

I'll never be *her*. And trust me, I'll walk away and it won't be like her leaving, because I'm. Not. Her. The end."

So she just gets to fucking leave? No skin off her back?

"No you certainly aren't her. She would never leave without saying goodbye. You know what? I'm sorry I tried to help." Fucking rue the day I ever talked to Jess. Because she's done nothing but put me through a special kind of hell.

Turning to my sister, I tell her, "It's not real for her either. She wouldn't know the truth if it smacked her in the face. She tell you yet?"

"Yes, now shut the fuck up before you ruin everything," Brit says to me coldly, but she doesn't fucking intimidate me.

"Well, just in case, let me fast forward the process for you. That best friend of yours," I nods towards *her*.

"Alex, stop—" *Screw you, Jess.*

"Yeah, her. Well, she fucked your husband." Brit and Jess both gasp in shock. The woman sitting at the table closest to them also gasps in shock. Sandy slams a tray of pastries on the counter and it jolts me to a reality I want no part in.

You could say it was then. You could say it was shortly thereafter, but I knew. I'd gone too far.

If it's not real for me, then why can't I stop being mad at you? Why can't I stop wanting to make you hurt? When is enough enough!? I want to scream all these things at her. But then Eden actually starts screaming. This gut-wrenching, horrid scream. Like some sort of fucked up symbolism for what I just inflicted on her mom.

It's also a fucking wake-up call. It's official. I've officially lost the last thing I had to lose. I take a step away, and then another. And then I'm gone.

———

Jess

Eden is screaming.

Loudly.

So loudly.

"Honey, hand me the baby," a sweet sounding voice with a southern twang says, then lifts my child out of my numb arms.

Everything is numb.

"Jess?" My best friend's voice finds me. (Ex best friend?) I blink. And blink. And all I can think is *ouch. That hurts.* What hurts? *Everything.* Where? *All over.* Why? *Because he hates me.*

"Jess?" Brit's hand takes mine and she rubs it back and forth over and over.

"I'm sorry." I say it blandly. Not because I don't mean it, but because I'm pretty sure I'm in shock and I can't focus. And I can barely bring my eyes to meet hers.

"I know," Brit says back in a soft, understanding tone. "I know you're sorry." She says again, while continuing to rub my hand. "Sandy, let's get her a coffee!" Britain yells over to her mother-in-law.

And then Sandy is yelling at Jim. "Jim! Get this woman a coffee and a goddamn pastry already." She says it like obviously the combination of the two things will make all of this better.

Who knows? Maybe it will. Maybe life is just that simple

if you let it be. If you cut off the feelings and just accept who you are. (What you are.) And you just live simply, maybe a coffee and a pastry really can make it all better. (That's called delusion, and honestly, maybe that's where I am right now.)

A gruff-looking, cowboy-esque figure sets a steamy cup of coffee down in front of me, and also a weird looking sticky bun. He sees me eyeing it and says, "It's a Queen-Ah-Mahn, dear." And then he's walking away.

"Brit," I look at the woman still holding my hand. "I'm really sorry."

She gives me a sad smile and says, "I know, babe. Drink your coffee, eat some food." So I do. While she holds my hand, I take a sip. And then a bite. She holds my hand like that's what's holding me together.

I think it is.

Sip. Bite. Repeat.

"He's gone *gone* now, isn't he?" I ask Brit after I've finished the pastry. She gets a sort of strange look, her mouth shoved off to the side.

"I'm afraid it's just who we are, Jess. We're runners." I know.

This moment is like splicing a film. I mentally cut myself off from the Jess of a second ago to the Jess of now. The Jess of now has no clue about Alex and the pain that brings because I've mentally cut my life in two. W.A. and W.O.A. (with Alex and without Alex). Those are the two time periods I'm operating in, and we are firmly in the W.O.A. now. I may have thought I was before, too, but I wasn't. That much is obvious.

"I'm sorry, Brit." I say again.

"Stop saying it. I've known." *WHAT?*

I slowly turn to face her head on, my face as white as a sheet.

"I knew the moment you stepped in my office. I hated you, but I was also so fucking curious about you, too." My stomach is just one jumbled pit of sour feelings and bad decisions.

"Why did you let me work for you?" I ask her because in my mind, no self-respecting woman would put herself through that kind of torment. I know she's a masochist, but...

She shrugs. "Honestly, it was for a lot of reasons. None of them are that great..."

"I need to know."

"Okay, fine. I wanted to meet the woman who turned my husband's head. Thought maybe I could learn a thing or two from you. And then more ashamedly, I thought maybe me being jealous would be good for our marriage because at that point I had assumed he was cheating on me, or sort of wished he was because our marriage was in utter shambles.

And also, I needed a friend. And, if you turned out to be a terrible person, I could make your life miserable." She tilts her head to the side, really examining me.

"But you weren't a terrible person. You were a great friend. You pushed me to be better, and stronger, and you never gave Damian the time of day, at least in my company. And I fell in love with you."

"Britain." I'm crying. She's crying, too.

She goes on. "He came home that night and told me everything. For as many things as Damian is, he was *never* not honest with me. He told me everything when it happened. With you. And honestly, learning how to forgive someone for something I could have done myself isn't as hard as it seems. It's just one foot in front of the other until, eventually, one moment, one day doesn't define us. Or them. It's just a blip. A fragment in time."

"A snapshot," I say.

"Yes! Exactly. And we wouldn't throw someone away because of one bad photo, now would we?" We wouldn't.

"You're the best person I know, Brit." I ugly cry. I mean, really. I'm sweaty. Hair is matted. Tears are rolling down my face and I can practically hear the plop they make when they hit the checkered tile floor.

"Well, I wouldn't say I'm the best...I've been petty recently. I didn't ask you to come to my wedding, I didn't greet you when you moved here. I have to admit I was mad at you."

"I know, and it was deserved."

"Well, I don't know that it was. Because I honestly thought you were lying to me about something much worse than you were. I thought you were cheating on Alex with Damian, and I was more angry for Alex than I was if you were sleeping with Damian." She sort of laughs. "So, like the fact that you're just friends, and I honestly think that's a really beautiful thing to be with someone, I really don't have a leg to stand on. And if it weren't for the fact that you were engaged to Alex, I don't think I would have cared at all if you and Damian were a thing. So as it turns out, I'm the asshole here."

"You are hardly the asshole," I scold her.

"Can we just agree to not keep any secrets? At all. Period. Please?"

"Agreed."

"Great," she says with a certain finality to it.

"Well, then, I am almost 100% positive that your brother is the love of my life. And well, you know how that just ended."

"I do. She rubs at my hand before continuing, "But things can change, things can happen. Just give it time."

I shake my head at her sadly. "I can't invest any more time into someone who loves someone else more than me." Brit rears back slightly at my comment.

"And who else would he love?" Her brows are furrowed with confusion.

"His wife, Amy." *Duh.* (The duh is implied in my tone.)

"Alex never loved Amy," Brit says sort of quietly, but with utter confidence while shaking her head.

"What?" I ask, stunned.

"Tally was an accident from a one-night stand, and he was just trying to do the right thing. But they were miserable. Both of them."

"You're sure?"

"The day she died, she was leaving him. She was moving out."

My world tilts on its axis.

Here's the thing about a snapshot, a photo: it's one dimensional. My favorite photo of Alex has always said the obvious things to me. About who he is. About what he must have felt. I assumed it was all grief. Not *guilt*.

Re-examining the picture, I can see it's more guilt than grief. I think back to all the moments where I'd super-imposed a filter of Alex loving Amy over our interactions. Moments where I would have gone further, I would have been braver, but I held back because I saw him as a one-dimensional widower who could never love again.

I never saw the man who maybe was in love with me, and if I look back, I think maybe he was.

I shrug anyway, though, because bygones are bygones. What's done is done. And to think we could come back after all *this* would be ludicrous.

The front door to the cafe opens, and my weak little heart beats double time before flatlining.

James strides into the cafe and nods over at me. "I'm ready when you are," he says.

Brit looks between the two of us, confused.

"Yeah, so I anticipated this morning going differently," I begin to explain. "Eden and I are supposed to fly to Taipei City this evening. James was my ride to the airport."

"James, I mean this in the nicest way, but please get lost. Well, get a coffee and something to eat on my tab, and then I'll see you later," Brit says to the teen.

"Yes ma'am," he replies breezily, then gives a fake salute before heading over to the counter to order.

"You are not going to Taiwan. I forbid it." Brit physically and metaphorically puts her foot down.

"Brit, I'm running out of options. I can either go live in my mother's apartment and work some shitty jobs and roll the dice on custody. Or, I can go live with 'the dads' and suck it up and at least know I'll never have to worry about losing custody."

"Uh-uh. No," she says vehemently. "I can't accept that for either of you. So no. You're going to *stay* and work for me and Liam. You're going to *stay* in the garage apartment until you can afford-slash-find your own place. And I will help you find and pay for the best family court attorney. And Damian will help, too."

"Okay?" I say feeling uncertain.

"Okay?" She echoes me back, an eyebrow cocked.

"Okay."

"Okay," she says, then leans over and gives me a hug.

TWENTY-SIX

JESS

When Caleb walks through the door, solo, my heart breaks again. It's in a less severe way than it was earlier, but it's there.

I walk over to him, noting for the second day in a row, he's come correct, aka not dressed like a Gen Z wannabe. He's got on black jeans and a gray sweater and sneakers. Completely normal, respectable Thanksgiving Day outfit.

"Hey," I say, offering him a cranberry Aperol spritz. (Carly's making, not mine.)

"Hey," he says a bit bashfully, if not sadly.

"I can't take the job."

"I know," is all he says back.

"Have you talked to him?" I ask. *Why did you ask, Jess?*

"Nope."

I nod, and without another word I walk away with my

knit dress from Dissh (borrowed from Brit) flowing behind me and my head held high as I head towards the kitchen.

"Carly?" She's finishing off a batch of sugared rosemary, but otherwise seems to have the kitchen under complete control.

"Yeah?" she asks me with a smile.

"Have you ever given a haircut before?" I don't know what compels me to ask her, except that she just seems like the type who knows how to do anything. Also, I equate good knife skills with good cutting skills. Meat and hair can't be that different, right?

"I cut James' hair all the time...and on occasion, my own."

"Great. Can you cut my hair?"

"What?! No!" Elodie walks in on the conversation. "Why?!" she exclaims, sliding on to a stool at the island.

"Just feels like dead weight. And I'm ready to shed what's holding me back." It's the most honest answer I can give that's not because your uncle may have loved me, but he hates me more, and we're too fucked up to ever work, but I'm quite sure I'll never meet another man like him, nor do I want to.

"Fine, but I love your hair. Caroline!" Elodie yells for her sister. "Caroline cuts all the girls' hair in the dormitory."

"Really?" I ask, surprised.

"Yeah, says it's her act of defiance...a lot of the girls at my school don't have good parents like us." Oh, that's sad.

"Oh, sweetheart. Are they okay?" I ask about the girls.

"They all have killer bobs now, so I'd say they're doing fine."

"Yeah?" Caroline asks then grabs a piece of goat cheese toast off a tray.

"Let's cut my hair." I pose it to her.

"Right now?" she asks with surprise.

"Yeah, why not? Come on." I reach for a pair of scissors from the junk drawer where there's a whole mess of condoms. *Eww.* I grab the scissors quickly and slam the drawer shut, hoping no one else saw that.

"That's my least favorite drawer in this whole house." Elodie cringes, and both Caroline and Carly agree.

"Oh my god," I laugh then reopen the drawer and move the condoms into the trash. "They clearly don't even need them, people."

Right on cue, my excessively pregnant best friend waddles into the kitchen to see me throw out a handful of magnums. She starts laughing. "I was wondering who would finally get the nerve to trash those. You know, those are the ones with the holes?" We all kind of laugh, but I notice Caroline not laughing quite as hard. I don't know if it's because it's not funny...or something else.

Though, to be honest, it isn't funny. Someone poking a hole in a condom is sexual assault. Brit should have filed charges against that crazy bitch.

"I have my own scissors, Jess. Let me get them." Caroline takes off towards the stairs.

"I'm cutting all my hair off," I tell Brit before she gets a chance to ask.

"Love that!" she says. And this feels good. Being here with her, with my people. It's not my person, but maybe I'm not a one-person type gal. Maybe I'm just a people person.

The mudroom door opens, and everyone in the kitchen collectively looks over to see Damian stroll in with a bottle of Dom Perignon tucked under his arm.

"Hey!" he calls out through the open entryway.

Brit pats me on the shoulder as she walks over to him. From the corner of my eye, I can see her go on her tiptoes to embrace him for a long hug. A *really* long hug. That's good, he must have told her about Summer.

They walk back in the kitchen and I do something I've never done before. I walk up to Damian, and in front of his ex-wife and his daughters, I give him a hug.

"Really happy to see you," I say quietly.

"Same," he says back, giving me a quick squeeze, then releasing me.

"E!" he calls out to Elodie.

"Hi, Dad," she replies but doesn't even bother to get up off her stool.

"Great to see you, too," Damian deadpans. Carly passes him a drink and a sympathetic smile, and he drifts off to the living room where the rest of the men are. Well, almost all the men. I'd be remiss not to mention Max who's been sulking about the kitchen silently while the rest of us talk.

"Got 'em'!" Caroline says, holding a pair of shears in her hand. Oh good, glad we won't be cutting my hair with crafting scissors, not that I would've minded if that's all we had.

"Perfect!" I down the rest of my spritz and waltz to the back deck where I sit for the next 45 minutes as a type-A, 15-year-old cuts my hair with the precision of an expert neurosurgeon.

"Who is that, Eden?" The grandmother of all grandmas walks out to the deck carrying Eden. She basically hasn't left her side since our epic meltdown at The Grounds earlier. And I do mean *our* meltdowns. We both lost it there for a bit.

"Maaa!" she exclaims, though doesn't make any move to rid herself of Sandy's arms.

"Your momma looks so pretty with her fresh cut, huh?" Brit asks Eden. Brit has barely left my side since it all went down, too. She kicked Liam out of their bedroom so we could get dressed. She's made me at least three cocktails. She even had Niko and Constantine pick up In-N-Out for us on their way over, which she insisted we eat in bed.

It's been simultaneously the worst *and* the best day.

"Almostttttt...done!" Caroline exclaims, circling me, examining the lines of my cut from different angles.

"Oh my gawd, you have never looked hotter," Brit says while standing and coming over to run her fingers against the blunt edges. "Eee!" She even lets out a little squeal of excitement. I look at the faces of the women on the deck. My best friend, her daughters, Sandy, my daughter, and each has a look of utter love plastered on their face. (See, who needs men, my friends?)

———

My sweet potato casserole would have been a joke stacked against the meal laid out before us. Carly already has sweet potatoes done two other ways. I mean, really. It's like she's got sixteen hands or something.

The table in the dining room has been extended and believe it or not, it actually sits everyone here. ("Everyone" being Liam, Brit, Caroline, Elodie, Damian, Sandy and her husband Jim, Carly and her brother James, Constantine and his sons Max, Niko, and Silas. Then there's Blanks, Eden, and me.) (Probably could have squeezed a few more people in, too, if I'm totally honest.)

"Hair looks good," Damian says, then bumps his shoulder against mine.

"Thanks, bud."

Under his breath, he asks, "Where's your fiancé?"

Under my breath, I say back, "Long story. Not enough alcohol and too many people." He nods in understanding and goes back to talking to Jim who is sitting on his other side.

"Well, it's not every day we get to have Thanksgiving with a billionaire!" I hear Sandy exclaim defiantly to Liam. Caleb blushes.

"Mom, inappropriate," Liam gently scolds her.

"Why?!" she asks honestly.

"Well, I mean you do sort of have a billionaire at the table...all the time." Caleb looks around at Liam, Sandy, and the rest of the table that has now clued into the conversation. He clears his throat. "Alex was, um, just here yesterday." This time it's me choking on my spritz. Damian pats me on the back to clear the passage.

"Sorry," I apologize and dab my mouth with a napkin. I just used a secret credit card my ex-husband gave me to buy airline tickets. I mean, the disparity between me and everyone else at this table feels even more vast.

No one else seems surprised by this except maybe Sandy and me. Everyone else just knew? Is being a billionaire like Fight Club? We just don't talk about it? *Cool.*

"You didn't know?" Damian asks out of the corner of his mouth.

"I hardly know him at all," is all I say, staring at my mashed potatoes still swimming with gravy.

It wouldn't have mattered. It doesn't matter. But I guess it all sort of makes sense. But it's also pretty clear that money isn't important to him in the same way it is to others. (When you have a lot of it, it rarely is.)

I shrug, then just give Damian a closed-lip smile. He pats my leg under the table and while I zone out and focus on feeding Eden, the rest of the table's talk resumes. The Scala boys are arguing over their latest golf scores. Constantine is telling Brit a story about her mom. Liam is just watching Brit, and attempting to force feed her every time there's a break in conversation. And Sandy is cutting up bits of food for Eden in tandem as I pick them up.

And then there's Caleb, who is just looking at me. I give him a genuine (looking) smile, one that I hope says, "See? I'm fine. This is fine. Everything is fine."

———

Things aren't exactly fine. But each day I wake up. I put one foot in front of the other. And each step takes me further away from the fantasyland that was my 40 hours with Alex. That's all it was. From the time I landed to the time I left his house. That's .006% of my life. A blip. (Yes, I did the math.)

My days all look pretty much the same lately, but right now, I'm grateful for the steadiness of it. I wake up when Eden does. We eat breakfast in our own apartment, then get ready and head to The Grounds where we get coffee. (I drive Brit's old car now.) (The Volvo sat parked outside The Grounds for about a week, until one day it was just...gone.) No one said anything about it and I didn't ask. But I wanted to. I wanted to ask Sandy if she'd seen Alex. Did he come get it? Did Caleb? But then some things are better left alone, too.

Sometimes Brit comes with us for coffee, sometimes we just pick it up and bring it back, and sometimes Eden and I sit and chat with the "rents" as Elodie and Caroline have lovingly dubbed Sandy and Jim. And then I go to work. Eden comes with me, and we sit in Liam's office while he doles out the day's to-do list. And then he leaves me to it to manage how it all gets done.

At first I pushed back on Brit because I didn't want her pity job that didn't actually include any work, but upon further inspection, there was actually a shit ton of work. It turns out Liam has started a custom build/remodel business, and is a bit crap at paperwork, just like most creatives are.

Paperwork? On it. *Logistics?* No problem. *Arguing with customer service over steel beams that have been delayed another 3 weeks?* I'm your gal. *Maintaining a healthy relationship?* Better look somewhere else.

Inevitably, we end up eating lunch at Brit's house and then I bring Eden back to the apartment to nap while I bang out the rest of my work. Once she's up from her nap, we do a FaceTime call with Tommy and Jamie that lasts 15 minutes, and then Eden and I get ready for dinner.

Dinner is, again, a mixed bag. Sometimes we just stay in. Sometimes we head to Colton's or pick up Maggio's, and then a lot of times, we find ourselves sitting down for a family dinner with Brit and Liam, a Scala brother or two, and "the rents." (The girls are back at boarding school now.)

Then it's the bedtime routine. You know the drill. Bath, lotion, two books, and a song. I put Eden to sleep in the Pack 'n Play in our room, and then I sit in the living room in my

Target pjs and watch *The Parent Trap* on an endless loop in the background while I try to get lost in the world of Pinterest. (This is on nights when I don't have an email from my lawyer that needs attention, because D-Day is coming.)

I don't actually get lost. I think about him under the pretense that I can't actually be thinking about him when I'm literally doing these other things. (But I can, and I do.)

Some day, when I'm old and gray, hopefully I'll be laughing at this weird time in my life. Or maybe I even use it as a cautionary tale in 20 or so years when Eden wants to get married, and I beg her not to do it. Who knows? But each day that passes brings me closer to that end goal. And that's the goal: Turn the recent past into a distant memory.

———

"What do you want for Christmas?" Brit has asked no less than 25 times in the last week or so.

"Honestly, nothing."

"Well, I can't get you nothing."

"You can, and you should."

"I can't and I won't"

"Some nice face cream," I finally say, still pouring over a spreadsheet on the laptop in my lap. (Expensive cosmetics are the one thing I refuse to spend money on anymore.) (Okay, not just the one thing. My new wardrobe is entirely made up of vintage or Target.)

Brit rolls her eyes. "Cop out." And I smile.

"Really, please don't get me anything. I'm so close to busting out of this joint (her house) and also, lawyer bills, so the only gifts I'm giving are ones that don't cost a lot." Like five nights of newborn babysitting to give Brit a break the first month. Or like me organizing Liam's entire office so it resembles something The Home Edit would do.

For the girls, I got lucky and thrifted the most amazing vintage bags and furs. (Mob wife style. I'm telling you, it's coming.) And for Damian, honestly nothing. My presence is his present.

Eden still doesn't care or comprehend Christmas, and I'm sure between her dads and the rest of the extended family, we'll have more shit than one kid could ever need. So from me, it's just a tea set. (Also thrifted.) (Look at me go!)

Sometimes, I get the strangest feeling. It's that hair raising on the back of my neck, it's a tingling awareness. And sometimes I can't shake it. And sometimes I don't want to, because it's the feeling I'd get when Alex was around and I'd know before I knew.

It unsettles me, and I shift on the sofa.

The front door opens, and I'm expecting to see Liam traipse in, but I don't. Alex walks in and he looks...different. He looks great. Honestly, better than ever. And it pisses me off. (Cue every shitty feeling.) His hair is slightly longer, his short beard has returned and is neatly trimmed, and he's wearing black slacks and a knit polo and...Ferragamo shoes(?) with a long black winter overcoat.

(And I'm sitting here in my thrifted Cal Poly Aquatics circa 1982 hoodie, a pair of $6 black leggings, and chipped toenail polish.) (I have to remedy that ASAP.)

This, it's just so not like him. And then I get irrationally jealous, because he looks like he's met someone and they made him over and maybe he has. I can just picture a skinny blonde, waif-like thing holding on to his arm as they walk down the streets of Vienna shopping the Christmas markets. Because he's carrying about 5 boxes and 10 bags of expensive-looking Christmas presents. Bright orange boxes and yellow bags. *Good for him.*

He freezes when he eventually notices me. (Still a nobody. *Check.*)

I've been frozen. I don't get up. I just turn my head and refocus on the spreadsheet. The spreadsheet that is now just a blurring of lines and numbers that have no rational meaning to me.

"What are you doing here?" Brit asks him sharply.

"Dropping off Christmas presents. Don't worry, I'm not staying." He says curtly, walking straight to the 12-foot Christmas tree where he quickly drops the boxes and bags and then is out the door again, never sparing me a second look. (I am nobody, it's officially confirmed.)

Maybe he's done the math too and realized I barely make up .006% of his life (maybe less) and maybe he has met someone else and he's already turned me into that distant memory. Again, good for him. (Shitty for me.)

The water floods my vision, making it quite impossible to read whatever it is this computer screen says. Then Brit is off the sofa and moving faster than she has in weeks. I hear the front door slam shut and then there's the muffled sound of arguing.

Of course I want to know what's being said, desperately, but it's best for my sanity if I don't. So I sit stiffly on the sofa, forcing my ass to stay put until Brit huffs back in and slams the door.

"Fucking idiot," she curses under her breath. It's on the tip of my tongue to ask. But I don't because in all likelihood there's a chance whatever that was about would kill me. If it was about me, that would fucking suck. If it *wasn't* about me, well, I'd be fucking obliterated. (You get what I'm saying?)

I'm still in that 'one is too many, 1000 would never be enough' thing with him. Or maybe it's more like if you give a mouse a cookie. If I ask about this one thing, I'll ask about more. And if I ask about more, I'm sure to get answers that will hurt. And if I get answers that'll hurt, I'll probably experience a setback. So no. Don't think I will.

TWENTY-SEVEN

ALEX

She's still here? The door clicks shut behind me.

She didn't leave? The door is opening behind me and then my peanut of a sister is getting in front of me as the door slams back into place again.

"Where the fuck have you been?" she asks me angrily. *Paris, Stockholm, briefly in Amsterdam.* Burying my idiocy in drinking, a little bit of recreational drugs, and way too many women. I'm not stupid enough to say that, though.

I shrug. "Buying my family Christmas gifts" is all I give her.

"Like fuck. Nobody needs an expensive 'sorry I can't be here, but let me buy your love' gift."

"Then give them away, Brit!" I raise my voice slightly back.

"You're just gonna leave without saying anything to her?" Alright, this is the real reason she's pissed.

"Why should you even care?" I ask.

"Because she's my best friend and she's so fucking in love with you and you've been a total dick to her!" *She's in love with me?*

"This isn't your battle to fight, Brit." I try to temper her.

"Yeah, it is because you're too stupid to say sorry. Because you're thinking one thing and she's thinking another and if you two idiots would just talk to each other already, this whole thing would blow over!"

"She's a liar, Brit," I say as my official shield, that's officially tired and basically a bullshit excuse.

"She is not. She had already told me everything when you came bursting in, ready to burn the world to the ground!" Brit stomps her foot down and actually screeches. "Ugh! She thought *you*," Brit's small fist hits me in the chest, "were still in love with *Amy*! My god, you're a fucking prick." With both hands on her hips she lets out an exaggerated sigh. "You know what? Be lonely. You deserve it."

And then the door slams again, and I'm alone. And rightfully so.

———

"That was quick. No issues then?" Blanks asks me from the hangar where his jet is parked, already fueled and ready to go.

I grunt in response to that. I wouldn't say *no* issues.

"Was she there?" I ask.

"What are you talking about?"

"Was she there at Thanksgiving?"

"Yeah," he says it plainly.

"You didn't tell me?"

"You didn't ask." *Huh.*

"H-how was she?"

"Do you really want to know?" he asks, looking down on me, like whatever he's gonna tell me is gonna hurt.

"No, but I think I need to." What was she like those first few days? I thought about it a lot, but I just imagined she flew back to New York after my explosive outburst. The one where I blew it for good. When I finally knew I'd ruined my last chance with her, I stopped keeping tabs on her like I used to. Had to, for my sanity.

"Well, I got there, and she immediately asked about you." *She did?* "And then she was outside for a long time and when she came back, she'd chopped off all her hair." *The fuck?* "And then at dinner someone said that it's not every day you get a billionaire at the table. And when I replied with, well, yeah you do because Alex was just here, she started choking because she clearly had no idea. And then she just looked sad, but pretended she was happy the rest of the evening. And I don't think she ate a single thing."

"Hmm." I get lost for a couple minutes. I'm thinking about what she would look like with short hair. She was wearing a big hoodie, and I couldn't see her that well earlier. I also only allowed myself to look once, because anything more would have been self-inflicted torture.

I'm actually debating. Am I getting on this plane, or turning my ass right around and running back to her?

But do you think she'll forgive me? Nope. And ultimately maybe it's all just too broken to be something.

"Are we staying?" Blanks asks, already preparing to nix Christmas in Hawaii.

I think about it, but the realization is blunt, and the answer is clear. "Not a fucking chance." As in there's no fucking chance of her taking me back either. He doesn't look exactly pleased and neither do I, but I haven't been pleased, at least well, in about a month. Who knows? Maybe Hawaii will do the trick.

———

It doesn't matter who. It doesn't matter where or how. If I'm fucking someone, I'm thinking about Jess.

I used to avoid long dark hair, but now it's the only thing that does it for me.

"Mmmm." Reina (I think) says around my cock, and I shush her. Again, don't like the noises, don't want to hear them now or later in my dreams. Well, nightmares. You know how it is.

Currently playing nightly is me fucking her senseless just to find out she was crying the whole time. That's my brain's current favorite. Has been for the last four weeks straight.

"Do you like that?" Big brown eyes look up at me, and I grunt and nod in affirmation. I don't love it, but it's a means, right?

A

> You should come join us in Hawaii for Christmas.

Yeah, I'm fucking texting right now. That's the level of investment I'm at with "R."

D

> Can't. Jess needs moral support to deal
> with the dads who are bringing their reign of
> terror to Spearhead. Have fun.

And then I'm pushing away. And then I'm walking away. And then my fist is going through a wall.

I said I'd be there. I said I'd help. And I'm not. I wonder how she felt when she told the dads we weren't actually getting married. Did I make her look stupid? Did she tell them the truth?

I don't want them to know the truth. I don't want her to lose face because of me. I don't want her to have to stand up to them alone. I quickly shoot off a text to Brit.

A

> Do Tommy and Jamie know that Jess and I
> broke up?

B

> Well, I think you'd have to be together for
> real in order to break up.

> You know what I mean.

> Well yeah, I think they figured it out when
> they showed up yesterday and found out
> Jess is living out of my garage apartment.

Fuck. It's too late now. And she's living in the garage apartment?

"Everything okay?" Reina asks. It at least definitely starts with an R.

"No, I'm sorry. I'm leaving." I stand up from where I absentmindedly sat down on the bed, put my jeans on, and

when I get to the door of the hotel room, I tell her, "Feel free to use the room the rest of the day." And then I'm gone.

A

Hey, how's it going?

Good day or bad day?

Did Eden like her Christmas gifts?

I'm not doing too great myself, thanks for asking.

Did you get a new number?

I'll text you every day if I have to.

I'd show up, but I don't think you want me there.

J

I don't.

Progress?

Did you get anything good for Christmas?

Divorce papers.

Please stop texting me.

See, divorce papers sort of sound like the best Christmas present. At least to me.

Happy New Year's Eve.

Happy New Year.

B

Stop texting her. She's moving on.

A

Is she really?

Britain sends me a photo of Jess in a dress so short you can practically see her ass. She's at Colton's while that spineless fuck of a bartender is holding her face in both hands with his tongue down her throat.

You had your chance.

———

I wake up in a panic. My brow is sweaty. I think I audibly gasp, too. It wakes up Blanks who is sitting on the other side of the plane.

"I have to go back," I say out loud and with no volume control. I probably look fucking crazed, sound like it, too. And it's probably because I am. It's vivid. It was so vivid, the image of Jess kissing another man feels burned on my brain.

The text messages, fucking someone named "R." It felt real. But it's *not real. It was just a dream. Just another nightmare.*

I should know better, I gave up trying to fuck Jess out of my mind with other women weeks ago. It doesn't work. She'll never not be in my thoughts.

My nightmares have taken on a life of their own lately, but on the tails of seeing her this afternoon, this one cut the deepest. The pain in my chest won't ease. I know it won't until I go back to her.

Blanks just unbuckles and raps on the captain's door, asking them to turn back.

He sighs as he passes me on his way to sit back down.

"Should've trusted my instincts. I knew you couldn't leave it."

"Sorry," I say brusquely.

"Don't be. Now I get to spend Christmas with Brit." He gives me a wink.

"Fuck off. You know she's officially married, right?"

"Yup, I know," he says with a smile, leaning back against his seat.

I look at the map on the monitor towards the front of the plane to see the little plane icon is now making a large U. We were a little short of half way. So three hours. I've got three hours to come up with a plan.

I pull out my phone and get to work.

———

It's almost midnight when I'm at her door. I knock gently at first. But after four knocks, I do it louder, and when I go to do it again, the door flies open revealing Jess in a little white nightgown. She locks up when she realizes it's me and I take it as a chance to look at her. Really look at her, like I wanted to earlier today.

Her hair *is* chopped short, and honestly, she looks even sexier without the flowing locks. Like you actually notice her nose that turns up a little at the end and the way her lips make that perfect little v. Or the freckle above her left eyebrow.

"Can I come in?" I ask.

She just stands there staring at me.

"Eden's sleeping," she eventually says back.

"I'll be quiet." She pokes her head out the front door and looks around. Then takes a few steps back, leaving room for me to enter.

"You shouldn't answer the door in the middle of the night," I say, setting keys down on the entry table. She watches me with a keen eye, like she's willing me not to get comfortable.

She crosses both arms over her chest to hide her hard nipples, but all it does is make her breasts pop in the sheer sleeveless nightgown. She notices me noticing and she reaches for a zip up fleece off the coat rack and puts it on.

"Why are you here?" she asks, leaning against the kitchenette counter.

"Because I promised I'd help, and I'd be here. And I haven't been."

She nods, and gives me a thin-lipped smile. "Don't worry, I won't hold you to it. I'm done with all that, and I don't want your help, okay? *But* I do have work tomorrow, though..." She trails off and holds a hand up for me to leave.

"Does Tommy know we broke up?" I ask.

She does the spine straightening thing again. It's one of her tells. "I haven't told him explicitly, but I'm sure he realizes it. We FaceTime daily from here." She gestures around the small studio apartment. "I'm too tired for this, Alex." She sounds too tired for this, which means she might be delirious enough to give me a chance.

I get down on one knee and her eyes go wide. I pull out a ring box that's been knocking around in my bag for longer than I'd ever admit.

"Jess," I start.

"NO," she says, flat out. I haven't even cracked the box open yet. "Get out." Her tone is harsh and she points a finger at the door.

"Jess, hear me out."

"No. P-please leave," she stutters, then stumbles back as she walks towards the bedroom. "When I wake up tomorrow, just p-please don't be here."

She shuts the bedroom door gently and I stand up from where I'm kneeling like an idiot. Right, deserved that.

———

Jess

When I hear the front door close and click shut, I finally take a full deep breath. He was here. *I think*. But maybe this is a dream. I've had dreams like this before. Except normally the second he gets down on one knee I jump into his arms and kiss him.

So maybe that's how I know it wasn't a dream, because lucid Jess knows better. I'm not pretending or doing anything for show, for anyone or any reason ever again. It was a fucking disaster and I don't have the wherewithal or the emotional fortitude to deal with it.

W.O.A Jess has to stay focused. On saving, on figuring out custody, maybe even on moving back to DC. W.O.A. Jess doesn't and can't focus on the man kneeling on her living room floor with a ring box.

I don't even know if he loves me. In fact, the more time I

put between myself and "the situationship" (that's what I'm calling it now), the more I don't think he could have possibly loved me. We've only gone on one date! (I'm only counting the deli.) No one should be asking anyone to marry them after one date. *Fucking psychopath.*

And that's how I know it's not real. He's just doing this out of some weird guilt-fueled obligation. No, thanks.

———

Eden babbling aimlessly wakes me up. This is how it goes most mornings. Like clockwork, really. At 7:00 A.M. it's either whimpering, babbling, or all-out screeching.

Before I pick her up from the crib, I double check the living room. Cracking the bedroom door the slightest amount, I peer into the small area and find it empty. Yeah, I mean, I knew it would be. (But hoped it wasn't because I'm a fucking psychopath, too.)

I let the door open entirely, then pick Eden up out of the crib for her diaper change. She gets a morning bottle in bed while I shower and throw on a light dusting of makeup. I foolishly put the same clothes I was wearing yesterday back on. I'm being superstitious. And silly. If I dress up and try to look good, I will absolutely not see him. But...if I don't, the odds increase that I will. Plus, no one here gives a fuck what I look like. It's one of my favorite perks of living here that I never anticipated.

Next up, it's Eden's turn to get dressed. We grab a quick breakfast, just yogurt and bananas, because today is Wednesday and that means it's sticky bun day at The Grounds.

"Do you wanna go see Miss Sandy?" Eden now knows Miss Sandy by name and by face. She might actually be her second favorite person.

Eden makes a little squeal and says, "Go!"

"That's right, we go!" I echo. "Up!" I say to her and she lifts her arms for me to carry her down the outside steps.

Diaper bag, Eden, yep, that's all I need. I open the front door and freeze because Brit's old car is just gone. *Oh.* In its place is the Volvo. That's not helpful. My shoulders drop slightly. I go to shut the front door, but notice the keys Alex placed on my entryway table last night are still there. The keys to the Volvo.

No. We are not doing this. We just won't get sticky buns today. Eden will most likely have a meltdown when we don't go see Sandy this morning, but what else is new? It's always something.

She knows it when we walk past the car.

"Go!" Eden says in between her paci.

"Yes, we're going to see Brit and Liam!" I try to impart enthusiasm into my tone in hopes she'll get excited about that.

"No." She knows three words now. Hi, no, and go. No is my favorite. (Not really.)

"Yes!" I say, readjusting her weight on my hip as she squirms.

I open the front door to Brit's house, and call out, "Hello!" like I always do. It only took walking in on Brit and Liam once, and now, never again.

I slip off my knockoff Boston clogs in the entryway, drop the diaper bag, then set Eden down where Luna immediately finds us. Then Eden and the dog are off toddling after one another.

"Hey." *Fuck!* A sleep-worn Alex sits up from the couch as I walk through the great room to the kitchen. He startles me and I jump back.

"Hi!" Eden bounds over to Alex without permission and climbs on to the couch, very slowly albeit, to sit beside him.

"Hi, E," Alex says to her, leaning back on the sofa. Weird. This is weird.

"What are you doing here?" I ask blatantly.

"Waiting for you." I shake my head and go to the kitchen for coffee.

I don't want this coffee. I want my coffee from The Grounds. The one Sandy makes me with pistachios. And I want him to go away. And I want you to be honest with yourself, Jess, because do you really want him to go away? Yes!

I know he's in the kitchen with me. I can feel it.

"You're messing up my routine," I say to the Nespresso machine warming up in front of me.

"Sorry," he says.

"On Wednesdays we get sticky buns and Eden gets to see Sandy."

"Then let's go get sticky buns and see Sandy." He's closer now. Too close.

"I don't have a car to drive anymore," I say through a tight jaw. And then his hand is on my hip. *No. No, thank you.*

"Jess," my name comes out whisper soft. The hair on the back of my neck rises. I'm wishing I had worn panties today because suddenly it feels like I wet my damn pants.

"I'd just like the car back," I say.

"You have a car."

"I do not," I tell him, slightly annoyed with myself for not pushing his hand away. At him, for existing.

"Jess, I—"

"What are you doing here?" Britain says too loudly, crashing the moment.

"Give us a minute, Brit, please?" he asks her. I'm still staring at the coffee maker like it's my lord and savior Jesus Christ. I actually start praying to it. *Please let me take one long blink and wake up. I can't do this, so please. Grant me this one ask.*

"Only if Jess wants me to," she says.

"Please do," Alex says as I say, "Please stay."

He whispers in my ear, his warm chest entirely too close to my back, "You want to do this in front of my sister?"

TWENTY-EIGHT

JESS

"Brit, do you mind just checking on Eden real quick? She's being too quiet." I turn to her and ask.

"Okay, sure." She gives me a look that says just yell and I'll be right back.

The hand on my hip spins me as soon as Brit clears the room. *Nooo*. Face to face is bad for me and Alex. I lose willpower and my autonomy when he can see me and I can see him.

Before he gets a chance to say anything I blurt it all out. "You hurt me. You think I'm a liar and a bad person. You've never even asked me out on a date. You don't love me. And you think you're so much better than me. I have $500 in my checking account that has to last me till the end of the month. You don't know me and I don't know you. And I'm still married to another man. Plus, you really fucking hurt me in case that wasn't clear at the start."

"Okay, what was all that?" he asks.

"It's the things I should have said to you when you asked me to marry you for the first time. And nothing's changed. So, it's all the reasons why I won't and can't marry you now." I try to turn back around to make coffee, but he won't let me.

"Well, you're fucking wrong," he says. I try to turn away from him again, but this time he has both hands on my hips and he's shoved me against the counter, his body pressing in against mine.

"About what part?" I ask too quietly, and too afraid to look him in the eyes.

"Come home and I'll tell you," he whispers.

"I don't have a home," I whisper back.

"Shut the fuck up, Jess," he says, and then his mouth is on mine. His warmth bleeds into me, liquid heat running straight from my mouth to my groin. A hand leaves my hip and is up in my hair. And his tongue is diving and plundering my mouth and it's like the kiss from July all over again.

With a sharp bite against the corner of my mouth, he pulls back barely a centimeter to whisper across my lips, "Did you know you're the only woman I've ever kissed, Jess?" I can feel his heartbeat in his thumb as he holds my cheek.

It's racing.

So is mine. But there's the part of me, the logical part, that's screaming at me like I'm an idiot. Nobody kisses like that when they've never kissed before. I don't know how many women he's been with, but when you look like him, I'm going with a lot.

And then there's the sap in me that says, that fucking means something. This fucking means something to him.

"Don't lie to me, Alex. I can't tell what's real and what's not." I say it sincerely.

"This is real. Me and you. Please come home." I shake my head and he rests his forehead against mine in turn. "What do I need to do?" I shake my head again. There's nothing he can do. I think maybe there is such a thing as too messy. I think maybe too much has happened, too many wrongs that we'll never be right.

"Nothing. Just leave me alone."

"Can't," is all he says.

"It's what I need."

"It's not," he replies.

"You don't know me, Alex."

"I know that your favorite colors are black and brown. I know your favorite movie is actually *The Godfather*, but you tell people it's *Casino* because you don't want to seem basic and at least with *Casino* you can say it's because of Sharon Stone.

I know that you sing your daughter classic Beatles songs at bedtime because that's what your Dad used to sing to you. I know Christmas is your favorite holiday because gift giving, not receiving, is how you show love.

I know that your favorite perfume is Flowerbomb because I couldn't get the fucking scent out of my head and I actually went to the store and smelled hundreds until I found it and then bought it so I can smell you whenever I miss you.

And I know that you're a pjs girl. But ironically, nine times out of ten you're actually commando in broad daylight. Shall I check now?" *No* because I'm not wearing any underwear. I give a quick shake of my head.

"And I know that you go to Serendipity when you're in

New York at least once a week because you saw the movie and dreamed of having a real-life meet cute which is why I wanted to propose to you there. And I know that *The Parent Trap* is your comfort film because the parents get together in the end, and you always wanted that for your dad and mom even though, again, you claim it's for aesthetics."

"And you're not a crier," he wipes a tear off my cheek, "but I seem to make you cry quite a bit, don't I?" I nod. Then sniffle. "Can I take you out for breakfast, please?"

"Umm, that depends," I say, then sniffle again.

"On...?"

"Well, are you asking me out on a date?"

"Yes."

"Okay."

"Okay, yes? Or okay and no?"

"Okay, yes."

And then he's kissing me again.

———

It's just a date. A casual breakfast date.

I'm nervous, but also feel like I should be more nervous. Somehow this feels normal, though I have to admit I wish he would've changed first.

"I still have to work today," I tell Alex who's driving us to The Grounds.

"No problem, I have a bunch of stuff to do today anyways."

"Oh yeah?" I ask, "Like breaking up with your girlfriend?"

"What?" He gives me a wild look.

I motion up and down his body. "You're telling me *you* put this look together?" He's still wearing the black pants that are cut Italian-style with a (most likely cashmere) long-sleeved polo.

"Believe it or not, these clothes are actually old. And I picked them out myself."

"I don't believe you." I don't.

"I don't *like* this look, but it's how Europeans dress, and we just flew in yesterday, and I haven't had a chance to change..." *Oh.*

"Oh, well, you clean up nice." I try to say it without instinctively looking down at whatever the fuck it is you'd call what I'm wearing. It basically equates to a trash bag, though.

"I missed you." He just says it. He just puts it out there and I feel myself blush uncontrollably. And my stomach drops in excitement.

I missed him, too, but I also think it's hard to miss something you're not really sure you've ever had. I did miss the tender moments. The way he touched me, when he did. But it was so short, I'm not sure there was enough worth missing.

I swallow the lump that's formed in my throat. (That's weird.) "What did you miss?" I'm not fishing. I'm curious.

He reaches across the car taking my hand in his and says, "I missed sleeping next to you. And hanging out with you. And I missed the time we could have had together, but didn't...I'm sorry."

"For what?" *This* I need to hear.

"For hurting you. And blowing up. And for the things I said to you and Brit."

"Why did you do it then?" He drops my hand at the question and the saliva in my mouth sours.

"Because I was mad at you." That's a stupid answer. And a basic one, too.

"Why were you mad at me?" I ask, because this is it. We're going to get to the bottom of it.

"Because you shouldn't have fucked my best friend!" There it is. And just like he does, he reverts. He retreats. He turns icy and it's like all the warmth gets sucked right out of the room. (Well, the cab of the car.)

Testing the waters, I reach out my hand towards his and he moves out of my reach. Just like I knew he would. Silly me had dared to hope anyway.

"Okay, please take me back to Brit's." I say, not looking at him, just facing straight ahead.

"Jess, come on," he pleads.

I shake my head. "You're never going to get over it, and I don't want to do this. You might know me better than anyone else. You might make me feel like I'm high as a fucking kite, but you also make me feel like a piece of shit. And I'm not. I'm not a shitty person.

I made a mistake and so did you, but the difference is that I don't let it define me. And I won't spend the rest of my life arguing my case just to be iced out over and over. I can't be with someone who wants to hurt me just so they have an excuse to run. So please, turn around and take me back."

He slows down and makes a quick U-turn, but he doesn't say anything. That took a lot for me to fucking say, and does he say anything back? *Nope.* Not even "I don't think you're a shitty person." So I guess that means he does, huh? I have to clasp my hands together in front of me to keep them from trembling.

It's funny how just one moment can change everything.

One wrong decision. One wrong word. It can change and shape the rest of your life. That one wrong thing could make you miserable for the rest of your fucking life. And it's clear to me, Alex plans to hold on to that pain as tightly as he can for as long as he can, even if it means he's miserable. In fact, I'd bet that's where he thrives.

I hate to break it to you, friends, but love doesn't *always* conquer all. In this case, (whether he loves me or not) he'll never be able to forgive me. He can't put one foot in front of the other and realize that night will never even round up to .001% of our lives. But it's like he never learned how to forgive, and therefore he'll be stuck in this vicious loop forever.

But I won't, because I was raised to have at least a modicum of self respect. I know my worth. And I'm worth way more than an existence that would have me constantly circling the drain with Alex.

And just like I expected, he doesn't say anything the rest of the drive.

When we pull back up to Brit's, I garner all the strength I've been keeping in reserves. I call on my ancestors, I send up a little prayer to God (the gods, whoever it is) for strength. Without looking him in the eyes, I tell him what I've known, and thought, and felt for years, because no regrets. (Right?)

"I love you, Alex." I watch for a reaction. I wait for a response.

When he doesn't give me a single thing back, I get unbuckled. "Please don't call me or text me or come see me. And please return Brit's car."

I slip out of the front seat, open the back door and unbuckle Eden who is just saying "Go, go?" on repeat.

"Not today, pumpkin," is all I say, then I close the door and he drives away.

And that's officially *our* end. (It's not the ending you imagined now, is it?)

I walk into Brit's house in a daze. I ask her to watch Eden for ten minutes, and I think she says yes because she takes her out of my arms.

I walk out the back deck and down the 25 stairs to where their dock juts out into the lake. I stand at the edge of it and embrace the cold wind coming at me off the water. In fact, I lean into it. And then I scream.

There's so much pain and hurt and anger, and it's all just sitting in and around my heart, crippling it. Crippling *me. I am not this person.*

So I scream because it hurts.

I scream because I can't cry over him anymore.

I scream because I can't get lost at the bottom of the bottle.

And I scream because it's final.

I only stop screaming when my voice breaks. So I sit on the dock, knees into my chest, and rock back and forth until eventually Liam drapes a blanket across my shoulders. He doesn't say anything. He doesn't stay. But there's a solidarity there. An understanding when you feel like you might have given it your all and still missed the mark.

I sit out on the dock looking at the gray morning sky. No sun (it's fitting). And I promise myself, for myself and for my daughter, that the next time the sun comes out, I'll be fine.

I won't be over it. I won't be better, but I'll be fine.

———

It's the Friday before Christmas and the sun has decided to grace us with its presence. So I shower, blow dry my hair, put on some concealer to hide the bags, and throw a merry-fucking-smile on my face. To top it all off, I've got on my ugly Christmas sweater, too.

With the dads arriving today, I take a deep breath in and out and repeat mentally: *I will be fine.* I am not good. I am not better, but I am fine. *I will be fine.*

Liam offered to pick them up from the airport, but I said I'd do it. It'll give me a chance to tell them they're actually staying at Brit's and not, well, not...mine and Alex's house. *Alex.* I don't really let myself think about him. Not since the day at the dock, really. (The holidays are good for helping you stay busy like that.)

I'd asked May to come as an added buffer around the dads, but her and Ellen had already made plans to visit *her* kids. It stung, but I got over it because I've maybe been a shit daughter lately, and May deserves to be happy, too.

You deserve to be happy also. I do. I will. (Just get comfortable. It might be a couple years.)

I'm leaving Eden with Brit and the girls because the dad's flight gets in right at naptime, and it just doesn't make sense to rock that kind of boat today. So as soon as Eden wakes up, I'll change her, make a bottle and head next door.

I throw a piece of sourdough in the toaster and wait. *Jam or just butter?* I open the fridge and get lost in what feels like the biggest question I'll face today. *Strawberry jam or blackberry jam?* (Second biggest question I'll face today.)

Shrill-sounding yelling has my stomach twisting with nervousness. It's Brit.

I slam the fridge shut and run to the front door, pulling it open.

"How could you!?" she yells. Alex says something in return, but it's too quiet and I can't hear. I look at the driveway to see a Maybach idling. *Huh, that's not really his speed.* And because I can't help myself (and because I think I already know), I slowly step down the stairs. The whole time, I'm willing there to be a different outcome, but it's like I already know.

When I get to the foot of the apartment stairs, I can see the whole car now and in the passenger seat, sitting like a princess, is some cute blonde. She sees me so I give her a polite wave. And she smiles and waves right back.

I turn back to look at my best friend and her brother because they've stopped arguing now and are both just staring at me. And I don't know what my face must look like, but I'm going to go with horrified. At best. Terrified at a minimum. However I must look, it's being reflected back at me by those two.

I loved you, flits through my mind lightning fast.

This is how the story goes, right? I always knew I wasn't the princess in the tower. I guess I didn't fully realize I was the wicked witch, or maybe the evil step sister. But as it turns out, I was just the supporting cast all along.

My mom senses kick in and I know I have to go. Eden's probably up by now. So I try to moderate my steps back upstairs. Not too fast, not too slow. (Look at me, I'm normal. I'm fine!) As soon as I open the door, I hear Eden crying. *Yup.* I pick her up, hold her tight to my chest, and I rock her, soothing myself probably more than I'm soothing her.

"We're okay. We are going to be just fine," I tell her in the softest voice I can muster. And then I tell her again. And again.

A gentle knock at the front door sends my heart racing and my thoughts spiraling. *It's not him, is it?* It's Brit. That gentle knock belongs to Brit.

Eden and I walk to the door, and I'd be lying if I said my hand didn't shake the whole way there. I open the door and my stomach rolls because it's not Alex. *It was supposed to be Alex.* I know I told myself it was Brit, but that was me trying to temper my expectations. But it's Brit with a completely shit look on her face.

I shake my head, begging her not to tell me.

"He got married." Of course he did. "I'm so sorry, Jess."

Still in an oversized robe (probably Liam's), Brit ushers me away from the door, but I step around her to see the Mercedes that cost more than most people's homes pull out of the driveway.

You knew it was over, Jess. You knew it was final. I guess I'm still somehow shocked that was true...

The cold stings my bare feet on the top stair, but I can't bring myself to step away. To lose sight of his car.

"W-why did he get married?" I ask, again dazed. *Thunderstruck. Ravaged.*

"Said he was wasted in Vegas and decided to take the plunge." That's fucking stupid. Men are fucking stupid. And Alex would never do something that wasn't calculated or strategic. No. I bet he wasn't even drunk.

"I'm sure they'll be wildly happy, won't they?" I say. Not to Brit, just more so to the universe. The universe will confirm it for me. (I don't doubt it because this is someone else's fairytale, remember?)

"I'm sorry, Jess. I just wanted you to hear it from me."

"Uh huh." I walk back into my crappy apartment (it's not actually crappy, but I'm feeling pretty sorry for myself right now) and I make a bottle for my daughter.

"When is it too much?" I lean against the counter, hoping it will help keep me standing.

"When is what too much?" Brit asks, worrying her hands together.

"When do you hit your threshold and you know you can't take anything more and that the only next logical thing is death? Because I don't think I can take anything more. I'm maxed out on life, Brit." There's no tears which is oddly reassuring, but then again it's a knife deep in the kidneys knowing that it was really, officially, and forever done for him and me.

"Okay, give me Eden." She takes the bottle and the baby from me. "It only feels like the end right now. It will get better. You have us."

"You have your own family, Brit. I have to find my own." *Do villains get their happy endings?*

"No, you don't. You *are* our family. Not him, don't count him."

I shake my head at her. "Don't say that, he's your brother."

"After today..." she trails off.

"He is. And he wanted this. Clearly. We would have been miserable together anyways." Brit rests her head on my shoulder as I stare out into the abyss, wearing my thrifted ugly Christmas sweater and that same pair of $6 leggings.

TWENTY-NINE

ALEX

Jess is a cancer.

I love you, Alex.

She's not a parasite like I thought she used to be. No, she's a disease. That infects you. She ruins you. She consumes you from the inside out. You have to cut out the disease so that you have a chance at living. You sacrifice the limb to save the body.

Well, I'm the one diseased.

And that's what I've done. For me and for her.

I love you, Alex.

She said stay away, but I can't.

So I gave myself a reason to. It came in the form of a gold band now circling my ring finger. I broke our contract so Jess can finally be free. She can take her trust, and her and Eden can live comfortably.

And Emma is nice. I can learn to care for her. I can make

her happy. *Money makes most people happy.* And I'll stay away from Jess because I'm married.

And if the wedding band *wasn't* a deterrent, how badly this hurts her is going to be.

I love you, Alex.

She'll hate me now. *Good.*

I need her to. I need her to know that we are dead in the water, and now she can be happy with someone else because she was right. I'm never gonna get over it. So I need her to get over me.

She's not going to be happy like we could be, no one could. But happy enough. Happier than me.

Men like me only get the amount of happiness they think they deserve. And I'd imagine I don't deserve shit.

"So, that was your sister?" The woman sitting in the passenger seat asks me quietly.

I nod. "Yeah."

"The one you were talking to? Or the one with short brown hair?" She saw Jess, so Jess must have seen her. Mission complete.

"The one I was talking to. The one with short brown hair is just some random friend that works for my sister." Random person, one I no longer know. *Believe that.*

I love you, Alex.

It's hard to believe when all I hear on repeat is those four little words exiting her mouth.

"Oh, cool," Emma says politely. "Where are we headed now?"

"Home." The home I built for the only person I've ever loved.

———

Jess

"Hey stranger!" Tommy shouts from across the small airport. *Lord, girl, give me strength.* I give a brief smile and head towards the two men pulling bags off the carousel.

"Hi there." I clear my throat for fortification when my voice cracks.

Tommy lets Jamie finish loading the luggage cart and scoops me up into a hug I'm not entirely sure I would otherwise consent to.

"I've missed you," he says against the side of my head. I just nod. I haven't missed him. I've missed the idea of him, but I won't be saying that to his face, so I just stay quiet.

"Where's my girl?" Tommy asks as he sets my feet back on the ground.

"Napping. She's with Brit and the girls right now." He nods, looking me over. No doubt noticing that things are...*off* for me.

"You look...different." (That's code for: you look like shit.) I smooth down my shortened locks, and realize he's probably looking more at my hideous attempt at holiday cheer that's come in the form of an overpriced, thrifted sweater. I want so badly to say, "Thanks! This is what being poor looks like!" But that would just be the bitter bitch in me talking and not the moderate bitch who's still interested in retaining custody.

"Ahh, yeah," I laugh insincerely, "this old thing." I dust invisible lint off Rudolph's pom-pom nose.

"I wasn't talking about what you're wearing," Tommy's

voice is a bit subdued. He pauses, then whispers, "Are you okay?" *Swallow lump. Will not cry now.*

Fake smile on. "Sure. Let's, um, talk in the car, though. Solid hour drive ahead of us." I even pat Tommy on the shoulder, like he's my chum. *Fake fake fake.* I give a perfunctory head nod to Jamie that he returns and we walk to the car in utter silence.

Thank god for the California sun giving me a reason to wear dark sunglasses three days before Christmas. They're like my armor, hiding all the weak, under-protected bits about me right now. So with my Karen Walker sunnies firmly in place, and both men buckled up, I rip off the bandaid.

"Alex and I aren't together anymore." I can practically feel the smugness rolling off of Jamie. I look in the rearview expecting to see his shit-eating smile, but instead I get a look of genuine sadness in return. *No. No. Not the pity. Fuck.* That's worse, so much worse than a shit-eating grin.

Neither of them say anything in response, so if we're going to play it like that, I keep going. "I'm staying with Brit and, umm, you guys can have the garage apartment while you're in town. Promise it's nice. And, umm, why don't you guys tell me about Taiwan? Enough about me!"

"I'm sorry, Jess." It comes from Jamie and not Tommy. Again a surprise, but it pisses me off.

"Don't pity me, Jamie. Today's not the day." I don't say it as rudely as I really want to. I try to just say it honestly.

"It's not pity, it's empathy, Jess." His voice is soft and quiet. *Yeah, alright.*

"Okay." I stare straight ahead at the road.

"Do you want to talk about it?" Jamie persists. I look at Tommy who's looking ashen all of a sudden.

"Not particularly, but I'll give you the details so you don't have to ask. He married someone else. Went to Vegas, got wasted, did the deed because he really wanted to prove a point that we were done. And so we are. The end."

"When?" Again, it's Jamie.

"Well, I found out this morning." Fake smile? *On*. No tears? *Check*. Cruising down freeway with the weight of the world on my shoulders? *Yup*.

"Pull over." Tommy looks like he might be sick. So I do, quickly sending gravel flying out behind us.

He lurches out of the car, emptying his stomach. This is shaping up to be the best day of my life. Lucky me.

I pull out some napkins from the center console and give him my bottle of water.

"The rest of the drive isn't any less winding. Do you need to drive?" I ask Tommy.

"I'm not car sick." Okay...

"Listen, I, uhh. You're, umm..." *What the fuck?* Tommy is stammering and rubbing his palms across his thighs. "You're going to get served divorce papers today." *Lovely*.

I don't say anything. I just wait for him to get buckled and continue the drive to Spearhead. It takes a half hour before he says something else.

"I didn't know about Alex...and everything." Like some sort of excuse. Like he wasn't trying to embarrass me in front of everyone here. Like this isn't three days before Christmas.

"It's fine," is all I say back, and Tommy squirms.

———

When the doorbell rings at 4:45 P.M., I know what it is. So I answer the door to a middle-aged man holding a manilla envelope. *Right.*

Brit is right behind me, though, so when I turn around, she just takes the envelope from my hands and throws her arms around me. I'm not sad about divorcing Tommy, I'm just sad at the state of my life. The hits just keep coming. What more can I take, really?

"I'm okay," I pat Brit on the back and say.

"You don't have to be."

"Sure, but I am. And I'm tired. There's no fight left in me." It's the truth.

"Okay." She releases me and entwines her hand with mine, leading me into their great room where her family is assembled like some odd Brady Bunch. She's happy. I want to be happy for her, but right now, if I let myself feel anything, it'll likely be rage. And nobody needs that today.

I settle into a singular club chair by the roaring fire and pretend to read a book on my phone while the dads dote on Eden and the rest of Britain's family organizes into teams for Catchphrase while Carly cooks dinner. A margarita finds itself into my hand via my best friend and I give her a warm smile.

If I can just get through Christmas, things will be fine. Things will be better.

———

As it turns out, all you need for things to feel better is six shots of tequila.

"I'm fine!" I shout over the loud music. "Never been

better!!" Warm hands encircle my waist and pull me off the tabletop.

"Alright, peaches, you're coming home with me," Sandy says, then turns to give instructions to the hunk who pulled me off the table. Her twangy southern accent could cure homesickness and insomnia both.

"I love sleepovers! Do you want to have a sleepover, too?" I ask the rock hard chest attached to the warm hands carrying me through the door of Colton's.

"Not tonight, buttercup," he says. *Ha. Buttercup.*

"You're so strong." I rub his warm, hard pecs feeling like he could fling me around like a rag doll if he wanted and in response he tightens his grip around my legs.

I hiccup. "Okay, well let's do a sleepover some other time, mmkay?" I give him a "Boop" on the nose and shut my eyes while I travel weightlessly into a pre-warmed vehicle.

———

Oh no. Oh no no no.

I rush into the kitchen to find Jim rolling up cinnamon rolls and Sandy fussing with the dishwasher. "Why did you let me get on the table?!" I screech.

Sandy starts laughing hysterically. "God himself couldn't keep you off them." My brain bounces off my skull painfully.

"Rick should really be worried about losing his liquor license. I was overserved." I massage my temples, trying to ease the vice-like pain.

"You were already like that when you showed up with the Scala boys, honey." *Ugh.* The spins. I have to sit down on a stool.

I vaguely recall driving with three very attractive men to the bar under the guise of wanting to dance. What I actually wanted was to get fucked into oblivion. What I wanted was to forget.

What I got was embarrassing memories and a hangover.

"Ughhh." I groan and lay my face against the cool marble counter. "I shouldn't have done that." I moan and Jim chuckles, just continuing to roll up pastries with my head laid right beside his workspace.

"Honey," Sandy rubs my back. "When's the last time you took a break?" A break? What's that?

"No clue." I finally open my eyes when the sound of glasses scraping against the counter wakes me up.

"Drink all three, eat the potatoes," Jim sets down a plate of eggs and home fries in front of me, "and then you and I are gonna have a chat," Sandy says firmly. I look at the cup of coffee, glass of water, and the bloody mary and my stomach rolls.

I don't protest, though. I just say, "Yes, ma'am." It's the only appropriate response to the queen. When I start lagging during the eating process, Sandy urges me.

"Damian is gonna be here to pick you up in an hour, so unless you start talking now..."

"Damian?" I ask, confused.

She laughs. "Oh honey, you really don't remember?" Oh god.

"No?"

"You don't remember him showing up and pulling you off the tables?"

"Oh gawd, that was Damian?"

"The devil himself." *Great.*

———

Thanks to a quick shower, and the generosity of Sandy, I no longer smell like the booze sweats. I toss Rudolph into the trash can in the guest bathroom, but on second thought...I pick the sweater back up. This thing deserves to be burned.

After a torturous debriefing of the previous night's events, I couldn't function without cleansing away some of my sins. Which included yelling at Rick for giving me shots of water, dancing on the bar, dancing on the tables (plural), dancing on the barstools, and losing my wallet and phone somewhere in the process. Oh, and I most likely made a pass at my friend.

The perfect end to the perfect day.

"Hey," Damian knocks on the doorway to the guest suite.

"Hey," I say back, then walk out of the bathroom and take a seat on the bed. He comes and sits next to me and my cheeks bloom with heat because I owe him one embarrassing apology.

"I'm sorry about last night." I drop my head to his shoulder to hide my shame.

"What do you have to be sorry about?" he asks.

"Well, for making a drunken pass at you." He chuckles.

"Was the highlight of my year," he says softly, then takes my hand in his.

"Why am I at Sandy's anyways?" I sort of sit up, asking the question that obviously should have happened sooner.

"Thought you could use a break from the circus." Ahh yes, the dads were on Eden duty last night.

"We're messes again, aren't we?" I ask him and he nods.

"Yup."

"I think I'm finally messier than you..."

"Well, not so fast here. I'm the one who got dumped by their fiancé a month before the wedding."

"Oh yeah, well my fiancé married someone else."

"He what?" Damian pulls away from me, shocked.

"Brit didn't tell you?"

"No, I haven't even seen her yet...I'm really sorry, Jess."

I shrug. "It's not like it was real. He was just doing it to help me win custody of Eden." Damian looks like he just found out Santa isn't real. "But listen," I put my head back on his shoulder because the full weight of my head on my body hurts. "I don't want to argue over whose dick is bigger here." It's his. Damian has a big dick. *Eww, stop.* Should not be thinking about his dick.

I stand up hurriedly at the intrusive thought, but Damian grabs my hand and pulls me back to sitting.

"It wasn't real?" he asks, disbelief still written all over him.

"Nope. I mean maybe it was at some point, but it's certainly not now."

"Huh," he says, staring at me intently. My face flames and I'm not sure if it's from the hangover or the discomfort growing in the bottom of my stomach. (Which could also be the hangover.)

"I'm too hungover to chat. Can you take me home?" *Home.* Hate that word.

"Yeah, let's go," he says, but he doesn't release my hand or make any move to stand.

"Do you ever wonder..." I see him visibly swallow. *The answer is yes,* but I can't do this right now.

"Wonder what?" I ask, playing dumb.

He gives me that one-dimpled half smile and says, "Never mind, buttercup." And I laugh then wince.

"Oh no, none of that." My hand holds my forehead. "No laughing or I might puke."

"Well, if you do, aim for the sweater." He picks Rudolph up off the bed.

"I'm gonna burn that thing."

"Really? I was thinking about framing it."

"So you can memorialize the worst day of my life?"

"Your worst, my best." *Huh?*

"What?" I ask because I didn't hear him.

"Nothing," a single dimple pops. "Are we heading straight home or do you need a little more time?"

I hesitate because the way he says home makes me feel funny. Hate that word. "Back to Brit's," is what I settle on, but that feels weird, too. *Huh.*

———

"How do you do it?" I ask Damian who's sitting on the couch beside me.

"How do I do what?" he asks.

"How do you be around someone you love? How do you watch that person move on and be happy and be fine with it?" I'm not even around Alex, and I can barely stomach the thought. Christmas at Britain's house has been challenging. And even though Alex didn't show for family dinner, thank god, Caleb did. And somehow that was worse. If Caleb's here, Alex is probably still there, too. Just a half mile away sitting in his dream house with his wife.

"Well..." he stares at the ceiling, "The truth is I haven't

really been happy or fine with it. But I've gotten good at pretending."

"Not there yet."

"You'll get there," he says and I take another sip. The ice cubes clink against the glass and I listen to the squeals of Eden as Jamie blows raspberries on her belly. I listen to Carly scolding Luna for eating food off the table. I listen to the chatter of the family that surrounds my best friend. There's grandparents and kids, big kids and little, and there's laughing, and Christmas music is playing softly in the background.

"I just always wanted this." It comes out without my consent.

Damian silently wipes a tear off my face. "And you'll have it, someday." He places a soft kiss on my cheek and as he leans away, he says, "Merry Christmas, Jess." And then he leaves, and I'm once again all alone. But now it's also Christmas. *Perfect*.

I don't leave my spot for the rest of the night, not until it's time for Eden to go to bed and Tommy and I take her to the apartment for the nighttime routine.

"It's nice having you guys around..." Tommy practically beams under my praise. "To help with Eden. She needs you guys." I'm not sure that's how he anticipated that going.

"I'm back in two months, and..."

I wait for him to continue, but he doesn't. "And...?"

"And I don't know how to say this without offending you, but I wish you'd move back to the house."

"I can't."

"No, I know you can't...like that. But you know, for Eden to have both parents around all the time? Listen, I want to be present, and I want you to be present. I don't want either of us missing out on anything. I mean, fuck! She can say three words and I had no idea."

"Fuck," Eden mimics and we both start laughing.

"Four words, actually," I laugh out.

"Right, but would you consider it?" As much as I detest the idea, Eden deserves what I never had. I know that. She deserves the big family, the happy household. She deserves to have a dog racing around under foot and to not worry about if she left her favorite sweatshirt at mom's or dad's this week. And maybe I want that for her, too...

"Okay, yeah...I think for Eden, it's the right thing to do," I say softly, but with a certain resolve.

"Does this mean you don't hate me anymore?"

I splash him with the bath water. "No...but I never fully hated you to be honest. I just hate not being number one. That's all. Fuck, I don't even hate Jamie." And that's the truth. He's been a fucking saint since that day in the car. Or maybe he's been like this all along, but I wanted him to be the bad guy in my story, so all his actions and intentions had that filter imposed on it.

"Fuck," Eden mimics me again, splashing her hands down into the soapy water. *Fuck*, need to stop saying it. This time Tommy and I both crack up under our breath so as not to encourage the little gremlin.

"You two are a bad influence," Jamie says from where he's now standing in the hallway.

"Alright, I'm done. You wrangle her to bed." I stand up and dry off my hands, but lean forward to give Eden a kiss goodnight.

As I leave to head back to Brit's where I've been sleeping in the basement, Jamie stops me.

"Hey."

"Hey," I say back.

"Thank you."

I just nod. I'm doing this for Eden. "Merry Christmas, Jamie."

He gives me a quick hug and kiss on the cheek and I set off to go tell my best friend I'm moving, for real this time.

THIRTY

JESS

I knock gently against the door before entering.

"Hey, Damian," I start, but the sight before me has me halting in my tracks. It surprises me.

Damian is sitting shirtless on his bed with his lounge pants pulled down around where he's fisting his cock with one hand, his phone in his other. "Fuck," I say, and he looks up at me. He's the one caught in the act, but it's me who blushes. My cheeks heat and my pussy swells. (A reaction that surprises the shit out of me.)

He doesn't immediately cover himself up, and I don't immediately look away.

I'm still standing with the door partly open when he says, "The door." *Oh fuck, right.*

"Right. Shit, sorry." I drop my head, turn around, and quickly slip out the door, even though a part of me is wishing he'd told me to come over and sit on his face. (Oh my gawd, what?!) My palms turn clammy and my body heats all over.

Fuck, that was so hot. And what was he watching? And why does that make me jealous? My underwear is instantly soaked and I need to go finger fuck myself while picturing Damian's cock. (I also need to get laid, apparently.) *This* is a whole new level of desperation.

I slip into my bedroom at the other end of the basement, but I don't even bother to get undressed. I unbutton most of my shirt dress, then lie back on the bed and move two fingers under my silky panties into my wet, quivering entrance. (Yes, quivering. Did I mention I was in desperate straits to get laid?) God, I'm so fucking needy for a cock, anything. I need that mindless release. I need someone to help me forget.

I'm grabbing and pulling at my nipples with the hand not in my panties, when the door opens. *Oh, fuck.*

Damian shuts it behind him, but I don't remove my hand from my pussy or my nipples.

He's just staring at me, so I say, "Stay, if you want." (And I do want.)

"Are you sure?" he asks, but he's already locking the door and then walking towards me. His hand strokes his cock through his thin pants as he gets closer.

"Yes," I say. And as he approaches, I can feel him mentally undressing me. *Yes.* It feels good to be wanted like this.

I need this.

I slide my fingers out and the sound of them popping out of my wet hole is vulgar, but watching Damian watching me with torment, and lust, and longing sends chills up my spine.

There's a thrill that we shouldn't be doing this heightening it all. (Knowing I shouldn't won't stop me, though.)

"What were you watching?" I ask, while I lean forward to slide my arms out of my dress, not even mentally aware that I've started stripping for him.

"Nothing." He pushes his pants down so I can see his cock straining against its own skin.

I laugh, "Bullshit."

"Fine. Come here and I'll show you." So I stand, unclasping my bra, letting it fall to the floor and then pad softly to stand in front of him in nothing but my thong. And when I get there, he pulls me up against him, my back to his chest.

"Now show me," I say, feeling my skin burn where he laces an arm around my middle. His dick is still out and sitting snugly against the crack of my cheeks when he slides one hand beneath the silky fabric covering my mound and then unlocks his phone with the other.

"*What?*" I ask softly, looking at the image on his now unlocked screen. "Really?" I ask again.

"Yeah, Jess. Really." His dick twitches against me when he says my name, and then his fingers find my clit, and I relax into the inferno now raging in my pelvis. With a gentle flick, he tosses the phone on the floor and directs all his attention to me.

My head falls back against his chest and I get lost in the pleasure of the moment. My skin tingles, my heart races. This is a new kind of high...and with *him* no less.

He was looking at me. A picture of us from a vacation probably three years ago. Why or how is it a picture of just the two of us? I don't know. But it was Mexico, and there were copious amounts of alcohol involved and way too little clothing. In fact, I haven't seen that bikini in years.

"Why?" I ask, and he slips a finger inside me, roughly. *Yes, please.* Then quickly adds another.

"Because I still think about our night all the time." His lips are on my throat now, but the burning isn't in my pelvis, this time it's in my chest. I want that...but we can't be that. *Fuck, we shouldn't even be doing this...*

So instead of talking, I flip around to face him. I push him back towards the bed, until he's lying down, and then I climb over him. Straddling his hips, I bring my hand down to his cock and fist it, running a finger over where he's already leaking. I catch the bead of cum and bring it to my lips, and he groans.

Without asking, I pull my panties to the side and slip down around him, and he stares at me in awe. He fists the lilac silk of my thong and rips the string, discarding the barrier between us easily. He pushes his pants down, then kicks them off, too. And I don't even care that there's a light on and he can see me, all of me. Every stretch mark. Every scar. Damian has seen my mess already, and he's still looking at me like *this*.

I slide up and forward and then ease back down, slowly.

"Were you thinking about this?" I ask, as I start riding him up and down, flicking my hips to grind my clit against him.

"You have no idea what I was thinking, Jess." He sinks his hands around my hips, splaying my ass cheeks. *God, the way he says my name...*

"Then tell me." I've never wanted or needed to hear this more.

"I was thinking of your tight cunt dripping my cum as you walk around your ex husband and ex fiancé." *Fuck.*

"I was thinking about these tits that I've felt, but only ever seen in my dreams." He palms my breast and leans forward to suck on my nipple, making me grind even harder against him. I let loose a little sigh as my walls clench around him over and over. Every nerve ending, every inch of me begging for more. *Closer. Harder. Louder.*

"Jess, I," he pauses, fighting for words, but I silence him with a kiss, because that's not what this is. It can't be. This is just fucking. It's primal. This is just about need. (At least that's what I'm telling myself.)

When I release his lips, he flips us, putting me beneath him. His pecs strain, and his arms flex and *fuck*, I've forgotten how ripped he is.

"I-" he tries again, but I put a finger against his lips and roll my hips against him to prompt him to move.

"I need you," I say. And he gets it. He understands. And he takes over.

"God, I fucking want you," he says back. And then he's thrusting into me, forcefully. And he's grinding down against me. He's gripping my hips and holding my neck, and he feeds me the whole time.

"Perfect, Jess. You're perfect."

"Didn't want to stay away from you the other night."

"This ass."

"God, you've fucking haunted me."

"You're choking my cock so well, J."

His lips brush against the skin below my ear and I swear I hear the faintest whisper of an 'I love you.' The way hope flares in my chest at that thought is despicable. I shouldn't want that as bad as I suddenly realize I do. Because if there's one thing Damian isn't, it's mine.

I ignore it. Was most likely a figment of my imagination anyways.

"So long, Jess..." he says louder against the sensitive skin at my neck.

I bring my hips tighter against his, gripping onto his flexed biceps, feeling him throb and notch deeper inside me. *Wow.* Somehow the feelings are quadruple what they were the first time we did this.

I liked Damian the first time I met him. I really liked him. But now...

"What was that, Damian?" I ask, breathy, as he slides his dick in and out again.

"Nothing, J." He shakes his head. "Nothing at all." The sense of loss teases at the peripheral of my mind, but then he moves one hand down to my ass, lifting my hips up off the bed to hold me up as he fucks me harder, and I gasp at the new angle.

He immediately freezes and stops. "Are you okay?"

"Fuck! Yes. Don't stop!"

The smile that jets across his face does something to me. *For me.* I wonder what it would be like for that smile to be mine. (Very dangerous territory, that thought.)

Please don't stop. Don't stop smiling. Don't stop looking at me like that. Don't stop...

I'm close. Too close to lose it now. Sensing I'm at the edge, he pulls me in tighter, making sure I can feel him rub against my g spot as he moves into me, and my head falls back. My hips grind against him. My inner thighs clench, my back arches.

"Look how fucking beautiful you are." And with that, he sends me to a high I've never known. It's an explosion that starts between my thighs and runs up to my taut nipples and down to my curled toes, rocking me. It's a fracturing of everything hard about me. This man has made me malleable in his hands.

"Christ, Jess." And then he's unloading in me and grinding to purposefully send me into a second orgasm.

"Fuck, Damian," I whisper out before the breath is stolen from my lungs. Again.

My hands are in his hair, and on his back pulling him tighter, closer, clinging to him like I need the feeling to last. Because I do.

"You've fucking ruined me, again," he whispers against my ear as his movements slow. "Fucking destroyed me, Jess." I just nod against him, because I feel a bit ruined, too.

———

With my head on his chest, and my body tucked against his, he runs a hand up and down my spine, sending with it goosebumps. I shiver at the sensation and try to get closer to him.

"Did you want to talk about something?" he asks.

"Like in general? Or?" I laugh.

He slaps my ass gently, laughing too. "No, earlier. When you came in, looking for a show." I smack his chest playfully and go to roll away, but he grabs me, and cements me back against him. "Stop, I'm kidding."

"I was going to ask when you're flying back to DC."

"Oh, umm, I don't know," he says a bit uncomfortably.

"I'm moving back...so Eden can be around 'the dads.'"

His hand freezes against my back. The even rise and fall of his chest falters. *Oh.* My heart sinks with realization. *Reality check.* "Oh, don't worry. I'm not expecting, umm, anything..." I pull my hand back from his chest, feeling a strange burn in my own.

He doesn't say anything about what I just said, but he takes the hand that I just vacated from his chest and places it back.

"Can I ask about Alex?" he asks in the gentle voice he uses with me. That voice has become my safety net over the last year.

"Sure."

"Do you love him?" he asks, hand at my back moving again.

"I thought I did."

"Why didn't it work out?"

"Because of you."

"Me?" He sounds surprised.

I shrug against Damian's warm body. "He thought you and I were...fucking." (The irony, I know.) "And he just couldn't get over that night."

"I'm sorry." He says it like he means it.

"It's not your fault."

"It feels like it is."

"Well, it's not." It's really not. Alex is his own worst enemy, even if he thinks it's me or Damian. "Tell me what happened with Summer. Please?"

"We're just in different phases of life."

"You sound like you're being polite." I chide him for giving me a politically correct answer when I gave him the actual messy answer.

He takes a deep inhale like he might tell me the truth, but instead says, "Maybe I'm feeling gracious at the moment." I look up at him, and he looks down at me and smiles.

"Has anyone ever told you how beautiful you are?" I ask, maybe teasing, but he is truly so beautiful. From his blue eyes and auburn hair, to the light dusting of hair on his chest, to his soul. We've all made mistakes, but I don't hold his against him.

"Go to sleep, Jess."

I laugh and go to roll over, but he doesn't let me. He keeps me pulled into his side, the same hand that was on my back is now in my hair, sweeping against my scalp. Back and forth, lulling me away from the day, away from this week, away from this year.

In a whisper he says, "I won't be here when you wake up. I just don't want you to be surprised, okay?"

"Mmkay," I say as the last bit of consciousness leaves me. It's like my body knew what was coming and insulated my heart, pulling me into a deep slumber. It knew if it didn't, my heart would be hurting.

———

He told me and yet, I'm still surprised. And disappointed. But it was just sex, right? *Right.* I take a quick shower so I don't smell like my best friend's ex-husband and head upstairs.

I'm tempted to knock on Damian's door, but it was just sex. So I don't.

"Morning sunshine," I greet Caroline already at the

island with a cup of coffee. "You're up early," I note before opening the fridge to grab the creamer.

"Dad woke me up early to say goodbye." *Oh.* My hands fumble the plastic bottle, sending it crashing to the floor. A literal representation of the ride my heart and stomach just took.

It was just sex. *You're not acting like it was just sex, Jessica.*

Maybe when you reach a certain age, sex isn't just sex. Or maybe when it's one of your closest friends. Or maybe when it's your best friend's ex-husband it isn't just sex. But that's it, right? He's ashamed, and doesn't want to tell Brit, so he left instead. *Got it.*

"Fuck," I lean down to pick up the bottle that thankfully didn't crack open. "Did you know he was planning to leave this morning?" I ask nonchalantly. (I'm coming to terms with the fact that I am actually *very* chalant.)

"No, we were supposed to go snowboarding for New Years, but he said something came up at work." Definitely ashamed.

I plaster my fake smile on and tell Caroline I'm sorry her Dad left. "It's okay, I think this whole Summer dumping him thing is getting to him."

"Hmm," I hum and nod my head while the inside of my body revolts. We were using each other then. "Maybe."

"No, I know it is. Summer texted me Merry Christmas yesterday and asked if I could tell him to call her."

"Oh?" Again, I'm playing it cool. "So there's hope for them yet?"

"I really hope not." She cringes. Well okay, that's a yes, though.

It was just sex. (Yes, I have to keep reminding myself.)

"Good morning, my princesses!" Brit waddles into the kitchen.

"Hi, babe!" "Morning, mom." We both greet her. "Can we talk real quick?" I ask.

"Sure," she tilts her head and I lead her to the office for some privacy.

"I'm moving back to DC." I blurt it out as soon as she's sitting so I don't lose the nerve.

"Jess, you don't have to do that."

I give her a warm smile. "I know, but I want to." And I mean that. "Eden deserves a chance at big family holidays in her own home, don't you think? And I can give that to her, and keep custody if I just relocate. It's an easy sacrifice to make in the scheme of things."

"Are you sure? I'm gonna miss you."

"I'll miss you, too, but I'm sure. It's the right thing to do."

"Dare I ask when?" She's bracing.

"Well, I was thinking soon, like in the next week or so..." Brit's face falls. "But I think I can stick around a few more months till the nugget comes." There's nothing there for us yet. "But once Tommy and Jamie are back from Taiwan, officially, I'll go."

"Okay. Thank god."

"In other news, I heard Damian left." *Wow, I just can't let this go.*

Brit rolls her eyes. "Yeah, he said he had something at work, but literally no one is working the week between Christmas and New Years, so I can almost guarantee Summer is giving him a second chance and he jumped." I nod. Yup.

"Well, good for them!" (I'm definitely overselling it.)

"Are you okay?" Brit examines me carefully.

"Oh yeah, never better." She arches an eyebrow. "Have you talked to your brother?" (I'm deflecting now, I know.)

She nods, but doesn't say anything more. That's fine. I don't need to know. What I don't know can't kill me.

"Do you think if you went to him, you guys could work it out?" she asks, but I'm shaking my head before she's even done talking.

"He's married, Brit. I also told him I loved him, and he didn't say it back..." Brit's face quakes like she's fighting back the tears.

"You did?" Her bottom lip shakes.

I give her a sad smile. "It ran its course naturally. I made my bed, and he made his and now we have to go lay in them. Separately." (Mine, alone-ly.)

"Okay, I just hate this."

"Why? Just pretend it was six months ago and we couldn't stand each other. Nothing has changed! It's just like old times."

"I guess that's true..."

"Still love you like a sister," I say, opening my arms to her.

She stands slowly and embraces me. "No secrets, right?"

I gulp audibly. *Bandaid ripping now.* "I slept with Damian. It was just sex."

"You hoe!" Brit breaks the embrace, then picks a throw pillow up out of the chair and launches it at me, laughing as she does. "I fucking knew it! I could see it on your face!"

"Oh my gawd, keep it down. Your children are in the next room!" I whisper-shout. "Truly, it meant nothing. It was just me trying to get over Alex and him trying to get over

Summer, and he already bolted. We can all mark ourselves safe from a Jess and Damian union."

"Mmmkay," Brit clicks her tongue and gives me a mischievous look.

"You're not mad?" I was slightly worried she'd actually be mad.

"Literally, Liam is my human Valium. I could not care less as long as nobody is hurting you, or him purposefully. And it was just sex, right?"

"Yup."

"Was it at least good sex?" Brit arches both eyebrows.

"Oh my gawd, I literally cannot talk to you about this."

Brit laughs in my face. "Well, too late you already are. And yeah, I can tell it was good, you hoe bag." She slaps my ass and heads for the office door. "Hey, maybe we won't be in-laws, but we'll be sister-wives instead?!"

"Gross." If she wasn't pregnant, I would pummel her with pillows.

THIRTY-ONE

JESS

Four Months Later

"We're home!" I call out like I always do. I haven't walked in on them...yet, but it's bound to happen. I'm just trying to prolong the "yet" for as long as possible.

"Hi, babes," Jamie says while he walks out of the kitchen, wiping crumbs off his mouth.

"Eden, go see Daddy." I set her down on the ground and she bolts straight into her dad's arms. I drop the swim bag in the coat closet, digging out our wet towels and swimsuits from our Mommy and me lessons.

"How was it?" Jamie asks, holding Eden under one of his arms as she flails and giggles uncontrollably.

"It was fine." He follows me to the laundry room. "It was the snarky instructor today. You know, the one with the nose ring?" I roll my eyes and he does, too.

"God, she's such a little bitch, right?" he asks, bringing a smile to my lips as I nod in agreement because he took the words right out of my mouth.

"Like how did she get a job working with babies?"

"I'm writing an email." Jamie's our keyboard warrior, I just laugh.

"Where's Tommy?"

"Having lunch with Damian." Oh. *Cool. Cool.*

"Fun. Hey, I'm craving pasta for dinner. I think I'm going to head to the store. Are you good to stay with Eden while she naps?"

"Yep. Take the day. Or whatever. We're going to eat lunch, nap, and then watch the Great British Baking Show until our eyes bleed."

I laugh. "Good God, man. I don't care about your eyes, but let's protect the baby's. But it sounds fun."

"It's gonna be a blast." He smiles at me. And I smile back.

Jamie passes me the other half of his sandwich once we're in the kitchen, then I swipe the running grocery list off the fridge, and head to the backdoor for my car.

"Text me if you think of something else we need," I call out.

"Will do, love you!" *Still weird.*

"Uh huh, bye!"

Jamie has decided to tell me he loves me, much in the same way you'd tell a sister. (Duh.) I'm not sold, but I'm also not *not* sold. Some day Eden will probably think it's amazing that all her parents loved each other. So I tolerate it because I love Jamie in that same entirely platonic way, too. I just don't want to tell him every time I go to the supermarket.

We've been cohabitating for two months now. And honestly, no complaints. Going from single parenting to having three committed parents feels like a vacation. There's always an extra hand, there's always someone willing to tag in when you want to tap out, and the free nights are actual bliss.

I don't even feel anything when I watch them kiss or cuddle anymore. It's all just very...normal. And Eden is happy. So I'm happy.

Maybe I'm not the happi*est*. But I'm happy. To be working for Liam still. To not feel maxed out on life every day. To not be shackled to a man who still resents me. Also not shackled to a man who doesn't love me. It's all good things. Honestly. And I'm even making my kale and walnut pesto tonight. Like, we are living. We are *good*. (Are you convinced yet?)

The Whole Foods gods have even smiled upon me today because I get first-floor parking in the garage. *Yes!*

I'm still pulling out my grocery tote (filled with more totes) when my name gets called out across the garage. I don't really have friends here anymore, so it takes me by surprise.

"Jess!" I turn towards the voice to see a cute-as-pie Summer in her spring best bounding toward me. *Oh.*

"Summer." My cheeks flush when I notice the bump she's rocking. *Ohhhh.* "Hi and, um, congratulations." She sets a hand over her little bump proudly. Very *awesome*.

"Thanks! Um, I haven't seen you in forever!"

"Just busy *mommin'*, you'll know." God, could I be any more awkward? "Well, Damian and the girls must be so excited. I can't believe I haven't heard about this until now!"

Her face falls a fraction. "Oh, no. Damian broke up with me six months or so ago. This," she pats her belly, "isn't Damian's!" *Oh, lord. Thank you.* I want to visibly sigh with relief, but I try to roll with it.

"Oh! I just thought you two reconciled..." The cogs in my brain start turning. "Well, he told me you broke up with him?"

She rears back slightly. "No, he definitely broke up with me." She sort of laughs, "Because he couldn't get over—"

"Brit?" I cut her off expectantly, already nodding my head like, *Girl, I get it.*

"Well, no..." *Huh...*

"Weird! I don't really keep up with him anymore, so it's news to me!" (I don't and it is.) "I should let you get going, but umm, congrats to you and your lucky someone again!"

Summer looks back over at her Lexus SUV where a tech bro is waiting for her. (Makes complete sense.) I smile and she smiles back.

"Nice to see you, Jess." I nod and she flounces away, her Ganni dress flapping against the April breeze.

I've kept my distance to mostly everyone except Tommy, Jamie, and Brit. And Liam. (Because he's my boss). I haven't talked to Damian since that night, and certainly not Alex. (Definitely fucking not.)

JESS

Hey, it's been a while. How are you?

CAROLINE

First home game of the softball season is next Saturday. Can you come?

You betcha. But you didn't answer, how are you?

Better every day.

Okay, love you.

> Love you more.

I pocket the phone and head into battle at Whole Foods on a Saturday, on the first nice day of spring.

———

When I get home from the grocery store, I find a priority mail envelope waiting on the eat-in table, and it's addressed to me.

"What's this?" I ask Jamie, presuming it's something divorce or custody related.

Jamie walks up, taking a tote bag out of my hands.

"No clue, honestly. Never even heard of the law firm before."

The return address is some generic-sounding Smith & Smith & Smith bullshit. *Weird.* I drop my other totes on the ground and start by opening the envelope. It's a stack of paperwork that resembles the now defunct prenup I signed.

There's a post-it note on top in a writing I don't recognize that simply says,

"I've always and only ever loved you, Jess."

I suck in a deep breath. The waves of emotion that radiate through my body make me want to faint, cry, keel over and die, all at the same time.

But there's no apology. There's nothing else. And I do look, quickly, flipping through each and every page hoping for some other nugget or message. But there isn't. Just paper-work and instructions on how to access a trust established in my name.

Did he? *No.* But maybe he did...maybe he broke our contract on purpose.

Is that why he got married?

Fuck you, Alex. For haunting me still.

"So, what is it?" Jamie asks, picking up the other grocery totes, scattered and spilling out on the floor.

"It's Alex."

Jamie's hackles immediately raise. His eyebrows shoot up, and he looks at me with shock and concern. In a haze, I pass the paperwork over to him. He drops all the groceries back on the floor and immediately scans and flips through the document with expert precision.

"I'm gonna go out on a limb here and say he really loved the fuck out of you," Jamie says when he gets to the page where the trust balance is displayed. "Or he feels really fucking guilty about marrying someone else." Yeah, that's probably it.

———

I still struggle to comprehend the amount of wealth swimming around Northern Virginia. That is until I come to Caroline or Elodie's school events, and then it becomes crystal clear. I am poor and they are not. (But I guess I'm not entirely poor anymore, am I?)

Still haven't decided if I even want to touch what Alex gave me. It's mine, free and clear, but it feels dirty. Like he's paying me off. Or like he's buying a clean conscience. And I don't know that I want any part of that.

And I'm not thinking about Alex today. That's not what today is about.

The campus where the girls attend boarding school looks like an English manor, if English manors also had sports complexes that were funded by the Kennedy family and rivaled NCAA fields.

Stepping out of my car, I feel it. It's butterflies, and a dry mouth, and an uneasiness I just can't shake. I slam the car door shut and dust off my trusty AGOLDEs. Like my pants are dirty and not that my hands are clammy because the nerves are getting the best of me. (It's definitely the latter.)

I may have given myself a blowout. And done my makeup well. And worn good underwear. Because, I mean, you never know who you'll run into, right? But if all this is is an outing to see one of my best girls (childfree, I might add) then I'll be content. (I left Eden with the dads so she could do swim class and nap uninterrupted. Really, this three-parent thing is so clutch sometimes.)

After the second inning, it becomes clear that *he* won't be here, which is why Caroline probably wanted me to come. *Right.* I don't let it get me down, I just cheer her on. When she gets an out at second, I'm screaming. When she makes it home, I'm crying. And when the game is done, I wait for her outside the locker rooms.

"*Hey.*"

I turn around to the voice that used to be my safety net, and is now just a stranger's.

"Hey," I say back, trying my best to mirror his tone.

"Thanks for making it today." *Polite.* He's being very polite.

"Oh, sure. Caroline asked, so here I am!" *Awkward.* I am being awkward. We both stare at each other for a second too long. "Well, since you're here now, I should go. Tell Caroline I said she played awesome today."

"W-wait." He reaches for my hand as I'm leaving.

"JESS!" The high-pitched squeal from the parking lot has me shaking his hand off. Elodie runs over and jumps right into my arms. "I didn't know you were going to be here!" She's still got her knee pads on from volleyball. "We just got back from our game in Pennsylvania. We won." She does a little happy dance. "Did Caroline win?"

I give Elodie a big hug back, then release her. "Yup, 5-2. She got an out and scored a run."

"Woo whoo, now I have to pee. BRB." Then Elodie bounds off into the locker rooms.

I smile at Damian and he smiles back, and with a wave, I turn to leave again.

"Would you go out with me?" he asks my back. "On a date that is. Would you go out on a date with me?"

I turn back around to find him with his hands in his pockets, rocking against his heels nervously. "Do you really think that's a good idea?" I ask.

He starts, "I mean—

"I actually ran into Summer," I cut him off, "and she told me there was someone else, and really, I've done that before and I'm *only* interested in being with someone who is *only* mine."

"The someone else was you, Jess." He pauses. "I am *only* yours." His mouth sort of twists nervously at his confession. *Oh.*

"Umm..." is all I can get out at first. I'm speechless. "But what about Brit? The love of your life?"

"She can't be the love of my life if I've fallen harder for

someone else." My cheeks flame, and my body thumps with each beat of my heart. "Do you ever wonder about what could have been...between us, Jess?" He finally asks the question he started in Spearhead. *Yes.* I nod in response, but I'm still speechless.

He takes a tentative step closer. "So, I'm asking again. Jess, would you go out with me?"

"You ran away from me...after Christmas..." That stung. More than I'd expected it to.

"I just couldn't be around you and act normal anymore." He pushes his moppy hair back. "Didn't think you were ready for that." I wasn't. Probably. "And you were still married." I was. I'm not now. "And I spent a lot of years pretending to be fine around you, and I was just done pretending."

If we weren't at a kids softball game I would kiss the absolute shit out of him. "How long, Damian?" I ask quietly, curiously.

"Since I checked yes. Since...always." He says with a smirk. *Fuck it.* I launch myself into his arms and he catches me. *PG, keep it PG.* I drop my legs so it doesn't look quite so bad, and instead of molesting him with tongue, I give him a safe-for-work kiss.

"One date," I tell him. "You get *one* date. We'll see if you can make it to two."

He laughs this big laugh that never fails to warm my insides. "I'll win you over."

"Did you just say you're going to bend me over?!" I ask in mock shock.

He laughs again and says, "Well, that, too."

———

I stopped counting after the sixth date because after that, he was just always around. Or I was always with him. We just never really wanted to not be with one another.

We started taking turns with who went to whose sporting events. Most of his clothes were now hung up in my closet. He even got a bigger car to fit Eden's car seat.

Then we told the girls, and Brit, and our families. And at that point, we'd already talked about all the biggest things.

Marriage: Sure. Kids: Done. We were both done. Houses: Not in the city, but next door to the dads. Wedding: Small. Honeymoon: Big. Ring: Bigger.

And then one night, I woke up with a strange sort of unease that I just couldn't shake.

"Babe." I nudge him awake with a hand on his chest.

"Mmm," he rouses sleepily.

"I don't think you've ever made me cry."

"Oh..." he says, running a hand down his sleep worn face. "Wait, are you breaking up with me?"

I laugh at him. "Oh my god, no."

"Okay...do you want me to make you cry?" He reaches out for me, letting a hand drift into my hair.

"Maybe..." I trail off, then move to straddle him. "Babe?"

"Yeah, sweetheart?" he asks, already moving his hands to my hips, one of them roaming up to my breast then back down again, slipping a finger through my damp folds.

"I love you."

He breaks out into the biggest grin. So big, he forces another dimple into existence.

"I love you more, Jess." He pulls me forward for a kiss

that's deep and long and it's like your soul meeting its other half and it's a fusion. His life with mine, his love for mine. It's a trade, and he gives himself to me, again and again. Just like he has since our first date. "Took you long enough, baby," he says with a quick nip at my lip.

I nod, knowing he's right. "It's time to make me cry," I push back and trail down his muscular frame until my mouth hovers over his hard cock.

"Jess, you're my fucking dream," he tells me as a hand weaves into my hair to grip the back of my neck as I lower my mouth around him.

And I do cry. When his cock hits the back of my throat and I start to gag, happy tears expel from my eyes.

When he pulls me up, flips us, and enters me he says, "I've loved you for a long time, Jess." And another happy tear falls.

When he brings me to climax three times and swipes another finger across my overly sensitized clit, I cry but beg for more.

When he comes in me and rests his forehead against mine and tells me, "You're my person, Jess." I let one more tear fall.

"Love you, babe," I tell him.

"Mmm, love hearing you say it," he bites my shoulder, as his dick twitches inside me. "Are we busy tomorrow?"

"Nope."

"Great." He slides out of me, leaving a gushing trail of cum in his wake, and he stares at me intently. Torn between my face and my pussy.

"Take a picture, it'll last longer," I tease, but he whips his phone off the nightstand and snaps a picture. Or two. Or five.

I love when he does that. I love that when he's away for work, he looks at me. He wants to look at me still.

I smile, and he smiles back giving me a quick kiss, then asks, "Are you satisfied?"

"Five stars," I say, holding up a hand. "Would come again," and give him a wink.

———

"Are we going to see the girls?" I ask once we pass the furthest point of civilization. (Not really.)

"Yeah, after." He slides a hand on to my thigh as he drives and it's completely non-platonic the way it nestles right up against the v between my legs. I put my hand over his, and just settle in. Relaxed. Happy.

"Love you." I love to just say it. I've said it maybe ten times already this morning. He's going to be so sick of hearing it.

"Mmm, never gonna get tired of that, babe." He smiles, still facing the road.

We turn off about 15 minutes short of the girls' school and into a private enclave of custom homes. We drive until we hit the furthest reaches, then pull into a cul de sac and park.

"Are you moving?" I ask, looking around at the lots marked sold around us.

"There's something in the trunk for you. Why don't you go get it?" he asks, leaning forward to give me a quick peck.

"Okay..." I unbuckle quickly, and walk around to the back of his SUV where he's popped the trunk already for me.

And there, sitting in an acrylic framed box like it's an artifact of great value, is Rudolph, the thrifted sweater from my literal worst day ever. A sweater that has been meticulously and professionally pinned into linen to be on display and preserved for all of time. And I laugh.

Beside the most ridiculous looking piece of art is a card.

Sleepovers forever?

That's all it says. But when I turn around, he's already there, down on one knee with a massive rock in hand.

"It's two lots, actually. Right beside each other. And you can choose whatever you want. I don't care, just as long as it's us. As long as you're mine"

"Y-yes!" I blurt out my answer mindlessly, then throw myself at him on the ground. He catches me, pulling me up into his arms and wrapping my legs around his waist as he stands.

"Promise it's just me and only me?" I ask. It sounds a bit desperate, I know, but with Damian, I don't care. He never makes me feel less than for any of my worries. And in turn, it has the effect of making me completely unworried. About him, our future, or who I am to him.

"Haven't been in love with anyone else since our night, J."

"Really?" I pull back, holding his face in my hands.

"Really." He has tears in his eyes. "I've loved others, but never *in love*. Never obsessed, never not thinking about *you*." Fuck, I love him.

"Do the girls know?" I ask, nodding towards the ring on my finger, then wiping a tear off his face with a thumb.

"You're kidding, right?" Yeah, the girls know. They exploded when he told them we were dating. (In the best way.) I think they described it as the 'step-mom jackpot.'

(Even Caroline came around to the idea pretty quickly.) "They're waiting for us." He drops a kiss on my lips and his short stubble slides against my skin deliciously.

"Well, that was a mistake," I laugh, "because all I can think about is staring at the rock on my hand while fisting your hair as you eat me out."

"Goddamnit, babe." He drops his forehead to mine and I laugh at his groan.

"Kidding, but later. Promise?"

"Promise."

EPILOGUE

JESS

I stare at the band of oval diamonds stacked against my pear-shaped rock, the light bouncing off the stones and refracting against the dark-tinted windows of the limousine.

"Is this mess for me, wife?" *Wife*. I smile.

My dress is slid up, and he runs another finger against my naked sex, then groans.

"You know it is," I say, then turn to kiss him as he massages my damp clit gently.

"Lay back." I do, tossing my bouquet onto a nearby seat.

He kneels down and pools the white silk to my abdomen, and then he's eating me, like I'm an oasis and he's in the desert.

"You taste so fucking good, baby."

"Damian," I moan, then slide my hand into his perfectly coiffed hair, watching the disco ball effect my rings send around the small space. My hand in his hair, his rings on my hand, his tongue on my clit.

"Baby," I moan again. "I want to make one of your fantasies come true." He stops feasting to stare up at me.

"Fill me up? Watch me walk around my ex husband and ex fiancé with your cum dripping out of me? Please?"

He pulls away, and I watch as his mouth twists into a smile. "You're my fucking dream girl, you know that?" he asks. I know. Because he's my dream, too. This is *our* messy dream.

He unzips his Tom Ford tuxedo trousers and my man is all ready for me. I instruct him to sit down and then I'm on top of him and sliding down.

"Mine." I say to him once he's filling me completely.

"Only yours." And then I start moving. He throws his head back in ecstasy before saying, "Fuck, baby...what are you doing?" Then his hand is on my hip, another in my hair pulling me down hard.

"I'm spelling my name." I smile then make an "s" with my hips.

"That's good because you fucking own me."

"I know," I say. Because I do. We fucking own each other.

"You've been ruining me since day one."

"I know."

"I fucking love you, wife."

I smile. "I love you, husband. Now shut up and fuck me."

"K," and then he does. He shuts up and helps me fuck him. He slips a hand in between us to stroke at my clit, and my pussy contracts.

"Is this cunt mine, too?" he asks, after giving my mouth a tongue fucking.

"Of course it's yours, D," I pant out as I pull closer to the finish line.

"*Mine*," he thrusts up into me and pulls my hip down on him hard, and with a swift shift of our hips I'm spasming. The high hits me, and I'm screaming my husband's name because I mean it.

"Damian, fuck me!"

"Jess, baby..." He fucking loves when I find my voice, and it's only for him. He's the only one who's ever sent me there. If it was a cliff, I'd fall off it. If it was a building, I'd jump. For him. Only for him.

"Only for you, Damian," I say because it's true. And then he's filling me with a grunt and a loud shout as he falls, too.

———

The reception is small (though the wedding was smaller) and it's only the best and closest and oldest. It's our kids, our co-parents, and the remaining parents we have left. And it's best friends. (So yes, I knew Alex would be here.)

I have to admit, I didn't think he'd actually show, though.

But there he is with his cute wife on his arm. I give them both a polite smile as we walk past and into the private dining room at the Old Ebbitt Grill. Then I proceed to (mostly) forget about him for the rest of the evening. (Oh yes, we returned to the scene of the crime.)

Damian pulls my chair out for me, but I shake my head and whisper, "I'll stain my dress if I sit down right now," and his cheeks turn bright red.

"Then let's get a drink." He tucks my chair back into the

table and with him at my side, we get a drink and circle the intimate room for cocktails.

We talk to the dads who are on Eden duty today, yet she still suckers Damian into carrying her around most of the time. We talk to Brit and the girls. We talk to May and Ellen, and then we find Damian's dad, Allan.

"Jess," he says, opening his arms wide and giving me a bear hug before turning to his son. "Damian, you never mentioned Jess' middle name is June before?" (His dad was our witness on our marriage certificate.)

"It was my mom's middle name also," Damian says to me, gently placing a hand at the small of my back.

"Amy June," Allan says with a sort of misty look in his eyes. "Pretty serendipitous you two should find each other, I'd say!" He booms and I smile at him. Serendipitous is right.

"Amy June is a beautiful name," I tell him, placing a hand on his arm as he fights back the tears. We talk a little bit longer, telling him about our new house, and when it's supposed to be done *done*. (Feels like forever, reality is five more weeks.)

And when the girls come to take their grandpa for a spin, Damian and I splinter off to head for the people I've been subconsciously avoiding like the plague.

"Hey, man." Damian pats Alex on the back, surprising him. He turns and for the first time I really get to look at him, and he looks...not well.

His wife turns to us, and I immediately extend a hand. "Jess. Nice to finally meet you." I give her a warm smile that she returns effortlessly.

She shakes my hand and beams right back, "Hi Jess! I'm Emma. Thank you for inviting us. You're a beautiful bride."

Polite, gracious, kind. She's perfect. I smile, then slip a hand around Damian's upper arm.

"We've gotta catch up," Damian says to Alex who just nods solemnly, silently. *Well, okay.*

"I think if we sit down, they'll probably start serving the food. Are you hungry?" I ask my husband who's picking up what Alex is putting out.

"Yup, let's, uh, circle back in a little bit, yeah?" The question is directed at Alex who again just nods.

We sit down before Damian asks, "Weird for you?"

I shake my head with a smile. "Not in the slightest." I run my hand up his neck and thread my fingers into his hair. "You're my person," I whisper, then lean in for a kiss that he meets me halfway for. And Damian *is* my person. It's never a struggle. It's never a game. His love doesn't hurt. *Our* love isn't based on pain.

"Good." And then his hand finds my leg under the table, squeezing me for reassurance.

We eat dinner all together at one long table, but before the cake is served, there's a clinking glass and my best friend is standing. *Oh, lord.*

"Friends, children." Brit gets everyone's attention. "I know this might be a bit unconventional to have an ex-spouse give a wedding toast, but I think that speaks volumes about these two people right here. They are my two *very* best friends, who deserve *all* the happiness, *together*.

If I go on for too long, I know I'll start crying, so I'll keep it really short. Congratulations, you two." She raises her champagne flute. "*BUT!* I'd be remiss to not also thank my brother, Alex. For introducing the two of you. So, to Alex, too!" And she raises her glass again.

The sound of a cracking champagne flute startles the table. We all turn towards the sound to see Alex with a bloodied hand cut by a broken glass.

"Sorry," he clears his throat and scoots his chair back from the table to stand. Then, without ceremony, he gets up and leaves. I hate to admit how my stomach sinks for him. I try not to acknowledge the feelings that are still there, but sometimes, they rear their ugly heads. Like right now, when I have to fight the urge to go to him.

And I do.

"Well, cheers!" Brit says awkwardly, and everyone devolves into clinking glasses and drinking, just as quickly forgetting about the broken glass. (And broken man.)

I smile at my husband and he smiles at me, and we both cheers ourselves.

"Someone was feeling petty today, weren't they?" I sidle up next to Brit once everyone disperses after the cake.

"Maybe I'm still salty about it..." Brit says, sipping at her tequila on the rocks slowly. "I mean, there's a reason my son's name is Constantine Alexander and not Alexander Constantine..."

"Have you checked on him?" I ask her.

"Nope, and I won't. He's being a baby. He's *been* a baby." I don't disagree.

"Well, I think I'm ready for a potty break. Need to go?" I ask her, but she declines.

I let Damian know where I'm heading, and then I slip out of the private dining room and head for the restrooms. My silky white gown flows behind me and I smile because today was perfect. It was the perfect amount of everything.

Nothing overdone, nothing underwhelming. It was just right. Just like Damian.

When I exit the bathroom, my stomach plummets because he's waiting there for me. The hair on the back of my neck raises and my heart starts beating faster.

Danger danger. Every instinct in my body is chiming with red flags, and blowing horns, and storm sirens. *Abort.* The mission is clear: *abort.*

"Excuse me," I say to walk around him, but he doesn't move.

"It was supposed to be us, Jess," he says solemnly.

And I laugh, almost viciously. "No, thank you to whatever *this* is. You have a beautiful wife waiting for you. Go home, Alex."

"Okay," he says, then he moves in and kisses me. For the briefest of moments, I let him in. Like a muscle memory, my body overpowers my mind and I start to return whatever this is that's happening. *No. No. Hate this.*

I push him off as someone pulls him off.

"What the fuck?!" Damian is there, yelling at him. *Or is he yelling at me? No. I don't know and I hate that most.*

"Damian, I told him to go home." I tell him, willing him to believe me. He doesn't acknowledge me, he just unbuttons and pushes his sleeves up, then takes a swing at Alex. And Alex lets Damian make the hit. The fist connects with eye socket and the crack and pop are loud in the small hallway.

"Damian?" I ask when he's just standing there, frozen and fuming.

"Did you kiss him back?" he asks with an edge to his voice that still never touches unkindness. I'm shaking my head, though, immediately.

"No! God no! I was pushing him away!"

"Okay." *Okay?*

"Just okay?" I ask, hopeful. Feeling desperate for him to believe me.

"Are you my person?" Damian looks me in the eyes, asking me wholeheartedly.

"Unequivocally." I say, meaning it.

"Then okay. Come back to your wedding reception." And then he simply holds out his hand for me to take.

Level-ten perfection. *This man.*

We leave Alex in the hallway, neither of us acknowledging him, but before we get back to the dining room, Damian pulls me into a quiet hall.

Before he can say anything, I'm kissing him as hard as I can.

"I love you so much, Damian." I'm crying. "I told him to go home and he kissed me. I didn't want it."

"Shhh," he soothes me. "I believe you."

"You do?"

"Yeah, I do."

And if I thought I couldn't be happier or more in love with this man, I would be dead-ass wrong at this exact moment. Because this was my end-all be-all. He was my pièce de résistance. He was my sun and my moon, my beginning and end. He was my serendipity. And he was all mine.

"Only yours," I whisper across his lips.

"Only mine," he whispers back.

THE END...FOR NOW.

ACKNOWLEDGMENTS

I'll start by thanking you, the reader. You took the time to read the book thus far, and for that, I owe you all my thanks.

Thank you to my beta readers, Alix, Kristie, Laura, and Ellyn. Your feedback is so necessary, and so important. Without all of you, these books would likely never see the light of day. So thank you. For taking time out of your amazing lives to read these little ol' books of mine, and for sharing your knowledge and insight with me. My books are always better because of you.

Thank you to my copy editor, Sara, who never ceases to amaze me. You always make time for my books, and for that I am eternally grateful and indebted to you. I owe you like 90 trips to Paris Baguette.

And of course, thank you to my husband, D. Thank you for believing in me, even when I don't believe in myself.

If you read the acknowledgements all the way through, thanks again. It's people like you that deserve the world. xoxo

ABOUT THE AUTHOR

 E.L. Stevens is a book loving low-key sneaker-head with a mild obsession for baked goods and Dr. Pepper.

Her love affair with reading and romance novels started in the seventh grade with Jane Austen's Pride and Prejudice and hasn't stopped since.

An overactive imagination and obsession with the genre led her to want to write her own books incorporating life experiences love of her hometown, and of course, baked goods.

When she's not writing, she's voraciously reading, walking her labradoodle, Maggie, chauffeuring tweens between sports and extracurriculars, shopping for sneakers, or baking in the DC exurbs.

ALSO BY E.L. STEVENS

Spearhead Lake Series

Georgia

BOOK 1, BRITAIN'S STORY PART 1

Constantine

BOOK 2, BRITAIN'S STORY PART 2

June

BOOK 3, JESS' STORY

Alexander

BOOK 4, ALEX'S STORY (COMING SOON)

Judge

BOOK 5, CARLY'S STORY (COMING SOON)

Say Something

NEW STANDALONE ROMANCE NOVEL (COMING SOON)